Carnal Sacraments

A Historical Novel of the Future

Perry Brass

Belhue Press

Belhue Press, First Edition
Copyright 2007 © by Perry Brass

Published in the United States of America by:
Belhue Press
2501 Palisade Avenue, Suite A1
Bronx, NY 10463
Electronic mail address: belhuepress@earthlink.net

The following is a work of fiction. All the characters, specific settings, and events in it are purely fictitious and have no relationship to actual specific personages, living or dead, or business entities except when described as part of a fictional narrative.

Cover design by M. Fitzhugh
Cover photo by Andre DeLoach
Inside book production by Robert Leuze

ISBN: 978-1-892149-05-3
ISBN: 1-892149-05-2

Library of Congress Control Number: 2006939266

Other books by Perry Brass:

Sex-charge (poetry)

Mirage, a science fiction novel

Works *and Other 'Smoky George' Stories*

Circles, the sequel to *Mirage*

Out There: *Stories of Private Desires. Horror. And the Afterlife.*

Albert *or The Book of Man*, the third book in the *Mirage* series

Works *and Other 'Smoky George' Stories,* <u>Expanded Edition</u>

The Harvest, a "science/politico" novel

The Lover of My Soul, *A Search for Ecstasy and Wisdom* (poetry and other collected writings)

How to Survive Your <u>Own</u> Gay Life, *An Adult Guide to Love, Sex, and Relationships*

Angel Lust, *An Erotic Novel of Time Travel*

Warlock, *A Novel of Possession*

The Substance of God, *A Spiritual Thriller*

"Let us not burden our remembrances with
A heaviness that's gone."
    William Shakespeare, *The Tempest*, Act V, Scene 1.

Q. Why does the human mind have to keep closing itself?
A. It's scared of its own dimensions.

To the men and women among us who are finding age, at any age, an impossible burden, and to those who want to lift that burden, and learn. Also, for Patrick Merla, the memory of Jeffrey Lann Campbell, and for Hugh, and Robert.

Note: A list of foreign words and phrases used in *Carnal Sacraments* appears on page 299, following the text.

Chapter One

*H*ow could he make himself stop thinking about it, stop remembering it? And how could he make himself forget? The fist in his face out of nowhere, its impact knocking him back, nose bloody, its sound like glass crashing in his eardrums, with him isolated, confused, and angry. The crowd packed and surging in front of him, ignoring him while hushed commuter trains skated in on invisible shafts of magnetic energy; and all of this while he'd been working to be oblivious, holding on to nothing, like everybody else.

There was only work in its many forms. Not even thinking about it was work.

Overstressed, brain-fried, and elbowed to the edge of a cramped pubtran platform, Jeffrey Cooper had been trying to coax himself into some small island of mental safety, even as his mind relentlessly chased his job through its big Byzantine flowchart of goals, purposes, and functions.

"Imagine," his therapist had suggested, "a calming mist made of your very self, of innermost peace, of everything that *you* would like to be."

He wanted that, an atmosphere composed of his deepest, calmest self, that he could enter when things became too stressful, when one stress spitefully mounted upon another. But it was almost impossible for him to achieve it.

Stress ate him.

Stress at work, stress in his life. As much as he tried to hide it, he was too sensitive, and too aware. Both had become handicaps as he got older. Too much awareness could be deadly, overloading the complex connections through the master files of his brain that supervised millions of other files and the images that went with them.

Jeffrey Cooper, Senior Project Stylist, was both a fixed shining star for an age obsessed to its last breath with "Image," and an agile, whip-wielding ringmaster in the mesmerizing flash and bareback-pony show of "Style." Arch-critic and super design consultant, archivist and heir to millennia of bright, smartly queerish, wisdom-keeping monks, Cooper, like almost everybody else, was hyper-tightened and overprocessing in the last quarter of the twenty-first century, an insecure but binge-level workaholic period unmarred by the almost regular, world-shaking explosions of the deadly twentieth.

But he had a problem he had to face.

He was getting older—*seriously*—and all this stress from work as well as the demands of living *luxe* on one of the upper rungs of the system's ladder had got to him. Canyon-sized signs warned you about it.

"STRESS KILLS!"

"STRESS & YOU: No Benefit to the Team. The System. Your Life."

"Give Yourself a Hand When You Kick Stress in the Butt!"

He'd been looking at such a sign with its beautiful flow of softly lit, lollypop-colored lettering:

"Be Happy. Forget Everything. Remember Your Past Only Serves the Present."

Ah, the present. Yes . . . an endlessly beguiling, mouthwatering visual, extolling a free, glorious, competitive lifestyle offering every possible, advantageous perk and reward. Super-*luxe*-upon-*luxe* resorts and all the rewards that came with them, some even *more* exclusive within other less exclusive resorts, always moving ever upward, more *luxe* premium, and always more rewarding. Something was guaranteed for everyone at every rung of this always-up-to-date, pushed-to-the-brim-of-its-endurance world.

Falling apart? Barely holding on? Remedial "catch-up" resorts.

First baby steps on the ever-accelerating Road to Riches? Cosmetically rebellious, dishy, and stylishly "youthy" resorts.

Recently divorced? Your kid's a murderer? You're still working hard, but it's time for detox? You're covered, with "quickie" specialty resorts at which to recoup from those nagging, little personal issues.

And of course, everyone's least talked about favorite: the Last Resort. The ultimate destination for the *ultimate* job change.

Very orderly. Antiseptic. Closely monitored. With appropriately distant, concerned attendants trained in the latest Compassionate Sciences. You were sent there when your brief time was over, and you never left. It was the workingman's last stop before his own particular Nirvana, Heaven, or Paradise.

But for others, there was another place, much higher on the social expectations scale, whispered about nervously as the final cocktail glasses were cleared.

There, "magical" chemicals awaited to nudge a wearied, overtaxed brain right up to the very doorstep of physical extinction, where Death's resourceful cousin known as "Suspension" played Solitaire silently with you.

Suspension was both a promise and a morbidly joked-about threat. If the system felt there were any possibility of you having some value in the future, you'd be kept in it for some time. The future was indefinite, yet, for practical purposes, defined by some limitations (your job "on earth"; a final reckoning of your worth, etc.). In Suspension, you could even be visited and kept lovely, if periodic reviews permitted it. It was mothballs, so to speak, where you were put into a dreamless coma, instead of what was tactfully called "the other thing." It had its odd glamour, as well as its drawbacks. The system, always offering choices, gave you an alternative to finality as it decided what best to do with you; but there would be no last poignant good-byes, only brain-waveless sleep.

Sleep could be difficult, so you wanted something restorative while being awake. Jeffrey had been trying to make himself drift into some anxiety-free, Hollywoodized mist of self-containment as he attempted to place himself above the threats and congested realities of life. Within the elbowing pubtran crowd, he was actually close to calm inside, ready to float right into one of those high-end "Escape" resorts, the kind promoted in every form of popular media and fabricated from the diaphanous wishes of dreams themselves. There young, gym-sculpted hunks wind-surfed through crystalline waters, then casually dined *à la* black-tie at five-star restaurants perched above landscaped jungles, all designed for their unimaginable beauty by youthful prodigies of Marketing.

Then a lightning-fast fist greased with beer-sweat had hit him in the face.

He'd frozen, too shocked to scream. His eyes popped open, his nose and head throbbing. Pain poured through him; reeling to stand up, he had grabbed at the man whose lips were now at his face, he was *that* close.

Closer than Jeffrey usually allowed himself to get to anyone, but he was only reacting physically. In pure shock, he had removed himself. He might have been dreaming, still floating down into one of those resorts with the trim young men either in black tie or bathing suits.

Then another salvo of fist smacked him again, snapping him out of his own body heat, back into the cold. Like a hurtling comet, the man's face got smaller, all dark ice, faraway, receding.

Absolute silence. A roaring wall of it, frozen like a Nordic-winter waterfall. Others on the platform had turned away, ears glued to their buzzing earphones. While blood and snot fell from his nose, the man's wolfish grin had spun in the warm prism of Jeffrey's tears, and chilled him like a stab with an icicle.

Some of Jeffrey's blood had spattered on that grin, which now zipped around memory itself, like the blinking electronics of a billboard. But not one with model-perfect young men, starched tablecloths, and aquamarine waters.

Jeffrey's breath came back to him, forming one word:

"Who?"

And why?

But the man was gone, pulled into the large crowd that gushed from arriving trains, then quickly got sucked back into leaving ones.

Jeffrey had touched his face, feeling the pain from his rattled teeth and struck nose, the blood smeared with snot and more tears clogging his nose and eyes. For a second, he felt like he was drowning, choking, lost. He needed to come up for air.

He did, he came up. Then a storm of anger had taken hold of him, an unexpected slam of barbwire rage with which he had too little familiarity. He should have glued his brains together, if only enough to scream and hold on to the guy until the crowd responded. Instead, he'd been out there drifting, not focusing. Just trying to calm himself in the packed menace of rush hour.

Rage stomped all over him, with big German military boots, jerking him about like a half-stuffed puppet: his own too-late rage.

Rage was hideous. It killed as surely as stress did. He had to control it. Yet there was something almost refreshing in its unexpected, stinging wash over him. The fiend had disappeared, a half-seen cluster of features, recalled from split-second terror and confusion. Jeffrey doubted if he could ever identify him again.

He pushed into the crowded train marked "Tiergarten," trying to compose himself as he managed to find an empty seat. No one noticed him; he wiped blood and snot discreetly from his face with some tissues, glad that nothing he could see had got on his nice shirt.

Jeffrey liked to dress well, with everything carefully chosen, but you had to be supervigilant at rush hour on the pubtrans. Sometimes you'd end up so wrung out by the crowds that your clothing couldn't find its way back to the creases neatly and beautifully programmed into it.

He tried to reprogram himself, to fade back into the train with everyone brainsucked into their own files or personal entertainments. Some were talking in whispers to home, office, or locations halfway around the world.

Ja. Ja. Ja. Nein. Nein. Nein.

Office was truly everyplace. Everyplace was *Büro*. Work was constant and unquestioned. The Germans proclaimed *universalarbeit*: Work universal. Work was good, its own reward. You'd be happy with it, and thankful. It got you into those "Escape"-filled resorts, showering you with an endless array of new merchandise.

But, always, rock-bottom worse was the alternative. Because without work you were nothing. *Zero*. Statusless. Just a negative number falling through the cracks until you ended up in some unspeakable sewer.

Occasionally in backstreets or alleys, away from street cameras, Jeffrey glimpsed the workless, half-crazy, foraging through garbage, their rags brown-stained with their own feces. Some tried to sneak onto the pubtran platforms, but were quickly spotted and removed. Maybe his attacker had been one of them, only agile and cagey enough to pass as "regular" and get himself in and strike.

But why strike Jeffrey Cooper?

The workless were an embarrassment to Jeffrey; their degradation and drop from acceptable positions secretly embarrassed him, reminding him of his own age, which was close to eighty.

Jeffrey Cooper—attractive, fashionable, mover through the global economic system, holder of big job titles, supervisor of so many— was, in fact, seventy-eight, but on most days looked closer to forty years younger: one of the most secret and well-kept perks of his professional life. His hair was glossy, mahogany dark; his skin healthy-looking, smooth, hardly lined, with an almost undetectable cosmetic glow. Most of the time he was amazingly strong and limber. Even his hands and feet, tell-tale signs of speeding decades, had hardly aged, with only a few sun spots and veins showing. At the most they looked only a few years past thirty, as did his teeth, which were white, healthy-gummed, and closely spaced.

Most of the time, he could pass for a much younger man, though there were days when the "weather" hit him from too much stress, too many deadlines, too many exacting people higher-up to please. Too much to hold in and then release, privately, at precisely the right time.

This holding-in had forced him to form a hard shell over his own rigidly held feelings and sensitivities. He looked young, but never exactly a hundred-percent real, like some very convincing window mannequin, made of a material that closely approximated human flesh.

Due to an exorbitantly costly schedule of drugs, dermatology, cosmetic dentistry, regularly monitored therapies, and secret operations, Jeffrey had been given an almost unlimited *extension* on life and youth. He was now alive and thriving at the very opposite end of Suspension, though it was all kept confidential, like so much else in everyone's private work dossier, that ultimate "sacred text," kept in the most Holy of Holy private files, whose confidentiality increased substantially with a sharp incline of status.

Everything done on him kept him producing day to day, moment to moment, at the very crest of a profitable, optimal flow of performance. It was as if his physical body had placed its hand at the razor-sharp edge of mortality, and in doing so was able to push most of the biological consequences of human existence forward repeatedly.

It might all stop at some point. But who could say when?

A large contingent of his cells as well as his organs (including his digestive, nervous, and lymphatic systems), his blood, fluids, and hormone levels were attended to in a constant process of cleansing, enhancing, and, even when necessary, replacement. But he was not going to be replaced; he was invaluable, and aware of it. But not cocky. His position did not come from education though he was fairly well educated, nor from any standout talent, though he had some talents. It came from a clear mixture of saviness, toughness, usefulness to the system, as well as how long and easily he would be able to stay absorbed into it.

In short, Jeffrey Cooper knew enough to keep himself shining brightly at the horizon of *appearing* irreplaceable, without ever becoming arrogant or difficult about it. He was clever, negotiable, and adaptable both to the demands of his superiors and the wishes and problems of those working alongside and below him (a number which ran to the hundreds, even thousands, when you counted factory workers). Like a smooth cog in a major pivotal wheel, he kept his own area of expertise within a larger system in steadily productive motion: when the attack came, he was on his way to an appointment with his German therapist Tony, another of his many perks.

Jeffrey saw Tony Rosenputter once a week, in Tony's spacious, tastefully bohemian, dimly lit apartment in an Art Nouveau building decorated with terra-cotta *putti*, classical bronze reliefs, and elegantly chiseled marble facings. The building had outlasted numerous wars against Germany, and its dwellings, secured through generations of wise investments and inheritances, gazed softly out at the world through a rosy film of stained-glassed eyes. The charming edifice was on a quiet, leafy street near a small zoo. The Germans loved animals, so living near a zoo was *spitz klasse*. Elegant *Tiergartenstrasse* was lined with these exclusive, private walk-ups, many with inside balconies overlooking back gardens or interior courts.

Approaching Tony's romantically inspired apartment, one could imagine daydreaming through meadows and mist-streaked forests, the sort Beethoven might have walked through, pausing to jot down *fortepiano* sonatas. But Jeffrey, an American originally from Alabama, in the Deep South, was definitely not German, but sent to Germany to be the head of an international consortium of design consultants. World business had made the planet one neighborhoody kind of place, where all the good neighbors could get along if they acted nice enough, and spoke an almost identical language of Production, Media, Marketing, and Sales. Successful Germans of the polite classes engaged in a fluid mixture of English and German, with some Hindi, Arabic, and even Mandarin thrown in, as well as many old French and Italian phrases that once upon a time quickly confirmed one's place and sophistication in "the great world."

Jeffrey was at home in this sort of *köstlich* neighborhood, knowing full well that no one could confirm their sophistication like the Germans when sophisticated, or be as boorish when they were not.

Tony rang him in when Jeffrey's troubled face appeared on the security system. The eyes of pivoting cameras followed him up the front quietly carpeted stairs to his therapist's beige and gray apartment in which the only bright colors came from flowers such as a tasteful arrangement of daffodils or tulips. Sometimes there were more exuberant displays of flowering cherry or quince in the heavy antique crystal vase Tony kept in the waiting room, which was also his living room. Tony's was a warm, protective setting that seemed yearningly reminiscent of old Teutonic knighthood and those once-patrician, outdated Germanic analyses of the Psyche, all watched over presently by the gaze of the system that pretended to bless it, since Tony was a specialist working for them through a highly-tiered government health plan, fed by a global consumer economy which Jeffrey Cooper, as one of its stars, stoked.

Tony was in his late-forties, square-jawed and nicely boned, but he looked as if he were edging into the vicinity of Jeffrey's actual age. He smoked, like many Germans, and, without ever mentioning it, drank a lot. He wore a plain gray tunic outfit that, except for its super-immaculate cleanliness, made him look like he should have been working under cars. He had a small beard and a tanned face with big teeth. He'd once been married and he and Elsie, his ex, had a daughter who was now twenty-two.

"How are you?" Tony asked Jeffrey seriously, after they were both seated in another, smaller cozy room that was his office. "Can I get you something to drink? Maybe some tea? I have some infusions that might work for you."

"Water, please. A man hit me on the pubtran platform today."

Tony stopped in icy mid-pour. "He *what?*"

"He grabbed me and hit me."

Tony paused, his hand suspended, holding Jeffrey's glass.

Jeffrey, still shaking, looked away from him.

"Any idea why?"

"No."

He finished pouring, then handed it to Jeffrey. Jeffrey drank it quickly, then put it down.

"Did you catch his eye, looking at him? Maybe you looked longer than was safe. People don't look at each other anymore. It's not con-sidered the thing to do, you know."

"I didn't look at him."

"Then you can't identify him?"

"Maybe. It happened fast. A lot of people were there."

"There're always a lot of people there, but that won't do you any good. How about the police?"

"I don't need an investigation. They'll investigate me as much as him. I don't want to be stressed by it. I'm not sure I could get through any investigation. I've got too much work to do and all the projects I've got to deal with. There'd be a big police thing, I'd probably end up needing a lawyer, and for what? It all happened so fast. He was young. Maybe screwy. In his thirties maybe, kind of scruffy-looking. Workless, even."

Tony put his fingertips together. Although often dressed in a casual street-type manner, Tony did not like the *strassenklassen,* as they were called. His wife had been a modern dancer and though divorced they still remained devoted to the arts together, to all sorts of artistic and bohemian endeavors; but both were cold to the nasty realities of the "street classes."

Tony tried to figure it out.

"He's a thug." His eyes narrowed. "Maybe even one of our little neo-Fascists. They're all over, like rats. '*Deutschland für Deutschen.*' *Scheisse,* it's crazy but they pop up. Truth is there's so little *German* left in Germany anymore. We're all so multicultural. Everybody does their little 'Dance of the Seven Veils' with the real Germany; they all want to look under the veils and sniff around. *Neges* from Africa. Asians with money. Arabs. We have more mosques than Mecca. It's not like in the old days when you had safety in the streets. Everything's changed, you have to watch out all the time." He shrugged. "Know what I mean, Jeffrey?"

Jeffrey tried to look at Tony the way Tony looked at him: eye-to-eye with a tad of intimacy, yet without aggression. The Germans always gave you the feeling that you should know what they were all about, because they were the norm and you weren't. You *should* understand their little quirks, their prejudices, their wounds from the past that never healed. You *should* understand every bit of that, using all of their own undoubting, self-described "intelligence" and "clarity."

After all, what was your problem *not* to know?

"I'm not prejudiced," Tony explained, going on one his little soapboxes. "But these people are not always the most liberated themselves. They have their own fascism, religious fascism." He paused. "I can't deal with it. You Americans—"

Suddenly Jeffrey saw his attacker's face again, totally clear, even if only for a second. Jeffrey's neck jerked as he refelt the impact— *bang!*—in the nose. He was scared he'd start to bleed again.

Tony, oblivious, could have been one of the unseeing multitudes on the platform, glued to their earphones, his voice that of a painfully sanctimonious, liberal preacher.

"—You Americans think in terms of business only. Naturally, business only wants everyone to be alike, so they can all buy the same things, even if you call it 'multicultural.' And, of course, being alike is important."

He gave a little shrug, and smiled.

"*Richtig?*"

Jeffrey performed almost the same shrug and smile.

"Tony. Listen. I know it's Jesus over here and Allah over there, but—" He paused. "The truth is, when he came up to me I wasn't even aware of him. I was so out of it. Trying to keep from being overwhelmed, too—"

"*Ja?*" Tony leaned in toward him. "Are we panicking *again*, Jeffrey?"

Jeffrey could not answer.

"*Are we?*"

Jeffrey could only nod.

"*Lieber* Jeffrey."

Tony's distinguished-looking head shook sympathetically.

"I thought we were going to work on that stress. *Schlecht.* Remember, my friend, we always need to keep your stress level lower than nine."

"*Ja.*" Jeffrey squeezed the word out. "I mean, yes. Sitting discipline. Yoga. Chanting. Meditation. No sugar, no coffee. Less meat. I'm trying really hard, Tony."

"But you panicked. *Richtig.* Sorry. *Zu viel Deutsch für* you?"

"No. I live here. You can use all the goddamn German you want."

"Don't joke, Jeffrey. This isn't about me, it's about you. Did you panic hard and stop breathing? Come on now, be truthful."

It was hard not to be truthful. Jeffrey was sweating copiously. Sweat trickled down his armpits, feeling like a high tide. But it was crazy to panic about being in a panic; he had to calm himself. He held out his glass and Tony poured more water into it, then Jeffrey gulped it down.

"Tony, we were right there, eye-to-eye. Then he hit me. All these people all over. Crowds bumping, pushing. Noise. Trains. He grabbed me and he hit me and—"

"What? Did he run?"

"No, he couldn't run. Too many people."

"So what *did* he do?"

"He hit me again!"

"*Gott.* Where?"

"In my face. Again."

Jeffrey started crying. Tony handed him a tissue, and he used it to wipe his eyes. A little more blood came out of his nose. It embarrassed him; he felt like shit.

"I could smell every hair on him. Beer. Sweat. Coarse kinds of smells. But I couldn't see him, much. My eyes just shut from fear. He hit me again, and people were so close that no one could see it. I wanted to shout, but I was scared and a train was coming in and then everybody jumped toward it, and he disappeared."

Jeffrey's heart pounded as sweat poured from him. Tony asked him if he wanted to lie down. In order to get paid by the health plan, he would have to do a stress test; there was no way around it. Everyone was closely audited, even people as credentialed as Tony Rosenputter.

Once Jeffrey's stress level had edged up to seven, and Tony told him he could fudge it a tiny bit. Mostly it stayed around five, but if it climbed up to eight or nine, the report would be very bad and some of the things that were done to keep Jeffrey really young and alive might—well, they could stop. Stress was to be avoided; it meant that you were compounding the pressures of too much input, too much Information in all of its daily, assaultive forms. It meant you couldn't hold any more: definitely a handicap in this always changing, competitive world where turn-on-a-dime adaptability and razor sharpness meant everything. You needed to know how to float almost effortlessly with Information, no matter what it revealed or what toll it took on you.

Now he was on the couch with Tony leaning over him, trying to comfort him.

"What would you like?" Tony inquired. "I could give you some herbal drugs; we could meditate together to slow down your breathing. I could even give you a massage. You like massage, don't you?"

Jeffrey grunted, too tense to answer.

"Lie on your stomach," Tony ordered.

Jeffrey turned over. Tony put his fingers on the back of Jeffrey's neck and let them drift down his crisp work shirt toward the base of his spine. Tony was excellent at this, applying orderly, neutral, professional pressure, tapping Jeffrey's tense, gym-and-hormone sculpted buttocks gingerly through the light material of his knife-creased pants.

Jeffrey sighed, feeling close to tears, just from the promise of relief. He wanted whatever Tony was offering, and wanted to embrace Tony if he could, as someone offering hope, if there were going to be hope. Tony went back up to his shoulders and Jeffrey became happy again. He felt miserably alone most of the time except for Tony. Benign, kind Tony. The perfect, always hoped-for, idealized father; the perfect, always hoped-for, idealized friend. His own valiant knight and healer: solid, sturdy, yet—in his most hidden and trenchant soul, beyond the psychic sciences and the system— artistic. Even though he worked for the system, Tony, in his tenderest heart (which Jeffrey wanted so much to believe), was there for him. And despite the happenstance of him being German, Tony did understand him, understood the very core of him, as much as Jeffrey tried to hide it.

Jeffrey was sure he could feel something between the two of them. Or was he merely feeling himself, liberated momentarily from his age and working role, relaxing in Tony's lovely, though somberly Teutonic, protective space?

He wanted to kiss Tony.

He wanted so much to take Tony's usually stoic, tanned face in his hands and kiss him, permitting his lips to graze Tony's always slightly withdrawn ones. But he couldn't. Tony was his therapist. And he worked for the system. That was the bitter shit of it, the *scharfscheisse,* as the Germans called it. So he kept his secret to himself, and it added a dangerous speed-bump all its own. And that particular, resistant blade of tension around Tony stayed with him, like an ambushing jolt of electricity.

"How's it now, Jeffrey? *Gut?*"

Jeffrey lied softly. "Yes. Very good."

But Tony saw through this. He took Jeffrey's left hand and eased his forefinger into the center of its rather deeply etched palm. Then, using his fingernail, he gently inscribed a figure-8 in it.

"Just relax," Tony cooed. "Relax and follow the feeling of my fingernail. That's all you need to do."

Still on his stomach, Jeffrey knew his palm was sweaty. No lying about that tension sign. Stress was not leaving; stubborn, spiteful tell-tale stress. It seemed that no matter how much closer he wanted to get to Tony, no matter how much of his always wary, professional self he managed to leave out at any time, no matter how young and resilient he looked, stress—rigid, tight, quickly recalcifying the ancient carapace around him—was always there, waiting below the surface.

"*Lieber* Jeffrey. *Was kan Mann tun?* We take the test, and it goes up to eight? *Nine,* maybe? There's not much I can do for you then. I don't like it"—Tony's face dropped into a splendor of solemnity—"but I can't change it."

"*Ich verstehe,*" Jeffrey groaned, meaning to accommodate Tony in German. He agreed. He hated it, but agreed. Then Tony motioned for him to turn onto his back.

"*Gut.* As God is my witness, I'm always your friend. But I'm afraid that's the way everything works."

There was genuine concern on Tony's noble face; in his own way Dr. Rosenputter was honest, though never too honest.

"*Ach!*" he went on. "We have your old problem. Your skills, your talents. What makes you useful, valuable. I'm afraid they exceed your abilities to cope with these gifts. Always the high-wire act: you're way up there, so very far up. But you can fall. That's the problem with us, the artistic people. You're up there, because only you can be *up* there. You, with the soul of an artist. I know that kind of soul. See, I admit it. I have one, too, myself."

Jeffrey smiled. At moments like this, Tony did become transparently full of himself, even if his face never showed it.

Tony nodded, shifting his shoulder blades.

"But it's easy, Jeffrey, to fall. I see it time and time again. You get scared. It's too sad. And let me tell you—very, very stressed!"

Those words, "very, very stressed!" sounded too threatening. Jeffrey didn't want to listen, though he knew that Tony's work within the system also included using threats. The threat was there; there was no denying it. Jeffrey had to balance these things: Tony was another cog in the system, as well as being his exquisitely, embarrassingly seductive therapist and "friend." Jeffrey tried to shield himself from any sense of threat or consequence, as he focused on only a calming string of sounds escaping Tony's habitually dry lips.

"We will do our best—!" Tony promised. "Get closer. I'll touch your head."

Jeffrey leaned toward him, and Tony's fingers, like soft rain, danced lightly over Jeffrey's forehead, oily with a mix of sweat and moisturizer. He closed his eyes but still saw the face from the pubtran, its mouth riveted into a hard, triumphant smile.

Tony's fingers did their little compassionate dance over him, but in the deep, obstinately punishing eye of his mind, Jeffrey followed a dark, twisting path down, very far down, as it became a maze in which he was quickly lost.

But he did not turn away; instead, he saw things clearly enough now to calm himself. He and the man were no longer on the crowded platform, but alone, like two beasts, two animals recognizing mutual strengths and prowess. Jeffrey's strength was visual and he realized, like finding one particular file within a sprawling metasystem of data, that if he wanted to he could recognize, and even memorize, the man's face.

Every detail of it.

He could retrieve the man's generous lips, the distinct print of them, their texture and alluring menace and savagery, ringed with white flashes of a near-nauseating excitement which intensified and burned, lasering through Jeffrey's tension and the cold recalcitrance under it. Then the man's nose, large, pronounced, not pretty but memorable; then his brow and cheeks, slightly heavy but handsome still, scored deeply with creases and dimples. He'd seen these same features on a long-buried, black-glazed Greek vase, showing naked wrestlers incised with such a starkly detailed, testicular realism that it spun off toward the excitement of pornography. The similarity of the Greek image sent a shiver through him; but he felt better now, as if entering a clearing after trudging waist-deep through brambles.

"How are you feeling?" Tony asked, jerking Jeffrey out of his clearing. "Tell me, how?"

"Better. I can be tested now."

"*Richtig?* Delighted. I'm happy, Jeffrey. I was scared for a moment."

"Were you?"

"Yes. I had a lot of fear for you. I was determined to do anything. I must tell you that."

"Really?" Jeffrey gazed into Tony's eyes. Normally, they gave little evidence of Tony's feelings, but he could see actual fear there. Tony wasn't hiding it.

"Yes," Tony answered quickly. "I was determined—" He paused, cleared his throat, then said, "To bring in other help. That's it! I admit it. I would even go into your—"

"Into my *what?*"

Tony looked flustered, very unusual for him.

"I would go into your—" He dropped the thought for a second, then resumed it with, "Your spiritual makeup, Jeffrey. If you'd let me do such a thing."

Jeffrey smiled. Tony looked vulnerable, perhaps even more vulnerable than Jeffrey felt after coming out into a clearing of his feelings.

"Why wouldn't I, Tony? By now you must know that I'd let you do almost anything."

Tony's tanned face darkened slightly more.

"Whatever you say. It's just not something normally covered in therapy. Not by the system. Some people get bothered by it. And others—" Tony's hands became expressive, like a dancer's miming a rising waterbird. "That's *all* they want. You'd think *they* invented God. Which, of course, is true. We all at some point do invent God."

"I haven't yet," Jeffrey said with genuine relish. "But what would this *spiritual* thing do? Tell me."

"Sit up," Tony ordered.

Jeffrey did.

"It provides a framework. It's like a contract. It gives you some-place to meet the higher 'Thing.' Fill in whatever blanks you'd like. Some people call it God. Others call it Ethics, Morality, even Imagi-nation. Yes," he added with insistence. "The very bull's-eye center of the Imagination."

Jeffrey rearranged his shirt, tucking it into his pants. "You never spoke to me about this, Tony."

"I wasn't so concerned before."

"And are you now?"

"'Fraid so. Believe me, I don't bring in the spiritual thing often, and never directly. That seems too arrogant for me. What I do is, well, bring in the ones who can help."

Now Jeffrey was indeed lost; Tony could see it.

"Jeffrey, I feel I know you well enough to speak. I can trust you, *richtig?*"

One of Tony's hands, completely out of character, suddenly dropped to Jeffrey; Jeffrey clutched it. It would have been easy to transgress the boundary then, to jump over the fence separating patient and therapist. Tony had large strong hands, and for a second Jeffrey drew his therapist's hand toward his face, dangerously close to his lips.

Tony pulled away. But their eyes remained on one another.

"O.K. We've gone this far. No going back, right? It's like this, Jeffrey."

Jeffrey held his breath, and looked at him.

"The spiritual . . . 'helpers,'" Tony said slowly. "They're like agents, see? Some people use words like 'saints,' but why burden the idea with such loaded words? Too many people have been hurt by words like 'saints.'"

Jeffrey listened. He had never associated hurt with "saint," but he could see the trap in that word.

Tony went on.

"I don't talk much about this, but Elsie, my ex-wife, got me to believe in them." He smiled guiltily. "The truth is, some humans have an oddly *godly* nature. This may be hard sometimes to see, since that very nature can be violent too. So, the truth is, you don't have to believe in God, whatever that means to you, but you can believe in these agents, the 'helpers.' And you don't need to call them saints, if you don't want to. They can be anything you want. 'Saints' is just an easy word."

"I see." Jeffrey's voice lowered to a whisper. "But you're like that. To me. I mean, saintly. You are, Tony."

"*Nein. Nein.* No, please don't say that. The truth is, I need agents, too."

Jeffrey smiled.

"I understand."

"Good. If you want, I can bring some 'helpers' in. They're around sometimes on an imaginative level, sometimes real. Maybe today's not the day. But perhaps sometime, when you don't pull out of your stress and it's pulling you in so badly that even I get scared, we can—"

Jeffrey nodded, eager to agree.

"Yes, of course. Someday, you're right."

He felt happy, just listening to Tony; Tony could sell him any-thing. The weird thing—too *weird*—was that Jeffrey, even at seventy-eight, felt his therapist to be immeasurably older than he was. This was not simply because Jeffrey looked and acted so much younger, but because his emotions had been, for the most part, deep-frozen in immaturity as he managed to stay a part of that relentless world of style that had, in fact, produced him. He was a comfortable part of it: that always new, always freshly reinventable *haute bourgeois* world and its vast, interlocking system, which kept Jeffrey function-ing smoothly, youthfully, at least on the outside.

So, even though on the surface he appeared to glide through his utterly professionalized life, inside, having a "Tony" there as his dad, protector, and captain was supremely pleasing to him.

"Tell me about these agents, Tony. Who are they?"

Tony shrugged self-consciously.

"Simple, really. They are . . . part of a belief mechanism. Kind of like the way we describe time. Time is only a function of perception, without perception there would be no time: you could go backward, forward; even remain stationary. That is, not backward, not forward. Just there. The agents then are another function of perception. If you can believe time exists, and we all do, then why not believe *they* exist?"

Jeffrey smiled. He'd never heard Tony sound like this. It punctured some of Tony's professional "artistic" superiority, that he could believe in something so basically irrational, like anybody else.

Tony got up and, making a quick gesture of apology, lit a cigarette. "Habit I can't break," he said, as he'd done so many times before. He settled down again. It was deliciously nice to see Tony like this, fully human for a moment.

"We believe," Tony picked up his thoughts, "that the pubtrans will run. Cars will work. Everything that biotech does, we believe in that, too. If you can believe in all that, why can't you believe that there are places in perception where *normally* you don't go? But the rub is you have to go *there* to believe them. In fact—"

Tony halted.

"What?"

"Well, you have to push a lot of yourself aside to go there, because sometimes the regular, working part of your brain can't follow it. Get what I mean?"

Jeffrey looked at him, not wanting to speak, not wanting to break the fragile bubble of that moment. He nodded, forcing a smile, putting aside any possible, reasonable doubt that might stand between him and Tony.

"*Primo*! Excellent." Tony shot some smoke out, like an ejaculation, up at the elegantly plastered ceiling. "You *can* follow, I knew you could! Let's make it truly simple. Let's call this a 'technique.' A *therapeutic* technique—and let's say you *need* it. There are things we normally don't allow ourselves to see, so we just dismiss them as unreal. *Zum beispiel*, you're not going to die, Jeffrey. Tell me, how real is that?"

It was a loaded question, hitting Jeffrey hard between the eyes. He became tense again, and wondered where Tony was going: it was someplace they'd never been before and Jeffrey, suddenly, was shocked by it. Tony's eyes became harder, losing that wonderful, soft, daddy quality that Jeffrey treasured.

"Let's be frank: You're going to have quite a life, Jeffrey. It's going to go on and on, until you can't absorb all your necessary information anymore. That's when you'll find yourself incapable of doing the work. We accept that. You have a place, you do it. *Richtig?* You've given up a lot to have that place. I admire you for it. I do. I couldn't do what you do. I admit it. As your therapist, I can tell you—I could not give up what you've had to give up just to stay alive. Please, forgive me, Jeffrey, for saying this now. But it seems this is the right time."

Jeffrey looked at him, stunned, feeling almost punched again; as if Tony were moving into a real forbidden territory of his own, and this declaration exceeded in intimacy and revelation any fantasy Jeffrey might have had about merely kissing him.

Jeffrey had to strain to pull himself out of his quiet.

"I'm sorry," he confessed. "I feel like my very existence bothers you."

"*Nein!*" Tony insisted. "Forget this. I'm the one who should be sorry. You don't know how helpless you make me feel! For all sorts of reasons, I can't be you and yet I'm supposed to help you. I'm here to help you stay alive. The system has put me here for you. To make your job easier, and without the system—well, we know what that would be like! Misery. Disaster. So what I'm saying is that even if I am at my wit's end, rational as *I* am, there are others of a less rational nature who can help you, if you let them."

"Yes?" Jeffrey blinked, feeling extra-confused now, as well as slightly blackmailed or at the very least manipulated, as if Tony's offer of some new intimacy had been yanked away. He wondered: Was Tony actually saying that, as a last resort, he had to bring in other forces, "spiritual" ones, to get Jeffrey back on to the good side of the system?

This definitely did not make Jeffrey feel better, or closer to Tony.

"What happens . . . once I *allow* them to 'help'?" Jeffrey asked cautiously.

Tony shrugged again. "You grow a second head."

"No, come on, I mean it! Do I start seeing things, Tony? Allowing strange hallucinations to hit me? How can that help?"

Tony looked at him patiently, as Jeffrey went on.

"Are you sure this isn't some kind of weird self-hypnosis that can get out of hand? I mean, isn't that what most religion is—self-hypnosis?"

Jeffrey had heard that stated once at a party; it had stuck in his head. Now it fell out.

"Jeffrey, that's not it at all. Besides, a little self-hypnosis in your case would not be so bad. Trust me on that."

Tony shook his head, smiled, and then suddenly winked so seductively that Jeffrey winced. The tables were being turned too fast, and he felt as if Tony were peeling away some very guarded and unappetizing layers of himself, and too quickly inviting Jeffrey to bite.

As if reading Jeffrey's mind, Tony said: "Why don't we go through a little bit of it now? A little taste of it?"

"But I was feeling better before."

"Relax. A small taste. That's all. *Ein geschmeck.* Lie down again. Breathe slowly."

It was getting late and Jeffrey knew that their session would soon end, and he had to be tested even if Tony didn't do it. Somebody else would; somebody less of Tony's caliber. It was part of the system. Tony was being really kind, which Jeffrey was also smart enough to know. So he did lie down.

"Now, let's suppose you're someplace you especially like being."

Jeffrey closed his eyes.

He was in a rural district outside of town, a mile and a half past the end of the main pubtran line, where a lofty forest, refreshingly light-soaked, smelling of moss and ferns, gave way to a great rolling meadow, and paths lined with oaks sand birches drew on to a lake colonized by lily pads, handing up gold and white blooms in the summer. Every winter he thought about the forest, the meadow, the ideally perfect lake, yearning for it like something in a beautiful dream.

Actually, the meadow was part of a public park and much of the woods around it had been reforested so many times after the wars that the trees grew up in perfect rows. Still, there were denser, off-path places that blocked out the sun, where at first Jeffrey had got lost, but now he was familiar enough with the area. He visualized the main dirt road cut through the forest, then more private footpaths, and finally deep stands of tall pines, waiting in silence. Sometimes noisy but harmless families intruded, but you could escape them. Solitary men often walked around shirtless with knapsacks on, wearing extremely short lederhosen exposing their muscular German legs. He liked all of this: the rich, living depth of the trees, the silence, the men; Tony had been correct, he could feel himself relaxing.

"Where's this place?"

"A forest outside of town."

"The Blichtenwald?"

"Yes."

"I like that place, too."

Jeffrey groaned happily, as peace flooded his mind like a summer sunset, all amber warmth glowing through the wood's dark greens. His body relaxed in a foreign, unfamiliar way. Then, like a reflex, it snapped back into rigidity: the recall of his first experience there. After feeling so alive, open, curious, and young in that beautiful place, he was suddenly lost. Darkness spread, bringing fear and confusion with it. Unable to find the path out, he became terrified that any move would only take him deeper into the forest. He panicked.

Then out of nowhere, a wrinkled old man in lederhosen, bearded and hunched over, but with sturdy tanned calves and an ancient hiking stick, appeared.

"*Sind Sie fürloren?*"

Jeffrey was embarrassed.

"*Ja,*" he whispered.

The old man chattered on in some barely understandable, thick German dialect, but indicated with a smile that was all glittering eyes and wrinkles that he lived in the area, had been hiking it for ages, and there was nothing to fear. Jeffrey could not keep his eyes off him. He was incredibly calming; even as the darkness intensified, Jeffrey started to see fireflies, silvery night moths, and the orb of a distant moon rising over the trees.

"I *vill* bring you!" the old man suddenly broke into English, then took his arm and led him all the way back to the platform of the station on the slower, connecting countryline, where they both smiled and said good-bye.

Jeffrey opened his eyes.

"Someone is taking you back, taking care you?" Tony asked, smiling. "How would you describe him?"

"I can't," Jeffrey said. "I can't, because I don't know how he got there. I mean, he was an old man and he got there just when I needed him."

Tony took his hand again.

"It's all right, Jeffrey. I understand. You feel terribly alone at times, isolated in your own years, don't you?"

"Yes," Jeffrey whispered, then started crying as more feelings swelled up within him.

He hadn't expected this. It was that difficult memory of his first trip to the forest, which he had erased and now had come back. He wondered what had happened to the old man; he was probably dead.

Why had Tony led him into this? It was hard for him to believe that the old man had served any special purpose, other than happy coincidence, but his wrinkled face was now illuminated in his mind by fireflies and moonlight, and Jeffrey felt as if he were breathing in the very air of magic.

As relaxed as he now was, he felt suspicious. If he had to, backed up against the wall of the system, he could control his panic and push down his stress numbers and go on working. But where was Tony leading him, and what even more pivotal place was he trying to dig out for himself inside Jeffrey's overworked brain?

Tony moved closer, wondering if Jeffrey could take this, and a bit scared himself. Definitely, this was not something he was licensed to do, or that the system smiled on. His therapeutic professional reserve melted.

"Do you want me to hold you?" he whispered.

Jeffrey nodded.

As Tony took him into his arms, into the crisp gray tunic that smelled of eau de cologne and tobacco, Tony's room with its distinctive furnishings, stained glass upper-window panes and jewel-colored glass shades, seemed to embrace Jeffrey as well, becoming his refuge. And Tony, a guardian of the system, somehow magically became the old man with the walking stick.

"Relax, *lieber* Jeffrey," Tony cooed, his voice pure liquid. "There are beings who will come to help you, just like that man in the forest."

"I was frightened. How did you know?"

"Your face. I could even see *him* there, believe me."

"Oh, God!" Jeffrey cried as if he'd been unmasked. "What can I do? I need you to help me, Tony!"

"I know." Tony hugged him kindly, cautiously. "I know that. The system has placed me here, but I can only go so far. That's why I say there are other 'good' forces, if you want them. I'd like you to think of me as someone who can bring them."

"I *vill* bring you!" Jeffrey heard the old man promise. He released a deep breath, then said to Tony, "I really want to do that—to think of you that way."

Tony smiled.

"Then do, my friend."

"Are they . . . ?" Then Jeffrey said it: "Saints?"

"Whatever you'd like to call them. But even saints are human. So when we call upon these forces, we must remember that a human element comes with them as well."

"But you know they are there?"

"I do."

Tony grinned, and impulsively kissed Jeffrey lightly on his forehead, as he'd never done before.

"Elsie has seen them. She made me believe in them. I couldn't at first. It seemed so lower-class: that's the truth. But when I began to really believe in them, I realized that they have a light and you can see it. It comes from within; maybe it actually comes from within *you*. But, for our sakes, don't tell anyone that I suggested this to you. I've gone very far out of my bounds, I know it. There's nothing in the system that talks about this. And one can never be too careful, as I'm sure the system would never consider this to be therapeutic. *Verstehsen allis?*"

"Yes, of course," Jeffrey said. "I understand it all."

Chapter Two

A moment later, Tony brought over the small gray instrument that measured Jeffrey's stress level. Its printout, done in little columns, was like a report card, except that exactly what the figures meant and how the genial but unseen "man behind the curtain" himself would interpret them, was still in most circles a mystery. All of it was "open to interpretation," meaning its significance varied with your position and how stress-prone that was, what exactly was being done to you, what investments had been made in you, and then how all of that would appear to the various business-suited analysts whose offices interpreted the results.

Basically, no one knew who they were, or what they actually looked like, yet one's very insides would run across their desks, appear on their data systems along with other anonymous comments, and then get filed away in places that only a select group of people, whose identities were often unknown even to each other, would ever know.

Once "accidentally," several decades earlier, through an obliging quickie "friend" whom he'd met one late rainy night on a business trip, Jeffrey had obtained a copy of his own complete medical transcript: something so forbidden that he was sure his fingers would burn just touching it. They were both drunk in a cheap bar at an end-of-the-road junction in Southeast Asia, one of those almost comically slimy sex-trade dives, eons off the "Escape"-resorts map, where factories teeming with child labor sprouted up at the edges of jungles, along with bootleg pharmaceutical labs and nomadic scam mills churning out unlimited opportunities for suckers. His "friend" was a horny little mole burrowed deep into accounting, but Jack "XYZ," sweet, chubby, balding with a hairy back, had other invisible mole-like "friends" who in turn could get him virtually any piece of information he wanted. After they both "popped," in Jack's roach-spattered rented room, as a favor to his good-looking guest and to prove that even as a pond-scum, frog-in-the-bog he had hidden charm and powers of his own, he offered, bleerily:

"If I can see you again, I'll get it for ya." He burped. "Bet you'd love t'see it."

Jeffrey swallowed hard and said, "Yes." He'd see Jack again, for that. It was all very sub-rosa. Nightmare scary. But after one more sex-drenched night in a third-rate motel in the States with this dodgy little mole, chunky little Jack in revolting striped boxer bloomers fished some papers out of a secret compartment in his briefcase.

Jeffrey sat at the edge of the bed, getting slightly nauseated just starting to read it. It was like looking at his own autopsy report. Everything was there in cold blood and type: so many organ and body system analyses, work done inside him, expensive but necessary preemptive cell replacements, all the procedures and their settings. The drugs, the meds, the therapies and consultations. Everything in neat rows of figures, beautifully captioned in matter-of-fact accountants' English, usually ending with the words:

"Need for Funding." "Cleared for Funding." "Forecast for Funding."

His head throbbed while Jack smiled anxiously. He handed it back, and Jack took it into the bathroom and burned it. He made sure he never saw Jack again.

His confidential medical file almost destroyed all the faith Jeffrey had in something he needed to keep some piece of faith in: the idea that he was more than just a business deal. He was a substantial "talent," an irreplaceable expert. Not something they might categorize at any moment as "Uncleared for Funding."

He hated thinking about their second meeting in that even more sordid room. It was painful to see the evidence of his worth spreadsheet like that in so many cold numbers, but he had been able to forget it, which also was a genuine part of the process of extending his life.

❧

"The Past Means Nothing Unless It Serves the Future," you saw that always on billboards, in training manuals, even on the pubtran platforms.

He was smart, well-placed, and liked having his long work history, though not the accompanying aging that normally went with it. Sometimes he would look into a mirror and could almost see this distant man furtively looking back at him from advancing age. Peering deeper, he could see the inner corners of his eyes showing the true extent of his years, like the underside of some well-preserved antique that had escaped the constant attention of its care takers.

He didn't use the exorbitantly priced cremes and other skin regenerators that fashionable people scooped up from department stores. Mostly what he used was fairly cheap, since almost everything on him worked from the inside out. Still, to his benefit, he had started out winning a good genetic lottery, with skin that didn't age easily, good joints, a near perpetually young stomach, and, to the surprise of the experts, almost Olympic-cyclist-level efficiency in the muscle fibers in his heart. His liver and kidneys, crucial for long-term health, were excellent, too. And he had a jump on vital youth-preserving hormones, simply because he kept secreting them full-blast, and was equally able to absorb them, all the way into his early seventies, only tapering off somewhat later.

His knees hurt sometimes after tennis, with a pain that was literally shocking.

"Where the hell did that come from?" he would ask himself. How could knees on legs that looked so young hurt so much?

He'd hurt his shoulders a few times lifting weights at the gym or working on the machines there.

"Those shoulders are really vulnerable!" a concerned trainer a third his age warned him, and he hurried off for physical therapy soon afterward. His physical therapist had no idea how old he was. No one did, since he used a fictitious age.

One's actual age and material status were classified items. The endlessly new global society was supposed to be democratic, egalitarian, multicultural, and as competitive at the same time as a school of piranha. One tried to keep as much private information to oneself as possible: not easy, since privacy was so porous. Still, the higher up you went, the more possible it was.

Higher in terms of location—and status.

In his mid-thirties Jeffrey had been summoned to a corner office above the clouds in the city where he was working, where a small, almost invisible executive recruitment team revealed that they were pleased with him. He'd been expecting something like this for a while, but was not sure what form it would take. He listened quietly. They liked his work, his looks, his manner, his adaptability, and the fact that he could float through most challenges, or appear to.

They spoke seriously, adding in jokes about longevity and performance. "Sometimes you need a shotgun marriage between the two!" A few women in black and pearls smiled at him, while the men, in severe suits, looked straight through him. They said they had an "idea" to present to him.

He glowed, attempting not to show too much satisfaction. But he had been driving himself like a demon and ended up profoundly good at what he did. His work was everything to him: his identity, his being, his religion, his *self*. He was unattached and totally self-starting, and physically he was in fine shape.

They went on warmly enough for people in such a cold, high place, telling him that he had an astounding future, maybe even more of future than he himself had conceived of.

He allowed himself to break into a smile.

"But, Mr. Cooper—" an older man in black-rimmed glasses broke into Jeffrey's praise-driven euphoria, his eyes riveting so hard on him that Jeffrey felt his heart rate accelerate. "Please be aware that some tests will have to be done"—to determine if Jeffrey were worth the long-term and costly investment in him they were proposing. The tests would be expensive. And if Mr. Cooper failed them, that would also go on his records.

The man did not explain further, but Jeffrey knew what this meant: failure would hobble him professionally, and he would be banished to some distant, inconsequential edge of the system, from which he would never return.

"You can leave now if you'd like," the man said, removing his black glasses. "It's up to you."

But Jeffrey had no intention of leaving. He sat down and they took out folders and looked at him with all the patient rapport of cannibals. He was a work in progress. The Golden Calf they would either idolize or throw back into the fire to melt down once more. Inside the folders, they scheduled him for two intensive days of physicals. They would look inside every part of him, cell by cell, organ by organ, system by system. Then the same man who had no hair and almost no eyebrows asked:

"Mr. Cooper. Tell us. Have you ever heard of the term *PICE?*"

Jeffrey nodded slowly, his hands clenching and unclenching in his lap.

They had given him a key as to what would happen. He had heard about PICE in rumors and whispers, mostly that PICE testing was never done on stay-behind people. The cost was prohibitive. Being asked to take it meant, at minimum, that those many levels above you felt that you showed the promise of being worth it.

PICE (Previous Influences Control Effects) measured exactly how earlier influences on your life factored into your present frame of mind, and what this did to your work.

Basic issues: What effects did your parents have, and how damaged did they leave you? Precisely what aspects of your growing up do you still carry with you? What permanent effects did your past leave on your present judgment? And how susceptible are you to the influences of religion, especially any faith of an orthodox, fundamentalist, or neo-Puritanical nature which, due to "ethically"-motivated restrictions on profit-generating expansions, might inject some subjective, "moral," and nonproductive tone into global business?

Other even more personal areas of PICE search: How easily can you let go of past relationships, hurts, or defeats? The system demanded that you never dwell on anything negative. Jettison it, or it would stick in you, compounding normal workday stress. Now that his past might extend into an almost endless series of decades, the executive group needed to know that no aspect of it would drag down his productivity.

Also in PICE: How deeply and definitely do you define yourself in terms of religion, culture, ethnicity, gender, or sexual orientation? None of these divisions, though useful for marketing purposes, were applicable in a global economy whose long-term goal was to flatten distinctions among consumers. In subsequent training, he would see over and over again the words:

"Leave It Behind, or Lose the Future."

The test took twenty-eight hours over three days, involving an exhausting written part; observed role-playing sessions with actors; and several meetings with a panel of psychiatrists, behaviorists, marketing experts, and other social scientists. The PICE data was fed through numerous interfacing programs, and its results were shared by another committee of medical and psychological experts, then teams of underwriters and financial consultants. After a last meeting, whose results would never be known to him, a final report decided that Jeffrey Cooper (not exceptionally "first-rate bright, but not neurotically vulnerable either"; definitely "sex variant," no hiding that, though "Sex variant candidates are adaptable assets to the system"; still, all in all, "outstanding in his field of Marketing-Design") was judged: "In peak renewable form."

General Outlook: "[Jeffrey Cooper is] Worth long-term investment. A very dependable element of Human Resource."

Or, in plain English: "A keeper."

Jeffrey never actually saw the final report; because of his PICE results, the system would maintain him in top form and on the cutting edge of Information, as long as he could keep "stress issues in control without recourse to production-conflicting pharmaceuticals." Although this message seemed to be specifically aimed at Jeffrey, in truth stress had become completely pervasive, leading to recurrent break downs of social and political structures, even to mass rioting and death. Stress was not only Jeffrey's enemy; it was the world's.

Everything conveyed a basic, buried "Anti-Stress" message. Anti-stress was planned into sealed, luxurious "no-problem" cars and magazine-perfect "no-problem" homes. Books, art, music, were all beautifully pre-packaged and easy on the brain to keep out stress. Even Jesus was prescribed by spiritual counselors and other professionals as a useful "stress-relief" alternative.

This was not done in Europe, where they sneered at the comic-book, linebacker-athletic Americanization of Jesus, and used "Art" with a capital "A" as their own favored de-stresser. In Europe, high-end, tastefully packaged Art brought feelings of security, education, and graciously elevated cultural superiority to "artistic" people like Tony Rosenputter and his dancer ex-wife, who looked down on the stress-prone lower classes. America, on the other hand, despised Art, in whatever form it came. Art could be stressful to the consumerate, no matter how much lip service corporations paid it. So "Art," high or otherwise, was replaced by corporate fashion and marketable style, at the sale of which Jeffrey Cooper continually proved to be his own wizardly self.

The lower classes got super-stressed, despite macho-"cool" illusions to the contrary, and violated each other regularly. Sports was a good release for them, though it could inspire mayhem and even cycles of murder. Kids, too, needed a stress valve and a well-designed and marketed "Youth Culture," idolizing rebellion and nonconformity, provided that, churning out pouty super-paid bad boys and stylishly slutty bad girls whose images were often beamed onto glass-walled skyscraper skins, giving the middle finger to "losers" and those disgusting hypocrites known as "parents."

Pop culture was a profitable branch of the system and Jeffrey had helped invent many of those petulant overblown images, dressing or undressing them like a master puppeteer, giving them an attitude he knew would work. Every rebellious face in those behemoth "edgy" video portraits flashed onto walls or malls spawned a trail of pricy "name" products, and the trail, no matter how super-badassed and unwashed it looked, climbed right up to the top, where the Big Money met, wondering when to replace their little dolls with fresher arrivals.

Those people, in their understated limos and climate-controlled, green-energy penthouses, in their country estates with live-in medical staffs, the absolutely *real* Money with few recognizable faces attached, were allowed inarguable room for Stress. They could bite their nails all they wanted and nobody flinched, since Jeffrey, in his own unwashed private moments, was absolutely positive that no one questioned *their* PICE for a second.

Sometimes, in his chillingly austere apartment, or his big office, Jeffrey smiled about all this, even though he was not supposed to think about it. Nothing was supposed to get inside him. No deeper questions, no detritus from the past. No grudges, no judgments. Nothing aside from the excellent performance of his job. But in truth, Jeffrey was smarter than anyone had given him credit for. And the proof was that he had cheated all over the place on PICE, using his own indomitable sense of style beforehand to figure out precisely what all the experts had wanted to hear.

Style, after all, once anybody had seriously picked the thing apart, was pure domination. Louis XIV knew it, and so did Adolph Hitler; so did Jackie Kennedy Onassis. And even in his early thirties, Jeffrey Cooper knew to a "T" how to use it. Gulping pills or taking his shots, even exercising, he would mull over the whole situation:

If you were smart enough, you were entitled to everything you grabbed for and got. And in this perfect (and stylish) world of high compensation and ever quicker gratification, it was predictable, even if not always openly acceptable, to knock anyone off the table who foolishly got in your way.

That was the system pure and simple. And any other ideas were, to put it bluntly, *shit.*

But he was a grateful part of it: this endless sea of digitalism and mutable technology that had to be mastered and remastered, as it changed for any number of well-publicized reasons, but mostly to recharge a waiting, passive market energrized only by change, as you gave people new diversions and excuses to consume, inventing new models of stylishness and fame (once called "celebrities"). One had to be able to absorb all these hair-trigger changes and direct tsunami waves of raw information that produced each change, with even more data subsequently resulting from it.

It was all pretty thrilling, if you stayed young enough to be thrilled. But to stay on top of it, you had to be smart; and the great mass had been dumbed down to such a numbing level of simple-minded self-appreciation, as it was constantly sold back its own mediocrity by people like Jeffrey Cooper, that "brains" in all of their unmarketable originality and complexity had become a more endangered species than any disappearing owl or chimpanzee.

Tony handed him the results. The little meter showed Jeffrey's stress level to be at an adequately comfortable *five*.

Tony smiled triumphantly.

In no way did he want to lose Jeffrey, whose brain was starting cumulatively to clog from stress, which was why the system had started sending him to Dr. Rosenputter in the first place. Still, as his German therapist put the meter away, Jeffrey stayed in a state of almost blissful self-containment, which he wanted to attribute to Tony, even though he wasn't exactly sure about this.

Sadly, at his very bone and gristle, Tony loved Jeffrey, though certainly not in any common fleshly way. He knew Jeffrey's story inside out; at least the part he, as Jeffrey's therapist and lifeline to life-sustaining, position-saving, emotional stability, played in it. Besides, he was already married to Robert Conway, a trim, cute-as-a-button English middle-market manager in his thirties, very on-the-go and excellent for Tony after his amicable divorce from Elsie. Tony and Elsie were still close; they had a daughter and both were too artistic and sophisticated for rancor, which the masses could vent in their own grubby way. Although sometimes Robert "vented," having a spunky little Cockney part of him that popped out, like when he came close to throttling a blubbering jerk at a favorite beer bar, who had no idea at all what "proper boundaries" meant.

"I'm so pleased," Tony said. "We have to report it; no way out. How do you feel?"

Jeffrey smiled back at him, almost too sweetly, with his usual highly developed professional's awareness that, grateful as he was, this was the time to make his therapist feel good as well.

"Good. Thanks for the tip about the 'forces.' I can use them. Can you help me more with this?"

"*Naturlich*," Tony said with his now-restored, utterly professional, supercompassionate smile. "*Guten abend.*"

❦

Jeffrey was out on the street with a heavenly sense of well-being, as if the man who had been attacked on the platform were a million miles or several light years away. The lovely, soft twinkle of the gathering evening lights on Tiergartenstrasse filled his walk and posture with delight. Little finches tweeted in the clipped linden trees. He was floating a bit, so he did not want to risk the pubtran again. It was always mobbed, as most of Germany worked 24/7 on shifts that fed and then relieved each other. This was hailed as the "ultimate freedom": You could work "anytime you wanted," but with little idea with whom you worked. Ultimately, you had to be willing to work about seventy or even eighty percent of your life away.

There were big rewards, of course, and, for Jeffrey, working around so many beautiful people, especially young men, was among them. They turned his eyes and made his heart flutter, even if it were mostly impossible for him to reveal any intentions toward them. But he worked around them, sometimes lunched with them, gossiped, dropped names and sometimes even small hints of his feelings. Office temptations, frowned upon as romantic stress, or "heartache" as it was once called, were as bad as any other form of stress. He'd brought some of his fleeting heartache to Tony, who quickly advised him:

"They are co-workers, Jeffrey. Not fantasy items. Never see them as that!"

That advice had worked. Until Rick came along.

Azure-eyed, golden-skinned, a German blond in his early thirties with a young gymnast's body. They'd met at the gym, not the office, so Jeffrey felt a bit more comfortable being attracted to him. Rick found Jeffrey "cool," and very much liked what he did.

"Your *profession* fascinates me!" he exclaimed, as they unwound in the sauna after a cool-down shower.

Jeffrey smiled. Everything about this young man fascinated him, especially with only a damp towel wrapped around his tight waist.

"You know from Komputer *Ahts*?" Rick asked seriously.

Jeffrey nodded. "*Ja.*"

Rick reported on a local art show he'd had in a cheap student bar, and his several attempts to rise up in the *Komputerkunst* world. He was very ardent and serious, as Jeffrey gazed at him. This was *Art*, Jeffrey thought: all those ripples, two perfect little nipples, mile-wide shoulders, elegant mustang neck. The young man's silky skin fit easily over the golden proportions of his frame like something Mies Van Der Rohe might have made, only more beautiful, more satisfying, more breath taking. Rick was a heart-stopper. As for *komputer* art? Fluff, whipped up and served on Jell-O, a cutesy sideline for the system. What Jeffrey did kept the global consumer economy going. Call it hardball merchandising or the fine art of persuasion, it was real, as real as this boy's navel or his very appealing chest.

"Imagine," Rick said, his eyes closed, smiling, "if *the* Leonardo had had such things. Just *imagine* what he could have done!"

Jeffrey nodded, watching Rick's gleaming body and the slightly coppery-rose hue on his shoulders. He had stored in his mind every Leonardo image. He knew where they came from and how they were used: Leonardo inside, Leonardo outside, and even the artist in some hysterically funny little places in the middle; he actually knew things Leonardo could not possibly have known about his own work. The vast influence of it, and its constant inflation as a worldwide commodity. He wanted to laugh, but didn't—*Imagine* Leonardo's magnificent creativity and intellect sucked dry and then spit out as simply more product by the bland merchandising steamroller of the system! It was impossible.

He almost laughed, but let Rick go on talking about himself. They made a date for later; weekend drinks in Jeffrey's upper-floor apartment, where Rick became strangely stony and silent, more impressed than he could admit and obviously not eager to take his clothes off.

Jeffrey smiled until it became uncomfortable, then suggested, "Maybe we should go somewhere else?"

Rick jumped in, naming one of those no-holds-barred clubs where chemicals flowed and nothing happened until four a.m. Jeffrey wasn't sure he should be seen in such a place, but Rick leaned in and kissed him, and Jeffrey found himself in a state of more help-lessness (and horniness) than he was used to admitting.

He excused himself and raced into the bathroom. There, using a small, painless pump that left no mark, he injected himself with a high-testosterone-and-mega-boosters supplement, laced with just enough long-acting, nitrogen-enhancing stiffeners: very useful if one were going to be out late with the possibility of recreational drugs and sex, activities in which he had not indulged in decades.

Slightly anxious, he came upon Rick inspecting his museum-quality art collection, and the latest, trendiest products in leather, crystal, space-age fibers, titanium, and other stylish materials that easily came his way. He suddenly turned to Jeffrey, as if exposed.

"You're very good-looking!" the young man blurted out.

Jeffrey felt giddy and delighted. This wasn't supposed to happen. He definitely needed to be more careful, and now . . .

The club was rocking with kids a third his age. Rick picked up a green glass beaker from a tray.

"Try one of these."

Pinpoints of light swam gently in the room, reminding Jeffrey of young dolphins off a private island in the Caribbean where he'd vacationed a long time ago.

He picked up another green glass and looked suspiciously at it, then he and Rick downed them quickly. Everything worked beauti-fully for a while. Rick got closer, and soon they were dancing bare-chested in a corner all to themselves. But the dolphins were now in his brain, along with an avalanche of images, some of them almost sixty years old, following behind.

Losing the veneer that held him together, Jeffrey started babbling uncontrollably, feeling frightened and *too* naked, as if everyone could see exactly what he really was and what he looked like underneath. The kids began to look almost fetal and Rick stared at him strangely. Stuck in some endless loop of confessions and small talk from his youth, Jeffrey pushed for whatever security he could reach in the words tumbling out of his mouth.

"Not everybody had their own little screens then or even cell phones and . . . people were scared of foreigners because of the wars and they'd blow things up . . . and Daddy . . . oh no . . . not Daddy . . . oil was all they talked about and how things were going to get hot. Big cars were everywhere and they still had little records and computers that couldn't see everything . . . and books were still on paper . . . don't you see he died because I—"

He couldn't shut himself up; he was too scared of falling into the isolating abyss of his own silence. What would happen if he did? There was only the big sorrowful noise of the club that made him feel tiny and old. He tried to pull Rick even closer to him. But the young man, beneath the ear-splitting sound, whispered slowly:

"You can't be *that* old."

Then he walked out, leaving Jeffrey sobbing under the noise.

He told Tony about the experience. He felt buried under his own years, facing a mortality that even he could no longer deny.

"You should have seen that boy's face. The contempt he had for me. I hate myself for doing what I did."

"Don't hate yourself," Tony said warmly, lovingly. "Don't blame yourself. It's never good to do that. You know as well as I do that you must act responsibly, without holding on to blame."

Somewhat consoled, Jeffrey nodded.

Tony looked sweetly at him. In a moment, he would suggest an anti-stress breathing exercise, but now he repeated: "It's never good to blame yourself, Jeffrey. You must know that."

"It must have been what was in the glass. I started seeing things I couldn't hold back."

"From too long ago? Places you don't want to go back to, and by all means should not?"

"Yes. Definitely, yes."

Jeffrey cried and Tony reached over and handed him a tissue. Jeffrey dried his eyes, while Tony touched his shoulder gently.

"This Rick. Does someone like that make you feel younger?"

"No. He made me feel older. He was so calculating, but childish. He wanted to use me, that's all. He figured out my age, and—I was really stupid, wasn't I?"

"*Kein so schwer.* Not so hard on yourself. He was a pickup. You just have to be more careful with your involvements. Maybe there's not enough free space"—he pointed to Jeffrey's head—"up there for that kind of complexity. Know what I'm saying?"

Tony was right. There was not a lot of "free space" inside Jeffrey, despite all the work done on him. Yet he wanted some free space, some space for his heart. But how could he ever admit it?

He'd been seduced by Rick's beauty, by the golden classical balance of it and the promise of the almost unbearable pleasures it might give him. That was where he had got himself trapped: He had waded into that beauty until he was way over his head. Work was different; there he knew exactly what the uses of beauty and style were—how powerful they were, how dominating. He could manipulate beauty without getting sucked into its icy-hot emotional vortex. At work, beauty was only a series of style elements, to be rearranged until they fitted the purpose of sales.

Free space.

Yes, Rick had crawled in where there was no room left for a private life, a life of the soul. There was only the cramped but well-catalogued warehouse of Jeffrey's mind, where he could extract and pinpoint the various forms and reactions ("tastes") associated with thousands of products and trends, creating precise charts of merging and diverging data on them, all for the benefit of sales.

Managers jumped on him, questioning: "How can this change? We've got to make it look new again. What do we do to sell it fresh?"

A small case in point:

A new dining room chair was to be produced in some cheap-labor alley of Asia by a big brand name Jeffrey would guide through dozens of refinements in form, style, and construction, as it tried to push sales through a fickle global market. Taste was hard to predict, but Jeffrey was so fluent in the various languages of product development that he knew how one item impacted on the sales of another, where price and style points merged, and how a can't-lose hit in tiny, class-conscious Singapore could be a washout with the masses of big, class-struggling Russia.

Money was so instantly, aggressively fluid that doing the right thing with it was crucial. Every barely conscious twist of this market cost something, so knowing what was feasible and profitable in this wild cascade of liquid wealth put you into an extremely enviable position.

In the old days men like Frank Lloyd Wright and Le Corbusier had said, "Form follows function." But "function" in this self-lavishing economy could be anything you made of it, and Jeffrey knew that ninety percent of any sales language was intention, which had to be guided and predicted, point by point, for something to work. He made it his business to know exactly how something was intended to be used. The question was, what would people pay for this intention, and what even more unconscious fantasies could he drive into the original intention to induce them to pay more? Status? Security? Power? "Spirituality"? Youth? Excitement?

In short, what might this ridiculous dining-room chair mean to the masses of people who'd buy it, and how could he make it *mean* so much more than they were willing to admit?

Now on Tiergartenstrasse, he felt excited, springy, younger—O.K., much *younger,* just from being with Tony and having come out on the good side of his stress test. Tony was right, there were *forces* you could call on if you knew them, and Jeffrey wanted to believe so much that Tony was one of them.

Tony, wise, fatherly beyond his years—father to an old/young man like Jeffrey—would protect him against an encroaching jungle of problems, including young men like Rick.

Jeffrey wanted to wipe the recent violence on the pubtran platform out of his head, to drive it away with something nice. Amusing. He recalled that Chris Stewart and Leonard Silverman, a well-placed queer professional couple, were hosting a cocktail party in their big apartment overlooking a desirable, well-tended park. Chris was fifty-six, but managed somehow to look like he was still in his late forties. This was not as young as Jeffrey appeared, but it was all fairly natural and Jeffrey was positive that there was no chance Chris's lifespan would be extended one year more than the stalking Reaper himself would allow.

Chris, an academic, specialized in English poetry of the Renaissance, a "frosting-on-the-cake" specialty that only some universities pushing for social cachet offered. Academic positions in the Arts were really about class and status, since for the most part you had to have means of your own to take them. Definitely an "old boy" system, it got more and more so as time went by, even if a few "old girls" were let in.

As a requirement, the artsy academics had to know how to converse in their special, jargon-laden, inbred, always-tripping-at-the-edge-of-facetious, "pinkies out" manner, as if ye olde brothers Wilde and Warhol were giving notes from on high, assigning Membership-Reward points toward evanescent immortality. Dr. Len Silverman was not a member of this club. He was an overbooked thoracic surgeon with a pronounced tic, making *gelt* by the nanosecond but crashing in on seventy and looking every year of it. Always on the verge of a breakdown, Len, according to some gossips, could be eased out. Maybe even be pushed into the ghastly twilight state of Suspension.

Jeffrey shivered at the thought of it. It seemed revoltingly cruel how certain key people were kept alive, their vitality and youth unrolled by the system like an endless red carpet, while poor Dr. Len was sliding into death, even though as a surgeon with genuine impact on human life, he had value.

Perhaps he could not take his own stress too much longer, and lacked Jeffrey's talent to glide (seemingly effortlessly) above so much pressure. Len was a neurotic, nail-biting perfectionist, a veteran of decades of therapy, but still nothing worked. He'd been born this way, the late-conceived only child of Sydney and Goldie Silverman, two abrasively over reaching, overdemanding, socially ambitious New York Jews who insisted that their driven-to-overachievement *boychik* become a medical specialist.

And in truth it fit him. It made Len happy: the status, the money, the parochial power. But he was *ganz* crazy, *total verukt*, as the Krauts would say, and he did everything to excess (back-to-back schedules of tense operations, smoking, drinking, jabbering on incessantly while stuffing his gullet till he threw up), while Chris hovered in the background like some diva waiting to jump into her aria, the one about being holy Mother Theresa to her darling Dr. Len—true—but without Len's money, nothing. No full-time North African maid. No beautiful white seaside house in Ibiza, plus another sweet but smaller apartment in New York overlooking yet another prestigious park. Chris and Len were both hothouse orchids who would have withered and died under the pressure Jeffrey survived every day, with hundreds of millions of dollars riding on his decisions, though Chris never admitted the importance of any other human being except himself. He had brought them to Germany where English Renaissance *Kultur* was ever *sehr hot,* universities still proclaiming it *spitz klasse,* a thing with which to be acquainted in the cultivated, High-Art-worshipping society of Europe.

It had worked. Here he was a *macher.* In the U.S. he would have remained an unimportant adjunct, bypassed for promotion by bland, stupid men who brought more money into the department, often coming with equally powerful corporate wives.

"*Liebchen!*" Chris greeted Jeffrey loudly at the door. "*Kom!*"

Chris loved a theatrical entrance, even if he didn't make it himself. He went on, in tribute to Jeffrey's background:

"Miz SCARLET!! Th' Germans are comin'! Th' Germans!" Then putting on a fat glop of Alabama accent, which Jeffrey, admittedly, occasionally lapsed into himself (though not nearly so hick-thick), added: "*Wie geht's,* ya'll?"

Jeffrey stood mute, squeezing in the visual aspects of the moment: Chris, perfectly ridiculous; distant slices of people milling past the foyer. He stepped forward as Chris announced:

"Ladies and gentlemen! We are pleased t' introduce *the* Empress of Aesthetic Information, Mr. Jeffrey Cooper!"

Jeffrey only nodded, as Chris, forever one to gild the lily to the point of blackening it, added, "How you be, *lieber knabchen?*"

Every face in the large living room turned disdainfully toward Jeffrey, with the look you'd expect on show horses when cheap hay was passed around. This convinced Jeffrey that some humble but suitably clever retort was demanded.

"I'm not *the* Empress, Chris," he began flat enough. Then, in a slightly exaggerated Southern drawl, finished: "Ah'm just one o' her ol' ladies-in-waitin'."

Chris's eyes, darkened with mascara, rolled to the ceiling as he boomed, "No, you ahn't, dear! You're *no* lady, and I'm Maria Stuarti."

Jeffrey shrugged, and said, "Sure. Distant kin, I guess. But she lost her head, didn't she?"

Dr. Len sped over to them. "What are you two girls gabbing so much about? Chris honey, *sehr unhöfflich* to monopolize our esteemed guest."

Chris, wearing his version of a regal Chinese hostess outfit (black silk pajamas, jacket mostly unbuttoned, twinkly ropes of gold and silver dripping off his chest), apologized in singsong: "So solly, Doccy Lenny. We no sure Missy Jeffey gonna make it t'night!"

Then he called out to the maid. "Azeena! See to it that Mr. Cooper gets what he wants."

The silk p.j. look had peaked about eight years earlier, part of a 1920's revival that hit every few decades. However, it was loose, looked good on men of a certain age, forgiving a multitude of faults that some of them could not correct at the gym or with diets and hormones.

Chris had lost most of his hair, but had dark implants which, though plugged surgically (and very expensively) into his scalp, always looked like they'd been borrowed from some other unfortunate's skull. His body, though, was in good shape, in contrast to Len's, a sad landscape of paunchy bulges, sagging slopes, and pathetic droops. With severe health problems, Len was around death too much, an occupational hazard for doctors which often made them super-hypochondriacal.

In contrast to Chris, Len was in conservative cashmere, tie, and brogues, like a lawyer dining with partners. He pulled Jeffrey into the living room, where the drinks were out and he'd left a big glass of scotch. Azeena brought Jeffrey a glass of wine, and he sipped it while Len introduced him to six other men and three women, all doctors of Literature, Art, or Medicine. Two were surgeons who glanced quickly at Jeffrey and dismissed him.

Jeffrey realized he was the only person in the room not addressed as "Doctor." The realization made him smile: he'd be around after most of them were dust. It was an evil thought, but it made him feel very good.

The Stewart-Silvermans were socially competitive, and bragged to everyone how they got the *creme de la everyone* of greater Europe into their place with its balcony presenting a stunning view of the tree-filled attraction below. It was known, if not too regularly discussed, that there were nighttime activities in the park, the Germans never giving up their love for *sex alfresco*, or at least in the bushes. But Jeffrey could not imagine either Chris or Len engaged there. They were too busy being convivial with opera queen friends, Big Art queens, medical worthies, and too many others graciously trooping through these rooms reflecting Chris's glory. He had just had a publication in *Rosenkrantz*, a prestigious, rarely read German art magazine, about Marlowe's extensive place in German culture. Copies of it discreetly peeked out from every table, nook, and corner and its editor, Dieter North, was expected any moment.

"It's in English, too," Chris informed Jeffrey gleefully as he pushed the article at him, like it were coated in gold and some of it might rub off on Jeffrey's gross, market-stained fingers. "I realize your German is still limited, even though you've been here forever."

"It only feels like forever," Jeffrey replied, "depending on where I am."

It took Chris a moment to frown. He did not like people to top him in any way, and Jeffrey knew that this little *stücke* could come back to haunt him. Then, Dieter North, a pale, fat young man poking out of dark jeans and a skin-tight black T-shirt under a dirty blazer, materialized at the door. Chris was ecstatic, though the editor for the most part brushed him off as the two of them circulated among the guests, until North found the food, Algerian hill country specialties which Azeena made exceedingly well, and several waiting glasses of strong drink.

Len grabbed Jeffrey by the arm and whispered, "Come out with me to the balcony."

The balcony was large and wrapped around a corner. Len pulled Jeffrey to the far side of it, out of sight of everybody. They could see the park and smell it, with its faraway glistening little lake almost like a ballet set, masses of trees, and the nighttime dew coming up. "I need to talk to you," Len said as he lit a small Dutch cigar, called Apfelgold, that he liked to smoke. "You mind?" he asked, politely, holding up the cigar.

Jeffrey shook his head.

"Good. I think I'm going to die."

Jeffrey's head bowed; they'd had this conversation before. It was the only piece of intimacy Len ever disclosed between them. Jeffrey knew nothing about Len's private life, if he had one, but death was always stalking the good doctor.

"Are you sick?"

"No. I mean, yes. Of course I'm sick! You know that. My heart's held together with chewing gum, a bunch of splints, some tubes and stitches. I'm dying from pressure, too much work, too much stress. I've got to make too much money, with too many social obligations I can't take and too many people I can't stand."

Len's face tightened with rage, while Jeffrey slowly exhaled, releasing any ambient stress into the air he possibly could. He was taking umpteen more drugs to keep himself in the excellent condition he stayed in than Dr. Silverman would ever know. He needed patience with Len, that was certain. Patience, and perhaps a certain saintly sense of humor. He remained quiet for a few seconds.

"I hate these things!" Len spat out, his tic causing his head to jerk (it came out double when he needed to make a point). "We got a bunch of *mumsers* in there who only *fress* on our food. Even the maid gets sick of it!"

"Why not talk to Chris about it?"

"Sure! Then she'd go into her martyrdom number: 'All I do is take care of you, darling! You know that!' Besides, Her Royal Highness doesn't like to discuss the life of the Court with *vekachte* me. If he didn't do this, he feels he'd get nowhere. So when he publishes some piece of dreck, we've got to have the high and the mighty here. That

Dieter North gives me the fuckin' creeps! I've wiped my butt with better, and Chris is licking him like he was coated with cocaine."

He paused for a second, drawing on his cigar.

"Not that I do coke anymore. Fuck, I wish I could!"

"I'm sorry," Jeffrey said sadly.

He didn't feel sad, but thought he should act it. Nobody there knew his real age, or the real consequences of his job. They had an inkling, but not the reality. There were things you didn't expose with social-climbing queens in Germany, and he counted his age, true professional status, and any proximity to deeper feelings among them. But he liked Len, despite his faux problems. Once Len revealed to him that the real tragedy of his life was that he'd never be able to acquire the yacht he coveted: it was sixty-eight feet long and required several crew members. "You should see it," he cried. "Breaks my heart. I could never afford something like that. Anyway, when you work as hard as I do, what are you going to do with it? Take it out once a year?"

"Can I tell you something?" Len asked, taking a slow drag from the cigar then releasing the smoke in a long, graceful oval, a skill he adored showing off.

"Shoot."

"I was operating this week. I had the poor guy's chest open; he wasn't going to make it. Sometimes you know that. He was a bottom-level worker and there wasn't much reason to keep him around. So there he was. We went in, did what we could, and suddenly I heard something. Prayers from my bar mitzvah. The old Jewish prayers I hadn't heard in ages. I mean, I'm not Jewish enough to be a real Jew anymore, just enough to *kvetch*. Here we are in Germany, where most of my family was wiped out in the old century. But 'bygones,' right? You're not supposed to dwell on that. It's always a new world. So I heard the prayers and they're marching up and down the *bimah*, you know the raised altar, with the Torah, showing it to the world, and I looked up and I'm smiling. I'm so young and my parents are there. Goldie in that pink Chanel knockoff she got on sale, and my dad Sydney, who's eyeing everybody like he's at the cash register and they're going to cheat him, and as usual they're convinced that their kid's a genius.

"I'm not. But they're convinced. Then suddenly I looked down, and there I was: it's me on the table. Me, dead. I can't take the sight of that. So I got somebody else to close up for me. I left the operating room. I swear, I just couldn't take it."

Jeffrey put his hand on Len's shoulder.

"That doesn't mean you're going to die, Len."

"Then what the hell does it mean?"

Jeffrey thought quickly.

"You're just scared of your limitations. We all are."

"Are you, Jeffrey? You never seem scared. Chris is. He's scared shitless. He's always got to be 'Dr. This' and I'm 'Dr. That'! He's got a fucking Ph.D. in Renaissance crap and who the hell gives a shit about the Renaissance? People think 'Renaissance' is a damn car!"

A familiar voice boomed out:

"Lenny! Jeffrey! There you are!"

Chris emerged with Angelina Harkness, a bone-thin woman in a short black-beaded outfit who sailed into her specialty, Baroque enamels, as if Len were genuinely interested or Jeffrey impressed.

"I've just come back from the Prado," she whispered, as if she were about to spill a dark family secret. "What those people have! The treasures! But you've got to get into the closed back rooms where they don't let the public in to see the *really* good stuff. They have this one exquisite little masterpiece of a pin: an Infanta from the time of Felipe Quattro. An absolute masterpiece in miniature, like Velazquez himself painted it. And no one *ever* gets to see it!"

Jeffrey nodded, then said dryly:

"It's nice, but I've seen better."

Chris stared at him icily. "Where?"

"The Metropolitan in New York has a similar one on display. I've compared them. Yours was done by André de la Ville-Martin, a minor but talented French artist who liked the Spanish court. They had so much money then. A lot of artists circulated in and out of the court to pursue it. Nothing's that different today. But if you look through the Met's extensive digital files on miniatures, you'll find some even better things, like half a dozen pieces. They all show up."

Angelina whipped back her thin shoulders.

"I don't know who you are, but you're nuts! The Prado enamel Infanta from that period is one of a kind. I'll bet you *anything* on that."

"They say it," countered Jeffrey, "but there's almost no such thing anymore. The duplicates come out of hiding; you always find something you didn't know about. No matter who you are."

Jeffrey tried not to smirk; it was difficult.

Len was gloating, while Chris went into a visible seethe.

Angelina Harkness pivoted on one heel, turning her back on Len and Jeffrey.

"Chris, I must go. Thank you. This has been *one* lovely party!"

She hurried from the balcony. Chris started after her, then stopped short. He bolted back to Jeffrey, his eyes flaming.

"Where the hell do you come off? This woman's made a lifetime study of that period. You don't even have a graduate degree! You're a high-class nerd with a good memory, that's all."

"I think," Len interjected, "someone's had a little too much drinky." He pulled Chris's arm. "Our guests are ready to leave. Why don't you say good night to them?"

For a second Chris stood frozen with anger, then Len managed to direct him off the balcony and into the living room. Jeffrey stayed outside. He could see what he thought was some kind of activity in the park, some subtle stirring in the bushes. Years ago he had scored there, but had since given up stuff like that. It didn't do anything for him, although the memory was nice, a pretty little glimmer of some actual physical excitement to keep around.

Shortly, Len came back to join him.

"Sorry 'bout Her Imperial Majesty. She got a little too worked up. I think that North creep snubbed him, drank our booze, *fressed* our *essen* and is going to skedaddle soon. So Empress Chris needed to take it out on somebody. He'll probably call you tomorrow and apologize, but let me do it tonight."

"I accept," Jeffrey replied instantly. "For both of you. And probably I shouldn't have mentioned the Metropolitan's holdings. Several years ago, I needed to do a deep search through their files on those kind of things. I went to the Met, they showed me pictures of every piece of enamel in the world, theirs and everyone else's. It's all in their files, including some private stuff they don't normally share with anyone. But I represented the right money, so I got in. I guess Angelina's position, despite all her degrees, just did not get her access to it."

"You know a lot," Len admitted. "An awful lot." He hugged Jeffrey, whispering, "I wish I could get away. Get that boat I want and just get the hell out."

The balcony door opened, and Len let go of him. It was Chris again, looking a bit more relaxed.

"I guess I blew it too hard, didn't I?" he said to Jeffrey.

"It's all right. We all do sometimes."

"I thought she was going to have a major conniption, and I couldn't exactly get pissed at her. She's a *grande dame* in my department, you know. She wrote the book on those enamels. But sometimes the nerds win, right?" He smiled, his look offering an olive branch.

"We don't win," Jeffrey said genuinely. "We still have to work for the people who really do."

Chris went back to his guests, and soon afterward Dieter North himself appeared, making a sweep of good-byes, including one to Len.

"You are *so* cultivated *für ein Arz*," he crooned. "Most doctors do not engage the good life of the soul as you do."

"*Danke sehr*," Len said with a slight smirk. A moment later he accompanied Jeffrey to the door. The two of them were alone in the foyer. He started to choke up.

"I don't want to die." Tears glittered in Len's wrinkled eyes. "Can you do something for me, anything? I get it that you know how to work the system, Jeffrey. I'm just a doctor, they'll find another one of me in a year. If not sooner."

"Do you talk to your therapist about this?"

"Yeah. She just says I'm a perfectionist, give it up."

Jeffrey felt genuinely sad. She was probably right. Maybe it was time for Len Silverman to give it up.

"I can't do anything for you, Len. I'm sorry."

"Are you sure?" Len whispered. The party was breaking up; soon others would be at the door.

Jeffrey gave it a quick thought.

"What is it you've got, Len? I mean knowledge. *Power.* What kind of advantage—leverage—do you have over anybody that you can grab at? And how can you keep others from getting to it, without them even knowing it? Can you tell me that, Len?"

Len took a step away, then burst into tears. He took out a hand-kerchief and blew his nose.

"Nothing," he sobbed. "I've got *nothing.*"

For a moment, under the bright street lamps, Jeffrey thought about going into the park and perusing the lit sidewalks.

It was a quick knee-jerk snap of curiosity, something he hardly indulged in anymore. Temptation he indulged in, when everything was dangled in front of him, but curiosity was rare. Curiosity could be dangerous, getting you into things the system did not like. He was close to a cab stand. With energy in any form everywhere in chronic, when not acutely, short supply, cabs were often a hard choice even for chosen people like Jeffrey. But Jeffrey was in a position to treat himself: he felt he deserved it. He had taken a cab from Tony's to the party, but he deserved another ride with all the games, news, movies, and entertainment cabs provided. You could even take some of it home, if you felt like it when the trip was over.

Ah, temptation.

Temptation was wonderful; it kept him, if not most of the world, in business. But if he deserved to indulge himself in the temptation of a comfy private cab, didn't he deserve, just for curiosity's sake, a walk in the park, too?

He might clear his head a bit, and then think extra-hard about work. That seemed perfectly right and innocent enough. And nothing, he assured himself, would make him stray even for a moment from the concrete walks.

He began walking, thinking, opening the big files in his head and pulling things out, as some new pressing design-consult projects were already lining up for him and his group.

There was a large Mormon chapel in Wisconsin, loaded with ancient biblical, D. W. Griffith-esque architectural details. And a low-end line of beauty products called "Goddess," aimed at a rapidly emerging Indian market of barely-literate village girls getting their first real paychecks and ardently desiring to be "in the know," featuring lip tints, blushes, and red and blonde hair colorings custom-mixed for dark complexions. Also, a high-end status car that was going be conceived virtually from *scratch.*

That is, if "scratch" meant that it would come with a deliciously, tinglingly transgressive, ever-so-slightly sexually naughty and ambiguous, "neo- Rudoph Valentino" romantic personality embedded into the actual material of the thing.

Since evidence of personality had been all but eradicated in most people, it was mandatory for products to have it. People not only wore their hearts on their sleeves, but also a lot of quasi-revelatory merchandise exposing various "intimate" aspects of themselves. You could "find yourself" in your own *exclusive* brand or line, something made "just for you." In everything from high couture to plumbing, an obligatory "Release" aspect was essential, like the promise of an orgasm. It never came, but that promise, and the covenant that went with it, that sacred sizzle pointing toward Redemption, was necessary: as in, after so much brain-sucking work and ceaseless effort, you were going to be brought to . . . *yes,* Release!

Yes. Yes. Yes: just give it to me!

That big, utterly waited for martini at the end of the day. Even teetotalers deserved one.

A new product had to be a kind of mini-resort, transporting you away from the everyday even if it were for everyday use. Jeffrey's various clients, consultants, accountants, and handlers, the ones who came to him and reported about him, barked over and over the importance of "Release."

Life without *Release* was just too cruel, and definitely did not lead to profit.

He extracted one report from his mind that stated this perfectly:

"'Release' is that thing that pulls the consumer out of herself and brings her closer to those fantasies of the real adventure, excitement, and fulfillment that she craves. 'Release' is that trip into the Unknown that we all want, though sometimes fear.

"In the marketing world, that trip can be controlled and designed into products and experiences that suggest adventure without risk, curiosity without failure, and pure wholesome entertainment for the consumer.

"This is the responsibility of all of us involved in product development, marketing, and world advancement through global humane entrepreneurship."

He walked through the park, staying on concrete under the bright lights, not even allowing his feet to touch the grass.

Release. . . .

Yes, even poor Dr. Silverman needed "Release." Jeffrey smiled: Len needed to *like* his own life a little. You could be too driven and end up like him: disciplined, perfectionist, about to die. Hell! Death was so distasteful, the ultimate failure and disgrace. He stopped, deep now in the park, watching three men in super-tight jeans quietly leave a thick clump of bushes nestled below the brow of a hill.

They were somewhere in their thirties to early forties, kind of natural-looking, not *tuntie*-types. Tuntie was German slang for queens. A certain class of Germans always loathed *tuntieness*; it did not go along with that hyper-masculine but baroquely mannered image of antique virility and nobility that so many German boys still romantically sucked up: fairytale mountain hunting lodges; anthracite-black leather pants. T-shirt-bursting, Tom of Finland muscles and super-big, uncut sausage cocks.

He waded into the bushes, dark and scented bewitchingly with wet leaves and the too familiar odor of white-wine-and-beer-soaked German breath. He would get messy, his nice clothes soaked in dew. He closed his eyes and loved it instantly, just allowing himself to. Then he flashed back to Len:

"Nothing," Len confessed. "I have *nothing.*"

Then he flashed to: I hope I don't get robbed. But with a click he could stop most of his credit, and tell no one at work. Or at least try not to. Then this thought came to him, like the text in one of those signs with glimmering, luscious lettering:

Relax, baby. Just relax, Jeffrey.

(Yes, he said inside: I'm sick and fucking tired of stress. Stressed out from it.)

Tony had told him about forces who came to help. Angels or whatever you wanted them to be. Maybe one was there. Carefully, he went darker and deeper, under thick overhead branches blotting out the soft inquiring gray eyes of night.

He took a narrow, well-worn path through brush, and immediately liked the freshness of it, so much fresher than Len and Chris's fancy party with everything stale except Azeena's cooking. He liked this dew-soft atmosphere. It reminded him of Alabama; of being a kid and secret walks at night filled with yearning and youth's sweet sadness. Sometimes the workless took stinky shits in the parks, in hidden alcoves like this. Luckily, this time they hadn't and all was nicely fresh.

He reached the last, darkest level, and the disembodied hand of a jinni, or some immaterial fairy whose magical intentions had been normalized by desire, reached out for him, then unbuttoned his shirt and took his shirt out of his pants. Another hand unzipped him. Then someone sucked him, just like that. The unseen mysteries in this fragrant chapel of foliage were luscious and equalizing, like sacred rituals of a sacrament before God. Who he was, his actual age hidden deeper and deeper into a closet of its own, what he was or was forced to pretend to be, meant nothing here. God would surely be thanked as this soft, experienced, pleasuring mouth and those gently groping hands asked of Jeffrey nothing. Which was exactly what Len Silverman was sure he had.

Nothing.

How sad that Len could perceive only this bitter end run around his true self, which contained, in truth, everything. Jeffrey felt *everything* now: the opposite of nothing. This vast, secret element, this mystery expressed in images shooting through his brain, going back to—anyway, they were there: knights and hieroglyphs, warriors, sacred monks, all bending forward, submitting to this one huge pulse, the volcanic phallus of . . . the supreme Eye. Yes, *It* saw him. Even in the dark.

The Eye of Jeffrey's brain was now looking at him as he was being "indulged," and Jeffrey, at this moment, free, continuous, and exposed to his own self, was happy with his guard down.

Tony's forces had come.

But who were they?

He didn't ask, as he felt his whole physical brain being sprayed with that calming mist of himself (yes, it had to be *of* himself!) that Tony had prescribed and told him to use to ward off stress. Ah, that elemental but so difficult to enter mist! Nothing like a delicious blowjob to bring it on. He felt mercifully suspended in it, like his cock were a trapeze and he was flying effortlessly through space on it, and even on his own body attached to it, and then even on the anonymous, sweetly attentive mouth sucking him.

He was suspended quite effortlessly (away from stress) in this gracious mist. But despite all the effort expended on him (both by Science, and those lips and that mouth with the talented, triple-trilling tongue), he wasn't exactly sure how far he could go beyond just getting very nicely hard, though this man was doing an exquisitely detailed job, reminding him of the refined, inside door-handle details on a few of the super-*luxe* cars he'd consulted on.

That alone was impressive, and "Release," no matter how far his rather retro-at-heart body took him, was going to be there. He knew it. And certainly could tell that ol' "Release" when he encountered it. This was definitely not something out of a supermarket bottle, or the stratospherically priced insides of a car. This was gorgeously real, and he could feel it in the wet dark. He had got into some wild, fugitive scenes in his twenties and thirties, but that was before a lot happened, both at work and in the world.

Everyone was so overworked now. It was sad. He needed to enjoy every second of this, every second that would not come again.

Then the mouth stopped, and the hands went on to someone else. He tucked himself back in, carefully making sure even in the dark that his shirt, wallet, and everything else were back where they should be, then he made his way back to the concrete.

His wallet was O.K., but several cops were now cruising about on scooters, going up the paths and even off them. Two had a man in handcuffs. The man, maybe forty with some gray in his dark hair and rumpled-looking dirty clothes, like he'd been either sleeping in them or on his knees a lot, quickly glanced at Jeffrey and smirked.

The man began to motion toward Jeffrey. But Jeffrey bolted away from him, dashing down a concrete walk to the entrance to the park.

Chapter Three

*T*he next morning, Thursday, was filled moment to moment with work, red-dotted with video-teleconferencing with people in Mumbai; Wal-doh, a recently sprouted manufacturing center near Shanghai; and Flint, Michigan, which seemed more foreign and archaically behind the global marketing culture than either of the other two. Flint had stayed stuck in time, like some large animal trying desperately to release itself from a freshly tarred road in August. Mumbai was another story. Once the glittering Bombay of the Raj, it was cosmopolitan, progressive, and the center of India's starstruck, media-obsessed, fabulously (but never too openly) queerish film world. Its large force of talent moved when it wanted to, married or didn't, and was more devoted to style than religion. India was outsourcing to the U.S., where people were not nearly so educated and Christian fundamentalism had detoured science and technology back to the time when Charles Darwin and his big theory were still hotly debated in school systems.

To Jeffrey the whole thing seemed too screwy: they were mining on the moon, but the Virgin Mary was the ultimate America beauty queen, and no one could relinquish his God-given right not to be descended from monkeys. Man was God's ultimate creation, but, Jeffrey wondered, since Darwin never went past Man, shouldn't the two ideas have met at some common "stylistic" point, that is, one freighted neither with orthodoxy nor theory?

As he stood amid the monitors in his office, looking at an endless catalogue of objects, their relations and histories, it was easy for Jeffrey to observe that in the world of style there was evolution, too, as well as "spontaneous creation," usually caused by some conscious-ness of an immediate necessity. War. Status. Both called for necessi-ties. So you had the advent of stylish officers' field uniforms and their accompanying necessary grooming kits; from these evolved much of the present "classic" clothing and status accoutrements, such as the sterling hip flask, the pocket comb, and the ever-convenient cocktail shaker.

Everything, then, that could be brought to human consciousness had evolved into a "style situation," hinging on how a need could be understood, refined, presented, then sold. Logically enough, thoughts and ideas went through the same process, with mock-ups, focus groups, and opinion surveys, as the results were disseminated through a media controlled by the same people who sold the products on it. This was the system's source of knowledge, and most people's as well. There was, of course, one ultimate secret: *People*, as the consumerate, were the *products*, and what was sold to them, *for* them, was simply another means of keeping them in that category.

The Flint Mormon chapel was Jeffrey's version of a private joke; sometimes he needed one just to prove he was still alive. He'd thrown in a slew of obvious pagan, Hindu, and Native American references, some so blatantly phallic or vulvar that if you were not oblivious, you'd blush. The various church committees, which had subcontracted to get expert advice to reconsider Jeffrey's expert advice, had no idea what was going on. They wanted the chapel to look "Modern," but also "Traditional." This was no problem, as terms like "Modern" and "Traditional" were interchangeable, since "Modern" had such a long tradition and "Traditional," in a politically conservative sales climate, saw itself as being the last outpost of the truly "Modern." That is, the one authentic place where all "superficial" fads stopped.

Therefore, real Old constantly reemerged as "real" New again.

Politics had become style exercises too, as the most painfully narrow interpretations of Christianity were judged to be completely up-to-date, while liberal or progressive interpretations were seen as throwbacks to violent, less controlled earlier periods. Genuine creativity was suspect; strictness and discipline were prized. So Jeffrey often stressed these terms in his reports:

"This curve, though decorative, conforms to the *strict* recommendations and buyer expectations of the product developers."

Or: "You will be gratified by the disciplined formulations of these cremes, and the purity and organic *strictness* of their formulas."

Everything he did was reported to someone else. There were spies in his own branch of the system, and from competing foreign branches. In a combustible, overpopulated, overstressed world, people used style the way they had once used religion: as a marker of class, nationality, and belief, and also as a sign of values dearly held in one's inner life, although private thoughts and desires had become almost extinct luxuries. People were too overworked, their minds too crowded for these kinds of unsharable feelings which might contain taboo pedophilic images or lead to outbreaks of new, foreign-born, sexually transmitted diseases. Fundamentalism easily rushed into this vacuum, presenting a ready outlet for the unsettling private fantasies and wishes many people once had.

"Jeffrey! Jeffrey Cooper in Germany! Is it ever a *delight* to hear your voice and see you!"

Jeffrey was on videophone with Ashok Rahman, a young, earnest, brand manager working in Mumbai on the "Goddess" project.

Jeffrey tried to keep a straight face.

"Thank you. Did you get the new colors? What's the feeling about them and the price structure, based on quality and packaging?"

"Cool! Everything is sooo cool! We're hot for it. However—"

Ashok's sweet, slightly fleshy dark face became several degrees more serious. He was wearing a very high-fashion, nipped-in French blazer, with a wide-striped tie that bounced with color. With his wry little mouth that could smile bewitchingly and a wavy mop of black hair flopping across his brow, he was not quite Nefertiti-gorgeous like some of the other always-emerging superstar manager kids, but he still had some genuine, old-school star sparkle to him, like an endearingly chunky Hindu Van Johnson.

Jeffrey smiled. Ashok did not.

"You were saying?" Jeffrey asked.

After dramatically clearing his throat, the young Indian confessed:

"I'm afraid there are some questions here about your pink."

"My *pink?*"

Jeffrey stopped smiling. He did not like being challenged.

"What about my *pink*? It's a regular *Indian* pink."

"Yes, sir. It's a little too *regular* Indian, if you ask us. *Too* Hindu, if you get my meaning. It falls into a provincial stereotype that the consumer is outgrowing here by the minute. Now, take *your* pink—let's say that particular *pink*: that slightly stomach-remedy pink." He tried bravely to smile, Van Johnson-like again. "I'm afraid, our studies show—"

Ashok hesitated. Deep water this was, and Jeffrey, who was perceived to be all-knowing when necessary, realized it. He had not been tested, raised up, and kept sparkling "in the pink" himself for nothing. He tried to seem routinely friendly, a bit supportive, and still not give up too much. He looked at the young man's face: Ashok was sweating hard; even dull Indian office illumination couldn't hide that. His hair looked streaky instead of glamorous.

Jeffrey increased the image size on his monitor as a drop of perspiration under Ashok's generous nose began to resemble a child's wading pool, with the quiver of Ashok's nostrils reflected in it.

"Be honest, Ashok. Come on now. Are these your own studies, or just a personal view of yours?"

"It's not personal. I beg you, sir, not to feel that way. We've gone over it, marketing has gone over it—the syndicators, the underwriters, the real money people. Know what I'm saying?"

"I do, Ashok, but any change has got to come directly from me as well as from you. So let me know *exactly* what you're getting at, Ashok. I need to know that now."

Ashok cleared his throat harder, spun his fingers through his hair, and took out a handkerchief, dabbing his face. Jeffrey did not like seeing this, but didn't want to go too gooey on the young man either. It would be easy to mother Ashok, but that was not Jeffrey's style or function. He wanted to get "Goddess" over with, and then get on to other major projects. India was a big market, but not a big priority to him. Ashok, and the Indians, could have kept this at home, but they had come to Jeffrey with it because they knew that without his support, big chunks of foreign money for the line would never materialize.

Now Ashok was hinting that the initial Indian money was going against Jeffrey, and he didn't like that. He lost patience.

"Well, Ashok, come on. What is this?"

"The packaging, Jeffrey." Ashok's eyes actually blinked from tension. "Your ideas, the motifs, the forms—how do I say this? A consensus here is that they're all a little too 'Ye olde Hindoo' for us. Way too 'Gunga Din,' if you know what I mean."

Jeffrey's face wrinkled.

"No. What *do* you mean?"

"Please, Jeffrey, come on. The line is for village girls. Say, ones still at home. First job. They wouldn't set foot in a high-end, la-de-dah shop. They'd be too intimidated by it. But they still want to feel classy, up-to-date, with-it, and just Western enough to impress their friends. See, your dark little pink elephants with the curlicues, the purple teddy-bear kind of Krishnas, the kinky Taj Mahal borders— to be frank, Jeffrey, it's *schmaltz*. Even these girls will find it schmaltzy. It'd be schmaltzy anyplace. Here, there. Like some kind of German *schlock* with busty *fräuleins* and cute dudes in lederhosen. You've got to understand: India is no longer the colonies, my friend. No matter who's doing the colonializing."

Ashok paused, a bit more secure now that he had got that off his chest, then added sweetly: "I apologize for this level of crit. But you get what I mean, old man?"

Ashok's "old man" was not a reference to Jeffrey's age, and he took no offense in it. It was like "buddy," with a bit more courtesy in it. Jeffrey's medical doctor, Bernd Ostreich, had told him emphatically that he could expect "at least another fifty years of productivity."

Jeffrey's eyes narrowed.

"What do *you* think should be done, Ashok?"

"Jeffrey, please." Ashok put on his nice smile again. "I don't mean to offend you, but I can only tell you what works and what does not here. *Es geht, es geht nicht.* Correct? In phantom India, our role is mostly to consume what the system gives us. So"—he cocked his head coquettishly—"darling, give us a bit *more!*"

Jeffrey had no smile in him. In fact he felt annoyed by Ashok's feigned attempt at intimacy.

"More *what?*" Jeffrey demanded. "I'm a bit lost here, Ashok. More Indian, less Indian? More European, more American? More Hollywood, more *Bollywood?* Hollywood worked with you for a while. We did *Gone with the Wind* to a 'T.' Everyone over there had seen the movie. It's so Indian, really. All your little working girls identified with Scarlett O'Hara. True, I can feed you, but you need to say *what.* The menu's too big not to have some idea what you're hungry for. So tell me. What is it you *want?*"

Ashok gasped, applying his handkerchief again as Jeffrey's patience unraveled. He had other projects, and he didn't like young Rahman taking up so much of his time. Time in India, though inflating in value by the minute, was still not worth what time in globalized Germany was.

Out of nowhere, Ashok released a torpedo:

"Jeffrey, my friend—"

His voice lowered considerably.

Jeffrey, his eyes glued to the monitor, wondered how he looked to Ashok, because Ashok was staring bullets at him.

"I'm afraid, Jeffrey—I get the impression that you're not being optimally, *genuinely* creative with me. If that's incorrect, forgive me. But are you holding back? And if so, why? Perhaps you feel this Indian project is not important? A lot is riding on it for us, and we're getting anxious. I, and some of our dear money people, are wondering—and again, please forgive us if this is not the case—if some distant latent *racial* attitude is not emerging here. Perhaps from someone close to you, or someone even farther out on your team."

Jeffrey's jaw dropped. This was a very *wild* shot on Ashok's part. Generally, you could only fire this kind of ammo once, and Ashok had now used it.

Why was this young man, whom Jeffrey had been following for several years, trying to back him into a corner? If the Goddess line failed (and new lines sometimes did), Ashok, with some nimble sidestepping, could hide behind Jeffrey and come back later for another try, whereas if it succeeded, Ashok would need to jump out of Jeffrey's shadow in order to write his own ticket. Consciously or not, he was giving Jeffrey an indication that he was trying to play this game one step ahead of his boss.

Jeffrey had seen this scenario happen before, and was good at keeping himself, and his team, in control of it. Ashok was trying something out of line and very combustible, and that bothered Jeffrey. He wasn't sweating, but Ashok's pressure on him (and the vulnerability behind this pressure), together with his ambition, were a dangerous combination in a young man, which Jeffrey knew could be useful.

Race was always an ugly card to pull out of the deck, because it was so difficult to put it back in. He decided now was the time to mother this young man, to give him what he wanted, or at least the appearance of it.

"Ashok, you've known me way too long and way too well even to *suggest* something like that."

Jeffrey smiled radiantly, with just enough hardness around the edges to let Ashok know he meant business.

And he did, because throughout the decades Jeffrey had made sure that the possibilities of any detectable racism coming from him were non-existent. For an Alabama man, his record was beyond scrupulous. Besides, if Ashok ever tried to play the race card again, he'd be labeled a troublemaker and/or a race *chauvinist*: someone who tried to maintain the biased, anti-global-consumerist isolation of his own race. This was as dangerous as being a genuine racist, which was illegal.

Both were distasteful, and both suspected racists and race chauvinists were quickly eliminated from positions of authority. For the most part, this left all fields open only to the blandly capable, or to keenly savvy people like Jeffrey. But it kept racial conversations outside the increasingly nebulous boundaries of Commerce, Science, Education, and the Arts.

Ashok peered in closer, so that Jeffrey could see the sincerity in his dark eyes and their rich, almost iridescent, obsidian lashes. What hardworking Indian lass wouldn't die of envy for those lashes? Jeffrey wondered, while feeling almost sorry for Ashok, for having the young man by such a sensitive area: his vanity, and perhaps his ambition, too.

Ashok tried to smile, like a dolphin coming up for air.

"You have my deepest apologies, Jeffrey. I mean that. Please accept it. It's just, I'm afraid some of us feel you've hedged on us. Forgive us. It gives us the impression that you are not taking India *quite* seriously. I'm saddened to say this, but it's *honest*. You do want me to be honest, don't you?"

Honest, Jeffrey thought. Now that was a new one. The honesty card was a bad one, too; though not nearly as bad as the race card. Jeffrey sensed innate goodness in Ashok, but he was not going to sacrifice his own control over this project because of it.

"Ashok"—he felt like he'd practiced this speech before, it came out so easily. "There are a billion and a half consumers in India, all thirsting for the greatest possible freedom of choice we can give them. I cannot *imagine* such an idea. But I'm indebted for your candor. Most managers wouldn't be this candid."

Ashok's youthful features on the monitor squeezed into some serious thought.

"I should reward you in some way, Ashok. Believe me, I should."

Jeffrey smiled sweet as pie, and Ashok managed a grin as well.

"Candid," smart people knew, was a code word for sticking your own neck under the ax. As in: "He was candid with his appraisal," or, "He was very candid with his reactions."

In other words, soon dead.

"Thank you, Jeffrey," Ashok said innocently enough, his face very plainly serious. "I mean about the promise of a reward."

Jeffrey felt home free. In fact, too free.

"Believe me, in the future, Ashok, you'll get a lot more of my time. And I'll call on you for input. I mean that."

Then he skated too far out on his own power.

"However, if you still genuinely feel this way, by all means I encourage you to file a report about this. I'd welcome it. In the friendliest manner, of course. It will give me a chance to rebutt your opinion."

Their eyes were locked on each other, until Ashok's softened.

"Unnecessary, Jeffrey. I mean that. Just send us what you'd like as soon as you can. Your own designers and product managers will be able to go to work and do what's necessary. I trust you in everything. I do, sir."

Ashok smiled sadly, one of those strained smiles you put on to keep from really smiling. Then, like some untouchable who'd been put in his place, Ashok lowered his voice to an embarrassingly modest level.

"I'll leave it all up to you, Jeffrey."

"Thank you, Ashok. You'll get something from us by early next week."

Ashok's face loosened, his self-flagellation over. Jeffrey admired that Ashok could bounce back quickly, always a prized quality in the system.

"Excellent! Tell me, do you plan to visit us in India soon?"

Jeffrey shrugged. He was good at this lie.

"I'll think about it very seriously, Ashok," he said dryly.

The young man's face became warm, and quite seductive.

"That would make me so happy, Jeffrey! I promise I'll do whatever I can for your visit here. I'll go out of my way, and arrange everything for your personal needs."

"Thank you. I'll keep that in mind."

Ashok's thick black eyelashes, like the iridescent eyes of a peacock's tail, made Jeffrey realize that he still liked looking at the young man, despite what had happened earlier.

"Yes, please," Ashok said firmly. "We have a lot in common, you and I. I believe that. *Honest*, I do."

There was that dreadful word again, but it triggered in Jeffrey a warm expression. He thanked Ashok once more, and clicked off.

The conversation had been recorded and would be preserved with the larger files of the creation and marketing of the Goddess line. At some point Jeffrey might be brought up on it. The threat hit him in the throat, like a sudden mouthful of saltwater after a perfectly executed swan dive.

He should not have pushed the race thing back at Ashok. Why did he do that, and why did he leave his group in the German part of the system vulnerable to *any* charge of race practices? He was too good a manager for that. Now he had doubts, which hit him as stress. Had he truly, stupidly, played into stereotypes?

Being an Alabama boy at heart, it was easy to fall into these things, and there was always some leftover guilt about it, as if they were in his DNA. He'd been trained to expunge so much of his brain, but there was always some furtive place he didn't know about, even missing to him.

He hated it. He was becoming stressed by it. He'd have to see Bernd and Tony soon: both would notice. He didn't have to tell Bernd anything, but it would show up in the hormone levels in his blood, even in his irises and other places.

He could feel it: tension approaching him like some Transylvanian vampire, all insinuations and half-veiled threats. He tried to get that black-caped image out of his mind. He needed to work on entering the mist, that quieting calm that Tony had coached him to use. But there were too many calls to make, reports to write, new files to see and archive. Then, looking at one of his monitors, he noticed lunchtime coming up, giving him an excuse to go out.

He left his office, hurrying in the warm afternoon light down to Afghanistrasse, a warren of flea-market shops, pungent street food vendors, and stridently foreign, native restaurants that seemed fish out of water in the bland American-German alliance, an economic-cultural cohesion, usually against the French and their occasional partners the Chinese, long-time wizards at petroleum. China could squeeze an ounce of oil out of anything and use even less of it, unlike the Americans and their too-close German allies who stayed ever-dependent on the Middle East.

The street jingled with student bicycle bells, there was friendly haggling from the shops, inviting smells, and amiable, diverse crowds of people enjoying themselves. Jeffrey had taken innumerable pictures there, between bargaining over the prices of things he bought for their colors and patterns. He liked the *Arabian Nights* texture of the place, even if undercurrents of resentful feelings sometimes simmered below the surface.

A small group of dark teens, some in sandals, most in black-and-white headdresses, pressed in around him, smiling and nodding. He nodded back; they gestured to each other, giggling, then hurried away. A few seconds later, not six feet from him, ear-splitting shots exploded off. The crowds scrambled for cover, screaming. Jeffrey jumped, very rattled. His ears buzzed.

It was only firecrackers, but high-power blockbusters obtained illegally by the boys, who must have thought they were being funny. Reminded once more of his stress level, Jeffrey ducked into a familiar shop that sold yard goods and fragrances and served tea. It was quiet. He loved the smell of it, and the lingering feeling of slow, relaxed time.

Several gray-haired men nodded to him, but a young, well-built man came from behind a counter. Recognizing Jeffrey, he asked, "Would you like a massage today?"

Jeffrey nodded, and was led into a private backroom with a table and a stand with bottles of oils, towels, and sponges.

Jeffrey took off his shirt, pants, shoes, and socks, and lay down on the table in only his briefs.

The masseur's name was Louis, an Algerian who'd lived in Southern France, Morocco, Turkey, and Egypt. He'd even had a sojourn in Afghanistan, which had stabilized and become outwardly modern, mostly with money brought in from the drug trade.

"How are you today, sir?" he asked as he began to touch Jeffrey's back.

"All right. Maybe a little tense."

"Don't worry, you won't be when you leave."

Jeffrey smiled as Louis began oiling him. His dark wide hands—a shepherd's hands, actually—were gentle but strong and skillful, knowing just where to reach in and stroke, or stay.

"Usual? Or do you want buttocks today?"

Jeffrey exhaled. "Everything. Give me everything."

Louis eased Jeffrey's white briefs down and off, then began kneading Jeffrey's buttocks. In his previous visits they hadn't gone this far, but now Jeffrey obviously wanted it. He moaned as a tense place at the top of his legs, where sore muscles reached into his butt, responded to Louis's fingers. He allowed himself to relax deeply, to be pulled into the mist, that dark grove illuminated by his deepest self. An erection stiffened between Jeffrey and the table.

Louis also felt it, and gently slipped one oily hand around the underside of the warm head of Jeffrey's cock.

"Is that good?" Louis whispered.

"Yeah," Jeffrey moaned. "Good."

Louis slicked the length of Jeffrey's shaft briefly with his oily fingers, teasing his glans, then returned to his buttocks and that sore place at the back of his legs. Jeffrey liked this. It was both extremely sensual and not too sexual at the same time. Teasing, seductive. Louis's stricter Arab traditions meant a shyness and coyness that left them always someplace else to go, and a promise that they might get there. Jeffrey eased his hips up a bit, then Louis found his scrotum, gently edging a finger up between his waiting testicles.

"Like that, too?"

Jeffrey was about to answer, when the door popped open and a man barged in, followed by one of the older Arab men who'd become furious trying to hold him back.

"*Nein! Nein! Nein!*" the man shouted at the old man. Then to Louis, he barked: "*Hey? Mein freund. Beschftig!?*"

Louis's warm hands released him, and Jeffrey felt a swoosh of icy-cold tension rush in in their place.

"Not now, Sir!"

Louis quickly threw a towel over Jeffrey's exposed rear.

"Sorry," the man apologized. "I'll wait."

Louis put his hands back on Jeffrey's shoulders, turning his back to the intruder.

"Listen," he said forcefully. "You must come back later, see? Maybe half an hour. O.K.?"

Jeffrey managed to turn his face to the man. His eyes had difficulty focusing, but almost immediately he was certain.

It was the man from the pubtran platform.

Jeffrey relived the attack. His ears stung just as they had from the firecrackers; he could hear the man's voice booming above the pounding in his chest.

"I'll be back," the stranger promised in English, then tossed in an Arabic phrase that sailed past Jeffrey, and left.

Jeffrey turned over, staring in disbelief at the closed door. He pulled himself up, naked.

"We're not finished. I want to do something. You'll like it."

Jeffrey shook his head.

"I can't stay, Louis. Tell me. Who was that?"

"I don't know. He's kind of strange. Been here a few times, screams a lot, gets crazy. I told him either be quiet, or don't come back. You know him?"

"I think so."

Louis's eyes searched his. There was no telling what conclusions the masseur was jumping to, but Jeffrey felt they had no secrets now. Why try to pretend they did? Louis's hands had already crossed a barrier, and this was just one more.

"I recognized him," Jeffrey explained. "From something that happened."

"Happened good or bad?"

"Not good."

"Good!" Louis said firmly. "Now you know to stay away. He's nuts. *Verukt.* I been at this for years, and he's"—Louis hesitated—"*ganz fremd.* Too fuckin' strange. You know, like his fruit fell too far from the damn tree?"

Jeffrey couldn't help smiling. He liked the image: God only knew where his own fruit had fallen.

"Do you know where he lives?"

"I know nothing and want to know less. But I work on him. He pays me good. I told him shut up or go. So he's back and he better be quiet while I work on him."

Jeffrey did not want to think about it anymore. He jumped off the table.

"I'd better go."

He got to his wallet, paid Louis, and hurried back into his clothes and left the shop, feeling utterly stupid, cowardly, and decades older than he'd been only a few minutes earlier.

He raced through the crowds, no longer thinking about boys, firecrackers, the sights or smells. A jolt of emotion had slashed him with the man's reappearance, bringing with it a streak of old memories he'd repressed, delivered by the hammer-blow sighting of the man's face. First came the cold dark eyes of Johnny Garfunkel, the sophisticated, emotionally dead Jewish beauty who'd broken his heart when he was young; then Jane Bruce, an insecure boss who'd humiliated him long ago, drunkenly accusing him of stealing designs—a bald-faced lie, but that kind of garbage gnawed at him for years until he trained himself to forget it. Both Johnny and Jane were gone. Like his father, Harold: always slightly heroic, but terribly tarnished; a distant landscape of silence, dead on the floor in Alabama after a suicide.

His PICE score, exactly where would it be at that moment? Why couldn't he cheat on his brain like he had on the big PICE, and just grab everything back? And why did that awful man bring everything back so fast? He hated this rush of helpless feeling.

He stopped at a public rest room. It was more Arab than German and smelled it, but he went to a urinal and took himself out anyway. He had to pee badly, but couldn't. He was shaking too hard, close to nauseated.

He made himself exhale, grabbing any shred of relaxation he could get to, and finally produced a slow, leaky stream of urine, like an old man's, some of which trickled down his leg onto his tailored pants before he could put himself back in. Embarrassed—he prided himself on being immaculate—he washed his hands in an ice-cold sink, then left the restroom.

Was the man casing him? Eyes were all over: wary shopkeepers' eyes, security agents' and plainclothes policemen's. Electronic eyes. Now these were joined by the man's green eyes that Jeffrey had gazed directly into, slightly more yellow-gold than jade. What a history was in those eyes! Unlike Jeffrey's, who had hidden his past, stashed it away, until it popped out with a vengeance at bad moments like this.

He felt tiny, vulnerable, reduced to being a scared child.

Everything returned to him, like Ellis, the bully who used to shadow him in intermediate school, grabbing him and calling him names.

Jeffrey recalled Ellis down to the last dirty-sweat crease in his neck and the dark hairs sprouting prematurely at the end of his stubby nose; he was comic-book ghoulish with a protruding overbite on an almost-flat face. Most kids avoided him, except for a few of his equally toxic pals. Once in the hallway, after Ellis had punched him exceptionally hard too many times on his upper arm, Jeffrey exploded, punching him back. Then he punched Ellis again, in his face, causing his front teeth to slice into his lower lip. It shocked Jeffrey; he'd never done anything like that before (nor would he again).

Jeffrey was introverted, too thoughtful; and when the run-in was over and his adrenaline was lying in puddles all over the floor, he panicked. The Jeffrey who'd socked Ellis in the kisser wasn't real: he was only a flash of rage, jumping out of the brittle cellophane of anger. Ellis would return and corner him, grabbing the real Jeffrey, a muscleless sissy.

In later years, when he tried to retrieve that rage, he was never successful. It was always gone, hidden in some corner he could never get to, with too much between him and it. He didn't have that raw male material that allows you to kill at will—and whatever it was, he lacked the tool to access it. Maybe the tool came between his legs, maybe it was in his testicles that Louis had been deftly fiddling with. But wherever it was, Jeffrey couldn't get to it.

Some of the other smart kids went nuts that day, laughing as a bleeding Ellis was sent to the school nurse, who called his parents. They came and got him, and Jeffrey became anxious about them, too. But Ellis's parents did nothing. No one said anything more to Jeffrey; even his parents tried hard to avoid the subject, though he could tell his father took a secret glee in it, like it was another key to Jeffrey's desired induction into the Real Boy's Club.

Of course, Ellis did return to heckle him. But nothing big this time, no punching or pushing. He merely narrowed his eyes at Jeffrey and threatened: "Cooper, I'm gonna get you. One way or another."

He and Ellis took separate paths after middle school, but Ellis's "one way or another" come back to haunt him sometimes, with every kind of anxiety and stress lurking inside it. Even the system, that protected him with its rewards and secret extensions on his youth, could not get around that threat.

And now this man appeared for the second time, as Ellis's surrogate, while Jeffrey was caught naked and exposed on Louis's massage table. That image of Ellis, stamped over and over again like a pattern on the drapes in Hell, made him know that if he were ever going to have a future of his own, he finally had to do something.

The sheer physicality of this decision shot an injection of pure steel into him.

He raced back to the shop, found Louis, and out of breath handed him his business card.

"When that man returns, tell him to come back tomorrow! Call me when he does."

"I can't, sir. I made a—"

"You made *nothing*, understand?"

Jeffrey grabbed some large bills from his wallet, twice as much as a massage fee, and pushed them at him.

"I'll pay you even more for this. Call me tomorrow. I mean that."

Louis took the money.

"O.K., sir. Whatever you wish. But he'll be back soon."

"Tell him you have an emergency. Family problems. Anything! You understand? But you'll be happy to see him tomorrow and you'll charge him half. Then call me when he comes back. Like I promised, I'll pay you even more tomorrow."

Louis smiled.

"All right. He's crazy, but I'll do whatever you wish, sir."

Jeffrey grabbed a French lunch at a popular place decorated in wool pillows and tenting, like a North African bazaar. The menu was in French and German, and cute but rude Balkan and Arab waiters interrupted customers yakking loudly on cell phones in a slew of languages, which Jeffrey understand much of since they always threw in some standard English or German words. It was always about the same things: business problems, home life, love life. A thought hit him: what he was doing with this strange man was *very* private. He would reveal it to no one.

Jeffrey needed to formulate a plan. He considered killing the man. Simply wiping him out. It seemed a logical enough idea.

The idiot was crazy; suppose he attacked somebody else? Jeffrey would be doing society a favor. The man was so far outside the system there was no way Jeffrey could be shadowed by it. In fact, no one but Louis could even suspect it, and, with the exception of the money he had given him, all of this was outside of Louis's business. Even better, given Louis's tight-lipped North African mores, it would remain there.

He liked the idea. A free, easy, untraceable killing.

But it left an odd taste in his mouth, like a memory from too far back to name. He shuddered; it would be like killing Ellis.

He couldn't do it. There was always that basic "tool" he couldn't get to. Even if it were in his balls, it stayed there and he couldn't get to it. No, he wasn't going to resort to murder. But suppose the man tried to kill *him*? He *was* irrational.

In any case, Jeffrey had to confront him; unless he did, he wouldn't know how to face his own life. And for the first time in ages, that life had something he could genuinely describe as depth. Jeffrey had put thousands of people to work, but this wasn't about Indian hair coloring or a new *luxe* car, or some stupid mock-Hollywood temple in Flint.

The depth felt bewildering, even dizzying, but good. It made him realize that depth did not mean only *deep*, but also high.

He was oddly high, like he was way up above something dangerous, above everything. Maybe that was what death felt like. His own death. He'd worked so hard to prevent it and suddenly the idea hardly bothered him, as if he were seeing it from so far *up* that it could be possible, but not at all that horrible.

This thrilled him. Not like one of those canned, marketed "Escape" fantasies on big billboards. This was authentic, a piece of the starkest, most authentic *reality* anyone could experience in his own lifetime.

He smiled to himself. *He* was experiencing it.

The other people continued chattering on their phones, a few of them annoyed at the rudeness of others as they themselves conversed with hands cupped over their mouths in more discreet voices. But Jeffrey did not have to do even that. He had the most discreet secret of all: his own life, suddenly, for the first time in ages, outside of the system.

He finished his *omelette au fromage* and *salat d' Africaine* with too much cumin in it, and returned to his office.

There, quickly, he got a call from Louis.

"Mr. Cooper, I *deed* it. I told him tomorrow *ist besser.* He said, 'Sixteen hundred hours?' I said '*gut*'. How's that for you, sir?"

"Perfect, Louis. I'll bring you some more money tomorrow."

He felt fine now, good enough to face Bernd Ostreich without anxiety. His stress-level read-out was superb. Ostreich's office was starkly white and incredibly sterile, even for a German doctor. But Bernd had some interest in *Kultur,* and he liked to talk in English to Jeffrey about art and opera.

"Have you seen the new *Rosenkavalier,* set back in the old nineteen eighties? The Field Marshal is a developer like that Donald Trump, and his pretty but fading wife works in real estate. She has to see her young lover between appointments. A big scream! The decor is so overdone. It's like those people were nuts!"

Jeffrey laughed. "Sure, the nineteen eighties. Anything went back then. There was Ronald Reagan, the bad actor's bad actor. Tell me, did they have big sleeves, mile-wide shoulders on the dresses, and huge hair?"

Bernd giggled so hard he started to drool.

"*Ja,* like something out of the *ancien régime.* Marie Antoinette set in Republican America. Like it's all old and new at the same time."

"*Allis ist,*" Jeffrey said.

"*Ja. Du bist perfect,*" Bernd assured him. "My report on you will be *spitz gut.* You want your shots now?"

"Any choice?"

Jeffrey unrolled his sleeve.

"Not if you want to stay the way you are."

Jeffrey smiled, preening in his happiness.

"I do."

"We'll up your dosage. It will make you feel much better. More lively. Tell me, how d'you feel in your groin?"

Jeffrey looked at him dumbly.

"Jeffrey, come on. How's your *sex?*"

'Not quite as good as *Der Rosenkavalier.* I don't feel old and new at the same time, Bernd. Sometimes I'm old and sometimes young. Make no mistake, I like being this way. But sometimes my *sex* gets lost in everything else I've got to do."

"Of course. You need to be productive, you've got to work very, very hard. So sex gets lost. *Entre nous,* I'll give you something for that, too. A little more testosterone and some other goodies. I love that word 'goodies.' It's so *American,* like 'dirtbag'! Now that's a word I love! Nothing like that in German!"

Jeffrey smiled, agreeing. The shots and drugs felt very nice, like an instant, though sky-high-priced pep-up. Few people even of Jeffrey's rank could afford constant, expertly monitored treatment like this, and most would never be given the opportunity, since the system kept it under strict controls. Some of Jeffrey's procedures could be done on the underground market, but there they could end up fatal, since there was no quality control, or proper follow-up care and monitoring: both extremely important.

Some of the drugs Jeffrey took could be dangerous and he had to be watched regularly. He had machines at home that did saliva tests or took minute blood readings and sent information to a panel of unseen doctors and underwriters. Bernd was merely their face; he, too, reported to them.

As the pharmaceuticals flashed through him, Jeffrey felt really marvelous, like the excitement and strength of a much younger man were now inside him, pushing up from his legs into his stomach and chest—his groin, of course, too—and then even farther, into his neck and face, which felt tingly but nice, like after an excellent glass of champagne.

He felt like a child, an enthralled young visitor testing all the gadgets and novelties inside someone else's body. He could not stop smiling.

"How is it?" Bernd asked after a few minutes, as Jeffrey, with no adverse effects, was about to leave.

"*Spitz klasse*," Jeffrey answered. "You know how to do this, Bernd. *Danke sehr.*"

Bernd nodded.

"We're all just part of the system, right? *Guten tag.*" He started giggling again as he lit up a cigarette. "See you soon, Dirtbag!"

Jeffrey waved good-bye. He needed to go to the gym, where he had an appointment with his personal trainer, a young Amazon-tough woman named Conny Dritte who kept him in shape. Sometimes she seemed more heartless than a man; one day he would just drop dead on her. But he did feel good as a result, a perfect physical lightness and strength that worked so nicely after Bernd's services.

Then there was more work to do at home. He wouldn't stop working until after eleven that night. Work was infinite, with a finite amount of time in which to do it. There were people to catch up with all over the world, some snapping at the heels of his team, trying to compete with it, others merely trying to keep up.

That evening he was sure he could do it all, with Dr. Ostreich's charming help.

And he did feel like a "dirtbag." Someone with a secret all his own. Someone who *could* "cut the mustard," whatever that meant.

He'd meet this guy and confront him. But, no matter what, Jeffrey told himself, at least this "dirtbag" was on the *right* side of the system.

Chapter Four

When he got the second call from Louis, at four o' clock on Friday afternoon, he'd already cleared most of the work from his desk. His chief assistant, Gregory Malace, had come in for a briefing on the new "Valentino" car project, nervously presenting to Jeffrey what he'd been doing. Jeffrey nodded as Malace pointed out his third reworking of details for interior lighting, some knobs and door handles, bits of dashboard styling, and then the separate rear and front entertainment systems.

Malace (pronounced "Muh-láce," emphasis on the second syllable, unlike "malice") was in his late twenties, reedy, slightly tall though he often hunched over. He looked bloodless and colorless, with long, lank, wheat-streaked hair and a bland, pinched, prematurely aging face. He was a total, peripherally sight-blind workaholic; that is, he could see straight ahead of himself and no more.

It was excruciating for him to originate ideas, but once a project came to him, he drilled straight through it, doing an amount of work that would have pulverized more creative, neurotically fragile people. He worked like a Trojan, maybe two Trojans, and made an excellent assistant, but would get no further professionally, even though he had some drafting expertise and a degree of taste. He had no heart to absorb all the dirty dealings of the system (the harsh money people, backbiting clients, numerous project collaborators; the platoons of sniveling, mediocre egos inflated to imperial proportions). Instead, he put his entire life at the service of the system. If needed, he could work a full seventeen hours a day, crash on Saturday, and then, when necessary, work on Sunday.

Malace's mother was a German geoscientist, his father an American ex-Marine energy manager, both relentless strivers. He'd been brought up near Mongolian oil fields, and had a striking lack of anything even approaching a personality. When he wasn't working, he was involved with various extreme sports, again avoiding human complexities by straining his hard, stress-tightened body to the near breaking point.

Jeffrey asked him if he had any plans for the weekend.

He grunted. "Nah much."

Jeffrey smiled. "Sounds safe."

Two months earlier, Malace had tumbled off the sheer icy face of some rock high up in Switzerland, broken three toes, dislocated a shoulder, and hair-fractured a leg. His new thing was combining windsurfing and spearfishing, including going after small sharks. On a rare four-day vacation, he'd flown to the Ivory Coast to do it. He loved these kind of *Übermensch* efforts, and spent large amounts of money on high-end sporting equipment that often ended up jammed into a corner of his already cramped office.

Malace cleared his throat, like he was ready for a confession under duress, then spit out, "Sat'rday. Maybe I'll do some cycling. Maybe something like Denmark."

Jeffrey nodded. Denmark was an excruciating distance away, and he could easily see Malace cycling it alone.

He took another hard look at Malace's working drawings and notes, nodded briefly, and left him with a "Don't break a leg" warning.

He said brief good-byes to three clerks who were sorting through files and cataloguing what Jeffrey, Malace, and the rest of the staff had already worked on, and strolled by the cubicles of six junior colleagues, including one from China who spoke almost no English or German. They were sweating over projects of their own. He wished them a nice weekend, and they looked up absentmindedly from their work, barely aware he was leaving.

He took one long, last look around the hallways of his office and had this feeling that it was looking back at him, like a possessive lover who did not want him to go. It was difficult for Jeffrey to imagine Malace having such depth of sentiment about his work, or any depth for that matter. Malace seemed like a cipher to Jeffrey, just a durable piece of office equipment. But Jeffrey's work had a magic and mystery for him, with something always else to know, some project to research, more plans and drawings to create or look at, then even more files to come out of that.

The files were infinite, always marching backward or forward in time, an endless looping stream of visual, historical, social, and economic information: how things looked or would look; how they were used or would be used; who used or would use them. An item used by the workingman in one era would be taken up by the elite in the next, such as the tweed hunting jacket that became the elegant sports coat. Cowboy boots, once scuffed and caked with manure, were now rolled out in exotic leathers chased in sterling, luxurious enough for heads of state.

Snap-on white linen collars had once been for Macy's shopgirls; Jeffrey sent them sparkling with precious stones into the wardrobes of media stars and socialites. He'd spotted them in an old *Herald Tribune* picture from the 1930s, had traced them to the Renaissance, with its gorgeous enamels and ornamentations, and ended up pushing them in a cheaper, fake version with Chinese jet beads. You missed nothing, or someone else would come up with a better idea. The lucrative life span of a fad was about twenty minutes, so your brain stayed on triple-time. Jeffrey's luxury collar fad was produced by a Dutch conglomerate with nests of guarded factories in the jungles of Malaysia. They could produce anything shockingly cheaply, then bring it out by boat to private airstrips. Anything could fly out of there in a twenty-four-hour turnaround, from a sketched idea into millions of finished units.

At times he felt frozen, with everything starting to look alike: a very bad sign. His body was way ahead of him, but he needed to kick-start his mind with pills and injections, which, while making everything crisp and fresh, screwed up a lot of neurons. Sometimes, a silent parachute of depression landed, like a jellyfish's quiet, poisonous descent, onto the freshly scrubbed surface of his brain. He had to watch out for this; the system wouldn't tolerate it. But at the moment he felt marvelous, as if some testosterone-loaded trajectory of decisiveness were pushing him out of his office toward Afghanistrasse, where he would surprise that bully supine on Louis's table.

And after that . . . ?

So he had the guy naked, what next?

Punch him? Make his nose bleed? Finally, and for the last time, get even with Ellis and all the others? Even if Jeffrey could make the man weep like a kid, he wasn't so much angry anymore as morbidly curious. He wanted to satisfy his curiosity himself, and find out *how* small, stupid, and shit-worthless the man was.

What else could this monster be?

He hurried to the shop with the additional money for Louis, then froze, waiting in the outer room, where imports were displayed, feeling utterly self-conscious. An old man in a baggy suit offered Jeffrey some mint tea, while he pretended to be interested in Egyptian beeswax candies and a small bright scarab pin, obviously fake.

He was paying for the scarab when the man, retucking his shirt, eyes off everyone, emerged from the backroom. Quickly, Jeffrey pocketed his cheap scarab, his heart hammering inside him, and without another thought of Louis, quickly followed the man outside into a noisy weekend crowd. For a moment he lost him, then spotted him again, with the loud noise muffling his fear as he hurried to catch up yet not be detected.

The man was wearing a gray workingman's smock outfit, like something Tony might have worn except that this was dirty, encrusted with paint and oil stains. He was actually taller than Jeffrey remembered, and his posture was noticeably straight-up, perhaps the result of one of Louis's superb massages. Jeffrey put on a pair of dark glasses and trailed him, making several stops and starts as the man's direction shifted indecisively. Finally, his quarry rushed into a jammed restaurant, sat at a counter, only to jump up half an hour later.

Jeffrey waited outside, a large, newly purchased copy of *Der Spiegel* in front of him, which he kept there. In his pocket was a box cutter he'd filched from Malace's office, out of one of his rat's nests of discarded mountain bike parts, ropes, and rock-climbing equipment. The cutters had industrial razor blades and Malace and the other assistants used them to make cardboard models. Jeffrey had no idea what to do with the one in his pocket, but the fact that it was there gave him a sense of last-ditch protection. If Malace could risk life and limb windsurfing for sharks, he could risk using a box cutter if necessary. After all, the man had his fists and his rage; Jeffrey had simply this little tool and . . . he had no idea what else.

In fact, he had no idea even how to pursue this, but there was no time to worry about it now as the man crammed himself into a packed rush hour train at the nearby pubtran station.

Jeffrey managed to squeeze in behind him, then follow the top of the man's head with its silken, chestnut hair streaked with glowing coppery highlights from the overhead lights. Stops came; interfering bodies parted. He could see the man's face clearly: his massive, narrowing forehead; his nose that began thin at the bridge then ended slightly too thick, like a clown's or peasant's nose, but with small nostrils at each side. His lips seemed too narrow for his face, but fine lines at the sides of his mouth suggested there would be knife-sharp dimples if he ever smiled.

He didn't. His eyes appeared to be focusing inward. Jeffrey felt sure the man was unaware of his presence.

As the train rode on, the crowd thinned until it ceased to be one. A few of the people left were dressed expensively, while a few others tried to look that way. In contrast were two men who looked like farmers, brothers maybe, in for a day in the city. They had fat fingers and bellies, and big arms and shoulders in tight, cheap knitted shirts. They joked loudly in a German Jeffrey could not follow. The man looked over at them, gave them a quick wink in their laughter, then returned to his reverie.

At the next-to-last stop the two farmers got off, along with everyone else, leaving only Jeffrey and the man remaining. Then the last stop came, and Jeffrey, perspiring now, had no idea what else to do.

He felt like an idiot. The sun was setting. Soft amber and red rays spread their warmth through the car. Then, with a jolt, Jeffrey realized that this was the exact line—at the very last stop—where he used to wait for the charming country train to Blichtenwald forest, that magical location, the memory of which placed him in Tony's calming mist of self-containment.

But this recognition did not comfort him.

Soon, in the low sun's last glance, he and the man were the only two standing on the platform, with darkening groves of trees and graying fields in the distance.

"Can I offer you a lift?" the man said in perfect, almost Oxford English.

Jeffrey had to catch his breath before he nodded, then said, "Yes."

"You're American?" the man asked. "You can take your dark glasses off. Are you trying to go *incognito?*"

Jeffrey removed his glasses, and followed the man off the platform to a small carpark a few yards away. The cars in it were old, beat-up, mud-spattered country vehicles, though their windshields were kept clean. The man got in to one, and opened the door for Jeffrey.

"Where can I take you?" he asked, once Jeffrey was seated and had adjusted the seat belt, adding, "I guess I should do that, too."

Jeffrey waited until the man was belted, then asked him, "Where were you going?"

"The forest. It's nice to run in at this hour."

"Then take me there."

The man smiled, glancing at Jeffrey's expensive clothes.

"You don't look like you're dressed for running."

"Then I'll walk."

The man put the key in the ignition and the old car made impressively loud, belching noises as it bounced down rutted dirt roads, through a sullen back lane to the forest. Jeffrey had never taken this route; he had always ridden the little country train, or walked a very pretty, one-and-a-half miles to there. Dumped cars and mounds of fly-infested garbage piled the roadside, while immigrant women and children stared at them from refuse-strewn front yards of darkened shacks.

"A lot of Turks live out here. Blacks. Albanians. People like that. You like them?"

Jeffrey did not answer.

"You don't talk much," the man observed. He lit a cigarette and offered one to Jeffrey, which he refused.

"I do like them," Jeffrey answered finally. "They're all right. Why do you ask?"

"I *don't* like them," the man snapped with an emphasis like he was marking territory, which did not surprise Jeffrey.

Jeffrey tried to shrug it off. "But you hang out with them? I mean, they're all around here. Right?"

"*Hang out?* Oh, yeah. Sure! Slang. American. O.K. I 'hang out.' Yes, 'fraid I do. Truth is: I'm not really a nice part of this world. But I know who my friends are, even if I don't always like them."

"It seems that you don't like Americans much either, do you?" Jeffrey ventured.

Suddenly he didn't feel so frightened being this close to the man, who, driving this old car, had at least to pay some attention to the potholes.

The man smiled. "No, I don't like Americans a lot. But who does? You like them? Come on, be honest! You don't seem the type."

Jeffrey lost his thought. Then answered, "Sometimes I like them. But you did offer me a lift."

"It seemed the right thing to do."

Jeffrey rolled his window down and looked out as they approached his beautiful forest from another end. It was like approaching the Garden of Eden from a garbage dump. He'd never seen anything like this, even in the States. More garbage. Dead animals along the road. He counted two large dog carcasses and something that might have been a horse or deer. It was hard to tell; all of it was stomach-turning.

He felt frantic and stressed again, and turned away from the window. The man smiled as he drove, and the promised dimples emerged.

"Don't worry. We'll be out of here soon. It's funny this way. I thought I'd take you, just to let you see it."

"Why?!" Jeffrey exploded. "You don't even like me!"

He wanted to jump out of the car. He hated this man. He hated going this way, hated even being there.

"Not true. I do like you," the man protested, suddenly pushing his free hand through Jeffrey's thick, dark hair. This was worse than any memory he had managed to conceal from himself. Ellis had been a little ghoul; this man was more attractive—and extremely frightening. Jeffrey's nerves were jangled and raw. Alarm hit him; he needed to save himself.

He flashed to the box cutter.

"Let me out! Stop the car!"

"*Nein, nein.*" The man's smile dropped. "It's dangerous here. This is no place to get out, as you can see from all the shit on the road. You'd be like one of those animals. Dead."

Jeffrey realized he had to hold on to himself, and not fall apart. He made himself talk.

"Was that a deer we saw?'

"*Ja.* They get run down like dogs. These people here don't care about animals. They're not good with animals, like Germans."

"I see," Jeffrey said, looking through the window, blinking a tear he could not help off his face. He sat back and tried to exhale slowly, to calm himself, as Tony had taught him. He was entering a sordid maze with no digital files to guide him. If the man tried anything, he'd use the cutter to kill him. He decided he'd do that.

Carefully, he turned to the man and watched him drive. The man returned his look, and said:

"I'm Johann. John. John van der Meer. You know about Vermeer? A Dutch painter. Van der Meer was his real name. My people came over here a long time ago from Holland. They were never really accepted; the Germans never really accepted the Dutch. It's not like America, where they think everybody gets accepted."

"I know Vermeer. I know him well. His colors. The pictures."

"I'm sure you do. You can call me John, if you want. You're American, so call me John."

"Thank you," Jeffrey said.

Now he felt some odd sense of completion. The man had a name. John van der Meer.

"My name is Jeffrey Cooper."

"Cooper? Like Gary?"

Jeffrey nodded. "*Yep.* Like Gary."

They drove into the forest. It was very dim there, and shortly John found a place along the main road to park. Then he got out, as did Jeffrey.

"What do you want to do now?" John asked. "It's up to you."

Jeffrey looked at him. John had a tight little smile frozen on his face, a smile that did not welcome any questions, let alone the one Jeffrey wanted to ask him: Why had he attacked him? John seemed a civilized man, even if he didn't like certain groups of people, including Americans.

"So what's it going to be?" John said.

"I'll walk," Jeffrey answered, with his question waiting there, lodged in his throat.

"Good. Just walk. Don't look back at me, understand? I don't want you to do that."

"Why?" Jeffrey had to ask.

"Because I've taken you here, and it's over. Get it? *Verstehen Sie?*"

Jeffrey stood speechless as John began taking his clothes off, first his smock, then his shirt, shoes, and pants. He was wearing oversized boxer shorts, like old men used to wear. They were a deep blue, emphasizing the moon-white leanness of his body, mapped with darker reddish-blue veins at the surface of his chest, shoulders, and legs. His chest was fairly wide and flat, with tiny nipples that looked like little paper cones. His shoulders, immense and obviously powerfully worked, gave way to long, pale biceps, then the taut muscles of his forearms and wrists. His hands were coarsely ruddy, like his feet.

"Go on," John ordered. "Walk!"

This was too ridiculous. Jeffrey *had* to walk. Either obey him, or lose every shred of dignity he had. He began to walk, and heard the door of John's old car shut; he must have put his clothes in it.

He walked a few more yards, then turned back.

There was John streaking into the forest, totally naked except for a pair of blue running shoes. In seconds he was gone, taking what felt to Jeffrey like the last remaining gleam of light with him.

Chapter Five

*I*t was so dark that the trees merged into one dense shape. He was on this unknown side of the forest, with no idea where the beautiful lake was, or the meadow he had loved so much. He was only sure that to leave meant taking that vile road, past mounds of trash and animal carcasses, with frightening people watching him, maybe to follow and rob him; maybe even to kill him.

After all, John had warned him. The situation seemed beyond absurd. He had allowed the man who attacked him to drive him to this strange place, where anything could happen.

He felt like a lunatic, like he had lost his mind.

Maybe that was the point, since he'd had no real plan in mind either. As if he could just improvise being there, not that he could have foreseen the present situation. This wasn't like one of those long structured digital files of various related images that he could follow until he got what he wanted.

But what had he wanted?

To confront this strange John van der Meer? To ridicule him, humiliate him? Wound him? How could he have imagined killing him? He felt old. He was way past seventy, even if he didn't look or show it. How could he turn himself into a murderer at seventy-eight?

He began walking, his scared jumbled thoughts ricocheting off the chain of events that had led him here: The attack on the pubtran. Tony and his "forces." Len's confession about his fear of death and Suspension. The carnal ritual in the park. The police raid later.

Louis's wonderful hands.

And now this John van der Meer.

How could Jeffrey think about killing him, even hurting him? You don't begin to murder somebody at seventy-eight. His age was a dirty secret, like the sordid backwoods route to the forest, like the secret of why John van der Meer had attacked him.

He should have listened to Tony and asked for help, even if he could not name where it came from. He could have used those unseen forces, if only to relieve the crushing weight of helplessness he now felt. Leaving the road, he crumpled to the ground near a group of trees and sobbed freely, wiping snot on the sleeve of his good shirt.

He couldn't fool anyone. Even with all the help it got, his seventy-plus-year-old brain just couldn't stop falling into an abyss of hopelessness. It was dark in the abyss, blacker than the trees, and it brought his end straight home to him.

He wasn't going to "expire" gracefully from age. No, he was going to burst like a bubble of overvalued real estate or those offerings of junk stock in foreign biotechnologies. His supposed "immense" value to the system would finally add up to zero. And he'd be cut off fast: just like that.

That was a negative thought, and very stressful. He should have had more control over it. As Tony had counseled him, there were "forces" that could help him. He decided he needed to put himself back in Tony's good hands as soon as possible.

To be on the safe side, he also decided he would wait until John van der Meer returned, then ask him, even beg him if necessary, to take him back to the pubtran station. If he had to, he could take a taxi from there. With sources of energy so limited as the world tried to spare burning carbon, it would cost dearly, but he had money on him and most taxis took credit, even those way out in the country. He tried to calm himself, and got back on his feet and dried his eyes. He would walk a bit to limber up his body, but not wander so far from the car that he could not see John when he finished his run.

The forest road seemed less frightening now, with a rising, almost full moon floating over it, silvering the trees and giving them separate shapes instead of that solid, threatening black mass. In the middle of the road, he watched moonbeams glide over him, and smiled. Everything *was* beautiful. Nature in its magnificence had no style. It contained what you wanted to see, while style only took something away, sucking out the living marrow of nature and substituting that with cold human intentions.

At this moment he had no intentions at all, and it was wonderful. He felt younger, content, and more delighted to be there than he ever imagined he could feel, as if he were tiptoeing on the very silver of the moon.

But he needed to pee and characteristically feeling inhibited about doing it in the open, ventured off the road. In the wooded darkness, he unzipped his fly and let himself out. Pissing felt so good, it was such a simple pleasure, something he felt he'd surely miss after death. But that idea was too negative. He wanted to let go of it like he did his own water as his body now, in this private intimate moment, reunited with his own youthfulness, that part of him he liked so much, that he could feel emerging from his fears.

He put himself back in and returned to the road, only to hear a boy's voice screeching out to him:

"*Wer sind Sie!*"

Immediately seven or eight teenagers surrounded Jeffrey, demanding to know who he was.

"*Wer sind Sie? Wer sind Sie? Schwul, Turk, or Ostvolk?*"

Was he a queer? A Turk? Or someone from the East (a Pole for instance, or an Arab)?

Stunned, he stared at them in their black jeans and T-shirts depicting chalky skulls, swastikas, broken crosses, and satanic pentangles. Their arms and faces were soot-blackened to make them disappear easily in the darkness. They were neo-Nazi youth, ignited by shared hatreds and their own uncertain futures.

"*Dumkopf!*" their kid voices screamed.

"*Schwul*-asshole! *Schwulescheissekopf!*"

He stood rooted in fear as they circled him. Then a deeper more mature voice asked:

"*Has du Gelt?*"

A black-T-shirted ringleader appeared. Slightly taller and older, already wrinkled, lunar-pale, muscular-skinny but with a beer paunch, he seemed like a more vile and sinister Dieter North. The ringleader smiled, revealing broken buck teeth.

"*Gelt?*" he repeated.

He might have been twenty-six. His skeletal face was a mere foot from Jeffrey's. Jeffrey blinked, swallowing hard, and the young man reached for Jeffrey's pocket, as the boys crept closer in.

Jeffrey immediately thought of the box cutter; he wanted to use it or run. But they were too close even for him to get to it. Boys grabbed him from the rear, snatching at his clothing, hitting and kicking him. The ringleader stood apart, watching and smiling.

"*Spas!*" he called out wildly—"Fun!"—as he pushed two of the smaller kids at Jeffrey like footballs.

Jeffrey grabbed at one about thirteen, trying to use him as a shield. The kid bit him on the hand and jumped away.

This gave Jeffrey a second to grab the cutter. He jerked off the cover and waved the blade in front of him, shaking hard but hoping for a moment's safety. The blade glinted brightly in the moonlight.

The ringleader shrugged.

"We got knives, too!"

Hands yanked at his jacket from the rear, trying to pull him down to the ground. He spun around; fists popped out and hit him hard. The ringleader snuck behind him and grabbed Jeffrey's wrist.

The box cutter fell from his grip, and the ringleader snatched it up, grinning with broken teeth, while the boys dove into Jeffrey's pockets and tore his clothes. He ended up in a ball on the ground, raising his hands to protect to his face as the kids screamed:

"*JA!*"

"*NEIN!*"

"*HIER!*"

"*GELT!*"

"*SPAS! SPAS!*"

Then everything stopped. Dead quiet. He looked up into the eerie moonlight and saw John return, covered with sweat, still naked except for his running shoes.

The ringleader and John exchanged wary glances, then the ringleader shook his head and he and his boys vanished in a sooty blur of curses and screams down the road and into the trees.

John, looking concerned, approached Jeffrey.

"*Scheisse.* You got beat up. It's really bad. That kid's name is Pik, like Pete. He and his boys and I have a truce, so they don't screw with me—not much, anyway." John shook his head. "Your fucking luck, friend! They're out tonight. I was afraid this would happen to you, if you didn't move fast enough."

Jeffrey remained balled-up on the ground. His clothes were ripped and he was in unholy pain, in an undiscovered world: the corrupt underside of the forest he loved. He reached out, clasping John's bare white legs, touching his muscles, the warm veins, his cool sweat.

John crouched, touching him softly on the forehead.

"Seems like you can use a friend. You're my friend, right?"

Jeffrey nodded. If he'd ever needed help, it was now.

"Let me help you up."

He felt very unsteady. Everything hurt. "Please," he begged. "Give me a minute."

"There may be more kids," John warned. "They have lots of friends, and I mean real nuts. Anything goes."

"*Bitte.*"

"O.K."

John crouched lower, hugging him. He seemed made out of moonlight itself. Nothing had ever appeared so beautiful to Jeffrey, or possessed such tenderness and kindness. He put his head on John's wet chest, feeling John's heartbeat and more peace than he'd had in his entire life.

"We must get up."

John helped Jeffrey rise and they went to John's car. He unlocked it with a key from his shoe, and the two of them got in.

"You want to come to my place?" he asked. "I don't live far away. Not exactly fancy, but it's yours for the night."

"That would be good," Jeffrey said.

John's small stone house was only a short drive from the forest, with a stream running behind it so that it looked as if it were on a tiny island.

"In the old days it was a mill," John explained as he parked his car. They walked in—John still naked and Jeffrey in his torn clothes—and John lit kerosene lamps and candles.

"I have no electricity but plenty of water, and I can get wood from the forest, stuff that falls from the trees. Want something to eat or drink? How 'bout a beer?"

The beer was warm but good. There were pictures in bright colors with extremely bold figures and designs in every room, even painted on the bare walls. They flickered in the lantern and candle-light, like old silent movies or medieval illuminations, with a vitality of their own. John took off his shoes and put on a pair of white briefs. Jeffrey felt ashamed of his shredded clothes, and John could sense it. He handed him a loose white peasant's shirt that fell to Jeffrey's knees, and Jeffrey stripped off everything but his underwear and put that on. John invited Jeffrey to make himself comfortable; then he pointed out some of the pictures.

"That's Adam, making Eve. I think Adam wanted to make Eve himself, so he would be complete. God showed him how to do it. I think we all want to be complete. The problem is how to do it."

Jeffrey gazed at the pictures in the soft glowing light. What were they? He thought of Picasso, Blake, Giotto; Gauguin, Matisse—all of them rolled into God's own breath. The paintings seemed not only self-taught but self-generated. As if in their brilliant, free, yet startlingly lucid forms they had created themselves, like a breath-taking piece of music that had always been there, only waiting for the composer to jot it down.

But from where did all of this come?

"And that over there," John went on, smiling handsomely, "is Jacob. He's dreaming of the angel, and then wrestling with him. I like to wrestle, touching a man like that."

Jeffrey looked at him.

"You do?"

"Yes. It's a pure kind of touching. I like that. See, I'm seeking something different. I call it the 'pure' image. An image greater than itself—it's 'real' self. If you look at things directly, what do they mean? Nothing, really. But somewhere there is the *pure* image, the image that is greater than the 'real' thing is. You know it when you see it."

Jeffrey drank in his words.

"So, if it's pure, we'll all recognize it?" Jeffrey suggested.

"Yes!" John shouted. "You understand me. I'm so glad."

Jeffrey went on, puzzled by this strange, gifted man.

"Are you saying that because we really recognize it inside, this image—this 'pure' image—that it's available to us, already a part of us—and simply only has various forms?"

John smiled greedily.

"Yes! I'm thrilled that you understand this."

Jeffrey looked at him; John's childlike glee at this morsel of understanding Jeffrey offered was touching but close to embarrassing. Jeffrey in his world rarely touched such innocence of feelings, with all of its generosity and pent-up force. He looked away from John, knowing he had to lay some of his grounded sense and cynicism aside.

Taking a candle, he peered closer at the pictures. Cascading ribbons of rainbows fell from flocks of vividly colored birds, naked children sat with wolves, and groups of naive but saintly-looking people were humbly worshipping simple field animals.

"You are a real artist," Jeffrey announced. "I've never seen anything like this."

John smiled incandescently.

"Thank you, sir."

Jeffrey nodded.

"Why did you attack me?"

The question flew out of Jeffrey; there was nothing to hold it back anymore. He had wanted some nicely stitched plan to confront the man, and now he was the one who felt confronted, both by John's amazing innocence of feelings and his own feeling that his normal carapace of control was having a hard time staying up against any possibility of salvation. Because he felt truly beautiful, and alive, simply being in John van der Meer's presence. The golden lantern light, flickering candles, and reflected colors from his paintings made John glow like a Byzantine icon, passionate to his core and powerful. Jeffrey felt there must be nothing false between them, and that he would forgive John anything.

John's eyes flashed for an instant, then they appeared calm, even resigned.

"Attack?"

"At the pubtran platform. Hauptwache, a few days ago."

"You?"

"Yes."

John sank onto a mattress covered by a sheet on the floor. He looked up at Jeffrey.

"You're sure it was you?"

Jeffrey nodded. "You hit me, then smiled at me. Then hit me again."

John looked down at his hands. His voice became strained.

"I don't know. I must have seen something in you that upset me."

"What?"

"I don't know!" he exclaimed. "*Gott*! Everything gets knotted up in me. I'm crazy, see?" He tried to calm himself, but was shaking. "I'm sorry."

Jeffrey nodded. "I see."

He couldn't actually, but he wanted to. He turned to the paintings again, so unflinching in their intensity. He felt truly dismantled by their honesty and intense emotional nakedness.

"I was married," John explained. "With the kind of 'successful' life somebody like you has."

Jeffrey turned to him, their eyes meeting. It was easy for people to think Jeffrey had a "successful" life; he was only too aware of that.

"I fell apart," John explained. "Everything was taken away from me. Or maybe I just couldn't hold on to it anymore."

Only listening, Jeffrey nodded.

"I had a good job," John went on. "In the city, selling things to people I'd never see, in China. I was in step with everything, but really never stepped on anybody. I just did like they wanted me to, and hid any questions I had until they stopped being questions."

Jeffrey smiled. He was beginning to understand.

"One day—on the pubtran—I'm not sure how it happened, but inside I became a stranger to everything including myself. It was this horrible al—"

John hesitated.

"Alienation?" Jeffrey offered.

"Yes! I knew it that moment; I couldn't hide it from myself. I was *the* Dutchman who never comes home. He's lost and knows it. Something parted inside me and I knew it. It was like I had lost the thing that allows you to go on with the lies and the forms, all the appearances. The pain felt unbearable. I was on the edge of being valuable, a huge 'asset' to the system; they were beginning to offer me everything and I could not hold on to it anymore. My wife was English, very pretty, nice. We were one of those bright couples you see in newspapers. We didn't have a 'relationship,' we had a romantic advertisement for a relationship. One of those full-color pictures that offer—"

"'Escape'?" Jeffrey suggested.

"Yes, that's it! 'Escape.' But how do I escape *this*? She couldn't see me at all. I mean, I really smiled, kept smiling like in those newspaper pictures; and we had two wonderful kids and I thought that if I didn't do something to get myself out of it, I'd kill *all* of them, and then myself."

He paused, looking guiltily at Jeffrey.

"Do you think I'm nuts?"

Jeffrey shook his head, then sat down with John on the mattress. It was so warm that he took off the loose peasant's shirt. He felt somewhat cooler, yet could feel warmth streaming from John's pale flesh hardly more than a breath away from him. He'd never felt so close to someone. He started shaking, with his sweat evaporating in the body-heated air between them.

John drank more of the beer.

"I put myself in a hospital; they told me I was schizophrenic, or some crap like that. They couldn't figure it out. Like one day I was a regular person and the next—they were going to chemicalize my brain. Numb it, operate on it. A doctor came in and told me how nice I was, how pleased he was to be 'working' with me. He gave me a distant, sugary smile, then left. So I had to figure things out for myself. What to do. How to preserve myself. How to fool the people I had to fool."

Jeffrey's eyes widened.

"The truth was," John went on, "I'd come to this moment, this awakening, and for the first time I found myself to be truly alive. It was wonderful, amazing. I saw that most other people weren't alive. They were trapped in their own deadness, no matter how 'rewarding' it was. They were on this constant. . . ."

His forefinger, pointing up, described a continuous circle, like a merry-go-round. Jeffrey watched, mesmerized. Their eyes met again.

"It was like a religious awakening, but I couldn't find anyplace in it for God. I didn't need God, not everybody else's God, the one that the system works with, one way or another. I needed religion, but I had to figure out where God stood in it. Later I painted these stories, made them mine, because I needed stories of my own. We all do, I'm sure of that. But at that moment, God, big, powerful, my own God, wasn't in it. Just the truth that *I* was alive, and they were going to kill that living part of me.

"So with some effort I tried to be normal again. I fooled them and got out of the hospital with my brain intact, and went back to my wife, Cynthia. Isn't that a proper-enough English name, Cynthia? But there was no way I could reach her. She had a good job and nice friends in her world. She tried to bury me in all her English busyness and drag me back with her into the system, so everyone would forget that anything had happened. She'd say, 'You'll get better, John. You will, darling!' and smile just like that dreadful doctor in the hospital. So I had to fool her too. I felt like shit. I couldn't even talk to my kids, they were brainwashed in their private school already."

"What did you do?"

"I went back to work and Cynthia went back to England for a while, to her wealthy parents. Then she came back to me. What else could she do? I was the father of her kids and she was very traditional. She made me feel that I had no choice. I mean, I wanted to work it out; you have no idea. But I realized I *did* have a choice. I could stay with her, inside a certain line tightly drawn around myself, and not fall apart too much if I held on. But—"

He stopped himself.

"But what?" Jeffrey asked.

"I'd die. Simple as that: I'd never have a moment of being alive. I'd just have everything that keeps you from being alive. Games. Entertainment. Too many things that do that."

Jeffrey's eyes narrowed.

"So you attacked me instead?"

"No. It wasn't that, I swear!"

John ran his hand through Jeffrey's hair again, then touched him on the shoulder and suddenly kissed him on the neck.

"I didn't want to tell you," he said crying. "I knew who you were when I asked you into my car. I recognized you. The truth is at the pubtran at Hauptwache, I wanted to warn you. I needed to."

"Warn me about what?"

"You're in danger. Something is going to get you."

"You attacked me to tell me that?"

"There was no other way to do it. I couldn't approach you. Why would you listen to me? Do you know what I'm saying?"

"No, I don't."

"There was no other way to reach you. You were so distant."

"I was trying to keep from going crazy in the crowd. You just couldn't see that."

"I saw it. And I could see you were struggling to reach someplace I'd—" he paused, then said—"already reached. But the only way I could get you there was to hit you. I'm sorry. It was stupid."

Jeffrey smiled. The man was crazy, but at least somehow he'd seen something Jeffrey was attempting to conceal even from himself. It was something that could be fatal; he tried to explain it.

"I was trying to be calm. I have a hard time with stress, John. Much harder that I let on. All those signs are right. Stress is a killer."

"Sure, you can die of stress; I almost did. The stress of not being yourself, of hiding, of trying to fool too many people. I could see all of that in you. Our meeting wasn't accidental, I swear to you. You were so handsome, beautifully dressed, trying to be safe in a guarded way, alone in yourself. I hated watching it."

"I'm not that," Jeffrey argued. "I wish I were."

John nodded knowingly.

"No. You haven't found what's inside you yet. That's why I hit you. I could have killed you, really. I needed to reach you; I mean that. What the hell else could I do?"

"I don't know," Jeffrey answered softly. "But if you did reach me, what else would you want to do?"

John licked his lips. His eyes seemed to Jeffrey as golden as the light.

"What else?"

"Yes, what?"

"God. I can't believe you asked that."

He put his hands firmly on Jeffrey's bare shoulders, letting his lips graze Jeffrey's neck as he whispered:

"Wrestle with you."

Chapter Six

John arched over Jeffrey, pinning him down with both hands as scalding electric body heat gathered between them, producing a charge that twisted the dark hairs on Jeffrey's chest like sea grass in a marshland wind. They were naked on the mattress. Slightly beer-sweetened sweat dripped from John's brow and neck, some finding its way to Jeffrey's lips.

Jeffrey turned his head, trying to resist, to throw John off him, but John seemed so much stronger than he. He almost gave up, so John would have his way, whatever that meant. But Jeffrey was angry, as much as he had told himself he shouldn't be, and this tamped-down fury—left over from the attack?—came roaring out, shocking even himself.

He couldn't hate John anymore, but something had penetrated heart-deep within him and he grabbed at its darkly throbbing energy as it screamed its presence and enabled him to push back aggressively at John, jerking himself forward and attacking, pushing John so hard that the taller man flipped over and fell off the mattress.

John got up from the floor.

Jeffrey eyed him, unsure if his newfound strength could keep up, but definitely not scared anymore. John jumped on him again, trying to pin him once more. Jeffrey caught him by the shoulders and, using every last reserve of strength, threw him off. John landed on the floor again with a flesh-bruising thud, then he quickly got up, smiling savagely at Jeffrey.

"You!" he screamed. "*Scheisse!*"

He jumped again, grappling with Jeffrey until he was out of breath. But Jeffrey wasn't. He was almost relaxed, scarily so, though he was not sure he could actually push John off again.

"I should kick your ass," John said. Instead, he fell softly on Jeffrey, hugging him, resting his cheek directly on Jeffrey's.

Jeffrey felt his whole body surrender, and he was grateful. That was all he could feel. Grateful that there was no more stress in him. He hugged John.

"Do you like this?" John whispered.

It tore Jeffrey in two; one part forgiving John anything, the other still angry. But the anger was no longer directed at John. He'd found it, the razor-raged tool of himself that he'd repressed for so long, the one he couldn't find with Ellis; and its dangerous, hard-on surging, intoxicating male substance was now racing straight through him.

Jeffrey moved his head and bit fiercely into John's neck.

"*Gott!!!*" John screamed. "Vampire!"

He jerked away, ready to slap Jeffrey, and immediately Jeffrey lunged at him and took one of John's paper-thin red Dutch nipples in his mouth, softly squeezing it with his lips, then putting the pressure of his teeth into it.

"*Gottttt,*" John whimpered. "*Sehr gut.* Wonderful!"

"Uh-huh," Jeffrey said, giving John a teasing slap on the ass, followed by a kiss on his large nose and his wide lips, until John surrendered his entire mouth to Jeffrey's hungry assault. Still embracing Jeffrey, John eased back the silky-thin sheath of his foreskin and jackknifed his cock down Jeffrey's throat, sighing as Jeffrey took it to the hilt.

"*Schön,*" John moaned, his hands all over Jeffrey, stroking him, his tongue licking everywhere, until he climaxed in loud bucking spasms in Jeffrey's mouth, and then lay spent, eyes closed, the sheet soaking in the weary bitter tang of lush male funk.

He reached out for Jeffrey, reading with satiated fingers his thighs, groin, stomach, drifting into something more solid than sleep, until Jeffrey slipped away and got up. The lamp and candles were still lit, and the small house glowed in its bohemian disorder, watched over by John's paintings.

Jeffrey wanted to be bathed in them, in the dazzling richness of their life. They were not primitive as much as honest. More honest, Jeffrey told himself, than he could ever have imagined himself being. He crouched on his naked haunches, gazing at them in admiration, absorbed in their magnificence. They seemed to spring directly from

God.

Yes, God. The God of the turbulent self. Van Gogh's God . . . as if the religion-besotted, sad Vincent himself had finally glimpsed the Creator he had always wanted, only to kill himself when he could not reach him actually. This was the unreachable God of Van Gogh, as well as of his protective brother Theo: the awesome Deity of power and of invulnerable tenderness, and of such forgiveness that even sighting such a God was not a sin, but brought one to the full splendor of the largest Self, immense, unguarded, which John had felt in his sudden, solitary, powerful awaking on the pubtran.

Jeffrey shivered; looking at John's paintings made Tony's suggestion that he try to enter a "calming mist" seem pathetic.

This was not calming. It was volcanic.

"You like them?" John asked, rising and putting his hands on Jeffrey's shoulders.

"More than I've ever liked anything in my life."

"Then surely I'll love you," John said. "I never thought it possible, but I will love you."

"Will you?" Jeffrey got up and faced him. "You know nothing about me."

John kissed him.

"I know everything. I do."

"My work?"

"Yes. It requires intelligence and great sensitivity, right?"

Jeffrey smiled. Close enough. If only John knew it had little to do with either, but only with the system.

"And my age?"

John looked puzzled.

"You're old, and young too. Correct?"

Jeffrey nodded. Again, true enough. It seemed the age issue meant nothing to John. There was nothing further he could say.

John took him by the hand and opened the door. It was much cooler outside and so calm that they could hear night sounds approaching from the fields and trees. Owls, nocturnal birds, fluttering insects; bats making single piercing notes in the blackness.

"There are wolves out here," John said. "They scare the people from the East, but not me."

"What does scare you?" Jeffrey asked.

But John would not answer. He merely smiled at Jeffrey as if he did not want to say it; in fact, did not want to say anything else.

For a while they lay on the grass on a knoll a short way from the house, looking up at the stars that seemed to fall in great handfuls of glitter; then they waded into the stream and washed themselves. The water was very cold and chilled Jeffrey. John held him, and guided him back into the house.

"I should make you some coffee," he said. "Or some tea."

"Tea would be nice."

It was very late. Soon morning would come, or at least the initial suggestion of it, that first cool light reflected from the earth. Jeffrey felt wonderful; he'd not felt so truly young or alive in years. Mostly, youth was this mask he put on which gave him the stamina to work more or was a reward for working more, like one of those powerful deluxe "Escape" cars from the fantasy ads, a car with more personality than the people in it. But no matter how fantastic it was, the car could be taken from you. Now he felt simply young; engagingly, wondrously young, authentically energized from within.

He wished he had a mirror, to see what he actually looked like. Then he realized that the real mirror was John's eyes.

John handed him tea, looking directly at him, and he saw himself in John's face. They both smiled. This seemed impossible, Jeffrey thought, even for Germany, a place where the past was erased and reinvented every day.

John smiled at him.

"Would you like to spend the night, or what's left of it?"

Jeffrey nodded, then the two of them fell asleep on the mattress.

When he woke up, his watch told him that it was noon. Even though it was Saturday, people would wonder where he was. He had some appointments, and work to do at home that he'd promised himself he would get to. The Mormons and the Indians and the car people would be sending him things. There were things to research, formulate, style. He did not want to go. John was still asleep. Jeffrey felt good just being there, walking naked through the clutter, looking at John's work in the pure, clear light streaming through the windows.

There was a knock on the door. Jeffrey put his pants on and opened it to find a small boy with a tin pail. He was maybe twelve with dark hair and blue eyes.

"*Ich habe milch,*" the boy said.

Jeffrey smiled. "*Danke.*"

The boy handed him the pail and left.

John got up, walking through the house naked.

"He's from a farm close to here. He brings me milk from the cow; eggs, too. I give him money when I have it. His name's Tommy; very American name. He's posed for me. Look."

John showed him some watercolors and drawings of the boy, all nudes, very natural looking.

"He didn't mind being naked," John said, drinking milk directly from the pail. "The nice thing about people out here is that they don't have a lot of shame yet. Those kids yesterday, the ones who attacked you, I guess they have it."

"Why do people attack each other?" Jeffrey asked, taking the pail and drinking from it. Some of the milk spilled onto his chin and down his chest. He winced, then enjoyed the careless feeling of it.

"They're scared. Sometimes, it's the only way they can address their own sadness. I think people become very sad."

"Depression?"

"That's it. And they are too scared to fuck or take their clothes off, to enjoy life. So they attack each other in the name of God even. God would like what I'm doing, I know that."

"How?"

"Maybe I've seen Him."

"What does He look like?"

"You."

Jeffrey tried to laugh, but couldn't.

"I'm only a sham. A false front," he said sadly. "I know it. I think you saw that. That's why you punched me on the platform. Did you see it?"

"No. I saw all the way down into you. And it scared me, what I did. Truly."

They began to make love once more, and John gave up any reticence toward him, becoming aggressive, kissing, holding, sucking and touching every part of him, lavishing Jeffrey with his feelings and his sturdy Dutch body, which Jeffrey received gladly. That marvelous, slightly too large nose; John's tender mouth, neck, and papery nipples; the sheer, thin skin of his stomach and silken cock; his firm runner's ass and long pale legs. He stopped, eyes glowing like jewels, and surrendered himself, surprising Jeffrey no end. He wanted Jeffrey to fuck him, hard, and he did. Then they washed up again in the stream.

Afterward, Jeffrey had to leave, but now felt no shame or self-consciousness about his clothes. They were torn and rumpled, but he decided not worry about it. John drove him back to the last platform on the pubtran line, whistling an old German song that Jeffrey recognized from *Fasching*, while Jeffrey attempted to sing it:

"'Please, handsome stranger! Make love to me, make love to me! But please, don't tell me your name!'"

"You really know it?" John asked as they approached the station.

"Yes. How can I see you again?" Jeffrey asked.

"Come back here. Or maybe we'll meet in the city."

"You have no phone, I guess."

"No, I hate that. They know every place you go and what you do. I used to have all of that, but not anymore."

"Don't you ever want to show your paintings or sell them?"

"No, I trade them sometimes. I do odd jobs for money. Only cash. I tell you, the less I have the easier it gets. And I want it to stay that way."

"You have a point. It is easier."

John took his hand in the car, after he had parked at the station.

"I'll go into Afghanistrasse on Monday," he said. "Maybe we can meet there if you'd like. There's a square. Do you know it?"

"Yes. Very well."

"About six o' clock? How's that?"

"Perfect," Jeffrey said, and he got out of the car. He walked around to the driver's side, leaned in the window, and kissed John good-bye. Then John backed the car out and drove off.

❧

It took Jeffrey a long time to get back to his apartment, which occupied most of the thirty-second floor of a new, full-block building with every kind of luxury and amenity in it: elegant shops, cleaners, restaurants, a cafe, even an exclusive games arcade for kids and their parents. Walking past the big front security desk with its bowl of artificial flowers pinpointed by spotlights, he realized how sterile it was: the staff unzipped starched smiles for him like fellow window mannequins. At Christmas, plainly American-style, one gave the staff money in sealed envelopes, producing a brief, artificial friendliness which wore off a few days after the holidays, when normal frigid formalities were happily re-established all around.

He went to his mailbox to see if anything had come in through the post. Only advertisements. He discarded them in a garbage bin set up for that purpose. In his apartment, some lights were on and music played low, preset for security reasons to give an impression that someone was there. He turned off several alarms, then went to his desk information system to see what had arrived. Six dozen messages had come in overnight, some from his office, some directly to him, many of them of consequence, although a lot were simply repetitions on the same theme of how to make something new again and bring in fresh money.

He poured himself a cup of coffee and began seriously reading. He was hungry but kept almost no food in the kitchen, so he called the cafe downstairs where he had an account. A few minutes later, a wrinkled Thai delivery man arrived with a turkey sandwich, French fries, and a Coca-Cola. It was not the healthiest lunch, but he felt like indulging himself. He signed for the food and tipped the man.

Suddenly he had this desire to take his clothes off and be as naked in his apartment as he had been with John. But once he undressed, it didn't feel right. Unlike John's rustic house, his apartment was carpeted in some areas and had polished marble floors in others. The marble felt freezing to his feet, and he wasn't sure about naked skin on his expensive upholstery. He slipped his underwear back on, then realized there were pills he needed to take and he'd better not chance anything by skipping them.

Looking at the tasteful ultramodern *objets d'art* he owned, the lights, the ultra-trendy, uncomfortable furniture that almost *sat* on you instead of the other way around, he felt old again, as if he were wading against a current he could not possibly overcome. At any moment, he'd be knocked down by it. He had assistants who were more up-to-date than he was. They were always joking and telling him about the most up-to-date thing in India, the Middle East, Asia.

Of course, they had their young fingers on the exact moment, the *now* that only happens *now*. But the real question was what would happen next? When one fad faded, there was always a glitch of uncertainty, and that was where Jeffrey came in—truly old, young-appearing or not. The problem with the utterly modern was how quickly it faded into the passé. So he'd reconnect the dots and tell them precisely what would happen at that point.

A lot of money rode on it. He knew exactly how easy it was to go from being with-it to being past-it, or passé—the one thing he could never *be* himself. To fade into the passé would mean to die, and Jeffrey liked sticking around too much, adored it in fact. Munching his turkey sandwich, he began dealing with his work, trying to keep it from overwhelming him.

He spotted a message from Chris Stewart and Len Silverman:

"Very important people coming over. Drinks and din-din tonight?"

Jeffrey smiled. Chris must have scored with another one of his hemi-semi-demi movers and shakers from the oxygen-deprived heights of "Aht and Lit-rature."

His first thought was to say no. There would be about two dozen of the Stewart-Silvermans' nearest and dearest there. They didn't need him. Then he realized that being alone after being with John would not be easy. The good thing about evenings at the Stewart-Silvermans' was that if he had enough to drink and stayed reasonably aloof, they could be pleasant in an innocuous kind of way, like playing bridge or shopping. It was only when Chris was being difficult, carrying his fragile ego on his sleeve, that things got testy.

He sent an info shot saying he would come, and got one back instantly: "*Wunderschön.* Lots of love to you, and a lot of *naches.*"

That must have come from Len, who used Yiddish whenever he could get away with it. The Germans did not like passing off Yiddish for German. "Naches," the word for "happiness," pronounced "nah-hus" but with a little guttural sound in the "ch," was not to be confused with the Spanish snacks, "nachos." But then Jeffrey was aware of this, having lived in the stylish world long enough to know plenty of Jews.

He munched at the sandwich on his couch, working on things to send out with a small keyboard, listening to some new music that he liked, interspersed with short pieces of Bach. Now that he was back in his own space, he could forget about himself, one of the major joys of familiarity.

He saw several memos from Malace, asking repeated questions about the luxe "Valentino" car and the Mormon worship-*cum*-dubious-pleasures palace. Then he got one requesting another rare (for Malace) piece of time off. "Four days. O.K.? Heard about something I need to pursue." Jeffrey's brow knit; he'd have to think about that. Things were jamming up, but (Jeffrey thought) maybe this might be a good time not to have Malace too close to him. "With Malace toward none" was one of his favorite brow-raising inside jokes, which he never shared with his dour chief assistant. Malace was a driven worker, but could mire things up with his plodding earnestness; he was incapable of making split-second executive decisions and had the social finesse of a baboon.

Four days? Maybe that wasn't a bad idea now.

Then came more trouble, in the form of another video call from Ashok Rahman in India rehashing dumb, rapid fire memos he'd received from some of the more difficult sponsors putting up money for "Goddess." Jeffrey did not like getting this, especially at home, but had to deal with it.

Ashok (in pleading earnest):

"Jeffrey, please forgive me for this intrusion, but you know how the Money works. It's not easy to direct its wholehearted attention toward us. I'm afraid some of these gentlemen, the key ones, feel that they want something a tad more—"

Ashok hesitated. Jeffrey could see glints of sweat again on the young man's face. The light picked it up and aged Ashok, making Jeffrey wonder what his own light, or the night before, was doing to him on Ashok's monitor.

Ashok went on, affecting a shrug: "They feel they want something a tad more—'elegant.'" Big sigh. "You know, 'Olde 'England' circa nineteen forties, nineteen-fifties maybe?"

"*Elegant?* Come on, Ashok. That was rationing, the Blitz. Then angry young men. Rotten food, cold water, and shitty plumbing. Elegant? Where on earth do they get *elegant?*"

"Jeffrey"—Ashok tried to put on confidence—"to be precise, we're talking about Greer Garson, *Mrs. Miniver.* Deborah Kerr. Joan Fontaine. Young Audrey Hepburn. Remember those swanky old Hollywood movies about poor girls marrying money—*Rebecca*! That's what every Indian girl still dreams of. We're talking elegant but *demure*, if you catch my drift."

"I'm trying to, but I'm not sure your drift is going exactly where the system wants it to go. We've already done a lot of prep work on the line, and stylewise we've done some very good things."

"You have!" Ashok exploded. "And please, I am aware that the provincial gaucherie of this may revolt you. But I think we need to consider a true turnaround on 'Goddess.'"

Jeffrey's eyes merely narrowed. A turn-around at this point would not be good. Jeffrey had already set a large amount of money into motion, and he wondered what trap Ashok might be setting. Despite the young man's earlier qualms, the Goddess line could work nicely in regional India, with few problems and an almost guaranteed decent return on its investment. But he let Ashok surge on.

"To begin with, a new name and a *complete* new design concept." Ashok smiled bravely. "I'm talking 'Good Olde England.' 'Creme high tea.' Attainable *luxury.* Our studies have found that the young women we've identified as customers prize certain elements of *properness* and *luxury* very highly."

"*Studies?* So you have documentation on them?"

"'Fraid not, old boy. They're pretty informal, but the money people have seen them and they liked them. In other words, they *want* this to happen."

"Who are you talking about, Ashok? Can you give me names? I need to hear names, Ashok."

Ashok lowered his eyes; Jeffrey could hear him take a breath.

"This is an Indian situation, and I'm afraid you really don't know India, old boy. No one wants to pop out as a name: It's just not done here. You need to trust me. My tail is on the line too, Jeffrey. I've told you all I am allowed to say. Our underwriters have identified the desired 'Release' elements, and we need to give them what they want. They want 'Old School' and a rename. They're thinking of 'That Woman,' as in: 'That Woman is one of us.' Or, 'That Woman is someone we want to be.' Frankly, I like it myself. So I'm afraid I have to tell you, the previous Hindu-India design with all of its funky but old-hat stuff is *out*."

Jeffrey tried to hold on to himself. "'Old hat'?"

Ashok shrugged and smiled beguilingly.

"Sorry. Maybe it was not the best choice of words, Jeffrey."

Jeffrey exhaled, trying not to look too nonplussed.

"I'll think about it. What would you like?"

Ashok became more formal.

"Can you bring in more informational models in something like two or three days? Sponsors need to be made happy. They'll thank you, believe me."

"I believe you," was all Jeffrey could squeeze out. They exchanged some closing formalities, then he clicked off.

Greer Garson? Deborah Kerr? Joan Fontaine? Who the hell came up with them? The idea, even for money people, was queer, still they had to be listened to, which had always been one of Jeffrey's major talents: listening to the money jerks, then, if necessary, doing an end run around them.

But *Deborah Kerr?* She had a kind of "no-style" that made her stylish, based on a quietly evident, pure "sincerity." This he could visualize, and quickly enough all of her little style motifs (the primly tied scarf, the simple blouse, the severe lady's jacket) came to him. Still there was a fishy smell about this radical turnaround. Why wasn't

Ashok steering the Money back toward "Goddess," instead of driving the whole line toward a different destination? That way the Garson-Kerr thing could come out later, as a side line. It made him wonder if indeed Ashok weren't smarter than he'd indicated in the past (mostly he'd been a toe-the-line lackey for the system) and was setting Jeffrey up, steering the line into a failure for which Jeffrey would have to take blame, thereby positioning himself for a promotion that would leapfrog him outside Jeffrey's reach.

It was interesting that Ashok was tipping his hand this way, and unusual for a project manager to deprecate his financial sources. There was a kind of holy, scary space around them. You had to approach Money with your shoes off, the way a wary Moses did the burning bush. This was true even in vast, stubbornly contradictory India, where money was still not like American money. In the States, unpredictable avalanches of moolah could destroy you. With all that pesky impatient Big Money out there being offered to you, at some point you'd start grabbing it for yourself. Then the real people behind it—dour, faceless, spoiled monsters who could snap your back on whim. . . .

Jeffrey shuddered. He was very familiar with these scenarios within the system. You could get wiped out if you didn't play your cards super-straight, and there was so much temptation not to. At some point, one of the smaller money jerks, like a court jester, would approach you and tell you that, now, *you* could be the "Star," instead of the brand. From then on, if you didn't know exactly what their game was, if you weren't schooled in their tricks, it was like drinking poison.

But if you were smart and *did* know how to play this game— which was as close to war as most people ever came—*and* you were used to its potent concoction of arsenic and world fame, you might survive, and even do well. Some backstage people, like Jeffrey himself, could, and even a few "little guys" like Ashok, who had become known "names."

You could push yourself up higher in the system. But you had to do it, as the Wicked Witch of the West in the timeless *Wizard of Oz* suggested, "carefully."

Being a (mostly) unseen power, Jeffrey had kept himself as far out of the immediate fire of the moolah-monsters as he could. This was part of his talent, and the source of the big luck he'd made for himself. Some of the empty-shell, brand-name "designers" he worked for got caught in the middle of it, but not Jeffrey. The system would pull someone up and start giving him colossal name recognition, making him an internationally recognized "lifestyle" arbiter, guru, force. Gargantuan "face" billboards. Media blitzes. Lines of products bearing his name. An endless spotlight. They'd stuff him to bursting with money.

Then, at some inevitable point, he would *burst*. The popular media would eat him: He was over, tired, worn out, stale. The unwashed masses of the consumerate, relentlessly fickle and needy for new blood, would sacrifice him on the altar of consumer hysteria.

The system giveth, and the system taketh away.

You had to feel sympathy for them. Jeffrey, in his godmotherly role, would see these "name" stars, and wonder when their hour would come. They were given help (including from manipulators like Jeffrey). And there were drugs that could steady and even inflate these poster kids for the High Life, to enable them to dance the night away and still come into the studio in the morning.

Most of the younger "name" people ended up like smashed piñatas after the party, with just a bunch of cheap trinkets and magazine exposure to show for it. He wondered if Ashok were using drugs already. The temptation was really great. Deborah Kerr? Greer Garson? *King Solomon's Mines. Mrs. Minniver.* Where the hell did Ashok get this? He was trying too hard, pushing too much. Jeffrey shook his head sadly, and decided to let Ashok play his hand, to guide and support him, until the proper moment.

Two or three days put him under the gun, which evidently was also part of Ashok's strategy. It meant dealing with thousands of images, finding and comparing them, rating them, and finally refitting them into a usable format aimed at a distinct new line of products: "That Woman."

Ashok Rahman's line.

Or so Jeffrey would try hard to make him believe.

He might try to rope Malace, already up to his ears in projects, into this. And there were also copywriters to deal with and then the final product designers, as well as groups of other independent consultants, all waiting like hardened mercenaries at various promotion and marketing agencies, many in far-flung locales, every one of them aiming a box cutter of their own at Jeffrey's throat.

He thought about the box cutter he'd brought with him to meet John van der Meer. Maybe he should have used it on himself.

He smiled, suddenly wondering if Chris Stewart in his ivory tower of the Renaissance ever got his hands dirty on something like this. The stairs running up that tower were narrow, and the important thing was to make sure that no one else could get up there, except for the chosen few like Stewart himself. What Jeffrey did, Chris couldn't do; but it was important for people like Christopher Stewart, PhD, never to see this.

Their work: saving tight-assed Western civilization, with its equally tight-butted, high-money culture.

His work: keeping the wheels of the everyday, happy-as-a-pig-in-shit consumer culture going.

Culture? This was *culture?*

It was more like hand-to-hand combat.

Then the strange, deliciously sexy Dutch guy crept back into his brain.

John van der Meer.

What was Jeffrey to do? He had been fairly good at being the gatekeeper of his own feelings; now one very improbable feeling had inconveniently snuck in. This feeling had reddish hair, fine pale skin, and green eyes, close to those of Van Gogh. The feeling (sexual; heart-stoppingly delicious) was attached to a painter.

A real painter. Not some *uber*-scheme of the system, with a bunch of shifty-eyed marketing vultures attached.

Suddenly it hit him like a stab of arthritis: There was no way he could go back to John.

Finito. It had to be. Just like the thing with Rick.

The system, the clients, the money people—all those who had kept him alive and young were telling him: "You've made your choice. You've found your pot to shit in. Do this and we might as well kill you. Forget it, or we won't even offer you Jesus as a consolation prize."

Terrified, Jeffrey realized that he'd better keep every compulsive, unbearably gorgeous nanosecond of his experiences with John dead quiet from Tony; or for that matter from anyone else. Any slip, and he might as well inject himself with one of those megapain killers that, upon exceeding its "normal" dosage, sped you express to death. The most respectable doctors did it all the time. Bernd Ostreich could do it to him, if the word got out and the system decided it was all over with for Mr. Jeffrey Cooper.

"*Hier*, Dirtbag. A little injection," he could hear Bernd say sympathetically, trying to smile.

Hadn't everyone done enough, just keeping Jeffrey young and attractive? He was exceeding his own dosage now: His talents, his skills, his abilities were being pushed far beyond his reach. He'd been floating way up there, and now he was ready for a fall. And he saw exactly where the fall ended if he weren't careful.

He'd wind up dead, dirty, and naked on that ratty mattress with John van der Meer next to him. Even as enticing as John was . . . though fucking weird.

He thought about tracing Herr van der Meer. What was his *real* story? He should know it, just for his own peace of mind, even if he were never to see John again. How cuckoo was he, really? Every human in the universe was now traceable: birth-to-death files existed for everybody. And Jeffrey, nicely placed as he was, had almost full access to them.

He went into his work files, placing passwords, starting digital signatures. Then in mid-stroke he realized: *Yep*, go ahead, idiot. And half the system will know.

Including Tony. His friend.

❧

"Jeffrey, *mein landsman*," Len Silverman cooed, as he let Jeffrey in. "Damn sweet of you t'come."

Len was in his cups, but he needed to be that way as there was yet another crowd of stylish and almost-stylish strangers in his living room. Jeffrey walked in and watched them do their usual dance around the bar and the canapés. But this time, a number of young people flitted about, their noses, ears, brows, navels, and nipples pierced with high-energy, flashing gemstones and optic-fine lights, some dressed in near-translucent outfits revealing just about everything. One milk-skinned, raven-haired beauty, shirt unbuttoned close to the fugitive hairs of his groin, generously displayed his family jewels repeatedly pierced, exhibiting but for the whispery cling of material neatly pouched over it, a ring hugging the fat circumference of his endowment, adjacent to its almost fully exposed head. It was an eye-catching effort at concealment that made the suggestion of what was underneath even more delicious; Jeffrey studied the full effect, captivated, until Len interrupted him.

"Chris has brought in some talent from his classes to entertain Mr. Magus," Len whispered, or attempted to whisper. Drunk, Len was as discreet as a meat ax, and always joked how he would "pay for everything in the morning, one way or another." This of course was Dr. Len's role: the harried, put-upon husband. He did it well.

Jeffrey smiled and whispered for real, "Who is Mr. Magus?"

"He ain't here yet," Len said, dropping any semblance of lowering his voice. "He's another *nafkee* whom Chris needs to ass-kiss. I better shut my *fakachte* mouth, right?"

Chris met them as they finished a full circuit of the living room.

"I'm so glad you could make our little soiree," Chris said, twinkling. "Reginald Magus is in town. He's the editor-in-chief of *World Affairs, Culture, and Art Development*. They're based in Dallas and have a gazillion dollars behind them. You must know him, right?"

"Not personally."

Chris smiled. "You mean, you really don't know Reggie Magus? I thought everybody knew Reggie. That's why I wanted you here, especially."

"I see," said Jeffrey, smiling tightly.

The chances of Chris wanting him there for that reason were thinner than the material of that young man's pants. If Jeffrey had indeed known this Magus, he would have upstaged Chris, something his host would never tolerate, if it were possible.

"I'll do my best not to embarrass you this time." Jeffrey offered

"That was unfortunate, that *contretemps* with Angelina. Sometimes these people have too much ego, you know. They don't have my self-effacing nature. But they could certainly use a bit of it."

"Yes, dear," Len said. "They could."

"Thank you for coming," Chris said. "Now like any good hostess, I've got to mingle."

Chris was dressed more demurely this time, except that around his neck he wore a showy multistrand rope of large baroque pearls.

"Like the pearls?" Len asked. Jeffrey nodded. "For his birthday. He *had* t'have them. I coulda bought another old picture or some nice piece of furniture or something, but he wanted pearls. So pearls I got him."

Jeffrey looked around the Stewart-Silvermans' show-off, frou-frou apartment. They needed more framed pictures or furniture like a long-haul trucker needed hemorrhoids.

"Very Renaissance," Jeffrey said, grinning. "All the best-dressed men wore pearls then; the women, too."

"Wuz that so? I just thought it was the Empress acting like royalty again. But I love all the talent in the room. I'd give half the hairs on my dick to suck some of this."

Jeffrey chuckled.

"Maybe you should, Len. You can always grow them back."

"Yeah, but Chris would go apeshit. They're here as window deco-ration for Magus from Dallas. That almost rhymes, don't it?" Len glowed warmly from alcohol. "I could be a poet."

"You could. Just don't give up your day job."

"Twue, twue. How 'bout a drink, or would you like something else?"

"Else?"

"Yeah, some of the kids are on the balcony, smoking. And it ain't Dutch cigars."

Jeffrey decided why not. He got a small scotch at the bar (tended by one of Chris's comely students) and took it out to the balcony, where the dark-haired boy with the pants was smoking something from a small metal pipe. The boy held the smoke in his lungs, then exhaled a slight whiff. It had a cinnamon fragrance, with a definite note of hashish.

"Want some?" he offered, looking only too sweetly at Jeffrey.

How could he resist?

Jeffrey thanked him, then drew the pipe to his lips and its contents very briefly into his lungs. He was not fond of drugs beyond the ones he had to take. Bernd Ostreich had warned him that recreational chemicals could pose a problem. ("No telling what conflicts one might have. One does not know the exact makeup of these street things!")

But one small hit; what was the problem?

"*Wie kennst du* Professor Stewart?" the kid asked.

"I'm a social friend," Jeffrey replied in English, handing the pipe back to the boy. "My name is Jeffrey Cooper. I'm American, but you probably guessed that even before I started talking."

"Yes, I guessed," the boy said. "You look American."

"How?"

"Your eyes. They're more open. I wanted to meet you."

"You did?"

Why on earth, Jeffrey thought. The boy was charming, dazzling. When he offered him the pipe again, Jeffrey took it and this time forgot all about Bernd.

"You're good-looking. I like older men. And I like Americans."

"You do?" Jeffrey could hardly keep from preening. "What's your name?"

"Joshua Goldmeister. I know, the name sounds Jewish. I think my father had some *Judenkeit* in his family. We are proud of it. You should not keep it a secret."

"I don't think you keep much a secret."

The boy smiled. "Why should I, or anyone? Secrets are not good for the soul."

"That all depends on whose soul. How old are you?"

"Nineteen."

Joshua smiled. He was definitely not nineteen.

"Okay," he confessed. "I am really twenty-two."

More like twenty-six, Jeffrey thought. But why not? Age was as fluid as culture now.

Joshua beamed. "And how old are you? Let me guess. You're forty-two."

Jeffrey darkened. Usually people thought he was in his late thirties. It was a sign he was still tired from the night before. He tried to relax.

"I'm a little younger," he said. "But I'm tired now."

"Partying last night? Do you like to party?"

The boy was now literally in his face, his body so close that his young heat seared Jeffrey.

"Yes, I do. If it's the right party."

"I don't think this is it," the boy confided, blowing into Jeffrey's ear so that his young, sweet breath sent a cool shiver through him. "Professor Stewart wanted some of his prize students here for this goofball from Texas. We joked about it. It's awful! I didn't know Professor Stewart was such a whore."

"What can Professor Stewart do for you?" Jeffrey whispered, his mouth almost on the boy's cheek.

"I need a scholarship to continue school. He can help me. I know that. This Dallas man is big in the *Aht* world. *Kultur,* that stuff. It's all about *gelt* and who gets to see it, right?"

There had been others on the balcony, but now Jeffrey and the boy were alone.

"You're very smart for a young man," Jeffrey said. "I wasn't so smart when I was your age."

Joshua smiled suggestively.

"But that wasn't *so* long ago."

He handed his pipe back to Jeffrey and relit it while Jeffrey inhaled.

Then Chris's voice boomed from inside.

"*Meine damen und herren*—everybody! Please, let me introduce you to Reginald Magus, who's visiting us from Dallas and is such a friend of the Renaissance—and a Renaissance man! Ladies and gentleman, my friend Reggie!"

Jeffrey peeked inside. Reginald Magus was overweight, dressed in a ridiculous, too nautically styled, expensive blazer too small for him, cinched in and buttoned tightly. He was balding, red-faced and appeared out-of-patience tired, like he had just flown in from some extremely important location, to which he would hurry back before he got completely bored. People hovered around him while he inspected the young students as if they were dogs at a show. He had a deep, sweaty, Northern Atlantic voice, with bits of Texas twang embedded in it.

"Ah'm very seriously looking for interns to take back to Dallas with me," he intoned as Chris introduced the kids.

"Rik is multilingual, and a specialist in several very obscure Italian masters," Chris announced proudly. "And Artur here"—a young man in placental-thin black leather—"he's excellent! You should hear him talk about the Northern Renaissance and what it did to capitalism. He's a wiz at that sort of analytical thinking."

Jeffrey had to witness this up close. He motioned for Joshua to follow him in.

"Yes, I can tell he has talents," Magus agreed, thoughtfully sizing up the boy.

Artur stripped off his black leather jacket, revealing a cut-down, tight silk "T" exposing lots of clear, muscular skin and several thin gold nipple rings in each site.

"What would you think about Texas?" Magus asked. "You'd have a place to stay. A car, of course. You can't live in Texas without a car, y'know."

"*Gern*," Artur said. "I'd be delighted. I've been to Texas. I like bar-be-que. Boots. Big hats." He smiled charmingly.

Joshua walked up to him.

"My name is Joshua Goldmeister," he said. "I've never been to Texas. And I don't like bar-be-que. How do you do?" He offered Magus his hand and looked him straight in the eye as directly as he had looked at Jeffrey on the balcony. He kept his hand in Magus's and got extremely close to him, whispering something into his ear, until Chris pulled Magus away.

"There are other people Reggie needs to see while he's here!" Chris announced. "Important people from the Arts and Culture Department, who've been waiting for him." Then to Magus: "My students are engaging, and I know you're interesting in all young people. After all, they are the hope of Art."

"Yes, they are," Magus said, looking at Joshua, almost but not quite winking, an authentic twinkle rising involuntarily from the depths of calculating darkness in Magus's eyes. Then he was whisked away by Chris, into the arms of an impressively large, blond young woman who babbled in German-accented French and then French-accented German, as Magus looked at her completely unimpressed and uncomprehending.

Joshua retook his place at Jeffrey's side.

"Want to leave? I am going to another party, in a better part of town. Much more exciting. You'll like it. Real artists, at a gallery so far underground it disappears sometimes!"

Jeffrey lowered his voice and somewhat loosened by the smoke he had inhaled admitted, "I have to be careful, or else I'll be on Chris Stewart's *scheisseliste* for life."

"He's only a whore," Joshua answered. "I'm taking his victory away from him. I already asked Magus if he wants to go. Of course he does. He felt me up when I was talking to him. Nobody saw it. It was—how would you put it?—*cute?*"

"I'm sure it was."

Magus made his way through the living room, with Len Silverman watching, bemused and besotted, and Chris guiding him from one hoarily important presence to another. There were no doctors this time, just specialists in one century or another, this school or that, this poet, dramatist, painter. Chris got more baroque with each eminence he introduced. "This is Wolfgang Anschlus, the world's foremost authority on fourteenth-century armor. And this is Anna Bosch. You must know her, or her dictionary of twelfth-century keyhole forms. The keyhole, you know, Reggie, was one of the great forms of that period."

"I was aware of that," Magus said. "I am deeply honored to meet you, Fraulein Bosch. Your reputation has certainly preceded you in all ways."

Anna Bosch, who looked like she came right out of her own period, in a heavy black-caped outfit with a dark, gargoyle-beaked, five-o'clock-shadowed face, beamed with glowing gratitude at Magus.

"You *naw* me, in Texas?"

"Yes, my dear," Magus answered. "But I'm afraid that as much as I'd love to speak with you about your holes, I must leave at once. I have another most pressing engagement to go to. Chris, it is has been a deep honor to be your guest at your lovely home. We must talk very soon. And as soon as I'm back in Dallas, I will be in touch. I have numerous projects that only someone with your qualifications, sophistication, and depth of knowledge can approach. I'll have my secretary contact you, to tell you exactly when to expect a call."

Chris looked immediately both elated and as if he'd been stabbed. The reception for Magus, expensive as it was, had achieved what he wanted it to: impress a very impressive man. But why was he leaving so suddenly, before the expensive catered dinner was served? Before Chris could say anything, Magus was doing the room again, smiling, kissing hands, offering good-byes. Then he was with Joshua Goldmeister and they were blatantly winking at one another.

Chris Stewart did not take this well. If he had seen it, so did everybody else.

Jeffrey was about to approach Chris to say good-bye when Len, who could barely stand up, intercepted him and pulled Jeffrey toward the balcony, where they could be somewhat private.

"If you're planning on splitting, boychik, I'd take French leave of Dr. Stewart. She's got her claws out, and she's looking for someone soft to stick 'em into."

"Thanks for the warning," Jeffrey said seriously. He did not want to antagonize Chris further, simply by leaving in obvious proximity to Magus and Joshua—obviously the department dish, a real catch, whom Chris had dangled in front of Magus as a tasty lure—now that Chris's little plot had backfired. "I'd hate for Chris to be pissed off at me again."

"*C'est la guerre,*" Len said, lighting up one of his Dutch cigars. "I guess it means no nookie for me tonight, but there ain't a whole lot o' nookie waiting in this world anyway."

"Tell Chris I'm sorry I left, and I'll be in touch soon."

"Okie-dokie." Len took a deep puff. "Don't eat a stranger!"

Jeffrey attempted to thread his way through the guests unobserved, but just at the door, Chris spotted him.

"Not you, too! What's pressing you?"

At that moment, Angelina Harkness materialized. She froze, looking at Jeffrey as if she were faced with a *real* vampire, naked and out of his cape, which meant that Chris had to say something.

"Angelina! Thank God you're here!—just as everyone is deserting me."

Immediately, Jeffrey slipped out the door.

❦

Jeffrey, Joshua, Magus, Artur, and one of the other boys were soon on the street.

"My car's over there," said Joshua, pointing to a new, expensive model.

"So where is this party?" Magus asked as they walked toward it.

"In a very artistic part of town, sir," Joshua answered. "You'll like it. It's at Pocus, a gallery. Very underground. You never can say where it's going to pop up. Lots of young people, entertainments, stuff of real substance. And real artists, not just academics who study dead art."

Artur and the other boy, who was all red hair and freckles and who introduced himself as Jimmy Schnulback, giggled.

"I like *real* substance," Schnulback said. "You have more?"

"Of course," Joshua said. Joshua unlocked the car and offered the front passenger seat to Jeffrey.

"Please, you should sit up front," Jeffrey said to Magus. "That way you can see more."

"You are very courteous," Magus said to Jeffrey. "Courtesy is the most endangered of the Arts, I say."

The boys laughed.

Jeffrey got into the backseat, between Artur and Jimmy, both of whom exuded a lovely fragrance Jeffrey could not place, until he realized it was only the genuine freshness of their young skin so close to him.

They drove for about ten miles, until Magus became anxious.

"Where are we? I don't know where we are at all. I've been to this town many times, but never came here."

The neighborhood had changed considerably from the elegance of the Stewart-Silverman abode with its adjacent park and streets bordered with front gardens. This place was deserted, except for swarms of rats and sullen men in flowing robes or other outfits whose faces you could barely see.

"Don't worry," Joshua said. "Your safety is in my hands. This can not be any stranger than Texas. I have been told that Texas is quite interesting, too, isn't it?"

"Nothing like this," Magus intoned.

They stopped in front of a building, and got out. Joshua knocked on the unmarked recessed door of a basement, and they were let in.

"I told you it was underground," he told them.

Chapter Seven

*T*he basement was a dank, winding catacomb of narrow halls and connecting rooms filled with dreary, hackneyed, foolishly cool and sickeningly amateurish art on the walls. They ended up in an extremely crowded large central chamber where a band played deafeningly loud and the walls were hung closely with portraits of young men and women, some in ethnic costumes but most in the fashions of various moments, such as shirts with comic-bookish military insignia on the epaulettes and pocket flaps, and belts heavily stitched with crazy colors, carrying triple rows of fake cartridge loops. Jeffrey recognized many of the depicted fads as things that he himself had concocted. Some portraits were paintings, done in a passable, paint-by-numbers style, mass-produced in art sweatshops in China or India. In some more backward parts of the world, they were still symbols of status to own. Other portraits were blown up, out-of-focus digital images that looked like third or fourth generation prints of the original exposures.

"Fascinating," Magus said, trying to make himself heard to Jeffrey and Joshua. "Who are the portraits? Why are they here?"

"It's a new show. Opening tonight," Joshua explained. "They are suicide bombers. Some go far back. The pictures are kind of sweet and homey, don't you think? It's the usual story, God and war. All kinds of wars. The show is called *Dying For What You Believe*. Very Texas, right?"

Joshua winked.

Magus looked at him, confounded.

"Have a look around," Joshua said, smiling at Magus. "Jeffrey and the other boys and I are going to another room. You may join us if you'd like. There are entertainments there that may interested you also."

"No. Please, I'll go with you," Magus protested. "This gives me the creeps. I had no idea there were pictures like this."

He indicated several images, among the more mundane ones, showing actual moments of detonation, with explicit pieces of human limbs in the air and silent screams trapped on faces. They were horrifying, but no one seemed to be especially bothered by them, as, oblivious, the young crowd bobbed to the earsplitting music, taking snorts from bottles and passing around tiny sniffing spoons and other implements; smiling glazily, but earnestly enjoying themselves.

Joshua led them to a doorway on the other side of the big room, where they went down another passageway to a smaller space furnished with several big mattresses on the floor, reminding Jeffrey of John van der Meer's house, but without its charms or naive decency. There were lots of kids on the mattresses, including a few boys who were down to their briefs and two girls of perhaps fourteen with their tops off, exposing very pretty breasts.

"This is nice," Joshua said. "It's quieter in here."

"I think I should go," Magus said. "This place is not to my taste. Can I get a taxi in this neighborhood?"

"Of course," Joshua said. "There's a chauffeur on every corner. Calm down, man. Chill for the thrill. This ain't Texas, pahd'nah." The words sounded really funny coming from Joshua Goldmeister, like he was in a play and trying too transparently to put on the accent. "Here." He passed Magus his hash pipe.

"Sorry. I don't do stuff like that."

"Then we'll get you a drink. How's that? How about a nice schnaps, or a beer or something?"

"Do you think they have any fortified wine, an Acquavite?"

"Sure. Jimmy, go get Mr. Magus an Acquavite. It's on me."

Joshua took a large roll of bills out of his wallet, and handed two to Jimmy Schnulback, who smiled, then disappeared.

"You're very kind," Magus said to Joshua. "I'm sorry. I kind of freaked out. Got a bit scared. I'm English, you know, but I've been in Texas a long time. Lots of money there, but it's really a small world. It's not like here in Germany, where everything's so cosmopolitan. In Texas, they figured out a long time ago what Jesus looked like. Tall blond football player. You see him all over the place, nuzzling up to black kids, getting business deals for you, telling you how to behave on dates."

"I couldn't live there," Jeffrey said. "I'd hate it."

"There's big money there, Mr. Cooper. You have no idea how much, and they love 'culture,' as long as they can just put it in a nice little box and wear it or show it. Strange, but I appreciate their honesty sometimes. Ah, here's my drink!"

Jimmy Schnulback came back with another group of dark young men who looked either Middle Eastern or African. They were all smiling, and Jimmy was speaking with them in a language that seemed freshly invented and yet was not. Joshua added a few words to their conversation, while Reggie Magus tried to follow it, but was quickly lost.

"I can catch some old Dutch-German in that," Magus confessed, "but very little. What are you speaking?"

"It's a South African tribal dialect," Joshua said. "Young people used to speak it in the shanty towns, so it was underground, like this place. It's fun. I should teach you some words."

"You should," Magus said. "When we get to Texas. I think you'd like Texas a lot." He took a sip of the clear icy liquid, smiled, and thanked Joshua with a nod and wink.

Joshua winked back. "We have some nice things to partake of here." He opened his palm, revealing several pink and blue pills that looked like little bird eggs. "You could call this the 'dessert' platter."

"I'd like one of those," Jimmy Schnulback said. "They make you very happy."

"Jimmy!" Joshua said, disapproving. "You are not letting our Texas guest have first pick. *Wie Deutsches ist es?*"

"I don't think I'd like any of those things," Magus said.

"They are not so bad," Jeffrey tried to explain blandly. "They're pretty recreational. The pink ones are mood elevators and the blue ones are sex drugs. I've taken them before. Not recently, but I have."

Magus smiled.

"In that case." He picked one of each, and downed them with his Acquavite.

"Why don't you sit on the mattress here," Joshua said, "and let them take effect?"

Magus squatted uneasily and plopped on to a mattress somewhat apart from the cavorting kids who were playing on it at the other end and starting to get seriously sexual with each other.

Joshua winked at Jeffrey, then nudged him over to some big rattan chairs farther away from the mattresses, leaving Magus to the other boys and Jimmy's very energetic darker friends, who had burst into a loud argument among themselves.

"I like you," Joshua said. "I'd like to be friends with you."

"Friends?" Jeffrey asked, with a little shrug in his voice. "That's nice."

He pulled Joshua's face toward him and kissed him. He'd wanted to do that, just kiss him, that was all. He was beautiful, there was no denying it, but it was not something Jeffrey wanted to go further with.

He took his tongue out of Joshua's mouth.

"You're very sweet to kiss," he whispered. "But I'm a lot older than you are."

"Are you sure? I'm older than I look. Or admit."

Jeffrey laughed. "How old could you possibly be?"

Joshua now pulled Jeffrey's ear towards him and said: "Forty-five."

"Ah, you must have started this a while back then. Staying young."

"Yes, I did. I'm doing it on my own, but it takes a lot of money. I'm frozen at a certain age, about twenty-three. So I never grow up any more than that. It bothers me sometimes. If I were a deeper person, I guess I'd be depressed, but luckily I'm not. That idiot from Texas thinks I'm going to be his little pussyboy. *Wirklich*, he's going to be in for a real shock."

"Why?"

"How much of my friend do you want to be?"

"A lot."

Joshua kissed him softly.

"But not too much," Jeffrey warned. "You may be more than I

can handle."

"At least you admit it, Jeffrey. None of those other shits would be so open about that. *Ich liebe dein sussekeit.*"

He kissed Jeffrey again, making his body accessible to him; in a moment, his bejeweled cock was out and in Jeffrey's hand. Jeffrey felt very self-conscious. There were people there, although the lighting was low, and the kids on the mattresses were doing everything against Levitical law and many other standards of social conduct, certainly the ones that the system espoused.

They kissed more intensely, and Jeffrey felt intoxicated with this boy who was not one. Then he realized he had no idea what was going to happen to Reginald Magus. He felt responsible for him, in a way, even if he did not particularly like the man.

"I should check on Reggie," he said, interrupting things.

"Why? Do you want Texas, too?"

"No, but—"

He got up and looked over. Magus was not there at all.

"Where is he?" he asked Joshua seriously. "What's been done to him?"

"How should I know? He was greedy. Acquavite. Drugs. He could end up in a canal someplace." The young man smiled beneficently at him. "But he won't. He's not worth anything dead."

Jeffrey tensed up, his heart pounding from stress. Why had he let himself be seduced so easily by this boy? He *was* a boy; he'd always be a boy. It was loathsome, and loathing it made Jeffrey hate himself for being there.

"You knew this was going to happen," he blurted out. "Those kids have taken him hostage. They'll sell him, right?"

"Jeffrey, that's a crude way to put it. But it's good enough. It was what Professor Stewart thought he'd do with me, *richtig?* He'd get in good with that pig if I went to Dallas and played Joan Collins. Or one of those other actresses from way back."

Joshua laughed. Jeffrey slapped him.

"I should go to the police."

"Oh, yes. You should. Listen, you're way past being an accessory, Mr. Cooper. You're in *total* cahoots. You made all this happen. I can tell you're knee-deep in the system; it's keeping you alive and damn pretty, I admit that. I'm not like you. It costs me plenty of money to stay this way. You're only a whore whom the system is feeding, another one of those 'big deals,' like in Professor Stewart's apartment. You won't go to the police, I'm sure. You won't do anything."

Jeffrey's jaw clenched. He looked at his hands. They were trembling and more wrinkled than he wanted to admit. He wished Tony were there and he could just load all of this shit onto his therapist. Instead, a rushing stream of images flooded his tired, stressed, half-besotted brain, pulling him with them: Torrents of Indian pictures and pictures from his intricately catalogued sweep of epochs and civilizations: lush Hollywoodized female faces, marabou, velvets, full capes of silver fox—inspirations for Ashok's beauty line. Egyptian, Assyrian, and Art Deco foolery for the Mormon chapel. Valentino, brooding sex god, emerged in full smolder from Jeffrey's new 1920s-ish auto *deluxe*, surrounded by scallops of silver-deckled clouds, as every second more photos, clippings, and sketches arrived, wave upon wave of them, replacing previous images.

He looked about him, past Joshua who was in his face, on his neck really, but not in his head. The images were still there, streaming like a zillion playing cards dropped from a plane into the stratosphere, each one unique, linked only by some purpose Jeffrey, the ringmaster of style, would assign to them. All around him throbbing human heat rose above tides of release and the violent drumming from the other room, as crinkly, ancient canned images fell through his brain. With all these deliciously young people squirming about, half-naked bodies on top of each other, popping sex organs and volleys of silvery fluids, releasing great, gorgeous tremors of sex itself: powerful, exposed, incendiary. The smell like gunpowder.

He was breathing hard. His head hurt. He closed his eyes.

Joshua took one of his hands in his.

"Would you like to make love to me now? Come on, Jeffrey, I have another blue pill."

Jeffrey unclenched his jaw and opened his eyes. He exhaled slowly. The images stopped.

"Over my dead—"

He did not get to finish. A loud explosion, blasting out of the large chamber with the suicide-bomber portraits, rocked the room, followed by another and another. Everyone jumped, screaming, trying to disentangle themselves. Bodies were trampled on the way to the only exit.

Jeffrey stood still for a few seconds as crumbling pieces of ceiling plaster and paint crashed down, hitting him on the face and head. The room went very black. He had to leave before the cops and the emergency workers arrived. The boys were all gone, chasing after Joshua, who was the first one to reach the exit. There was no telling what had happened to Magus; maybe he did end up in that canal. But Jeffrey began carefully and quickly to move as flashlights approached and more debris fell. Then he knew he really *had* to do something. A plan, crystal clear, came to him.

It was the only thing that made any sense to him after this tense, awful evening; the design of it seemed perfect.

He'd go to India with John.

Chapter Eight

*T*he system's information centers and publishing networks were filled with accounts of the terrorist attack at Pocus, "a putative center of illicit drugs, sex, and radical thinking."

Below the lead story, this sidebar often ran:

"Reginald Magus, editor-in-chief of *World Affairs, Culture, and Art Development,* based in Dallas, Texas, was found dead among the wreckage at the terrorist bomb site. How Mr. Magus got to the club is unknown." [Some details of Magus's day were given, and, also, that he was last seen] "at a reception given by Christopher Stewart, PhD, an American professor of Renaissance literature, and his partner, Leonard Silverman, MD, at their impressive apartment in the elegant park section of town.

"Said Dr. Stewart, 'Mr. Magus left our reception early. I have no idea where he went from there. He told us he had a pressing engagement. The whole academic and artistic community is extremely sorry to hear about this tragedy.'"

Jeffrey spent the day working from home, as he normally did on Sundays, sometimes breaking up the day by going to the gym in his building or outside for a bite to eat. He wondered if anyone could trace him to that sordid club, which was also known by a daytime name, *Gallerie Welttanz,* and where the body count was set at close to a dozen. It was very sad. Most of the dead were kids. Kids were always idealistic and easily led. A list of the identified dead did not contain Jimmy Schnulback's, Artur's, or Joshua's names, so they must have made it out all right. As for Reginald Magus, his kidnappers must have miscalculated and dallied, not knowing what would happen.

On the other hand, perhaps they were in league with the bombers themselves, who felt that the tawdry slick hipness of the scene cheapened their cause, whatever that was. It was hard to say; the only conclusion was that Reginald Magus was dead, another victim of worldwide terrorism.

There were dozens of terrorist groups, especially in Europe, a crossroads of so many cultures. There were fundamentalist Muslim groups, Catholic fascist groups, antigovernment libertarian groups, neo-Communist groups, right-wing pro-life groups, and left-wing pro-nature groups who'd kill for trees while doing nothing to replant forests. The system, though, that continuous mechanism that kept the whole thing running—currencies and banks, markets, endless networks of buying, selling, reinventing, and re-marketing—had managed to outwit and outlive all of them so far.

Maybe it was just superior packaging.

No matter what system of belief captured you, there was always that glimmer of hope, that not-to-be-completely-dismissed feeling that just up ahead lay something *wonderful*: something that in exactly the right packaging would make you happy.

Which, strangely enough, was how John van der Meer had made Jeffrey feel, only without the slick packaging. He found it almost impossible to think about John and work at the same time, yet there was so much work to do. It seemed endless, like those underground passageways at Pocus-Welttanz that were now tombs. Maybe work *was* the tomb. The tomb you got locked into while still alive.

At three in the afternoon, he gave himself an injection and took large doses of medicines to counteract the effects of alcohol and stress. Then he went down to the gym. The machines were loaded with people. Conny Dritte, his personal sadist, had the day off, but Carlos, a short, dark Brazilian soccer player with endless piston energy in his calves, was there. Jeffrey gave him his card and Carlos swiped off ninety minutes of training, then put Jeffrey through a hard bench-and-aerobics routine. Jeffrey was winded through half of it and felt very foolish: he'd been out too late twice now, once up most of the night with John, then at Pocus.

After a while he got his wind back; then Carlos did some extra spotting and quick massages on him. His chest and legs felt good having blood pumped back into them.

"You slow," Carlos noticed, grinning. "You party last night?"

Jeffrey nodded, face down, feeling like a kid caught stealing cookies.

"Eez okay. You hear about the 'splosion at th'club? Very sad. Too bad for boys and girls. Who want to hurt people, 'specially people who ah so much like you?" Carlos broke into softer Portuguese-inflected German. "*Schade. Zu viele scheisse. All'ist scheisse! Politics, auch scheisse!*"

Jeffrey felt bad for him. He was all dark, hairy muscle, with a sweet little grin on him that stayed natural. In a place where few people talked to each other, he was a nice go-between, a neutral point. In the past, he and Jeffrey had ended their sessions rubbing one another's back in the steam room. Today, he just wanted a shower before returning to his apartment.

When he got back, there was a message from Chris Stewart.

"We need to speak *immediately*. It's important."

Jeffrey felt that he would rather have one of his fingers amputated, but he called him. Chris and Len had separate lines, so there was no way Len could answer and soften things up.

Chris got down to it fast. "Where were you? Were you at the club with him? Is that why you left?"

"No." It was none of Stewart's business, Jeffrey rationalized. "I had a date, that's why I couldn't stay."

"With whom?"

"Why do you need to know, Chris?"

"Because, Jeffrey! They're going to ask me who was at my party and where they went afterwards. Get it, Jeffrey?"

Jeffrey tried to do something resembling a laugh.

"Chris, none of your friends are terrorists. They're all high-class, professional, academic people. Tell them to see that Harkness woman. She'll bite their dicks off."

"Very funny. I have not been having a good day, Jeffrey. Last night did not go the way I wanted it to. My guest of honor left early and then was found dead in a club frequented by scum, and you're making a joke! When are you going to grow up, Jeffrey?"

"I guess when I finally become Dr. Cooper. How's Dr. Silverman? How's he taking all of this?"

"Len always has his head up his butt with a drink. I don't know.

My whole career could be rocked by this. Those kids he left with—Joshua Goldmeister, Artur, and Jimmy What's-His-Back—"

"Schnulback?"

"Yeah. Funny, you remembering their names. I don't even remember you talking to Jimmy."

"We talked outside your building for a minute, then I took the pubtran back to my place. I told you I had a date."

"I don't—" Chris hesitated. Jeffrey was sure he was going to say, "I don't believe you." Instead, he said, "I don't dispute you, Jeffrey. Really. Why would you lie to me?"

"I'm glad you see that. Good-bye, Chris."

Jeffrey knew then that Stewart would turn him in. He'd say that Jeffrey had left with Magus and the boys, even if they had not gone down in the same elevator. Chris would do anything to keep his own status intact. Maybe that was what kept him and Len Silverman together: this symbiosis of shared vanities and illusions of status, with little pieces of love thrown in.

He did some more work, wrote a style/marketing recommendation for the car people, which he thought was excellent and should bump the finished auto even further up in its price category. Then he called Ashok Rahman in India.

"I am overjoyed to hear from you so fast!" Ashok said.

His face was beaming. Jeffrey was not sure how *he* looked in Ashok's monitor, but Ashok flattered him.

"You're looking superb, my friend. It must be the cool weather in Germany. Here it is too hot to breathe. Even breathing here in India is work!"

"Work is not bad," Jeffrey said without humor.

"Not if it's only to breathe!"

Jeffrey cleared his throat and dove in:

"I want to come see you, Ashok. We need a face-meet to deal with all the new color and style issues from 'That Woman.' And I need you to prepare the situation for me—where I'll stay, use of a car, things like that. Can you do that?"

"I can," Ashok said softly. "But the system usually—"

"I want you to do this for me personally. Can you?"

"Is God not good, my friend? Will you be alone or with a colleague? Will you take an assistant?"

"Yes." He paused. "I'm taking a . . . colleague. A very nice young man. A painter, actually."

"A painter? Yes! I see." Ashok's face lit up with a smile that was florid but also sweetly natural looking. It went all the way up to his iridescent eyelashes. "How *very* exciting for you. I love art. Don't you love art, also?"

"Of course. Art is good. He'll stay with me."

"I see."

"I mean in my hotel."

Ashok's face became slightly more serious.

"Of course in your hotel. What's his name?"

"John van der Meer."

Ashok looked puzzled.

"The name has a ring to it, have I heard of him before? Is he advanced in the system, too?"

"No," said Jeffrey bluntly. "He's not advanced, not at all. But he shares the last name of a famous painter, Vermeer. It's like being named Van Gogh. Many people know the name, maybe that's why you thought he was familiar."

"Now I see. Van der Meer, *Vermeer.*" Ashok nodded. "That is so smart of you, Jeffrey, taking this colleague—here to India, I mean. I'll be very happy to meet him as well. I'll think warmly and good of him."

"I hope so," Jeffrey said, his eyes slightly narrowing. He was in no mood to joke further.

"Such a wealth of knowledge you have, Jeffrey. No wonder we all learn so much from you!"

"Thank you, Ashok," Jeffrey said without blinking. "If you have any problems, let me know."

"What problems, Jeffrey? God is good. I look forward very much to seeing you and your friend."

❧

Jeffrey clicked off. The dice were cast now; the question was how difficult would it be to travel with John, and would John go for it? He didn't feel stressed, as much as elated, as if he were coming into contact with some hard-to-capture delight, like an exquisite, momentary sighting of rare butterflies or the magical aria of a mostly boring opera whose entire production was focused on those fleeting notes. It was all John's wonderful effect on him, despite Jeffrey's rage and pain such a short time ago. He was excited, elevated, purring inside like a happy cat, and wondering if he'd be able to sleep that night from excitement.

But he did, smiling as he drifted off.

He still felt excited the next day at work, even dealing with Malace who dropped a hint or two about his time off, and his other clerks and numerous colleagues. New clusters of deadlines came up, projects that were being shot like projectiles at him; there was no stopping it.

The Danes wanted a new line of discount stores to sell everything, and they wanted them to "look Danish, but not in the old provincial way. More like Danish *Arabian Nights.*" The Italians wanted a new car to promote a famous multibillionaire designer with stores on every continent. The car would bear Antonio Zbatti's stylish "A-Z" trademark, but had to be sellable to "real men" types who'd never buy anything blatantly "Italian designer."

Zbatti, waving his signature lacy hankies and traveling with his too-too, frou-frou retinue and flock of pug dogs, was blatantly queer, even if he were one of the richest men in Italy, if not in all of Europe. So the "A-Z" car had to look "pumped" but not pissy, rich but not effete, extra-high status but not vulgar.

Jeffrey wondered if Malace could handle some of this, especially since Jeffrey was waist-deep in the "Valentino" car already. A thought flashed: maybe he could bleed some ideas from one project to the next. He dismissed the idea. That way could be fatal, as dealing with Ashok had showed him. Everyone wanted their own distinct pound of flesh. He brought the young man into his office, and tried to make him understand the basic Italian concept, and how they would pursue it.

Malace looked confused, then asked:

"Who's gonna buy it?"

"We're not sure yet. But whoever it is needs to know they are getting something no one else has. Even after everybody else has it."

Jeffrey switched to the Danish project, running cues he kept at his fingertips through a projector: flashes of images and details, stuff from the nineteenth century, twentieth, and earlier decades of the twenty-first. Danish paintings, design work, Hans Christian Andersen, movie stars, Royal Danish ballet opera rugby painters sculptors travelers writers cheese butter pastry cows—

It became headswimming for Malace. Jeffrey could see that one of his own files had close to a million Danish images in it. They needed to get it down to a mere thousand.

For the car, he brought up leather, wood, the polished gleam of silver ornaments from great homes and their stables, and of course some of Zbatti's own designs.

"The point is," he said to Malace, "You need to incorporate a lot without overdoing anything."

Malace took notes, and Jeffrey could see the strain showing on his young face and the way his back and neck tensed up. He wished he could touch his assistant in a friendly manner, but there was no way he could. Malace assured him he would put fourteen or fifteen hours into both projects, then said, before leaving, "About my going away? I really want it, Jeffrey. I gotta do it. I'm serious this time."

Jeffrey nodded. Coming from Gregory Malace, this was an amazing bit of intimacy, about as up-close as Malace had ever been with him.

"Is there something you need to do?" Jeffrey asked, as kindly as possible. "Some personal problem or conflict?"

"No. It's just time off. R 'n' R. Know what I mean?"

"Sure. Give me a little more time, and I'll schedule it."

"Thanks," Malace said. "But I need it soon. The time's right for this, and I gotta jump on it."

"You'll get it soon, I mean that."

He did mean it. He could understand how Malace might need to get away. Jeffrey was exhausted, too, his brain filling up. With the door to his office locked, he meditated and did some yoga, trying to let his mind go blank. But there were too many pictures in it: the "A-Z" car, the Danes, the "Valentino" thing, Michigan. And the almost chilling promise of this Indian fiasco, now labeled "That Woman," about to come up.

Finally, six o' clock approached and he put on his jacket and left the office.

The outside seemed to glitter with three-dimensional magic after he'd been cooped up for so long, buried in so many canned images. Living trees, the energy of lights, the pulse of signs, furious traffic, people going home. He went down toward Afghanistrasse, toward another reality that seemed almost mystical, where men in various aspects of native garb talked softly, stood still, exchanged looks or looked warily at him. Then he saw the square; it was deserted.

Cops were all over, on the alert after the bombing at Pocus. He was afraid to sit down, afraid the German cops would ask him why he was there. Sitting was not against the law, but the area was suspect now. He stood on a street across from the square and watched, moving slowly and casually, to give the impression that he might be browsing or looking for a shop. He saw no one.

At six-thirty, he decided to go into the shop where Louis worked in the back. He was not sure what else to do. It was too late to take the pubtran out to John's house, if he were willing to risk the long, dark walk beyond that to his place. He felt lost, alone, stupid, and really wished he could talk to Tony, tell him everything, no matter how implicating it was.

He walked into the shop, and there was John, sipping a mint tea. Jeffrey smiled at him and John approached, placing his face near Jeffrey's, without embracing him.

"I'm glad you're here," Jeffrey said softy. "Let's get out of here, and have dinner."

"I'd like to finish my tea first."

John's nose nuzzled his cheek, then he sipped his tea.

The men in the shop watched them, nodding as if this were completely correct.

"All right."

Louis emerged from the back.

"So, you two have met."

He winked at Jeffrey, who smiled, embarrassed, as Louis shook his hand.

John finished his tea, and they walked out together.

"There were too many cops in the square," he explained.

Jeffrey agreed, nodding mutely.

"Everyone here is a terrorist, they think. Or maybe they don't think."

They were now on a small side street, kind of an alley, full of a casual, un-German quaintness, more conducive to intimacy. Jeffrey pointed out an old Indonesian restaurant with a big, faded, once colorful sign. Inside they were seated by a young man in a sarong who brought them water, menus, and tall cold bottles of Indonesian beer.

John looked at the menu.

"Rijsttafel?" he suggested.

"Yes," Jeffrey said. "That would be fine. Would you go to India with me?"

"Yes. I would."

"You would?"

"Yes. I told you that."

Jeffrey drank some of the beer. He wanted to kiss John so much it was hard to drink it.

"You don't need to think about it?"

"Why would I think about it? I'd love to go to India with you."

"Do you have travel documents?"

John shrugged.

"I have a fake I.D. card. I destroyed my real one. They could find me too easily with it."

"How do you get on the pubtran?"

"At rush hour it's not a problem. I try not to use it outside of that. My time is my own. I don't have to be productive all the time. Your American poet Whitman said, 'I loaf and invite my soul.' He was right. I thought about you a lot."

Jeffrey watched John's eyes. They were animated, truly young. He knew his own eyes rarely looked like that. They were too cautious.

"You did?"

"You wanted to find me. I don't know how, but you did. I'm powerless sometimes. I can't control my own impulses, but I know I can help you. I feel that I've been charged with that purpose. In fact, I would love to help you."

Jeffrey watched as the waiter brought in the countless small dishes that made up rijsttafel: rice, meats, some chicken, smoked fish, fish cooked in various sauces, very savory cabbage as a condiment, oils, a form of vinegary tomato catsup, and several other sauces dotting the table, the dishes appearing on the white tablecloth until there was almost no sign of cloth under them. His life was like that: a continuous, often congested pattern, no matter how interesting the individual dishes appeared to be. Now John, this mysterious man, was clearing away some of them. He felt an unexpected clearing in his own mind, just looking back up at him.

"I can get you the proper documents," Jeffrey said, smiling at John. "I have friends who'll do that for me."

John ate some fish, then some of the vinegary rice. "Won't that put you in—" He searched for the word. "Jeopardy?"

"I won't think about it."

"Good. Did you try this?" He lifted some very spicy fish.

"No. I think it'll kill my stomach."

"Yes, but it might tickle your tongue. And your brain."

Jeffrey liked it. It felt strange on his tongue, lemony and hot at the same time. He smiled. He'd have to take something for his stomach later, but that was not a problem. The next step was.

"I want to sleep with you again."

"Where do you live?" John asked.

Jeffrey told him.

"If I go into your building, security will pick me up instantly. I'll feel like a terrorist. They may even decide I am one."

"Are you?"

John's face clouded over. The glitter of youthfulness died.

"Why d'you ask that?"

"I don't know. There are all sorts of terrorists. That's why the system has to clamp down on them so much."

"It offers you everything, doesn't it? Everything except yourself. That they take away from you in little pieces until there's nothing left. I need to settle this with you: I don't think I should sleep at your place."

"Then we'll find a hotel, someplace that will take cash. Not fancy. All right?"

John smiled, young again. "Sure. Not fancy would be good."

❦

Afghanistrasse led into a small Chinatown area, where they found a hotel frequented by Chinese workmen. The place smelled of soy, beer, laundry starch, and open toilets with a rank disinfectant haze wafting from them. John spoke to the desk clerk, an old man with nicotine-yellowed teeth, in Dutch and German. At first the clerk would only say, "Neet," Chinese-inflected German for "nicht," pretending to know nothing. Then John offered him a pack of German cigarettes, and he smiled and told them in good German what the price of a room would be.

Jeffrey had never stayed in such a cheap hotel, but he produced the cash and John signed some name in ink on a tablet of lined paper. No passports were shown, no credit cards or I.D. cards necessary.

There was no elevator. They walked up to the fourth floor and found the door to their small room, a narrow section of one long rectangular space partitioned with cheap wallboard. The wallboard was replaced by wire mesh several feet from the ceiling, to provide ventilation, since there were no windows in the rooms. But each room had a small sink. The bathroom was down the hall, the toilet a hole in the floor with indentations for your feet. Jeffrey found the place quaint and repulsive. He hated it, actually.

Inside their room were two narrow beds, which they pushed together.

"This would be a palace in India," John said.

"Not in the India we're going to. Have you been there before?"

"Yes. Once, when I was married. My wife's family took a place in Goa, at a big hotel by the beach. We went with the kids for a week, in and out. But it could have been Disneyland. India was around us, I just didn't get to see much of it."

They took off their clothes. Jeffrey thought he should wash around some, and did. The towel, only one to a room, was scratchy and thin. He felt like he was no longer in Germany, but some other place. Maybe the long-ago Asian Diaspora of manual-labor Chinese, not the New China, all glitz and aggressive Western-style luxury. The room was dark, but light from the hall crept in over their heads; they heard distant tired voices of other men.

John went to the sink, ran some water into his mouth and spit it out, then he got back onto the bed. Jeffrey pulled him to him.

"What would you help me with?" Jeffrey whispered.

"Finding yourself. You're smart, aren't you? You know it's missing."

Jeffrey nodded. This huge, strange power came over him, like nothing he had experienced before. Certainly not with Tony. Tony was just a Band-Aid, something to patch him up so that he could go back to the well-rewarded grind of his work. In truth, Tony was part of the reward, and part of the grind. Holding John to him, he realized how much he'd been seduced by Tony and Tony's lovely little world of culture and therapy, all of it so "normalizing," and he realized how much he hated it—deeply, authentically.

It was stunning, an instant physical revelation. Perhaps it came from being in this place, the smells and the stark, prison-like lighting easily cutting through any illusions. Here poverty, exhaustion, and pain were certainties attested to by the hacking coughing, spitting, and loud farts Jeffrey heard down the hall, by weary whines and groans and the acrid odors of tobacco, piss, shit, and sweat.

Someone knocked on the flimsy door. Jeffrey froze.

The knocking stopped, then restarted a few doors down. The knocker was let into someone else's room.

"It's O.K.," John explained. "Men here pair up. They're looking for something and they get it."

He kissed Jeffrey. Jeffrey felt suddenly totally whole.

They had nothing to fuck with, and used spit. John wanted him to fuck him again and he did, with John sitting on top of him. There was almost no privacy. They tried not to make any noise but the bed springs creaked; they ended standing on the floor. Its filthy coldness felt wonderful to Jeffrey's bare feet. He had not felt so alive in ages, every pore of him taking in its own ration of wonder. He came amazingly fast, then sucked John off.

They left the hotel before dawn and went to a German student cafe that was barely open except for a few kids. John looked at them and smiled.

"You like young people?" Jeffrey asked.

"Yes. I like boys. I like the boy part of me."

"Don't we all?"

John looked serious. "Not everyone. Some lose it, and they hate it when you don't hate it, too. I know that."

They parted casually, without any demonstrations of affection, but Jeffrey was sure someone, somehow, would be able to connect him to John van der Meer. There were cameras all over the streets and there would be one he had overlooked. Or someone on the street, keeping his eyes open too long and seeing "something unusual," would report them to the cops. You were allowed a right to privacy, but it had strict parameters, and he and John were already outside of that. Two men, one of them in the system totally, but—as Jeffrey was aware—engaged in some underground work for himself.

And the other, who was just not "right" at all.

The thought made Jeffrey smile. Jesus was traditionally, remarkably "right." You could be remarkably private when you were with Jesus. And war was "right," as long as it was not formally declared. Sex, used to sell something, was perfectly "right." But in reality, every physical sexual act was either too forbidden, dangerous, or uncontrollable to overlook. So everyone knew your business about that.

You had none truly of your own, except "the" business: the system's relentless, culture-blind, cultureless movement.

Hurrying to his apartment to dress for work, Jeffrey felt tired but had to appear cheerful for the morning lobby staff, who eyed him as he sauntered in, pretending to be as bright as a star in some old movie musical. He flashed I.D., then strolled in a controlled, dancer's motion toward the elevator bank.

He showered and changed, then on a whim decided to call Tony for an appointment, just to see if he could fool his very intuitive therapist.

Tony's scheduling program told him in a formal but reassuring tone that Dr. Rosenputter was in, but unreachable. "If he has a conflict, he will get back to you. Thank you. Your call is important to Dr. Rosenputter. Please understand that." The same message followed in German, sounding even more portentous.

Jeffrey made an appointment for that evening, then tagged into his office communication system, saw what was happening there, and relayed to a clerk that he had a headache and would be in late. There was another message from Chris Stewart, but Jeffrey didn't care enough to listen, and put it into his save box.

Out on the street, he noticed something that was actually happening to him: everything stopped looking like something else. The real world was no longer an approximation, or reminder, of another sequence in an endless homogenous digital file. Even people on the pubtran looked individual—real—though they still interacted with their personal electronics, ignoring each other. He watched them, smiling at no one in particular, with a smile coming from his very depths, called forth by his closeness with John.

He realized he did not need to enter Tony's "calming mist," but could call up his own real self, which made him feel something truly forbidden: that he actually loved himself, no matter how old he was or what in truth he wasn't. He could still love being Jeffrey Cooper, this person who'd been so successfully hidden from everyone else and was now making an attempt to peek forth.

Unfortunately, the feeling did not last, as the day, jammed with more work than he could possibly do, quickly accelerated into manic frenzy. He tried to preserve his earlier calming state, but by two o'clock it was unraveling and by three he was tense, flailing about, trying madly to hold on to a hundred ideas and the constant rat-a-tat repetitions of images before him.

Then Ashok called.

"I am prepared for your arrival, Jeffrey! We are all most happy! You can't imagine the esteem we all hold for you and your talents!"

"Wonderful," Jeffrey replied tensely, trying to hold on, then asked:

"Can you get me some travel papers and a visa for my friend John van—" Then, suddenly, off the top of his stressed head, trying to dodge a bullet even if in an amateurish way, Jeffrey decided that John van der Meer would be better off known as—"John Vann, with two 'n's'?"

There was a short silence from Ashok, then: "John *Vann?* He has none of his own?"

"John has, but his coming may be tricky. Some complications. Nothing to do with the system, so I won't burden you with them. It's just that . . . his name *is* John Vann."

"Ahh." Ashok smiled seductively and said, "Jeffrey, come now! There is no burden between friends. Here in India, friendship is sacred like family. No burden is too much for me. Please, don't think in those terms."

Ashok paused, then lowered his voice. "Jeffrey, be assured. Your needs are very *safe* with me."

What the hell have I got myself into? Jeffrey thought. Everything he said, every idea and statement, question and request, was documentable, and could be used to terminate his position and state of health. It was obvious to him that he was out on a limb, one that from the very beginning, decades ago, he had put himself on.

What the hell, he was in this far. Swallowing his fears, exhaling slowly, he asked as matter-of-factly as possible:

"Then you'll be able to get the papers, and send them to me?"

"Of course, Jeffrey, I will. And I know how much this will make you happy, so I insist that I accept only your gratitude as thanks. As you know, I'll need a photo and some information about Mr. Vann.

His age, address, stuff like that."

Jeffrey nodded, then thanked Ashok, who beamed as if his own life were going to take off, now that he was ingratiating himself to a more powerful person.

And perhaps that was the case. Jeffrey wondered how much Ashok knew or was able to figure out, and where this would leave Jeffrey soon enough.

It would be easy to create a picture from the extensive images in the "Face" files Jeffrey kept. Being so visually sensitive, he remembered every aspect of John's features. He could have assembled a complete full body picture of him, even a naked one. He smiled; it made him feel as if he owned a substantial piece of John already, his image, just as John owned a piece of him: his soul.

He couldn't deny this. He had never believed in the idea of a soul, it always seemed too primitively Christian. But now he felt that it had to exist. The soul, he decided, was not that part of you that went on after death; it was the part that made you want to go on being alive.

He pushed everything off his crowded agenda and assembled John's picture. The completed file was large; he sent it to Ashok. Ashok quickly sent a message back to him:

"Very acceptable friend."

"What is it?" Tony asked sympathetically, in the comfort of his office.

Jeffrey was seated across from him; their knees were almost touching. He had an urge to reach over and touch Tony, just to see his therapist react. Though Tony often touched Jeffrey therapeutically, Jeffrey never touched him. Now Jeffrey wanted to do that, maybe even shake him.

"I was feeling very—" Jeffrey shook his head. He couldn't finish the thought. It was being strangled by other feelings, which included something normally foreign to him: anger.

"Stressed?"

"Somewhat."

"Only somewhat?"

"More frustrated. Pained, maybe."

Tony's eyes narrowed at him. "I see. *Schmertz* is a bad one. So what have we here? Psychic pain? Spiritual pain? Physical pain? Tell me, Jeffrey?"

What was this, Jeffrey wondered, a Chinese menu?

Why not bring up the forbidden thing? Much as he wanted to spit the truth into Tony's eyes, he needed those eyes. Those ever-comforting, endearingly sweet, Daddyish eyes that Tony was so good at placing upon him, except now they were looking at him with a real question that needed answering.

"For the first time in my life, I feel whole, Tony. And I also feel so much that's not whole about me."

Tony's eyes were not Daddy at all. They were genuinely penetrating.

"This *is* interesting. Exactly what made you feel this?"

"Remember your talk about beings who can help you? A 'force' that can come to you? I think I've found one."

Tony's face softened. He exhaled, unleashing the full, delicious shower of his smile.

"Wonderful, Jeffrey! Did you use some of the techniques I gave you? We can practice them together, you know."

"No."

The smile stayed frozen for a heartbeat, then fell with a crash, as if it had yanked some of Tony's expensive glass and ceramic bibelots down with it.

"No?"

"No," Jeffrey repeated, his body stiffening slightly. He was not used to this, but still enjoying it.

"Are you sure? Sometimes you can use them unconsciously without knowing it. I must say I was skeptical for the longest, but now I see that in the scheme of things, there is a place where our rampant materialism stops and some pure, almost unseen goodness comes in."

Jeffrey riveted his eyes on him, something he rarely did.

"I'm sure it does, Tony."

Tony cleared his throat, swallowing hard.

"So how did you connect with these 'forces,' Jeffrey?"

Jeffrey's heartbeat raced. He broke his glance with Tony. After a moment, Tony asked again:

"How did you connect, Jeffrey?"

Jeffrey felt like he had fallen into his own trap. He'd been such a mess when he first ventured up those carpeted stairs to see Tony. Even though he was a part of the system, Tony had been there to help and *had* helped him. The system created, aided, and, when necessary, destroyed. Destruction, surely, could be curative; Jeffrey knew that. It was all part of the organic free flow of the markets. Tony, with his highly refined aesthetics and stylish wash of spiritual enlightenment, easily presented himself as an agent for the system's responsibility to create and aid.

However, if Jeffrey's stress levels continued to spike, he would turn Jeffrey in; if not at the drop of a coin, the drop of a shoe. Either shoe.

It was now Jeffrey's move.

"Sexually. I connected sexually, Tony," he announced.

A sour expression tightened Tony's tanned face, making Jeffrey feel like a lap dog that had left a significant calling card indiscreetly on Tony's carpet.

"Sex-*zu*-ally?" he said slowly, drumming together the tips of his fingers. "I'm afraid, Jeffrey, that is not the way it's done."

Jeffrey squirmed. This had been harder than he had thought.

"Sorry," he said, his eyes on his fashionable shoes.

"No problem. But tell me, what made you think you'd found a 'force'? It's easy to misread these things. Someone offers you something and you take it, not knowing the price. Sex is a basic drive, but to embellish it with some deep, spiritual dimension is not good. *Es geht nicht,* I'm afraid. And this person—it's a *him,* I guess?— you're aware that he's only taking advantage of you, right?"

Jeffrey tried to suppress a guilty grin: it was only too evident that every step he took away from Tony would be considered ill-advised, and he was now stepping on very unsafe ground. He had to be a spy for himself now; and a very good one, he knew it.

"Yes, I'm aware," he answered softly. "He is taking advantage of me, you're correct. But I'm enjoying feeling this way, feeling open and good."

"All right," Tony said, springing to action. "Let's see how good you really feel. We'll test you right now."

"Now?"

Jeffrey felt nauseated, tense, unprepared.

"*Now*! I want to see what kind of physiological effects this person has had on you," Tony continued. "On your stress levels. Your status. The system needs you to keep that level down, and I don't think a sexual involvement is good for that. Sex, to be frank, is part of the 'Escape' thing, like a reward resort. But that's all it is. It's a selling tool, a fantasy item."

Like a condemned man, Jeffrey rolled up his shirt sleeve, undid some of his chest buttons, and then took his place next to the machine, feeling vulnerable after a night of making love in that awful Chinese hotel and a hard day at work. Tony was testing him, without doing any of the customary things he did to calm Jeffrey and reduce his stress level.

Check, Jeffrey thought. The bitter game.

Check, check, and *mate*. Tony is going to get me: if I get up to nine, the system will stop me from going anyplace. Even seven would not be acceptable at this point.

Jeffrey lowered his eyes and counted slowly to ten as Tony hooked him up. Before any numbers reached the monitor, he pictured John with him and the radiantly celestial pictures on John's walls, those intense, rapturous pictures that John did not want to show in galleries or sell at all. He felt John's soft, endlessly beseeching lips on his, felt John's naked body, sensuous, palely handsome, lower itself on to him. They were holding one another, and allowing their shared secrets to seep into the deep-reaching, entwining spaces between them.

Jeffrey exhaled, his eyes mere slits where silver light collected, feeling relaxed and genuinely good, like a fresh pool of water after a spring rain.

Tony yanked off the attachments.

"You've been spared!" he exclaimed. "Nothing bad has happened to you. You must not have got too involved with this robber, this vulture of your real soul!"

Jeffrey asked the number as he got up, rebuttoning his shirt.

Tony looked uncharacteristically embarrassed.

"It's okay. Fine, Jeffrey. I'm glad"

"What number was it?"

"Why do you need to know?"

Jeffrey only smiled.

If there were angels, Tony was now revealing which side he was on. His face had a definite cast of shame across it. He tried hard to smile, then finally succeeded.

"It's a three," he said. "You're down to *three*. Any more questions?"

Chapter Nine

*I*ndia! With its sounds, smells, and intense colors, there was no preparing for it. It took you over. Jeffrey hadn't been there in several years; at one point he had gone at least annually, so the changes that came with each visit, pushing the subcontinent into more and more "consumer participation" as the global system called it, hardly amazed him. Germany was like a warped America, seen through a hard prism of Western narcissism, self-armpit licking, and brutal salesmanship, without, of course, America's basic self-reliant redneckiness, which survived decade to decade. But India was so foreign that he never really bothered to penetrate it. Why would he bother? Most of it was off-limits to him anyway.

Where the global system ruled and knowing what to expect, he could be somewhat comfortable. But the *real* India—teeming, vast, with its countless beggars, venders, peasants, chai-wallahs hustling tea on the sidewalks or mango-wallahs or taxi-wallahs hustling rides, the men on bicycles bringing tiffin tins then disappearing into puffs of hot air with their ragged, wide-eyed kids and wives in saris? The part of India still so poor that all they owned were a few yards of sun-bleached cotton and faith? The India outside the big chain hotels that offered Western-style serenity, freezing air-conditioning, "State-of-the-Art" health clubs, and "Most Up-to-Date" diets for celebrity-style bodies? The India that sometimes surfaced from below the old muddy tidal currents of the British Raj? He dismissed it.

It was unimportant, part of the big, unseen, barely literate market that people like Ashok Rahman were paid to tap, whose rupees alone, by sheer numbers, gave them bullet-point validity as that most recognized and prized of all commodities: customers.

"Jeffrey—and your friend! Welcome!" Ashok boomed once they were out of the dreary Customs-and-Immigration lines.

Jeffrey tried to make reality fit the flat image he was used to on his monitors. In person, Ashok was darkly attractive, glisteningly alive, even if somewhat pudgily baby-faced. As he came closer, he seemed to morph into a rampantly seductive, energetically handsome presence, East-West in a stylish denim sports jacket with loose, dark Indian pants flapping around his legs. He was all over the place, helping them with their bags, charming John (who was jet-lagged and already in culture shock), herding them toward his new Indian-built car, a status sporty Rumi, named for the thirteenth century Sufi mystic who'd cried, "I have put duality away, I have seen that the two worlds are one!"

"Too long!" Ashok cried to Jeffrey. "Too many years without seeing your face, my friend!"

Jeffrey managed a grin; Ashok always talked like that. At the little sedan, Jeffrey remembered that he'd had some role in styling the Rumi: he'd wanted to put a little more high-powered design "cockiness" into it, but the Indian money people had said, "Not yet. Give us time. We're approaching it." The joke about the Rumi, of course, was that it was not *roomy*; they'd be cramped in it, especially with John's long legs.

"This is the mother of all places," Ashok said confidentially to John, as if imparting a secret. "And the newest! The wildest! We're so pleased to have you *both* here. It's an honor! It truly is, Jeffrey."

"Thank you," Jeffrey said, while John merely folded himself into the backseat, emitting growling, throat-clearing noises.

"Perhaps your friend is jet-lagged," Ashok said.

Jeffrey turned to John and decided to try a little German:

"John, *wo ist deine höfflichkeit?*"

"Sorry," John said. "Thank you for picking us up, Ashok. I'm sorry. I'm John. Vann. Or Van der Meer. Like Vermeer." He smiled sheepishly, like he were letting a cat out the bag. He shrugged. "Anyway, names are not so important here, right?"

"Whatever you say!" Ashok said gaily, raising a hand in the air. "Vann? Der Meer? I knew Jeffrey would bring something wonderful back to us. A painter? I am so *utterly* delighted by your being here with us, no matter what you say."

Jeffrey smiled, promising himself not to pay so much attention to Ashok, who'd be licking his hand one moment and biting it the next. Mumbai, an ultra-fast state-of-mind rammed into an older Indian cityscape that could no longer be termed simply "Third World," offered too much to see and too many head-spinning contradictions. Too many people. Too many stores. Too many signs in too many languages. Too many prosperous young people screeching on cell phones, thumping to music, jumping into and out of cars, taxis, motorcycles, and mopeds, hauling everything in wild shopping bags with colors so neon-intense they stung the hot, polluted autumn air around them.

Ashok sped up to stoplights, drove on through crowds that surged in and out, and made several amazing turns into streets barely wide enough for a bicycle. They were stopped again in traffic.

"Look!" he shouted, too excited to contain himself. "Look! You can buy anything you want here! See that bag?"

Jeffrey stared at a lone nicely dressed teenage boy with bleached hair carrying a big bag printed in enamel-sharp colors, the design of which began with a muscular male butt tattooed with flowing Hindi script. These tattoos graphically waved off into white peonies, then swirling pink clouds. Farther up, the clouds rose into a Himalayan landscape full of Nepalese design motifs, which finally soaked into a glimpse of an Italian beach featuring nubile, near-naked youngsters.

"That's something," Jeffrey admitted. "But what's the bag really about?"

"India!" Ashok exclaimed. "And the whole world! It's from a new housewares and furniture shop called 'Neat House.' Cool, right? I worked on Neat House a lot. I'm very proud of it!"

"Doesn't seem too neat to me," John observed.

"John," Ashok said sweetly. "In India being *neat* is cool. Because the country is not. At least not yet. 'Neat House'! Tell me, Jeffrey, is this not *genius*? The system just landed it into my lap. I was grateful! I tell you: *genius*! 'Neat House'! Everything is here!"

"It is genius," Jeffrey answered blankly. Ashok didn't get it. John, too frayed for irony and now shuttled between chilly Germany and heated India, glowered in the backseat. Ashok smiled at him, full-wattage, in the rearview mirror.

"I could use something to drink," John announced.

"Excellent!" Ashok said. "When we get to your hotel, you'll have all the drink you want. Tea, cool drinks, alcohol? Whatever you want. We have excellent beer in India. Some will surprise even you, a German."

"I'm not German. I'm Dutch."

"Please forgive me. Then they will surprise even a Dutchman!"

Ashok continued smiling.

John had sunken into sullenness. The weather, stifling to him, though not Mumbai at its worst certainly, did not help. Beggars and poverty were everywhere in sight, even on ever-jammed sidewalks and streets filled with big stores, American and European fast-food places, and chic restaurants. Suddenly amplified electronic sounds, the notes long and simple, floated above the ambient noise.

"Soundclears," Ashok explained. "They use it at certain hours to keep people quiet. The notes are based on old ragas, Indian classical music. It's nice, like having Gregorian chants piped into the air in your country."

"Not my country," Jeffrey said. "But I get the idea. Sound as an environment to calm people. That's interesting."

"You get it, but some people here don't. It almost caused a riot at first. They complained about 'perversions' of our culture. They're always going on like that. Sometimes people just go nuts. I'm a Hindu, but I believe that religion evolves, even if it remains basically the same—the way people do. India is old, but now we're used to the new. We can't imagine living without it. Still, there's always Mother India; it remains eternal, like Shiva—and like Shiva it takes many forms. But inside," he winked in the mirror at John, "there's always Shiva, the One Form."

John listened until the sound disappeared. Then breaking out of his sullenness, he announced: "I like that. I think I'll like you, Ashok."

"Good! I'm delighted. Tell me, John, have you ever been interested in Metaphysics?"

John's brow wrinkled. "That's like magic, isn't it?"

Ashok turned around, grinning to John in the backseat, making Jeffrey nervous. Cars were all over the place; people dashed into the street from the crowded sidewalks.

"Why don't you have this talk later, over drinks?" Jeffrey suggested.

"We will!" Ashok promised, giving the street his attention once more as it broadened into a wide boulevard, then narrowed again. "Metaphysics, John, is what lies underneath the world. It's the science of the unseen. In India, we take Metaphysics very seriously."

John sighed, smiling now as if mountains had parted, making Jeffrey wonder exactly what new game Ashok was up to. "Then I'm looking forward to that drink."

Ashok turned sharply into the street of the hotel.

"You'll like it here, John," Ashok announced as he cut the motor. "Personally, I'll see to that!"

❦

The Bombay Princess, using the old name from the Raj, was on a quieter backstreet in the Nariman area, which was modernized and business-oriented, even as the hotel tried to present an atmosphere of marked gentility. Uniformed men quickly collected their bags and parked the car. The place looked fairly new, although it featured an old-fashion verandah with high ceiling fans, Kiplingesque rattan furniture, and English magazines like *Peer and Peerage* stacked on cocktail tables. The lobby was cool but not freezingly over air-conditioned.

"I thought you'd like this, Jeffrey. It's not Taj Mahal Hilton, but the service is good and the system approves of it for some of their high-up people."

Jeffrey smiled gamely. He didn't want a Hilton. He'd stayed in them enough times and had met the same kind of brain-dead people there, all deals, status, and money.

Ashok had put them in separate rooms across a narrow hallway. He accompanied them with the bellboy to Jeffrey's room where he made sure that everything was O.K.: large plump towels, a sparkling bath, and a very commendable level of desired neatness.

"It's tip-top, isn't it?" he asked Jeffrey.

"Yes."

"Good." Ashok handed a bill to the bellboy, who looked about sixty. The bellboy made a short bow, and took John and his bag to his room, leaving Ashok and Jeffrey together alone.

"Your friend is interesting."

"Yes," Jeffrey agreed.

"Do you think he'll really like me?"

"He said so. Do you like him?"

"Yes, of course. He's your friend, and I want him to like me. I understand this is business, and I don't want to mix things up too much. It's never a good idea, but—"

"No, it's never a good idea," Jeffrey clocked in, as he looked at the light on Ashok's close-shaven cheeks. The light traveled up to the young man's dark eyes, and his lustrous, almost mesmerizing lashes. "Unless it *is* a good idea, Ashok. Sometimes that happens."

John came back in, beaming.

"My room's fine. How about that drink?"

They went to a small bar off the lobby with windows that looked onto the verandah, and sat at a table. Jeffrey ordered a gin-and-tonic, Ashok rather demurely asked for a *lassi*, a salty-sweet yogurt drink, and John a large Indian beer that arrived ice cold. He was pleased, taking deep swallows of it, looking around. Suddenly his eyes landed squarely on Ashok. This flustered Ashok, who turned away and then looked back at John. John put his hand on Ashok's shoulder.

"I'd like to see the real India," John announced. "This India of your Metaphysics. Can you show it to me?"

Ashok squirmed with obvious embarrassment. He cleared his throat, then said, "You're very direct." His face colored under his dark complexion. "In India, people are not so direct."

"They're not *so* a lot of things," Jeffrey said. "But when they are, it really knocks you out."

Ashok smiled bashfully.

"It's true. My country sneaks up on you. Suddenly you relax into it. Have you ever done that, Jeffrey?"

Jeffrey tried to think.

"No. There's too much that's off-limits for me, and too much is about business. I find it fascinating though."

Ashok sipped his *lassi*. "Good. Then even if *you* don't, perhaps your friend will relax and understand the Metaphysics of India."

Jeffrey sipped his gin-and-tonic. "What are you talking about, Ashok? This Metaphysics stuff? You've never spoken to me about it. Not on the phone, or when we've had any face time."

"I'm afraid I didn't know you that well."

"And you do now?"

"I know John, I can tell. That's metaphysical too, I'm afraid."

John's strained bluish-green eyes lit up, as if most of his exhaustion, jet lag, and even culture shock had evaporated. He did not say a word, but Jeffrey could tell he was pleased, just as he could see Ashok's almost involuntary moves of seduction at work.

"This is my idea!" Ashok blurted out, licking a coat of *lassi* off his lips. "We'll go to the area where I grew up. It's not like this. There are forests and temples without tourist guides. Real Indian villages. You'll love it."

"Think so?" John asked.

Ashok smiled with a distinctly bashful quality Jeffrey rarely saw in him. Obviously Ashok was insecure in a different way around John; Jeffrey absorbed this passively, as if he were looking at a file.

"Yes."

"Good!" John exploded. "Mumbai's too American. Too German-American! Anyone can see that."

Ashok nodded. "It's all only a game, John," he said seriously, trying to climb up to more secure ground. "Just think of it as that. What Metaphysics does is tell you how the game is played. It's the game of the Universe, and Metaphysics puts a face on the cards. If you can't read the faces, you can't play the game, so believe me, you're out of it. But the game goes on anyway. See what I mean?"

"I'm not sure," John answered. "I mean about reading the faces." He looked at Jeffrey for an answer, but Jeffrey had none.

"Sometimes it is difficult," Ashok said. "Seeing the faces on the cards. Of course, the ultimate face card is Death, and how we use it. Or react to it."

"Use it?" John asked warily. "How do you use such a card?"

Ashok lowered his eyes; Jeffrey could detect a tiny dark rainbow from a mist of feelings settling around his lashes.

"That is what Metaphysics is really about. If you allow yourself to, perhaps you'll find out about it here in India. Death, certainly, there is that card, and of course, Love. Love is such a troublesome card. But we are aware of that too here, very much."

John finished his beer and was ready for another one.

"I see," he said. "But it seems to me you're good at this game."

"No," Ashok said firmly, shaking his head. "But I would like to be." He smiled. "I would."

John smiled, too, and Ashok said nothing more.

In truth, Jeffrey had stopped listening to the conversation and was simply watching John's face with casual infatuation, like watching, in the midst of some daily drama of weather, the afternoon light changing under a beautiful Dutch sky. There was a mysterious quality in John's face that skipped triviality. He was indeed like a Vermeer, and his face never bored Jeffrey.

Suddenly the word "game" registered on him.

"What is the game?" Jeffrey asked, popping out of his reverie.

"Human aggression mostly," Ashok answered. "What people want, and what they will do to get to it. Also, their desire to merge with something else. We all seem to want that, know what I mean?"

"Yes," John eagerly answered.

"And that's a *game*?" Jeffrey asked, suddenly out of patience.

"Certainly, Jeffrey."

Ashok looked at him with more confrontation than Jeffrey was used to from him, or comfortable with.

"The game is how it will be played, and who has the cards: the power. You must know that. The system is always about the game, keeping it going. It has to go on, no matter what. It can't stop. Right, Jeffrey?"

Jeffrey said nothing, wondering how far underneath Ashok's charms, eyelashes, and talk of Metaphysics he could trust him. Ashok might use the system anyway he could against him; that was always a risk in the global economic system, which changed second by second, even if it always remained basically the same. Normally, Jeffrey could have dinner with anyone and at the end of it know how far to trust him; but he did not feel that way about Ashok, although he had thought Ashok would be fairly easy to deal with, even perhaps to use.

That was why he was in India.

But Ashok, despite his occasional rushing in like a fool, was no idiot, and now Jeffrey was convinced that the Indians, here in their huge, far-too-Bollywoodized country of multi-limbed gods and extraordinarily multi-functioning human beings, were perhaps smarter than even the Americans *or* the Germans.

It was not a thought that made Jeffrey terribly happy.

The silence was becoming sticky. Finally John asked, "Are there holy men where you'll take us?"

Another beer was brought to him. The waiter bowed and left.

Ashok smiled, lifting his hands behind his head.

"India is full of holy men. Everyone here pretends that he's one. But I know some who really are. You will meet them."

"Good!" said John. "When will you take us?"

"When Jeffrey and I have done enough work. How does that sound, Jeffrey?"

Jeffrey nodded, realizing he could not play this game any other way.

"Sounds excellent! We have your project to work on, and I want to get on with that as soon as possible. There are things we need to say to each other in person that we can't say any other way. That's why I'm here."

Ashok got up.

"And I am so pleased that you are! I can't tell you the honor you've done me. Shall we start tomorrow at eight? I'll come by and pick you up."

Ashok shook hands with Jeffrey, then winked at John. It was a funny wink, like something you'd give a kid. He signed for the drinks and left the bar.

John slowly finished his beer. Jeffrey smoldered a bit, wondering what was going on, "Metaphysically," between John and Ashok.

After the horror show at Pocus, he had thought that India would provide a little more room for them, some immediate element of safety that he needed with John. Now he was not the least bit sure. He did know some things about Ashok. Like many Indians, Ashok was married; it was still hardly acceptable there for a man not to be. His wife was also a working professional. She made considerable money in banking, and individually they had very private lives.

Ashok had told him that his wife Miryam was religious and did not always approve of everything he did. "Man is meant to play, as well as pray," he said, flirting with Jeffrey as usual. Ashok's flirting had always seemed fairly pro-forma, the seductive East's delicate dance of insinuation toward the West, implying an intimacy not really on offer, certainly not in the Western manner. In the West, intimacy meant opening up what was closed; whereas in the East, it seemed to be closing up a relationship that had once been fairly open and replacing a common, jocular heartiness with something else. This something was rarely overtly sexual, though in fact it was still quite amazing. The closest value Jeffrey could assign to it was a revelation, perhaps, of a genuine, endearing kinship.

Jeffrey returned to his room, showered, took his pills, and injected himself with his little painless pump. He was on the bed doing a calming exercise when John arrived at his door, wearing only a towel.

"I like it here," John said inside, dropping the towel.

"Do you?" Jeffrey asked, trying hard not to be infected with stress. They were on his bed, entwined naked around each other. He wanted John to spend the night with him, their first night in India. He thought about having supper brought to the room. It would be easier than going out; urban India easily got to you. "Not everyone is like Ashok."

"That's good." John smiled purely. "Wonder what he wants."

"It's pretty obvious. He's smitten with you."

"He knows nothing about me."

"He knows nothing about either of us, really. He works for me, but in a distant way. I think he would like to kick me off the board, but the system won't allow it. Talk about games. All that Metaphysical bullshit."

"I don't think it's bullshit, Jeffrey. I like it, it appeals to me."

"I see that." Jeffrey kissed him. "Just be careful. Nothing here really is as it seems."

John smiled. "How do you know I am?"

Jeffrey tweaked one of John's delicate red nipples. "You seem pretty real to me. No matter how we met."

Jeffrey got up. He ordered dinner, and they ate it in the room, dressed in terry robes. Then John went out, promising to come back soon. He returned much later, around two, and let himself in with Jeffrey's borrowed room key. Jeffrey was asleep. He woke up, feeling John next to him in bed.

"If this is a dream, I like it," Jeffrey said, half asleep. "What's it like out in the big, unreal world?"

"Very strange here in India. People come up and talk to you, even if you can't understand what they're saying. I walked a long time. Very strange, really. People sleeping on the sidewalks. I wanted to find the beach; instead I found a girl who had sex with me for a dollar."

"What?"

John smiled sheepishly and shrugged.

"Why'd you do that?"

"I don't know. Fun, maybe. Something I can't do at home. She was maybe fourteen. Younger even."

"God, John! You know there are laws, even here."

"It was O.K. We didn't do anything dangerous. She just sucked me a little and jerked me off."

"Cute. What happened to all this Metaphysical shit? Was this child part of it?" Jeffrey needed to sleep; he had a full day ahead with Ashok. "I hope you kept it all kosher. I mean, it happened in some dark street alley, with her pimp waiting?"

"No, not at all." John grinned sheepishly. "It was in my room."

Jeffrey almost jumped up out of the bed.

"JESUS CHRIST! YOU'RE KIDDING?"

He lowered his voice. "John, what in hell—don't you know everything we do here can be reported? Ashok probably knows about it already." He could feel his neck snap. "It can be used against me."

"I thought Ashok's your friend."

"There are no friends in this business. Only illusions about them."

John's face looked like a tractor had rolled over it.

"*Scheisse*! No different than Germany." His chest tightened and shook. "But you're my friend. Please, tell me that's true."

"Yes," Jeffrey answered, pulling him close and caressing him. "If you want to play, fine. Just don't do it here. Especially with fourteen-year-old girls. I've got to be up bright and early tomorrow. What will you do?"

"*Weiss nicht*," he answered.

John didn't know what he'd do; they had not thought that far ahead.

"I'll see if I can get the hotel to provide some entertainment for you," Jeffrey offered. "Mumbai is wonderful. Big art museums. The old English cathedral. Markets along the Port. A million things to see." His brain was tired, but he thought for a second. "Hey, how about a tour of a film studio?"

John smiled like a little boy. Jeffrey loved that. He forgave him everything. He adored that smile.

"That sounds good. Total make-believe. I can dig that. Ah, India, quite a funny place for boys and girls."

But Jeffrey had stopped listening. He needed to be wrapped again in some of Tony's calming mist, wandering through his own land-scape of files, images, and product concepts: a game in which he was still the undisputed master.

Chapter Ten

"So this is what we have here," Ashok said. "And this is what we want."

He showed Jeffrey the old prototypes of the Goddess line, then showed him a series of market surveys that ended up with a declaration: "The customer is ready for something else, something more sophisticated and pointedly Western than she has been given, although not too much more so. It must be familiar to her, and yet enticing with newness and immediately believable promises of status and recognition."

Jeffrey thanked Ashok for showing him the material, then they went over "That Woman" point by point, from the color and texture of the packaging and the new style devices used, down to the package lettering and names of the colors.

They began with Jeffrey's introductory "show-and-tell," as he explained design elements, where they came from, and how they would be used. Ashok watched, registering little feelings, although occasionally his eyes narrowed.

First, Jeffrey had come up with an extraordinary packaging device extracted from the sleeve of a Cristóbal Balenciaga gown from the early 1950s, beautifully tucked and swirled in wool, hued in pale yellow and garnet, banded with understated satin ribbons: the visual core of the concept.

Additionally, he had appropriated some wickedly chic style ideas from classic 1960's Hubert de Givenchy collections (that almost intimidating color sense and cut; the nose-bleed high fashion, lost-Hollywood-glamour, perfect-cheekboned "Audrey Hepburn" look) which Jeffrey transformed into some accompanying elegant plastic shapes, with additional style cues from Yves Saint Laurent's "Mondrian" phase, when Yves was using cheeky, thin window checks on simple but elegantly constructed dresses.

The checks idea had turned out literally too stunning; in fact, all of Jeffrey's work was *plus d'chic*, with an almost oxygen-deprived level of peak quality, bringing everything together in a consummately magical way, exactly as it should look. This was Jeffrey's role: the adroit, whip-cracking ringmaster of style. After some head-pounding hard work from Malace, Balenciaga's ruched sleeve device had been transferred into a fuller packaging concept, using the "Hepburn" and Saint Laurent refinements. In these prototypes, everything looked gorgeous, with the flow and sense of unity and sophistication that were Jeffrey Cooper's hallmark. From these initial style elements, he and others on his team had been able to dicker around until the repeated concepts fit all the projected products of the line: gift boxes, compacts, tubes, jars, shopping bags; even the shades of the products inside the packaging. The only thing missing would be the scents, perhaps; and of course the finalizations of the line and its promotion.

Jeffrey had the files with him, and they loaded them into Ashok's personal information system, which he assured Jeffrey was shared with no one else. Jeffrey doubted this, but let Ashok go on with that part of his game.

"I like this," Ashok finally said, thoughtfully placing two fingers on his lips. "I like the direction you've taken us into. Very, very much."

This was exactly what Jeffrey wanted to hear from Ashok, and no more.

"But let me speak freely," Ashok went on, moving his fingers away from his mouth. "I'm fairly confident the Money will feel we need to be"—he hesitated, then said it: "More aggressive. Certainly slightly *more* aggressive. If you get what I mean?"

"And that is?"

"The line still does not *sell* itself, Jeffrey. And for these girls it had better."

Jeffrey closed his eyes. He was tired. It was past two, and he was ready for lunch.

"So tell me, what would you suggest, Ashok?"

Ashok's brow furrowed.

"Rhinestones!" he spit out. "I mean it. In very strategic places. Lots of them. Glitter, glitz, let it pop out! It adds a jewelry element to the line, and in India that goes a very long way."

Jeffrey could not believe what he had heard. They had asked for class, Hollywood, and refinement, and he was giving it to them in spades. Now Ashok was going back to "Ye Old India"; they could have just stuck to "Goddess."

"You're kidding, Ashok? This doesn't sound very *Mrs. Miniver*, Deborah Kerr, or Audrey Hepburn to me."

"Ever heard about *Breakfast at Tiffany's*? That was all glitz, wasn't it?"

No, it wasn't, thought Jeffrey. *Breakfast* was something else. Something more fascinating, more interesting. And Audrey Hepburn/ Holly Golightly didn't go to Tiffany's for a fat slap of rhinestones. But Jeffrey said none of this to Ashok. He just let him go on.

"We need to do large 'TW's in rhinestones and throw some big flash into lots of other places, then add some extra embossing in gold. And that ribbon—it's dowdy! Dowdy, dowdy, dowdy! Value has got to pop out for these women—announce itself *big* so that they can show it off to their girlfriends, who'll be envious as hell and go out and buy gobs of 'That Woman' for themselves. I want them to talk about it incessantly, to chatter about it as only Indian women can. I know this adds price points, but I'll let you decide that, Jeffrey."

Ashok paused, either out of breath or out of confidence, then said, as a kind of *coup de grace*:

"It's really all your decision, old man. That's why we're here together, and I thank you for it. Strictly speaking, your position is high enough to get these things done, and—"Ashok lowered his eyes humbly—"I'm only here as an adjunct to you."

Jeffrey smiled coldly, his face frozen like a mannequin, as he hunted for a strategy. He had wanted to say, "Cut the crap" to Ashok's fake humbleness, but didn't. The stakes on the beauty line were climbing by the hour. Ashok was getting more ambitious, and the Money monsters behind him, who could have been anywhere from Brussels to Beijing, were obviously pushing him much harder than he had let on.

Jeffrey detected a simple-enough subtext: The Money, rapacious as ever and eager to pounce, was getting ready for a huge product blitz, as in *millions* of pieces of "That Woman" pouring out for sale, flooding from factories in Asia, Eastern Europe, South America. "That Woman" was definitely not going to remain in India, but would quickly shoot outside its initial market of young working village ladies with small disposable incomes. They were positioning it to become part of the international language of consumers, who could identify brand names in any language. It would spark a clothing line with freshly-minted celebrities pitching it, even celebration days such as soft drink and automobile companies had, with high-hysteria, mega tie-in events all over the world.

The truth was becoming evident: Ashok needed a super-big "kill" on this. True cash register carnage. And he needed to run with it, not just walk gingerly, as he had in the past. For all of his "Metaphysical" posturing, Ashok could be planning a real *coup* here, forcing Jeffrey, from his higher position, to sign off on a dummy concept that might be jettisoned later. The system would back Cooper's prototypes, with Ashok taking the line higher and higher, quickly killing or disfiguring Jeffrey's ideas one by one. Then, if at any time the line failed, Jeffrey, due to his "spontaneous" visit to India, would be fully blamed for it.

And, if "That Woman" succeeded? Mega-BIG?

Ashok would emerge with a real name for himself: "Ashok Rahman, Creator of 'That Woman'!"

The scenario sped through Jeffrey's head, from the rejected spunky irony of "Goddess" to the sublimity of what he had pulled together for "The Woman," to Ashok's almost admirable deviousness swathed in rhinestones and glittery gunk. Check. Check. Mate.

Ashok was a good-looking boy. Jeffrey could see him becoming an Eastern "face," one of those media design celebrities the system created like a new food source, pitching as much buzz, energy, money, and hype into them as human endurance would allow. If you survived it without becoming a monster, it was close to superhuman; if you did not, it was all part of the game. And, definitely, part of Ashok's "Metaphysics," as well.

Jeffrey had been in tight jams before, but this one seemed more diabolical, if only because he had walked directly into it. He had rushed into this trip for his and John's sake; after the recent chain of events, it had seemed like the only idea worth having. Certainly John was. Jeffrey's glacial smile warmed, and Ashok looked at him with a delicious, slightly arch, Mona Lisa air of mystery.

India now. What next? And how much *more* could Jeffrey use this appealing young man?

Ashok had been part of Jeffrey's group for something like eight years (he could not pinpoint Ashok's arrival to the day), and now the kid was growing up. In the beginning he had seemed a deferential kiss-ass, but not totally. He had a perceptibly Western, preppy-aristocratic edge to him, marked by a gung-ho aggression that Jeffrey, who liked strong men as long as they did not get in his way, had found charming. He had dealt with other Asians who had been either so cold and hard that he got rid of them, or so weak that they only held things back. But not Ashok Rahman.

Obviously, it would be easy for anyone, no matter how high up in the system, to fall for Ashok's lighter-than-air promises of delectable profits to come. In the final tally, Jeffrey was convinced, Ashok had been leading the Money, not the other way around. Evidently, he was good at this, poised for something big. And the system would recognize it mostly on the outcome of how well Ashok played his hand in the development and sales of "That Woman."

They looked at the prototypes again, with Jeffrey editing out elements that might stand in the way of the product message and tweaking other details to make them even more appealing. He coughed and winced, his stomach hurt, but he stuck in Ashok's rhinestones and gold embossing, with the terrible feeling that if he did anything to kill this line, he would die along with it.

It was the price he had to pay for this time with John.

"I think," Jeffrey said seriously, "we need more 'Release' element. The customer needs to feel that when she buys this, she'll go straight to heaven as soon as she gets home."

"Think so, Jeffrey?" Ashok looked hard at a box of dusting powder. "Hard to see 'heaven' in this. Maybe at a certain point the customer may think that she can go to dinner with the boss's wife.

Now that might be *heaven* for her!"

"You told me you needed a harder sell, Ashok."

Ashok backed down.

"All right, Jeffrey, you're correct. I did, and I agree that you know more about these things. Certainly more than we do here in India."

Touché, Jeffrey thought, and he relented. Perhaps Ashok was right. A harder, more sexualized sell might be too much for these women, wherever they were, and a detailed, approachable appeal to class instincts right. There was a universality to this, and Ashok had got it correct. This would be about recognizing attainable, perceivable value (glitter) and quick upward mobility (glitz); it was not about outsnotting the girls with Givenchy/Hepburn's old-century chic. Jeffrey had always been able to take a lot of responsibility and even blame for his actions, no matter how badly the cookies crumbled. He could do it here, and he smiled as he watched Ashok put in his two-cents worth of rhinestones for every nickel of quality Jeffrey took out.

Lines like this came and went for any number of reasons: factories out in the jungles, where the workers had been headhunters a generation earlier, screwed up gluing rhinestones on little bottles; or, after umpteen go-rounds with the prototypes and the Money, subsequent product managers did not get the message and misinterpreted Jeffrey's directions; or some half-wit distributors messed up orders. Or, finally, worst of all, everything was perfect but didn't fly economically because price points were too far off or something else in the world, like an overnight currency collapse, took attention from it.

There were myriad reasons why products didn't sell enough to keep money circulating. The important thing was that Jeffrey Cooper, well seasoned at seventy-eight, could take the fault without either self-destructing or allowing others to destroy him. He was sure he could assume overall responsibility for this, cushioning Ashok enough to keep him happy and in bounds, and the line working.

"All right," Jeffrey conceded. "We'll take this *my* way, as you wish. But if you feel that we're going too far at any time, then you'll stop me, right?"

"Of course," Ashok said shrugging. "It's my line—I mean *ours.*"

Sure, thought Jeffrey, till Death, or a quick mudslide of money, do us part.

They had a late lunch at a fashionable Italian restaurant on the edge of Colaba that Ashok liked, while noise outside from crowds, car horns, traffic jams, beggars, screaming kids, and vendors pummeled the senses, despite the frigid air-conditioning. Ashok ignored it, eating his linguini and clams with gusto. As a modern Hindu who was mostly vegetarian, he had decided that things like clams, scallops, and even lobster did not count. "I feel they have no real eyes or heart," he declared, sipping from a large tulip-shaped glass of red wine.

They spent a long time at the restaurant, until Jeffrey wondered what John was doing and decided to call it quits for the day. Ashok drove him back to the hotel, leaving him at the verandah. Jeffrey waved to him, started up the stairs, then decided to wander the streets a bit, attempting to let some other aspect of Mumbai beside work sink into him. He had been strolling only a short time when he met John, who was walking back to the hotel.

John immediately embraced and quickly kissed him; some Indians on the street stared hard at them. John was tall and red-headed, which alone could cause heads to turn, but his sudden embrace, even in Mumbai, caused Jeffrey to feel out of place there. He had to watch himself. One way or another, the system was all over the world and his position in it, bland and for the most part personalityless, had to remain established in it.

"We've been invited to a party," John said as they walked.

"A party?" Jeffrey smiled. "Already?"

"Yes. I took your advice. I went to a film studio. It was a bit out of the way, but I didn't go for a tour. I just told some men at the gates that I was a film director from Holland, and that I was looking to cast a new Dutch movie with some Indian actors. *Gott*! The reaction! Everybody wanted to meet me, and this young woman—a very nice girl—asked me if I'd like to go to a party. 'Everyone in the movies will be there,' she promised. So I said, 'Sure! Why not?' Here, I have the address of the place."

The address meant nothing to Jeffrey, but the desk clerks at the hotel could help them.

Jeffrey showered again, then lay down to rest quietly. At some point, a fusillade of jet lag would knock him down, but for the moment he was still running high on adrenaline, oxygenated with some of Bernd Ostreich's chemical boosters, plus his desire both to get his work done and spend as much time as he could with John. While he was trying to let his mind wander and delete some stress from his head, John came into his room and got into bed with him.

"I do like it here, Jeffrey. Maybe it's because I know so little about it."

"But you told me you were here once."

"*Scheisse!* When I was with Cynthia, I never really looked at anything, just like she didn't. Everything was 'quaint,' 'adorable,' 'cute!' All those dear little underfed children. That was another life. Besides, we were in Goa mostly. It could have been Miami, or Spain."

Jeffrey sighed; he needed ten more minutes of quiet, but now John was there and that made rest unlikely.

"It is different now," he said. "Isn't it?"

"It is," John agreed. "Very different."

"It's hard to know anything about India," Jeffrey said, his eyes closed. "It's so big. People are kind yet brutal. Maybe that's the way every place is at heart, but here it just seems so—" He ran out of thoughts, then said, "If we go to this party, John, you can get into real trouble setting up people's expectations."

John smiled softly.

"Then I'll have to act *very* mysterious."

"That should be easy. You're mysterious to me."

Jeffrey opened his eyes, pulled John closer, and kissed him.

"We're both mysteries then," John whispered, and took his clothes off. He got back on the bed naked, and drew apart Jeffrey's robe.

Jeffrey felt both chilled and hot at the same time, just from having John near him. John's body gave him an instant erection, something he'd not experienced before in decades. He loved looking at him. The savage, raw, sweet tenderness of his body; the almost Flemish pallor of his skin and ivory-smooth groin; the purple testicles sinking deeply into his near-translucent pink scrotum; his beautiful uncut penis, the head sneaking out like a furled morning glory. There were armies of professionally cute young men out there, but John van der Meer had true mystery about him, a depth, something too forbidden to be exposed without effort, and yet fresh and direct as his paintings.

They kissed and Jeffrey went down on him. Then John said: "I want you to fuck me," his voice deep, secretive, and revelatory. Jeffrey took lubricant from his bag, and John coated some on Jeffrey's cock and put some inside himself, then straddled Jeffrey's hips and eased himself down smoothly, like a celestial fireman descending from heaven. They changed position several times, and it always felt as if John were on top, even though he was getting fucked. He was monstrously good and totally wild about it, letting himself go completely, without any holding back. Jeffrey forgot about the endless files, the cruel machinations at work, how he was fooling most of the world with a fictitious age. He deleted it all, except himself and John. John was monstrous in the most beautiful way, all great green eyes and pale white skin, and sheaves of flaming hair that looked almost transparent, like strands of red crystal.

Relaxed, loose, agile, fire-stoked, kissing and sucking John, even while fucking him, Jeffrey felt wonderful; the two came together. Then it was time to go to the party.

The desk clerk was familiar with the building, which was not far away; an air-conditioned taxi arrived, and the driver took them quickly to the location, a nondescript office building that could have been in Omaha. The party was in a suite on the fifteenth floor, but it was India as soon as they got off the elevator. A handsome boy with dark swirling henna patterns on his hands, arms, and face bounced up to them out of a crowd of younger people. He was wearing baggy pants and a black sleeveless shirt that exposed much of the left half of his chest where a small, intricately jeweled ring sparkled from his nipple.

"Hello! You must be th'Dutch filmmaker Sonja told us about!"

John bowed, smiling.

"Now's the time to be inscrutable," Jeffrey whispered.

"*Ja,*" John said. "I yam. Who ah you?"

"Dira. Dira Gambino. I'm an Italian Indian. My mom was Indian, my dad Italian. I love India, don't you? It's so modern. It makes Italy look old-fashioned. They are so Catholic there, even when they don't want to be. Come! Have a drink. What d'you drink?"

"Anything vet und s-trong!" John crowed.

At the far end of the packed room was a bar, with a barman in white uniform pouring Indian vodka, scotch, wine coolers, and nonalcoholic fruit sodas. The fruit drinks looked interesting; Jeffrey had one with pomegranate concentrate, while John downed a scotch. The boy bounced up and down, barely able to contain himself.

"What are you on?" Jeffrey asked softly.

"*Paan*! You just chew it, you know. Betel with some sweet stuff and other good things. Mine has some coca, too. I have my own *paan*-wallah. Another good thing about India: here you can get high and everybody just smiles!"

They were smiling, this array of gorgeously bejeweled and madeup young women in bright saris or cocktail pants and good-looking young men, some in expertly cut suits that looked faintly Italian, but in more saturated colors like turquoise-marine blue, or a rose-crystal pink that stole Jeffrey's eyes as they followed the mingling egos of these creatures, some jumping into a V.I.P. group of generously puffed-out, leering older men—producers obviously—then released into the waiting arms of their lesser-plumaged hangers-on. From out of all this energy, *the* Sonja appeared, in her early thirties, rather plainly pretty but nice looking, in a simple dark dress, her hair colored a sun-streaked, honey blond.

"Hullo!" she said, smiling, delighted to see them, and quickly introduced them to dozens of eager young faces who also smiled, although some of them were smashed enough not to remember most of anything later.

John was spirited off to another corner, persuaded by two actors who felt that they should definitely be in *his* film. One looked like a beefy Bengali wrestler, the other a sensuous court dancer, though the big one was actually a comedian and the thinner one already had a reputation for playing sinister gangsters and philandering husbands.

Jeffrey glanced at them, then turned to Sonja.

"I like the way you look," he complimented her.

"Thank you. I'm not an actress. I just work in the film office, reading scripts."

"I like your hair. Is this from India, the hair color?"

"Oh, yes, it's called 'Natural Beauty.'" She sighed. "It's been around for years, like something you'd expect from the Raj. I could see Deborah Kerr wearing it in one of those funny old English movies. It doesn't feel like India, but I like it. A lot of young women like me would never buy it, though."

The "Deborah Kerr" thing kindled Jeffrey's interest.

"Why is that?"

She hesitated, then explained, "Because they think only foreigners would use it."

"I see," Jeffrey said. "Tell me, personally, would you rather have something that—looked more Indian?"

"What do you mean?"

"Well, not quite so . . . Deborah Kerr."

"Personally, yes! I think that 'We're-proper-ladies-from-the-Old-School' crap—it's ridiculous. It's O.K. for village girls, but the truth is I'd prefer something *very* Indian-looking. We're proud of the fact we're Indian, but it's got to be our India, at once modern and old."

"I see," Jeffrey said, trying to put this together while sipping his pomegranate drink. "That is interesting."

"Are you also in film?"

"No. I design things. Products, cars, buildings. Actually I tell designers how to design them. The whole world's designed now. Nothing's left to chance. Even chance is designed, if you understand what I mean."

"Of course I understand. You mean questions like how long you'll live, things like that?"

Before Jeffrey could answer, John appeared with Ashok, who was all extra-high voltage, even for Ashok.

"How did you get to this party!!!" he cried, loud enough for the whole room to hear. "And those men believe John's a Dutch film-maker! Very clever! I love you, John. You're so clever!"

"I am a Dutch filmmaker," John said solemnly. "I just haven't made any films."

"Good! You can be what you want!" Ashok lurched forward and kissed John, without anyone's head turning.

A second later, the fast beating of little drums and ding-dings of finger cymbals interrupted the clink of drinks and career commingling. A group of dancing girls in loose saris and scarves, jingling bangles and anklets, swirled in, quickly surrounding John, Jeffrey, and Ashok, making ear-splitting noises with tambourines and high, nasally singing voices.

"Hijras," Ashok spoke into Jeffrey's ear. "You know, eunuchs. Transgendered boys. Indians love them, especially the ultra-hip Indians. They're great at parties."

Some of them were no longer boys; up close they looked past forty, even sixty. About ten hijras worked the room like politicians facing reelection, three of whom had small video cameras and directed the action, making sure that no possibility of an offering was overlooked; everyone gave the dancers some kind of money, which disappeared instantly into hanging purses or bra straps.

Ashok conversed in Hindi with a short, chubby one, who looked about thirty-two, as he handed her an offering.

"Her name is Reeta," he told Jeffrey.

Reeta smiled brightly at Jeffrey, lifted her arms dramatically while she was being videoed, then said something else in Hindi. Ashok smiled, and beckoned with his fingers that she should speak more.

She did, flexing her shoulders seductively at Jeffrey, like an aging movie star demanding a close-up.

"What did she say?" Jeffrey asked.

"She said you are handsome as Krishna, boyish, always young, and she could go for you!"

Jeffrey smiled, embarrassed. "Tell her thank you."

Ashok bowed to her, pointed to Jeffrey, and said something, then Reeta answered him, her palm out.

"What does that mean?" Jeffrey asked.

"Oh, the usual. She's telling you that for a small consideration, she'll make a date with you. She'll dance for you alone."

Jeffrey laughed. "Tell her I'm all dated up!"

"Maybe you should—" Ashok stopped himself. "All right."

Ashok told her something, and Reeta glared at Jeffrey. She spit a few words out, pointed the camerawoman to another group of people, then hurried on to them, singing in a screechy voice that sounded like it came from an ancient record player with a worn needle, her hands moving suggestively in circles mimicking smoke rings.

Jeffrey watched her; their eyes met. She turned curtly away from him.

"They're interesting," Ashok said. "Kind of like American street drag queens, but much—" he paused—"deeper. Like India itself. You can hardly compare them to anything; things only appear to be like other things here. That's our great strength. We only *appear* to take on the colorings of others. I think the hijras go back to temple prostitutes, who were also priests and priestesses."

His eyes turned away from Jeffrey, then returned to him.

"I'm afraid you insulted her, Jeffrey. Her come-on to you is something you either accept or joke off. It seems you rejected her."

"I'm sorry. I had no idea," Jeffrey said, wondering why Ashok hadn't warned him about this—or had not done it for him, since he had served as Jeffrey's interpreter.

"They're sensitive to rejection. I'm surprised she didn't put a curse on you. Perhaps she did, and you just don't know it."

"I'm sorry," Jeffrey repeated. "Really, I am."

He went over to Reeta, whose back was toward him. When she turned to him, he handed her a large bill. She took it, and without acknowledging him walked over to her other friends. Jeffrey could see John with two of the oldest hijras, who were doing an impromptu audition for him, singing, dancing, and laughing. A few minutes later, he returned to Jeffrey's side.

"They're crazy, those people!" John spurted, giggling. "They speak some English, some German even. They wanted to know all about me, what kind of camera I use." His voice went up several notes: "'We are in many movies, sir. We will show you the old ways of India. Please, let us show you!' So, of course I told them I would."

"I hope they don't find out you're a fake. Ashok told me they're famous for their curses."

"Curse? *Curse!*" He let out something that resembled a mocking laugh, that shocked Jeffrey in its coarseness. "Screw them! You can't curse the cursed," John said bitterly. "You can only try. No, I don't accept their curse! But I hear they do blessings. I heard about them: they bless weddings, bar mitzvahs or the Indian versions. All the good stuff." He smiled. "I like the funny Jewishness of India. People pretend they're all your family. That's really funny Jewishness, I believe."

"Are you drunk?" Jeffrey asked, but then Ashok re-appeared, wrapping his arms around both of them.

"I should take you boys out. That's it! We'll have dinner tonight. I know this really good restaurant. You'll like it. Lots of Indian gay guys go there."

"Sounds fine," John said. "I think I've had enough time being famous."

"Good."

They were at the door when a pale-looking young woman in a black tailored business suit strode in. Her small but intense face bore an extravagantly distinctive, almost Semitic-looking nose, lending a flash of credibility to John's Jewish-India theory. Ashok excused himself, and went to her. They talked seriously, but he did not bring her over to introduce her.

A moment later he rejoined them and they waited at the elevator.

"Who was that?" John asked.

"My wife, Miryam. I didn't expect to see her here, but she must have got an invitation, too. Meeting socially is nice. We go out together too sometimes."

"You don't live together?" John asked.

The elevator arrived. Ashok got in, and then they did.

"We do," Ashok said. "But we have our own lives. It works out nicely."

"Sounds like a good idea to me," John said. "More people in the West should be married that way."

"Oh, you're right!" Ashok said, maximum wattage. "India is absolutely *full* of good ideas!"

☙

The restaurant, miles away in one of those many parts of Mumbai alternately seedy and trendily overpriced, was no problem with Ashok driving. The trip was like watching a movie about teeming urban India. Sinister areas of darkness, then startling lights. Tall buildings and squalid tenements. Crowds of near-naked people, some asleep on sidewalks, others drifting or sleepwalking among people doing business as usual, shopping, moving on. Eerie night noises of water trickling through gutters and wandering bits of exotic music. Loud talk and piercingly ugly bird calls and animal screeches. Great moans from cows. All old-hat to Jeffrey, yet for the first time in years new, as he tried to look at it through John's eyes, which gorged on everything, mesmerized. John sat up front. Behind him, Jeffrey watched Ashok casually place his hand on John's knee. He accepted it. What else could he do? Being jealous seemed silly, perhaps even a touch insane.

The restaurant, decorated in "India-meets-Paris" motifery from the final glamorous pre-World War I twilight of European high society, was named Le Cocque d'Or; and the management, in an attempt at *tres haute Art Moderne,* had mobilized an onslaught of pearl-gray ostrich feathers, pearl-gray dinnerware, pearl-gray uniforms, and starched pearl-gray oversized table linens: *elegant* pearl-gray overkill, comic verging on depressing. There were intimate banquettes and deep sullen alcoves, like war trenches, for seductive goings-on; and a dimly lit display of framed (in pewter, pearl-gray) ebulliently queer photos of Vaslav Nijinsky and the Ballets Russes, its dancers of both sexes dripping Mogul jewelry and frozen into "Hindoo" poses, exposing just enough anatomy to show how Europe processed the "anything goes" East.

In contrast, most of the Cocque d'Or patrons looked demurely preppy, although Jeffrey noticed a few lads in too-tight, taffy-colored cashmeres displaying flamboyant rumba wiggles in their walks. Other men arrived in subdued leather and disappeared into private alcoves. But mostly the clientele looked like it reflected eras much older than Nijinsky's: centuries of self-effacing, deeply-ingrained Eastern sexual reticence.

Perhaps that was good, thought Jeffrey, at least the more discretionary aspects of it. He needed to recompose himself with Ashok there, who was getting wilder by the second, waving his arms about, trying to get the young, for the most part oblivious, waiters instantly to their table, as other tables cast looks of coy embarrassment at him.

"I thought you boys would like this!" he announced, smoking a slightly clove-scented beedi. "Want one?" he offered.

They both accepted and Ashok lit them. The place had a nonsmoking area, but there was enough smoke for everyone.

"I like these," John said, exhaling. "I think I like everything about India."

Ashok smiled at him. "You should. The nice thing about India is that there is so much history here that no matter what you've done in your past, it just dissolves here. Poof! It's gone. Now, if we could just get one of these *poofs* to take our order! I need a drink!" He beckoned to a waiter, who ignored him. "Scotch! Scotch!"

"I'm not sure he saw you," Jeffrey said.

"They try to ignore me! Goddamn poofs! Why shouldn't I drink? I'm with friends, right?"

"You are," John said, getting up. Since he was tall and, in this setting, very striking-looking, the waiter appeared immediately and took their drink orders.

'Do you two like boo?" Ashok asked, as soon as the waiter was gone.

"Boo?" Jeffrey asked, trying to appear innocent.

"Come on now, Jeffrey. Nice little drugs. I can put some in a beedi for you, or you can sniff it. Here at *Le Cocque*, things like that are O.K. if you're not too pushy about it. Actually everything's O.K. Actually I'd like to stick a little something up my own nose, actually."

He winked his beautiful eyelashes.

"I think I'll just stick with this," Jeffrey maintained.

With a few exceptions, he was not used to smoking anything and could only imagine what Bernd or Tony might say: all their dire warnings. But Bernd and Tony were not in India and were not being tempted by their own feelings working so seductively against them.

Jeffrey could hardly imagine Tony Rosenputter or Bernd Ostreich in India. Bernd would only see everything as a vile joke on the "dirtbag" races. Tony would feel compelled to appear compassionate about the poor while doing nothing, not even caring enough really to look at them, in fact. Tony, he was sure, didn't actually like *real* life. Suddenly the truth came crashing down on Jeffrey, smacking him hard. But, strangely enough, without any reason he felt genuinely good, as if he were floating within himself—and naturally, beautifully happy.

Perhaps this was what Tony had always wanted: that Jeffrey would enter that mist of himself, that place where he could experience himself calmly, in peace, without judgment. The truth was, he liked being at Le Cocque d'Or, overdone pearl-gray as it was, and in India, with these two younger men. Looking at the handsome men around them, he had a moment of feeling absolutely sparkling within himself, like an earned reward for what he'd have to go through: Ashok's shark-in-the-water machinations; John's almost unchartable flights of psycho-fancy, or infancy.

The beedi made him light-headed. He had a cocktail, a Beefeater martini, and forgot about Sonja, the young woman he had met who frankly contradicted most of what Ashok had maintained so firmly about his beauty line. Jeffrey felt distant from all that; now he was back in Paris with Nijinsky. The furs and jewels of the women, the clandestine behavior of men perfectly dressed for the evening (their dangerously romantic kisses of honor, that yet contained the flint of sincerity), and the torrent of madness under the inscrutable mask of Nijinsky's face. Unwatched, he stared at John's face, and all the atmosphere at the Cocque d'Or that had momentarily bewitched him—the clouds of ostrich feathers, the blurred, dark faces of the men, even those sepia Nijinskys bringing back the intrigues of the Ballets Russe—came crashing down around him like so much Venetian glass.

And one more thought exploded in his face: Suppose Ashok were *really* trying to sabotage him, and all this was an artful setup, fabricated to get him into a hole he could never climb out of? He gripped his pearl-gray napkin so hard that he could feel his knuckle bones pop.

Ashok was speaking, but Jeffrey could not hear a word coming from his mouth. Instead Sonja's voice like a warning flag spoke in his head. He wanted to rush back into his chinchilla-gray, misty Paris morning with the magnetic Nijinsky at his side. Ashok was flirting with John, and John was basking in the cardamom-oiled charm of Ashok's effusive attentions, positively glowing from it. Was John such a fool?

Or was it Jeffrey now?

He excused himself, unable to watch any more, and went to the bathroom, walking through a tableaux of throw-back queers, some of whom were dyed Jayne Mansfield blond yet still looked classically Indian. The martini had kicked in on top of the beedi. He felt dislocated. Where the hell was he? He could have been in Germany, leaving Chris Stewart and Len Silverman's tacky ballet-set, over-decorated apartment.

Suddenly, he hated them, hated everyone who took from him without giving anything back—including John van der Meer. And Ashok Rahman with his flirtatious, iridescent eyelashes. Chris Stewart had a narcissism you could distill, but why should he hate him for that? Narcissism and its favorite form of expression, the constant need to buy something and then discard it, was keeping him alive. So Chris and his sick-doctor boyfriend were just accessories to. . . .

John appeared in the bathroom, just as Jeffrey finished zipping himself up.

"You okay. *Woll?*" John asked, genuinely concerned. "*Complet?*"

Jeffrey liked hearing that. Yes, he was complete. Somewhat. At least it was nice to know John cared.

"I think our friend Ashok has had too much cocaine. He doesn't want you to know about the cocaine. He got a little clearheaded and said I shouldn't tell you about it. I'm not, understand? But I thought I should come and find out if you're O.K. You are, *richtig?*"

"I'm fine," Jeffrey snapped. "More than fine."

"Good," John said, reaching for Jeffrey's fingers then bringing them graciously to his lips. "Ashok keeps trying to flatter me into something. I think he's nuts."

Jeffrey melted.

"You do?"

"Yes. I don't know what his game is, but he's good at sucking you into it. Believe me, I won't be!"

Jeffrey smiled and thought he'd faint from sheer pleasure. John's clear-sightedness reminded him of the "horse sense" he'd been brought up on in Alabama. But instead of fainting, he tipped the attendant who was not at all interested in their business, and waited while John peed. Then he knew it: something as close to being in love as he would ever get was hitting him, and it was with John. Just watching John, a vast, powerful electrical charge hit him. It was stupendous. He was *outrageously* in love with him. Why didn't he know it before, or at least admit it to himself? The impact was immediate, and it scared him. John might as well kill me, he thought. That was how dangerous the feeling was, pushing him right over the edge— but of what? His static, enduringly youthful self?

Then he dismissed the thought; he told himself not to let it bother him. Not at that moment. He wanted to be happy, to embrace that beautiful, floating feeling of happiness from a few seconds earlier. He wanted to be folded in it to the point of tears.

Back at the table again, they ordered dinner. The food was from everyplace and seemed to work together nicely, because mostly it was terrible. The European entrees, greasy and over rich, tried too hard to be too Continental, while the Indian food was surprisingly bland with stringy meat, something good Indian cooks never tolerated.

"I like everything here," Ashok said, patting his stomach. "Mostly because it's different."

"Do you come often?" John asked, wiping his mouth with his pearl-gray napkin.

"Often as I can," Ashok said, smiling broadly, then said: "Oh, you mean to this restaurant? No, I don't come here *often*. But I thought you guys would like it."

Ashok paid for the meal, which was not cheap, and on the way to the car he said to Jeffrey: "I hope you don't take this night too seriously. I'm afraid I went too far. After all, we do work together. I hope you'll judge me not as a fellow worker, but only as your friend."

"I'm not judging you at all."

"Good," Ashok said sincerely, and kissed Jeffrey on the cheek.

It was dark in the parking lot, where a single attendant guarded the cars. A shower of stars appeared as the crystalline sky cleared itself of lower clouds.

"This is so beautiful!" Ashok exclaimed. "It's like where I want to take you. Listen, I have a wonderful idea! Why don't we go tomorrow, instead of waiting? We can finish our work when we get back. I mean it! I want to show you both the *real* India. Especially John. I want to show him things that he won't forget. How does that sound, Jeffrey? Are you up for it?"

Jeffrey hesitated. To seem afraid would have played easily into Ashok's hands, but he did not want to agree too fast either. He had serious qualms.

"I'm not sure. I feel like I'm putting off what I need to do."

"Nonsense! Maybe you *need* to do this. What do you think, John?"

"Maybe he does," John agreed, cocking his head slightly, smiling and looking at Jeffrey.

"I was afraid he was not doing well in the toilet. Nerves, travel maybe. But you're right, Ashok. Maybe Jeffrey needs it. Just to rest, to relax."

"Let me think about it," Jeffrey said, stalling. "And I'll call you early tomorrow."

Chapter Eleven

*T*he next morning Jeffrey decided that the trip would give him more time to figure Ashok out. "Metaphysical" or not, what was his game? On one hand, he was showing a few more warts on himself: the drinking, the drugs, boys, his wife. On the other, with enough crafty flip-abouts on this project, he could turn Jeffrey into a distant "consultant," a rubber stamp for attracting the kind of big Western money that might turn Ashok into a superplayer while pushing Jeffrey off the board, certainly in India. Ashok was making a lot of sudden, contradictory, maybe even decoy moves: First, classy Greer, elegant Audrey, and demure Deborah, then *Gentlemen Prefer Blondes* glitz and bling. What gave?

Everything was going to add up to something, but to what? He called Ashok, who seemed not at all hungover.

"It's settled! I'll pick you up at noon!"

The village they were going to was slightly more than two hundred miles away, though mostly along fairly good roads. They were only going to stay a night or two, so they waited for Ashok with small overnight bags on the verandah of the hotel. John was having a beer already, and Jeffrey a lemonade. His stomach was not doing great, but he'd fortified himself with pills and injected himself after a shower. The important thing was to let Ashok and his India unfold for them, and if along the way, Ashok revealed himself to be playing some kind of warped "karmic" game, Jeffrey would give Ashok just enough rope to hang himself, and then personally slip the noose around the young man's neck.

John was all gung ho eagerness. "It's going to be pure Gunga Din!" he announced between swigs of beer.

"Kipling?"

"*Wirklich*! Wild! Free! One *crazy* adventure!"

Jeffrey laughed, then embraced John right there. John was wild, free, a crazy adventure himself, no matter where he was. Ashok drove up in mid-embrace, his small car piled with boxes and shopping bags, so that loading even their overnight bags was not easy. Jeffrey released John.

Ashok, wearing a kurta, loose pants, and sandals, jumped out. "I have to bring presents," he explained about the jammed back. "Hope it's not too crowded for you."

John squeezed himself uncomfortably into the backseat, his face out the window for air, permitting Jeffrey to sit up front. They drove off into the full slam of Mumbai congestion, which Ashok took fairly calmly, although sometimes he looked ready to burn.

"Did you see that!" he said about a big truck driver who almost killed them. "Idiots! Any idiot can drive a truck in India!"

"Any idiot can drive anything," Jeffrey moaned queasily from stress. He wanted to hit the real countryside, but this seemed to take forever as the packed, miserable, charmless outskirts of Mumbai only bred more packed, miserable, charmless outskirts. After enough of this punishment, Ashok stopped at a service station, where Jeffrey had a cold Coke. He drank it slowly and very gratefully.

"How are you feeling?" Ashok asked as a man pumped gas for them. Ashok paid with a credit card, then tipped the attendant.

Jeffrey only nodded, then decided a trip to the bathroom was in order. It was in the back of the station, and so filthy and foul-smelling that on entering it he thought he'd throw up. A water bucket was provided for "hygiene," with tattered pieces of bleached newsprint nearby. The toilet was a hole in the floor; there was no way he could use it. He left and found a spigot and hose outside, and after throwing some water on his face, convinced himself he'd feel better soon.

The last outskirts of the city were not so bad. People had small gardens and the poverty did not hit you quite so flat in the face. There were beat-up cars, faded signs and billboards for Bollywood extravaganzas and American products, cheap shops and American-style greasy fast food. Neighbors gossiped on the streets with half-naked children playing around them and older kids in school uniforms walking by. Jeffrey felt that he could have been on the decaying edges of numerous American cities holding on to shreds of dignity.

Except that people dressed differently and the Indian women, their faces covered or elaborately painted, watched them, their piercing eyes landing squarely on Jeffrey.

Then the country quietly overcame them; the road more pebbly, the air dryer after Mumbai's dense coastal humidity, with great rolling vistas of bluish brown and scrubby hills in the faraway distance. They were hungry and stopped at a grocery and snack shop that stood alone, a tin-roofed hut. The eager owner spoke rapid sing-song English while his wife, in a dusty red sari, said nothing. Ashok went through the short aisles and told them what to buy.

"You have to be careful! Even I get stomach problems out here sometimes."

He suggested boiled eggs, bananas, Indian tea biscuits, and soft drinks. They stood by the car, eating. Ashok noticed John picking up his egg with his left hand.

"You must always eat with your right hand," he said, and John switched, clumsily dropping some egg.

"This is not easy," John, who was left-handed, said as he practiced eating with his right. "How much further to go?"

"Only a short way," Ashok answered. "Maybe four or five hours." He laughed. "In India, that's short!"

They got back in the car, with Jeffrey in the back this time. They passed by several villages, saw signs for Internet cafes and almost-naked young men using cell phones, boys leading groups of cattle, and women with blue and yellow designs on their faces, crouching in front of houses by braziers with cook fires.

John was fascinated by everything.

"This is India!" he kept exclaiming. "India! *Schöne* India! I wish I could paint it. I should!"

"Yes," Ashok said, smiling openly. "You should stay here and paint. Really, I'm sure you'd do some lovely work. The whole country is beautiful!"

"But I brought no paints with me," John complained.

"It's O.K. Paint in India is very easy to get."

After several hours they slowed down by a river, where a large gathering of people walked in slow procession. Ashok stopped the car.

"What is it?" John asked Ashok.

"A cremation. They're bringing the body back to be released into the water."

"Released?" John asked, his mouth dropping open when he saw the corpse wrapped in a simple white cloth, leaving the tips of several dark, shriveled toes exposed. "That's awful. Don't people wash in it?"

"It's only ashes, the current takes it away. Along the sacred Ganges, they do cremations all the time. Here, too. It's part of the cycle of life, really very beautiful. Want to watch? We'll get out, but not too close."

"I don't know," John said. "This is very strange."

But Jeffrey decided he did want to see it; at least some of it.

They got out. A load of wood had been brought to the top step of a ghat. The body was placed on the wood, and smaller pieces carefully arranged over it. A priest chanted, then using a firebrand set the wood to torch. John averted his eyes, but Jeffrey could not keep his eyes from it. The white covering flared up, and they could see the still features of the man under it. Jeffrey was stunned by the coarse simplicity of it, feeling an elemental, quirky union with this ceremonial event marking the end of a life. His own life would go on and on, ever further until it unraveled beyond his control, exactly the way the shroud did. One sudden burst and it was gone, leaving the deceased naked, burning.

Jeffrey stared, warmed by the heat, then felt a funny dropping in his stomach, as if this fleeting exposure to death had taken some piece of him and he were now hollow inside, not really there.

"When it's over," Ashok explained softly, "the man's son will take the ashes and mix them about. If the skull is not reduced to ash completely, he will crush it down. Then they will push everything into the water, and leave."

"I don't want to see that," John protested. "I think I'm going to be sick."

"Then we'd better go!" Ashok said. "I'm sorry this has upset you, my friend. I genuinely am."

John turned from the river, and quietly they walked back to the car and drove off. Jeffrey put some of the boxes and bags on his lap so John could stretch out in back, with the windows open. The charred smell hung in the air, and Jeffrey was glad when they were away from it.

"Are you feeling better?" Jeffrey looked back and asked.

"*Ja.* I don't know why I feel so *schlecht.* Perhaps I wasn't ready to know death on such a nice day. It's sad, looking at death like that. I don't know why—"

"It's O.K., John," Ashok said. "In the West nobody likes to look at death. No 'Escape' in it, that's for certain. You can't sell it, so the system hates death. Right, Jeffrey?"

Jeffrey ignored the question. He hated it, and hated Ashok's amateurish method of putting him on the spot. He looked out the window, then at John, who was getting a bit more warmth into his normally pale face.

But ten seconds later, Jeffrey uncontrollably exploded.

"Is this your 'Metaphysical' analysis, Ashok? Death's such a nice ol' thing, so we should all embrace it? I guess you've never dealt with violent deaths, the deaths of kids, or men who suddenly don't come back? Screaming, crying, and—"

Ashok's fingers tightened on the wheel.

"Come on, Jeffrey!" Ashok protested, trying to put on his best game face, though it was difficult. "You know the system thinks death's just for losers. Even here nobody's saying it's a day at the beach, but we don't feel it's only for the creeps who don't get to make it. We don't have Suspension yet in India, like you do. Here, death's part of the cycle. Part of the Great River itself. Maybe," his face softened, he was now on firmer land, "that's why we love our rivers so much."

❦

They arrived at Ashok's village around seven that evening. It was pleasant, full of trees, and surprisingly prosperous looking. They parked in front of an impressive wooden house with a stone and concrete foundation, two floors, and a courtyard in the back. His father came out to meet them.

"Shokie!" his father cried. A short but distinguished elderly man with snow white hair and an almost wrinkleless face, he had fine features and a thin mouth that rippled easily into a smile. "These are your friends!"

Ashok got out and his father embraced him, then Ashok introduced them to Neji Rahman, a retired mathematician and physicist. Several servants came to carry the bags and boxes, and they followed John, Jeffrey, Mr. Rahman, and Ashok into the house.

"This is my father's study," Ashok said proudly at the door of a spacious but very neat room furnished with a large desk and monitor, some old laboratory equipment, and tall bookshelves. "This is the parlor, where we gather." It was smaller than the study, but cozy with large tinted family photographs of eminent *sahibs* in stiff jackets and regal-looking turbans and their *begums* in formal saris and pearls looking down from the walls. "Over there's the kitchen, the dining room, a breakfast place that goes out onto the courtyard. Upstairs are bedrooms. You can each have one, because my sister's away. She's married now, but it was her room. My mother's room is still not used; it was her private study. She died ten years ago." He paused, then said, "Anyway, you can each have a room!"

"I am so glad your friends are here," Neji said. "It's nice to have young men in the house. Would you like a drink, or some supper?"

"Supper would be good," John said. "And a drink. I like Indian beer. Do you have any?"

"We have everything," Neji answered. "Beer and cold drinks. I like a cocktail every now and then myself. I studied in London and Chicago. Nice places, but *too* cold. I love this village. It's the family house, but I also keep a small place in Mumbai. Village life is good, but it's the same everywhere: too confining."

He smiled in this innocent, beguiling way, so that Jeffrey had no idea what he was referring to.

Ashok took them upstairs, and showed them their rooms. Jeffrey's was large, overlooking the front of the house, and John's, smaller, was in back. It seemed that John's room was more of a servant's room.

Jeffrey offered to change rooms with him.

"No!" Ashok insisted. "You should have the big room. It's only right. After all, you're my boss!"

Jeffrey shrugged and they went downstairs, where Neji had drinks and a light supper ready for them. The food was vegetarian and nicely prepared, with homemade flatbreads, vegetable kofta, assorted pickles, dahl, and a cooked pudding for dessert. John drank beer, and Jeffrey had some tea. He felt tired, but wanted to go for a walk, to stretch his legs and also to have some time alone with John, but Ashok insisted on joining them.

"It's too easy to get lost, and there are animals around."

John asked what kind of animals.

"Wild dogs. Wolves. We used to have tigers, but they're all gone."

They took flashlights. The village was quiet and dark. Part of a river was nearby, and they walked along it.

"Is this the same river where the cremation was before?" John asked.

"No, but it's always the same river, one way or another." Ashok laughed. "The cremation really bothered you, John. Why? You don't seem like the kind of man to be so bothered by something like that."

John became serious. "There are a lot of things I don't look like. I'm afraid I wasn't ready to see it. Stupid of me, wasn't it?"

"No," Ashok answered patiently. "It's not stupid. It's just India doesn't let you become ready. It throws a lot of stuff at you. So does America. It just throws different stuff, that's all."

"And Germany? Europe? What stuff does it throw?" John asked suddenly belligerent. Jeffrey, enjoying the quiet, simply listened to the sound of their voices and some dogs—or were they wolves?—howling in the distance.

"Oh, John!" said Ashok. "They only throw what's been thrown at them, and then tell everybody how smart they are! How's that for an answer?"

Ashok laughed again.

"Sometimes I think you're laughing at me," John said.

Ashok put his hands on John's shoulder, and drew him closer.

"Not at all. I'm laughing at myself!"

Jeffrey looked at the river. "Do people swim here?"

"Oh, yes. They bathe here a lot. We can do that if you'd like. There's a wonderful temple in the woods, not too far away. It's old, but still used. John asked about *sadhus,* holy men. They are there. You'll find them fascinating, too. We'll go tomorrow, after lunch."

Jeffrey looked at Ashok. "That sounds good. I'll take pictures."

"You can. But don't take pictures inside. It's not allowed, and only tourists try to do it. Everything's very phallic, like those old Tom of Finland pictures; Shiva, you know. The lingam is one of his big symbols." Ashok winked. " But you'll find some interesting pictures and statues. My father first took me there when I was a kid. He said, 'The world is not like this, but the inner world is. And that is the real world.' My father's so smart. Sometimes much smarter than even I want to know."

Jeffrey nodded, realizing that it would be harder than he had hoped to figure Ashok out.

They went back to the house, and Jeffrey used a small bathroom to prepare for bed. Despite the long drive he felt suddenly relaxed and peaceful. There was something about being out in the country, no matter where, that made him feel happy: simply the air, the quiet, and the faint, distant noises like those he eerily remembered from railroads and cows in Alabama.

He'd been a kid in the country there, another world ago: part of those forbidden Previous Influences he was not supposed to carry with him, counter to the life-changing PICE ordeal he had been chosen for, which he had passed for the most part because he wanted to. That was his own bitter secret, and he had voluntarily jettisoned his past to keep it. Now, without warning, here in the haunting nocturnal quiet of India he felt free enough to revert to that primal human instinct to recall the long-ago past.

Things were only starting to happen then in America. The great cities had not become privately secured, smaller walled towns. Cars still ran mostly on gasoline, and information wasn't so controlled that it didn't come basically from one source. The huge, hardly spoken of, wrenching transitions hadn't begun yet. The system wasn't in almost complete control throughout the world. Neither of his parents had been particularly devout Christians; they even had a few gay friends who worked in the local shops or in medicine. One was a nurse, another a veterinarian. The concept of gay marriage was still ludicrous to them, something they could hardly imagine.

His father asked, "Why would a man *want* to marry another man? You could just as soon marry a horse!"

Jeffrey was nine, and already felt something alien inside, something about boys: their incandescent smiles; their warm, tremulously touchable skin; that yearning like a tiny planet approaching some hidden sun. He could feel it inside him, despite everything that forbade it. In summer, his parents would drive him to the country, where his pretty mom's family came from a town that never changed. A few stoplights, stores, a small white wooden church, the longed-for shade of a woodsy picnic area by a stream. Everybody talking so hillbillyish, he could barely understand them.

But Grandma adored him. They would shell peas together on the front porch, and listen to the moon.

"If you be real quiet, you'll sure 'nuff hear it. Jes' lissen," she'd say, pointing one of her wrinkled fingers up at it.

He was convinced the moon was talking to him in the fiddling sounds of crickets and cicadas, the buzzing of flies, the whisper of the wind. After a storm, the bullfrogs made their belching-and-popping sound. He knew they were not the voice of the moon, but loved listening anyway.

"Jeffy is th'nicest boy in th'whole world!"

Grandma patted his sandy-colored hair with her thick fingers, and waddled. She was country fat, unlike his mother who had gone to the university in Birmingham and zealously guarded her weight, trying to look like the models in fashion magazines. She was a style person, attuned to the captivating look and feeling of things. But there was captivity in it as well. Style, once it captured you, wouldn't let go. And it never offered what Grandma did.

Love. The big, protective, infinite lap of love. Simple and basic, which you could not explain and which was not there to be questioned either.

Jeffrey did not think about Grandma often, but now in the foreign freedom of India, her wrinkled face and the way she smiled and touched him came back to him. He lay down in his room on the cotton bed covers. The room was attractive, painted with a thick, sun-drenched Indian yellow you could only find there, with thin white muslin drapes and a small shelf of dolls left by Ashok's sister.

He gazed around him, trying to penetrate the story of the room. He always believed that every room contained a story, something not to be duplicated. Yet when we left them, the stories disappeared with us, especially in the case of featureless rooms like hotels on a high-way. Their stories were mostly about people forgetting being there, and leaving.

This room, he could tell, had a story of its own, and he liked it. He thought about reading, then switched off the lamp and watched some bean-shaped phantom illuminations from the street outside sneak their immaterial selves in. A breeze fingered aside the drapes, streaking the night-dulled yellow of the walls with a brazen flash of light. He was sure he could hear the yellow hiss in reaction to this cold exposure to reality. It was a noise like the moon made, remind-ing him of Grandma's revelation that all things made a sound if only you were still enough to hear it.

He waited to hear another sound: John's knock on the door, dressed only in a towel. He wanted that very much.

Finally he got up, put on a T-shirt and shorts, and went to John's room.

The door was closed. He knocked; John answered.

Ashok was inside. "I'm telling your friend about India. Why he should stay!"

"Are you?" Jeffrey squinted. "Why should he?"

"I think it is more like his kind of person than Germany."

John shrugged. They were both dressed, but John looked flushed with embarrassment.

"I keep telling him, Jeffrey. I'm not German. I'm Dutch."

"It's all the same, the West. Here, it's different."

"How?" Jeffrey asked.

"You'll see tomorrow!"

Ashok smiled coyly, and after wishing them a good night, left.

"Do you want to stay in India?" Jeffrey asked John.

"No. But I feel something about Ashok, I don't know why. Just a—"

"*Metaphysical* thing?"

"Yes, that's it."

"It's easy. He's taken with you."

"You think that's it?"

"Some of it has to do with me. He wants to be me, which of course means taking you."

John smiled sincerely.

"You think so? I don't get that feeling at all."

"Of course, you don't. But I know something about the Indians. They can be charming, but they don't let on what they're all about. Except when they do, and then—"

"Then what?"

Jeffrey looked straight at him without smiling. "Watch out."

"Isn't most of the world like that? Would you rather sleep here with me, or should I sleep with you?"

"Yes, most of the world is like that. And yes again: I would rather sleep *here* with you. Or sleep *there* with you. Come to think of it, how about there? The bed's bigger."

❧

For some kind of decorum, whose exact nature he wasn't sure of, Jeffrey woke John before daybreak, so the tall Dutchman could return groggily to his room. Ashok knocked on the door an hour later, to ask what he would prefer for breakfast. He walked into Jeffrey's room, as Jeffrey squinted at him.

"Coffee, Jeffrey, or tea? Eggs or porridge?'

"Tea. Porridge."

"Good! That's what I have. Did you sleep well?"

"Uh-huh."

"Sometimes we get noises from the street. Did they wake you up?"

Jeffrey was hardly in the mood to answer. "Nuh-uh," was all he could get out.

"Good! I'll see you downstairs for breakfast."

Jeffrey wondered why Ashok was waking him up this way, then realized it was probably to see if John were there. He closed his eyes and tried to relax. A cold edge of tension came over him; he hated it. Why couldn't he just dispense with it, shoo it away, like a fly in Alabama? But he couldn't. He wanted to be wrapped in John's arms again, to hold him. He didn't care what John was. He didn't care about his past, which seemed as useless to him as Jeffrey's past in Alabama. He was a long way from Alabama, a long, long way. It might as well have been a thousand years ago. He could dispense with that. Still, like some unbidden ghost, he could not help but wonder what Ashok had really said to John in John's room before he interrupted them. The question floated in the Indian–yellow air above him, winking at him.

And it said: "However this question is answered, Jeffrey, watch out."

Chapter Twelve

*I*t became very warm in the early afternoon, and the sky was thickening, but not dark yet. They drove several miles toward the temple, into a forest Ashok told them had once been a royal reserve.

"That's why it was protected. The pasha preserved it, then the British did, and now it's government land for the most part. There've been tigers here, but they are mostly gone. Every once in a while, one is seen. But too many people live close by, so they've killed them all off. It's sad, but being eaten by a tiger is no holiday, believe me!"

A short way from the temple, he slowed the car, then parked it in a small cleared space off the road. They got out and walked down a footpath that at places became almost lost in the feathery closeness of the trees that canopied much of the sky. They crossed a rough wooden bridge over a brook, then the temple appeared in the distance.

At first it was only a pile of ancient weathered stones, then other details emerged: heavy, smoke-darkened wooden gates creaking ajar as if entering a dream. Stunning, action-filled reliefs turning blatantly sexual, with lingams everywhere repeating, even in the tops of blackened stone arches. As they passed through the gates, Jeffrey gazed at everything, trying to absorb every figure and the colors worn by ages of weather, thickly layered in blistering paint. He wanted to look deeper and took out his camera, but Ashok urged them to come farther inside.

The sadhus were there, dressed in sarongs or loincloths; one especially striking was in even less, hardly more than a strip around his genitals, his lean body coated in gray ash, his hair stone-white, both from nature and a powdering of ash.

John grinned at Ashok and Jeffrey. "This is really India!" he said, his voice almost cracking from excitement.

"Yes," Ashok said. "It is India. Do you like it?"

"I love it. I wish I could be as naked as this man is."

Ashok frowned. "You should not. It's not pukka, John. They can do it; it's part of their vow, their life. I need to give them an offering."

He took some bills from his pocket and handed them to a large man whose stomach spilled over his sarong. The man, palms together, made a blessing toward them. He said something in Sanskrit, and Ashok uttered something back. He then said something in Hindi.

Jeffrey asked him what he had said.

"I thanked him for the blessing, and asked if we can go inside, make an offering of prayer on the altar, and then leave."

"Can we?" John asked.

Ashok nodded, and the holy men, five of them, walked with them into the temple. It was much darker inside, but there were numerous small oil lamps and the fragrance of flowers, sandlewood, and burning oil.

"Who is this temple to?" Jeffrey asked.

"It is now to Shiva as Nataraj, the Lord of the Dance. It's been here for so long that the gods sometimes change, but the temple remains. All the gods are manifestations of Brahma, which is all we can know of life. I think what you find here you cannot really talk about. It is part of life's Metaphysics. The unseen, the truth."

Ashok bowed his head, then touched three fingers to John's forehead. John smiled, and took Jeffrey's hand in his.

"I like it here!" John exclaimed. "I do! I do!"

"Good," Ashok said, lowering his voice and smiling into Jeffrey's eyes. "I hope Jeffrey will like it, and he'll allow himself to be taken by it."

Jeffrey did not answer, but merely contented himself to look.

There were paintings, old and peeling, near the altar, on the stone walls or screens of wood. The figures were hard to understand, but the atmosphere, with the holy men chanting, making gestures of blessing and doing what seemed like a dance watched by the thin, almost naked, ash-covered sadhu, was so totally at peace that Jeffrey quickly found himself lost. Which seemed a strange contradiction: "finding himself" and "lost."

In truth he had stopped looking critically at everything, stopped seeing solely with his eyes, stopped being what he was: Wary, picture-snapping tourist. Mega-stylist. Representative of the global system whose decisions put nations to work, that produced things sold throughout the world; that actually kept the world moving.

He allowed himself to close his eyes.

Without even attempting it, Jeffrey found himself entering that mist, that bloom of his deepest, most intimate self that Tony had tried to place him in, if only to preserve him from the stress that might kill him. Time, measured purely in stress, *would* kill him, as it did everyone; but he had been so good at outracing it. Now it stopped: simply peeling itself away from his efforts, the way the thick paint on the walls and the figures was peeling, revealing layer upon layer of vast, wonderful, timeless quiet with chanting at its edges. And there he was: gorgeously, timelessly, truly young, trembling with the endless promise of something about to fill him, even create him: his *real* self, a self he could feel as truly as he could feel . . . what?

Oddly, nothing.

Yet he was not falling, drowning or blind. He was not even simply, physically, happy. But this insane, separate blissfulness that bypassed fear and events and came from deep within him filled him, even as he could hear the chanting get louder, roaring in from the edges of his calm like the river cleansing itself of ashes.

After what seemed an impossible amount of time, he opened his eyes.

One of the holy men stood before him, placing a garland around his neck, then placing the two first fingers of a hand on Jeffrey's forehead, slightly above his nose.

He smiled at Jeffrey, a wry, inviting smile, and Jeffrey, the old Jeffrey, returning much against his will, wondered bitterly: "Does he know everything? How old I am really, and what I have to do to stay this way?"

Ashok approached.

"He wants you to stay here with him for a moment," he announced. "He wants to pray with you. Do *satsang.* Will you?"

Jeffrey nodded and bowed his head. He distinctly heard the priest chanting with a voice that sounded almost comical. Then he looked around, trying to see John. At first he thought John was lost among the numerous columns and areas of the temple. But he wasn't there. He asked Ashok where John had gone.

"He left suddenly. But it's O.K. Just stay here. I'll find him."

"You'll—" Jeffrey tried to form a question, but it became difficult. Noises flooded in, chanting louder and louder, drums and tinkling bells. And thunder outside. Jeffrey could hear it crashing, its stormy *boom* smashing any remnants of enchantment left in the temple. That exquisite mist, that bloom of his wondrous, deepest self, ripped open, producing in its tatters only panic.

He was wordless; then the words blew out of him.

"*You'll* find him? *Where?* Where *is* he?"

"Don't worry, I'll find him. I want to find John."

"No!"

Jeffrey raced out of the dark into pouring, wind-lashed rain. All the holy men had gathered under the protective eaves of the roof, except for the almost naked thin man covered in ash.

"Where is John??" Jeffrey screamed once more to Ashok. "I've got to find him! There's something about being here that's upset him!"

Ashok tried to put his hands on Jeffrey's shoulders, but Jeffrey jerked away.

"Jeffrey, my dear, he's fine. He loves India. He loved being here at the temple. You saw how excited he was."

Jeffrey lost his composure, his resolve to float over this, and screamed, jumping at Ashok, his voice shrill to the breaking point.

"You don't know what he's like! You have no idea! Even I DON'T! God help me!"

Ashok smiled that wry, knowing, bittersweet smile he did so well.

"I know you need to find him; we both do. That's what I love about him, Jeffrey. He's that 'Escape' we all want. There's this need inside both of us, with John waiting just outside it. You want him, sure. But I do, too. And I think he understands that."

Jeffrey stared at him. He wanted to slap Ashok, but that was impossible; too much of the system held him back. Ashok's smile was so set, so revoltingly condescending, with all of India on his side. Jeffrey hated it. He was sick of it.

"He's crazy about India, Jeffrey. Believe me."

Jeffrey said nothing. He leaned against an ancient, blackened gallery of columns, to regain his breath. The stones were thickly carved with entwining arms, breasts, buttocks, and thighs. Most of it had eroded, with the rain-slickened paint peeling off. Some of the wet color got on his clothes.

He had to find John. His eyes returned to Ashok, who was still smiling.

"Maybe we should go back to the car. Maybe he's there."

"No," Ashok assured him. "He's not. I know where he is."

"Then take me, goddamn it!"

Ashok shrugged, as if out of patience but not at all offended.

"All right."

He led Jeffrey through the front gate of the temple, and they treaded along a soggy path into the woods.

"In the past they had animals here," Ashok said. "I hope none are around."

"Tigers?"

"No. I told you there are no tigers. More like wild dogs, but they can get nasty, attacking cows and people. John's with that yogi, the man in ashes. They went out together. I saw them."

"And you just let them?"

"Jeffrey, he's a grown man. He wanted to go. I imagine they're in the sadhu's hut. I know a bit about him. From what I've heard he enjoys the company of good-looking young men. Some do, you know." He smiled sheepishly. "In India, boy-play is a Ganesh activity, like elephants do. People look aside of it, as long as it does not interfere with family life. So John may be blessed and receiving *darshan* with this man. You know—*darshan*, a vision?"

Jeffrey panicked. "A vision? What kind of vision?"

"God, in some very plain form. Or the deep inner truth of life. *Darshan* is amazing. I've never had it, to be honest with you. Metaphysically, John may be ready for it. I believe he is a real candidate for *darshan*. I only know that when *darshan* comes, you cannot stop it!"

Jeffrey stopped to catch his breath.

"How much further?"

"We're almost there."

"Good!" Jeffrey said, picking up speed again. "We need to hurry."

The rain, which had been torrential, lessened to a steady drizzle. They saw the small hut within a grove of spindly trees. A smell of fresh rain came from it, and also of stale sweat and smoke. Ashok knocked on the door. The sadhu appeared, bowed, and invited them in.

Jeffrey lowered his head and entered. The hut had a dirt floor in the center of which was John, naked, sitting with his legs crossed and his head lowered to his hands.

His face rose to meet Jeffrey.

Jeffrey tried to smile, but there was concern in his voice.

"Are you all right?"

John nodded.

"I don't know how I got here. I had to leave the temple. This man took me here and I took my clothes off and just sat with him. I feel so—" he paused. "Naked. I mean not just without clothes. Naked inside. Why does India make me feel this way?"

"It makes everyone do something, doesn't it?" Ashok said.

John sniffed and swallowed hard. "It's not funny, Ashok."

The sadhu took John's hand, and with his other hand touched John's forehead. He was still in ash, with the strip of dirty cloth around his genitals.

"Can I speak to you alone?" John said to Jeffrey. "Leave us, Ashok, for a moment. Then if you like, I'll spend time with you."

Ashok smiled.

"Your wish is fine. You know I am always here for you."

"Thank you," John said, and Ashok left the hut.

The thin sadhu stayed for a moment, then also left.

Jeffrey squatted next to John on the dirt floor. They did not speak for a while. Then John started crying, sobbing loudly.

Jeffrey took his hand. "What is it?"

"I can't let you know. But—"

"What?" Jeffrey looked at him, holding his hand.

"If I tell you—"

Jeffrey waited. Whatever John would say, he was prepared to accept it.

John released a huge sob, then said, "I murdered my wife."

Jeffrey squeezed John's hand, looking at him, then he released it. He took off the temple garland still around his neck and crushed it, slowing stripping red petals from it.

"We were on a summer holiday. I was going crazy. I simply couldn't be the lie I was supposed to be. Do you know what I mean?"

Jeffrey nodded, then took his hand again.

"She couldn't understand anything about me. And the act, the pretend of it—I just couldn't do it anymore, I swear. It was about six years ago. Our two boys were with their nanny, and we were out at the beach. It was an overcast day, but warm and I said why don't we go in for a short swim? We went out, I took her pretty far with me, and an undertow came. She panicked. I held her down, then pretended almost to drown, myself. I'd been planning it; then the time came and I did it. I am *so* guilty. Even God, whatever God is, knows it."

Jeffrey could not take his eyes off him, no matter what John said. John's eyes closed; tears fell from them.

Jeffrey took his hand away.

"You could not have done anything else?" he asked. He had to know this.

John opened his eyes and looked at him.

"You mean 'escape'? There's no 'Escape,' Jeffrey! It's modern marriage, hell for two. 'Escape' is only in advertising."

Jeffrey felt slapped, but he had to take it. He could not stop loving John.

"And that's why you killed her," he said, stating it as a matter of fact, not an accusation.

"I *had* to. The system had me. It still does and I know it. One false move, and—"

Jeffrey stopped him, kissing him on his mouth.

"Yes, I see. I do see."

John put his hands around Jeffrey's face.

"Good. You see me as no one else has. I love you for that."

Jeffrey nodded mutely. Later he would wonder what did that mean, "I love you for that"? Now, all he could say was:

"You had to live with this?"

John lowered his head, without answering.

"God, I feel bad for you, John. I do."

John started to choke. Jeffrey was afraid he'd throw up, just from the release of feeling. Then John composed himself.

"I need freedom," John said. "I'm trapped in my terrible need for it. I need it as much as I need you."

Jeffrey stroked his hand and the reddish hairs above it, then brought it to his lips.

"I'll give you that, that freedom you want."

"You will?"

"Yes. As much as I can."

John attempted to smile. Jeffrey touched John's lips which were stiff and unyielding, feeling terrible for John's wife and for John, and for all the terrible things the two of them must have done to each other. But he had betrayed many people himself; it was part of the system. He'd even betrayed himself, erasing himself until the only left thing was this figurehead of sales and production. The light rain outside flashed him back to Alabama: being young, ambitious, and queer there, with everything he'd ever wanted and with so much constant work attained, getting thrown back, stinking, in his face.

He winced hard at the thought of that, turning his face from John. John squeezed his hand, and Jeffrey returned his eyes to him.

"You must be revolted by me," John said bitterly.

"No." Jeffrey whispered. "It's just—you have something horrible to live with. I couldn't live with that. I would do anything to forget it."

"I'm sure you would. Do you hate me?"

"No. I love you like you're my own skin. Maybe even more."

"You should not, Jeffrey. Not after what you've heard. I warn you, I don't believe you should even trust me."

Jeffrey lowered his eyes. He was not used to this kind of stark honesty. Perhaps John was right, he shouldn't love him that way. The stress alone would surely kill him. Tony had tried to warn him.

"All right then," Jeffrey admitted. "Do you want to stay here in India? Ashok would like that; he'd take care of it. Something tells me he wants to do something with you that he can't do with anyone else."

"Like be alive, really?"

Jeffrey nodded.

"I know," John said. "He's got something for me, I can tell. He can offer me India, but I don't know how good that is. I'm not sure I want my demons out all the time, and I think they come out here even worse than in Germany."

"You may be right," Jeffrey whispered. "Even the demons here seem to have games of their own."

John finally smiled and so did Jeffrey, getting up, leaving a mass of petals strewn on the dirt floor. John put his clothes on. It got very hot in the hut as the sun came back full. Ashok and the yogi were outside. The yogi bowed a *puja* to John and Jeffrey, then Ashok gave him another offering of bills and they left.

They had dinner that night with Neji, who was very charming and a good host. There was beer for John; Neji and Ashok had cocktails. Jeffrey only drank an Indian soft drink that tasted like salty lemonade. Neji asked Ashok about his wife, and Ashok talked about her as if they had a close and intimate marriage.

"I love her more and more," Ashok said, "But unfortunately she needs a life of her own. That is the way modern women are!" He smiled. "They can't help themselves. This modern world. It tosses everything up in the air, and then lets it all fall!"

"It does that," Neji agreed, smiling affectionately at his son, then at Jeffrey and John. "I have a hard time keeping up with it. Sometimes I think it doesn't understand people at all. It gives you things to keep you from understanding yourself. Not very terrible things, not very taxing, but not very sustaining, either."

He looked at Jeffrey, who was drinking his lemon pop and trying arduously not to think about John's revelation. Most of his life, he'd been good about the past, dispensing with it, letting it disappear when necessary. Now John had lassoed him with a past that was violent and disruptive, like their meeting on the pubtran platform.

So John was what? A criminal?

Jeffrey shuddered; his skin crawled. He hoped no one noticed it; he had to keep his revulsion to himself, try to stay in control. He hated that feeling of revulsion; it was better not to have any feelings at all. But that option was no longer open to him.

"I think it's good that Ashok works with you in the system," Neji went on, no longer looking at Jeffrey. Jeffrey watched him. It was obvious the old man was staring inward, at his own disappearing hopes and his disappointments. "He is making good things happen. He's smart and likes to have things happen." Neji smiled weakly. "Right, Ashok?"

"Of course, Father. I like to make things happen. To be a part of what's now, and not in the past."

"That is true," Neji agreed, his smile broadening. "The past— India tries to forget it, but cannot always." Neji and Ashok smiled at one another as the servants cleared the table, then Neji suggested that they go outside to the courtyard, where they could sit and look at the moon. "I'd like a smoke, too," Neji said. "I will not smoke in the house with guests here."

"I'm tired," John said. "I think I'd like to go to my room."

Jeffrey looked at him; he could understand the exhaustion. Every part of him wanted to go with John, but he felt he shouldn't. He'd look in on him later, he told himself.

Neji got up and took Jeffrey's arm, leading him toward the garden. Ashok said he'd stay to make sure the dishes were put up well.

"I'll bring you tea later," he said, as Jeffrey and Neji went out.

The moon was beautiful, not quite full, but clear. The garden smelled of jasmine; there were masses of the white, night-blooming flowers. Jeffrey could hear crickets, reminding him again of being back in Alabama.

"I'm glad you are not so American," Neji said once they had settled into ironwork seats with pillows on them. Some of the pillows had little mirrors sewed onto them, catching twinkles from the moon. "I mean, you don't seem to have that attitude that you know everything, and can make all sorts of decisions for other people."

"No, I don't know everything. That's one thing I've learned."

Neji lit an Indian cigarette.

"I hope this doesn't bother you, that I smoke."

"No. We smoked beedis a few nights ago with Ashok."

"Did he smoke other things with it?"

Jeffrey did not want to answer.

"It's all right. Ashok can be wild at times. I know that. I was wild a bit too, in America when I was young. Then I came back to India and I realized that Americans want everyone to be American. They will bring us all democracy, American fast food, their gadgets and whatnots. They make it very hard not to take it. In the East, democracy becomes like a bad joke. Most people don't understand what it means. They think it means that either their wills will be ignored and the wills of other fools listened to, or that they will get their way and others won't. Here family, clan, tribe are everything. People are lost without them."

Jeffrey looked at him, but somehow he had stopped actually listening. Mostly he was looking at Neji's mouth, the way words came out of it, beautifully formed, very deliberate. Neji seemed intelligent, thoughtful, sequestered in his own little world, unlike the more impulsive and ambitious Ashok. Yet there was something deliberate about Ashok, too, and in this deliberation there was something more than simple obstinacy. It was the potential for power and advancement, which attracted Jeffrey, if truth be known.

Neji smiled, as if he were opening some great intimacy to Jeffrey.

"Here you don't need secrets. You have family! The family is always a secret, a mystery. Freud knew that! It makes no difference where you are from; do you think anyone can ever really escape it?"

Jeffrey said nothing, then realized he'd been asked a question and shook his head slightly.

"Escape what, sir?"

"The family, Jeffrey! The family?"

"Ah." What a hard question. "If only . . ."

"But why would you want to? All my science, when I was younger, told me that the answers don't necessarily bring you happiness. Ashok, difficult as he is, does that for me—I am very happy with him. He is a wonderful son, and I'm glad he is close enough for me to see him."

"Yes," Jeffrey said blandly. "That's good."

He looked around at Neji's softly scented night garden and felt the dark descend on him so delicately that he forgot for a moment about John, in his room, going through something he would not know how to share. Neji started talking about democracy again, blathering like an old man, even though he and Jeffrey were probably the same age, give or take a year.

"In America they talk a lot of about the equality of humans, but I think—"

Jeffrey was not listening, only nodding. He was too young to listen. That was his problem, he was always young. Once he hit sixty-five, still feeling and looking like a young man hardly more than thirty, he had cut himself off from most of the entanglements of other people. His inner life was like a fisherman's very loose net, pulling in almost nothing, letting go of as much as he could. No personal intricacies or beliefs; no heavy intimacies. Personally, he traveled lighter and lighter each year, with nothing wearing on him except his own place within the system. Here he was, this kid—O.K., old man—from Alabama who'd lived in New York, Chicago, San Francisco, Los Angeles, Hong Kong, and now Germany, though most of it seemed numbingly the same. The same people rushing about, doing business, signaling their importance among themselves no matter what they looked like or where they came from. Some had spouses, children, partners, even long affairs. But he? He had been a monk, and the religion he served . . . he did not want to think about that.

"Democracy is really only a front for others things that go on," Neji said, waving a twiggish wrist holding his now-dead cigarette. "The truth is, it has its own caste system, like everybody else. And they'll do anything to keep it going."

Jeffrey blinked a few times, trying to pick up some lint from Neji's thoughts.

"Anything?" he asked.

"Yes, my friend. Anything. Like I said, it's all just a front for the other things that go on."

"What other things, Neji?"

Neji relit his cigarette. Smoke rose from it; a small group of gnats flitted within its pale gray cloud, catching light.

"Yes, Jeffrey, that *is* a question."

He exhaled, appearing stark white in the moonlight.

Jeffrey looked at him. "What does go on?"

Then he saw John's face again, that instant on the pubtran, punching him.

Neji tried to concentrate his thoughts.

"History. It's about history, frankly. What they call 'democracy' tries to hide it, to make it all go away. Americans think that I am like them, with only a little more color in my face. They'll bring us more things to buy, and we'll buy them and become even more like them. I think even Ashok believes that, though not deep inside. The truth is, we still have some real private life here, and real history, even if you can't see it. All of India has. We can touch it. Smell it. Eat it! Though it's getting harder to find, I know."

Jeffrey nodded mutely. He was all right until the word "history" came up. The damn word seemed to sit there, mocking, gloating at him as if Jeffrey were playing pickup street basketball clumsily and the word itself were some uncouth jerk standing on the sidelines, heckling him:

"*History, baby! Dig it? You ain't got none! Y'gave it up!*"

Instead, he had a great PICE score.

Jeffrey shook his head. To have a real history, something had to penetrate him. He didn't want history; he wanted style. And style— static, ruthless, and yet fickle as it was—was pretty blank in this conversation. To rely on it would only reveal the shallowness of the cards in Jeffrey's hand. All Beau Brummell jacks, maybe. Nothing durable, powerful, uncontainably wild. John had that, and it attracted Jeffrey. No other ways about it.

Neji gazed at him, as if expecting a comment. But Jeffrey could come up with nothing. He couldn't even get angry at the old man, the way he did at Ashok, who was so good at these little "Metaphysical" games, greatly annoying Jeffrey.

"Do you see what I'm saying, Jeffrey?"

"Yes," Jeffrey finally said, after some silence, gazing at Neji's unnaturally smooth face, wondering what his secret was to looking this way. Any useful grip he had on Neji's concepts—a good term, very sales oriented ("And what is your *new* concept?")—seemed too shallow, if not moronic, to expose then. Jeffrey could come up with acres of the right words, but he was usually lost when it came down to any intelligence outside his own specialty. And "History," something that could start vast multitudes of people galloping brainlessly in horrifying directions, as it had in the twentieth century, was not inside his specialty.

Images, files and more files of them, were. Suddenly several very incriminating ones fell on him like a dislodged house, all depicting his Dutch friend. John's naked vulnerability and rage. His crimes. The images were there, but like all pictures, they gave Jeffrey little information about how to deal with them. Feelings, real ones, were necessary for that. Maybe that was why John had chosen him: knowing instinctively that Jeffrey had given up real feelings to keep on living. John was *instinct*, passion; Ashok, very old games for a young man, and cunning; while Neji—he only *seemed* to know so much.

Jeffrey could tell that was true, looking into Neji's smooth face and his eyes with their placid, clear moon whites and great, contrasting darkness.

"I'm sorry, "Neji said, sincerely, "I've been so much in the realms of the abstract. Personally, I dealt with precise things. The mathematical, the physical. The biological sciences seemed too disordered for me. They lacked the mystery of numbers, precise symbols, physics. As for psychology? It's impossible, if not often ridiculous! Still, I'm happy that Ashok's doing what he's doing. Making things happen. With all my heart I hope he gets what he wants."

Jeffrey watched a trail of moonlight reflect in the little mirrors.

"Wants?" he asked, his eyes narrowing.

"Yes. I hope he gets that. It seems even now foreign to me, but I hope he gets it."

Neji blew out some smoke. Jeffrey cleared his throat; now he could say something concrete and precise enough even for the old man:

"Then he'll have to learn how to ask for it, Neji. Instead of expecting others to figure out what he wants. Which is what he seems to be doing at this moment."

"Yes. Precisely. I'm sure you are right. That does seem to be *the* American way, after all."

"Or the world way," Jeffrey said, getting up. He wondered where Ashok was, and why there was no tea. "Maybe I should look after the tea," he suggested.

"A good idea! See if the servants have it."

Jeffrey went back into the kitchen, but no one was there. Then he went to John's room and knocked on the door. It was quiet, but he could hear breathing. He wondered if John were all right. He knocked again.

John cracked open the door slightly.

It was dark, but John obviously was naked.

"It's all right," Ashok said loudly. "He should know."

Know *what?* Jeffrey wondered, but couldn't say it.

"Shut up!" John ordered, and shut the door.

Chapter Thirteen

*J*effrey staggered back to his room, feeling old, out of his depth, stupid, and stressed again. There was too much here to understand, and nothing he could put into his customary categories of files and styles. Files and styles were easy, no matter how difficult the money pricks could be. But something definitely "Metaphysical" was going on, and now Ashok was using his own seductive, sexual nature as a way of speeding the game ahead. He had played Jeffrey for a fool, getting him into the garden with Neji, knowing he would prattle on, giving Ashok an opportunity for a brief but compromising interlude with John.

Lying in bed, Jeffrey tried to work it out as some kind of schematic flow chart. He had gone to India with John, in order to give himself more time with him, away from Germany and the dead-eye range of the system. He'd also come to deal with Ashok, thinking that with proximity and with some possibility of real "honesty," Ashok might perhaps turn into a genuine ally, if there were such a thing in this world.

"'Metaphysics,'" he remembered Ashok saying, "puts a face on the cards. If you can't read the cards, you can't play the game. You're out of it, but the game goes on anyway."

So he had positioned Ashok and John to play with one another. And by going to India, had fallen into this trap. John, he feared, was a trap, too, though he found him indispensable to his life now, his real life. Before John, his only "real" life had been with Tony. Every week he'd try to construct some kind of simulation of a private life, a life of the soul and of the moment, with his therapist. But Jeffrey knew that his particular "real" life had to be very limited; or else, as the price of not aging in the hands of the system, he would end up dead.

"Private" life: it seemed a bitter joke to him. Ages ago, a few men, their physical appeal, their personalities, had penetrated him (one way or another), tossing him around like a beach ball in a storm. Then their time was over.

"Over." "Lover."

The "L" standing between the two words loomed significantly. How could someone carrying so many secrets of the system have a private life? Hardly anyone had one anymore; and now John had opened up this once tightly closed door, nudging Jeffrey into that very "mist" of himself that Tony had encouraged him to enter: that blissful, dew-soaked, promised environment easing all stress, but which, quickly enough, could just as well be sealed into some transparent, perfectly closed bubble of self-containment. That once lovely mist now felt like blood sprayed directly into his face.

There was a knock on his closed door. It opened.

John, freshly showered, came in wearing shorts and rubber sandals. He got onto the bed with Jeffrey and kissed him.

Jeffrey turned away, feeling encased in steel. He made himself say it:

"What do you want?"

"That man's crazy! *Verukt!*" John exploded. "Gibbering his 'Metaphysical' *scheisse*—all this was 'meant to be!' He yanked my clothes off."

"*Yanked?*" Jeffrey's eyebrows rose; his eyes met John's. "Come on! I think he *yanked* something, but it wasn't your clothes."

"O.K. We had some cocaine. I admit it. It helped. Too much is going on here in India. They mix it all up too fast. Death. Sex. The world above and below. I've met my own demons here, and they all have paint on their faces, mixed with ash."

"Interesting image. Right out of that temple and the man in the hut. Tell me, do you want to stay in India?"

"No," John declared flatly. "Ashok wanted to go to bed with me, so I did. India is charming, but I can't stay here. It's not something I can do."

"Yes," Jeffrey agreed slowly. "The charms here are real, though complicated. Nonetheless, Ashok can offer you a lot. He's ambitious and much smarter than he appears. Believe me, you won't have to go back."

John looked puzzled. Something was gumming up his mind; the question was how to flush it out.

"It seems like you have to think about it, John."

"No, I don't!" John answered. "It's O.K. here, Jeffrey, I know it. But I'm not free here, simple as that. Not like I am with you. Ashok would fuck me until my brains fell out. But nothing about you is like that, even when we do it."

"I make you feel free?"

Jeffrey smiled. It was hard for him to believe that he, such a part of the system, could make anyone feel free. But it must be so: that John had seen something in Jeffrey that he knew would allow him to tell the truth. "But you make *me* feel free."

"I'm glad." Now John was all over him, holding him, kissing him, releasing all of his feelings to Jeffrey. "Ashok would only want to control me. He'd make me some kind of—"

"Amusement?"

John bolted up.

"That's it: an amusement! He laughs at us. That strange, wicked smile of his, that—"

Jeffrey watched John's eyes. They were frantic looking.

"He scares you, doesn't he?"

"Yes. I'm scared."

"Because of Ashok? Why?"

"Because I can't hide anything here, and I think Ashok knows that. He's impulsive. He'll use anything he can dig up to control me. You won't."

Jeffrey didn't want to ask this, but he did; he knew that if he didn't, he would always wonder.

"Are you in love with Ashok?"

John put his face in his hands.

"No, but I feel helpless with him. He's very—he manipulates me. He—"

"Does he know about your wife?"

"I haven't told him. Maybe I should, just to scare him. I've scared you, haven't I? You'll always look at me like I'm a murderer. I saw it right after I told you, when you turned away from me. But that's my own *geschichte*, my past, my story."

Jeffrey drew closer to him. He was enraptured with John, and relieved to know that if John were in love with Ashok, at least his Dutch friend had not figured it out.

"The past means nothing to me," Jeffrey confessed. "Yours or mine. I was only looking at my past when you told me. And it hurt."

"Then you'll forgive me?" John asked, his voice straining with shame.

"I love you," Jeffrey said, kissing John's hands, then his face. "I'll accept your past, whatever of it you want to give me. And I won't demand that you give me any part of it you don't want to. I mean that."

John looked up, his face aglow like a powerful light had been turned on behind it.

"Thank you, my friend. My real friend."

Jeffrey nodded.

"Maybe it's the most I can give you, John. But it's true."

John touched Jeffrey's face.

"But without a past, you're not much of a person, are you?"

Jeffrey shook his head slowly, happy simply to look at John. Everything else, from India to Germany and back to Alabama, disappeared.

"And my past," John asked. "*Wirklich,* you can accept it?"

"Yes. But you need to tell Ashok you're not going to stay."

"He knows, believe me. He knows I've come back here to be with you. We'll return to Mumbai tomorrow. He said you'll finish your work soon. 'Jeffrey's work is almost done,' he told me."

Jeffrey nodded.

"He's correct. My work here is almost through, and I haven't done enough. What I really wanted to do was be with you. I'm glad you told me what you did, difficult as it was. We keep trying to erase the past and it keeps coming back. I think I'm too scared of it, really. You see, I've had to give up my past."

John touched Jeffrey's face.

"How old are you, Jeffrey?"

Jeffrey shook his head.

"Old enough."

"That's all I want to know."

He unbuttoned Jeffrey's shirt, discarding it to the floor followed by his pants, then removed his own shorts and made love to Jeffrey as if he'd never been with Ashok, and perhaps in truth he hadn't. Kissing him wildly, sucking and licking every part of him, while Jeffrey felt dumbfounded, lost in John's passion, his mystery. They repositioned, reconfiguring into a sixty-nine, partaking mutually in the host each offered the other. Jeffrey adored this, floating endlessly in the engorged, filmy, iris-petal-soft stream of John's foreskin and genitals, rushed with a spreading warmth of veins, enticing Jeffrey's tongue and brain.

This was all the history he wanted, reading it in the flexed muscles of John's body—in his intensifying belly bucking, tremors and spasms, while pushing, forcefully, toward some deep, unmarked ease—and then, in the ultimate, dark-shooting deliverance of the act.

Ashok insisted that they leave after an early lunch. He did not appear for several hours, while Neji, barechested in only a pair of white cotton drawstring pants, smoked and sipped tea as his servants brought rice cereal and freshly baked warm paratha served with dahl for breakfast. Neji's trousers were like pajama bottoms, loose and comfortable; he wore light rubber sandals that he discarded when he felt like it. Jeffrey observed how comfortable he was with himself, the way Neji sat and moved about, his sweet smile. He could not imagine this in Germany, where there was always an aggressive push for status, or in repressed Alabama when he was growing up.

"My son is a late sleeper, when he can do it!" Neji joked.

"Sometimes I need the recharge," Ashok said, arriving unexpectedly. He smiled at his father, then at John. "Sometimes life is not what it appears to be, and then it is."

"That sounds 'Metaphysical' to me," Jeffrey said, winking at

Ashok. "Is it?"

"You could say that," Ashok answered. "I'll get the servants to bring us something for lunch, then we'll go."

"How is Miryam?" Neji asked suddenly. "You never talk much about her. How's the bank, what's she doing?"

"She's fine. Always busy. I'm the perfect husband for her."

"And is she the perfect wife?" Neji asked, shifting his legs.

Ashok hesitated, pouring himself some tea.

"I need to see about our lunch," he said, and left with his tea cup.

Neji shook his head. "No children. I don't understand it."

"Maybe they don't want them," John said. "I had kids once. I'm sorry I did."

"Why?" Neji asked.

"Because I can't see them. I'm no longer with their mother. Her parents are raising them in England. It's the price for my freedom."

Neji blew out smoke. "Most freedom is an illusion," he said, watching the smoke trail off. "Nature has none of it. Everything fits into a pattern that goes on and on. Even changes are a part of this pattern."

"But who produces the pattern?" Jeffrey asked.

Neji smiled, the same elusive smile as Ashok.

"Does it matter?" He shrugged his bare shoulders. "The pattern produces itself. It's God, you know, one way or another."

John smiled.

"*Schön*," he said. "Very beautiful. I see what you're saying. Then everything within the pattern is God, too? Is that what you mean?"

"In India it is," Neji responded. "I'm not sure about the rest of the world. But I always say, 'You take your India with you.' That's the one truth I know."

The servants came in with lunch, and they ate it while Ashok chattered on about family gossip, cousins and what they were doing, things in the village. In the midst of this, Neji said:

"You're going to leave me an old man without grandchildren. Neither you nor your sister want them."

"I think Miryam is not interested," Ashok said. He got up abruptly. "I don't want to discuss this, Father. We need to make sure everything is packed for the trip back."

He left, and a few minutes later Jeffrey thanked Neji for his hospitality. He and John went to their rooms and packed, then went out to the car.

Ashok was not there. Jeffrey went through the house looking for him, then he found him, alone, in the garden, sitting where Neji and he had sat the night before.

Ashok looked up and saw Jeffrey. His hands were shaking; his eyes filled with tears. His body shook, and his face was terribly furrowed.

Jeffrey felt bad for him, but was not sure where to begin.

"Ashok," he asked. "What is it?"

"I feel like a shit. No one understands me, my father's angry at me. I've been stupid. I shouldn't have spoken to him the way I did, but he doesn't understand these things. It's so hard to make people understand, even when you speak the same language."

"Yes, it is," Jeffrey agreed. "We each speak our own language. The system knows that. It tries to bridge it with what we do."

Jeffrey smiled to himself. At least about the system he was on sure ground.

Ashok cleared his throat. "Neji said to me, 'If you don't like women so much, you can still produce a child. Lots of men do.' The truth is, I don't want kids. Neither does Miryam."

Jeffrey stood near him, with no desire to touch him. Strangely, he felt closer to Neji, who seemed so guileless, than he ever would to Ashok. He brought his hands together and then to his face, looking down, trying not to stare at Ashok; it was a useful "meeting" technique he had learned, allowing people to take a breather and relax around him when things got tough.

"I need to stay here for a moment," Ashok said bitterly. "Sorry to hold us up, but give me a little while more."

"Take all the time you need," Jeffrey offered generously. "But tell me something, Ashok. What is it you *do* want?"

Ashok exhaled, and looked directly at him.

"I'm not sure."

"I think you are, Ashok. Tell me what it is you want. I think I need to know."

Ashok shifted his gaze without smiling.

"O.K. Since you've asked, I'll tell you. I'd like to be like you. Move to Germany. Leave India."

"Whatever for? I wouldn't want my *worst* enemy, if I had one, to be like me."

"That's the thing, Jeffrey. You can't even believe you have a *worst* enemy, you're that powerful. To me you're like some—" He paused. "Like some god! You have an image, but no one really knows what your substance is. All they see is your effect on others. What you produce, and what that produces for them. You're only images. Effects. And I want that."

Jeffrey looked at him sadly. "You do?"

"Yes. You asked me what I want, I've told you." His eyes became impatient, as if real anger were in them. "I'd give up everything I believe for it."

Jeffrey gazed around at the garden feeling anxious and wary. Ashok, who could appear so dizzy, ditsy, and callow, had unmasked him. He'd seen perfectly that there was almost nothing under Jeffrey. All the drugs, the therapies, the protocols, the PICE, even the system he worked for—everything that he had mastered and that had kept him alive—had robbed him of almost every bit of substance he'd once had. The only thing left was what he produced. He had virtually designed himself out of existence.

And now he was used to it. He even thrived on it.

The only thing between him and this totally blank state was John.

It was awful. India, enigmatic, charming, so powerfully revolting and revealing at times, had disclosed this to him. Or had Ashok? But he couldn't allow Ashok to go on thinking he was a god, or even in the position of one. The idea was too silly, and too naïve. He was about to set the young man right, when Ashok broke into one of his awful, bemused smiles, that screen-of-a-smile that seemed to contain half of India. The hijras had it, even beggars. It disgusted Jeffrey.

"You can't be like me!" he insisted. "I wouldn't want anybody to be like me. I'd stop it if I could."

"I'm sure you would, Jeffrey," Ashok said sweetly. "That of course is also in your power, isn't it?"

"No, it's not, but—"

Ashok cut him off. "Then will you give me John?"

"Ashok, he's not mine to give. I—"

He couldn't tell him. John was not just a decoration in his life, John was—whatever it was, he couldn't tell him. It was impossible.

"Jeffrey, please," Ashok went on. "Listen to me. I don't know what power you have over John, but I've become much more than fond of him. I need him; I feel like a—a child when I'm with him. It doesn't seem Indian to be so given over to a person. But he has this deep thing, this—"

"Soul?"

"No, it's more than that. He can act freely and powerfully, yet he's vulnerable and easily hurt. I see that. It attracts me. It attracts me very, very much."

"I see," was all Jeffrey could say.

"You do? Do you *see* how he's pulled me in? He is more than just a 'soul.' He's warm, yet he's so beautiful. I'm glad he has come to India, because men like him are very rare here, if they exist anyplace at all."

Jeffrey smiled. "You're right. John would be rare anyplace."

"I have a Metaphysical connection with him; I knew it as soon as I saw him. It vibrated all the way through me. I can give him the freedom he wants, and all of myself at the same time."

"I'm not sure that's what he wants, Ashok. Believe me, John can claim his own freedom."

"In that case I'll hold nothing he's done against him."

Jeffrey couldn't help smiling. This was a strong card for Ashok to try to bluff with. No matter how much of the truth Ashok would ever learn about John, at some point he would use it. And then what would John do?

"What *has* he done, Ashok?"

"I can tell he has a past he's trying to hide. I knew it as soon as we met, but believe me it makes no difference to me."

Jeffrey looked straight at him.

"How could you tell?"

"Why did you want him to be known as John 'Vann'?"

"That was my idea, to preserve privacy." Jeffrey pretended a smile. "But I saw that it really wasn't necessary."

Ashok's eyes brightened. "Yes, you realized that. Good."

"It is, Ashok, but I'm not sure John feels the same way about you. To be frank, I'm not sure that he sees anything here that you can give him."

"Then, please, Jeffrey. For your sake as well as mine, you must make him see it. I'm begging you."

"Why?"

"In your heart, do you really love or care so much about him? Let's be truthful. I don't believe the system will ever allow you to."

Another strong card for Ashok to bluff with.

Jeffrey imagined Tony's words, his benign, fatherly Teutonic face carrying disapproval over the stress Jeffrey was going through. He could see it as surely as he could visualize Ashok's glitzy "That Woman" and all the other projects that would consume him. Just as surely, he could see John's fierce green-eyed features that he loved so much, and his mysterious, lightning-fast assault on the pubtran platform, which had set all of this going.

At some other point, in the not too unseeable future, if he did not stop this connection with John, the stress from it would overwhelm him. He'd fail hugely, and the system that protected him would stop keeping him alive. End of story. His pulse pounded in his temples.

"All right," Jeffrey assented. "Let me talk to him when we get back to Mumbai."

Ashok smiled triumphantly, looking very much like Neji, secure in his intelligence and its age-old sources. As if the young man's beliefs, quirky as they were, in whatever testing life had put them through, had been thoroughly strengthened.

"Tell me," Ashok asked, his face cocked confidently, slightly to the side. "Does he know everything about you?"

Ashok's eyes glittered.

The pounding hurt. "What are you getting at, Ashok?"

"Who you are? Your real age?"

"What are you talking about?" Jeffrey's voice rose and he had to squelch it. "How—how do you know *any* of this?"

"Don't worry, Jeffrey. It's no problem here. But after you called and we talked about your coming, I had some friends of friends, who'll do anything for a favor and who're good at digging, do a little digging for me. Your secrets are no problem. Here in India we hold the false fairly easily, because, understandably, it makes it a lot easier to see what's underneath."

Jeffrey's mouth dropped.

"Don't look so shocked, Jeffrey. You look like our friend Deborah Kerr in one of her movies. She could be *so* indignant!"

"What are you getting at?"

"O. K." Ashok smiled blandly, as if to reveal the security of his position. "Let's say, I know *everything* about you and John. The upshot is, I want you to talk to him *now*, not later in Mumbai."

Card number three, and this one was too dangerous to bluff with. Jeffrey knew it was there, ready to come out; but he didn't expect it to hurt so much or that he would respond so quickly to it.

"All right."

He tried hard not to choke on his words, or the anger and disappointment that came with them. "I'll talk to him first. Just the two of us. Then I'll come back, Ashok, and get you to come to the car."

"He wants you with him," Jeffrey said to John, as several boys on bicycles went by. It was getting very warm and muggy, and they were both sweating.

"That's crazy."

"No, he's right. I mean it. You should stay here."

"Now you're crazy, *mein lieber freund*."

"I mean it, John. I can't share my life in Germany with you. You probably know this: the system won't allow it."

"The system won't allow a lot of things," John asserted. "It won't allow *me*. That's a fact. So I tell you: leave the fucking system now, I mean that. Live with me. You can stay in my house and I'll take care of you. But it's simple, I can't stay in India. Would you be with me?"

"No. You've got to see, I'd die fast one way or another, if I did it. I haven't told you all the truth, John. I'm a lot older than I—"

John interrupted him.

"Please, Jeffrey! I know, that's why I don't really ask about it, just," he paused, "hints."

It was becoming difficult for Jeffrey to speak. He wished he could have it over with and get rid of John, just—

"I don't want to die this way," he confessed, close to breaking down. "You hate the system and everything about it that keeps me alive. Don't you see, you can stay here in India with Ashok. He'll even move to Germany to be with you. He's crazy about you."

"He's crazy all right!" John insisted. "And I know about craziness. But I won't do it. You and I will go back to Germany, and then—"

"Don't make me do this," Jeffrey snapped. "I'll have to give you up. It's the only way. Ashok won't be happy unless he has you and he'll do anything to get to you."

"He's married to a woman."

"So were you."

"I see," John said. "So that's it? I was married, and I killed my very pretty little wife, and there was no other choice for me, so I must pay for it every fucking day. That's it. It makes me want to kill myself: I get down into that shitty hole and—O.K., I get it. You're in the system, so you don't want to be around me 'cause of what I told you. Is that it?"

Jeffrey did not hesitate.

"Yes," he said. "John, nothing I do can be kept a secret. At some point, my therapist, the doctors, the money people—somebody'll find out and they'll rat on me. I've made this bargain and I've got to keep it. There's no other choice for me."

John's eyes dropped. There were more boys on bicycles, and in the steamy distance people who looked suddenly so foreign that they could have come from Mars.

"I didn't make that bargain," John said.

But he could tell, when he forced his eyes once again onto Jeffrey, wanting only to look at him, that the argument was over.

❦

Jeffrey went back to the garden where Ashok waited.

"I've spoken to John. It's all right now. He understands what has to happen."

Ashok nodded, smiling, and they walked toward the car where John waited, his eyes on a group of buzzards perched in the trees above. John did not say a word.

Neji came out and embraced Ashok, and said good-bye to John and Jeffrey.

"It has been a pleasure having you in our house," he said to Jeffrey. "You're indeed a fine young man. My son is honored to work with you."

The three of them got into the car, Jeffrey in the back and John in front with Ashok.

"We're off!" Ashok announced. Neji, the house, and the servants who'd come out receded in the distance. He said to John, "I hope you liked being here,"

John looked out the window at cows and scooters and kids. He liked watching the kids.

"You've gotten to see some of the real India. It hardly exists in the cities, just in a little place here and there. But out here, we still have it."

John abruptly turned to him.

"Can we go back to the temple?"

"Would you like that?" Ashok asked, glancing at Jeffrey in the rearview mirror, who seemed lost in thought. "You want to see that naked yogi again, don't you?"

"I want to see the temple. Only the temple."

"Is that it? We can go to other temples."

"I want to go back to that one."

"All right. Whatever you say. You can be the boss now!"

Although it was out of the way, Ashok drove them through the forest to the temple grove, and then they walked in the gathering heat through the trees.

"This is like my forest in Germany," John said to Jeffrey, who could not face him.

Ashok smiled, as if everything he wanted was now in his hands.

"Would you show me your forest? I'd like to go there."

John did not answer him.

When they approached the temple they saw that it was empty, the outer gate locked.

"There must be a festival nearby. That's why the monks are not here. I admit I don't know all the festivals, but we can try to find it. It's getting hot. I know a place further up, by the river. Perhaps we can bathe there, then start off again."

John's eyes looked panicked.

"They won't have another cremation, will they?"

"Not where I'll take you. I promise."

The car was surrounded by small kids. Ashok tried to shoo them away like they were flies, but Jeffrey reached into his pocket and gave them some small change.

"You're only spoiling them," Ashok said, starting the motor. The heat was now terrible, with no promise of a shower to relieve it. The small Rumi had air-conditioning, but Jeffrey didn't want to ask. He didn't want to say anything. He lowered his window fully and put his head out. As they drove down a country road, he was back in Alabama with his grandma and stylish mother. Time just rolled back on its own, and PICE or not, he couldn't help it.

He realized there was something physical about time; it had its own physical presence, like an amazing chair you can find some way to bring back after it's been out of style for a long time. He saw Harold Cooper's utterly naked face that had escaped being "pretty" and sailed quietly into the shelter of "remarkable," drawing intense love to it. It had haunted him earlier for years and it hurt him now. He adored it. Huge, it floated, billboard-size, over his thoughts—a celebrity face, like a politician's or a god's, more true, more real, than any depiction of Jesus.

He wanted to touch it, to hold it, to give his daddy a soft, forgiving kiss of time.

At the service, his mother had kept a remote, steely look that Jeffrey himself later learned to imitate and could see in certain unguarded mirrors, and in the probing eyes of others as he remained young. He was fourteen and had been pushed into a cold approximation of manhood when he opened the garage door, finding his father lying on the floor in a glistening pool of blood left from the explosion in the back of his head.

Love. It was too painful to have anything to do with it. And unlike style, its pain always hurt the same. Style was about domination, but love—there was no certainty in it.

Now there was the heat and the traveling to nowhere along a river that went nowhere that he knew. Everyone takes his own India with him, Neji had said. "Your very own India," he heard himself say. Or was it just a dream of India—a *nightmare* of India? He saw the party with the hijras dancing, and then the starched collars and dark neckties and heat outside the service for his father who'd been truly foreign to him, speaking a language of his own. A big, blunt, flat-natured guy with the hilly woods of Alabama pressing close to him while he and Mom had drifted farther into their own India. Golly! Golly! Golly! An invention of India! So fragile and artfully constructed, just like the old Ballets Russes, where Mom, inside her own stylish *parc* of topiary perfection, always appeared onstage at precisely the right time. Always there to show him the right thing to do. To wear. To buy.

Daddy had found a girl eighteen years younger than he. Country sweet, soft, approachable in her waiting innocence by someone who was filled, himself, with difficult and unsortable intentions. Maybe it had begun as a lark, but it was only to end in a cemetery vault bought for one. The rest was blank, locked like the garage door against the afternoon heat. Harold wouldn't allow his "funny" son inside, where it was all extremely secret and to share it they would have to speak a language foreign to Jeffrey: Southern football. Near-death drinking. Pretty girls with doll-like faces; boys built out of the turbulent fantasies of young gods. A language of sighs and secret kisses that nobody ever shared with Harold Cooper except this girl, and perhaps an empty bottle of bourbon.

She left him flat out: one of the pieces of the puzzle Jeffrey managed to pick up. Got smart. Perhaps there was another boy waiting someplace; perhaps even pregnancy or the fear of it. Later, in certain moments with himself, Jeffrey had tried to piece the thing together, imagining what his father had had to go through: that she had left Harold with a crying pain in his heart, where there was nobody else.

Sometimes men, hurt and angry past their own abilities to reason or even feel, kill themselves as the only reprieve from a pain that no amount of not feeling can heal. What a Hell-pit to fall through, Jeffrey early on decided; one he'd never fall through, no matter what. Fate, and his own talents and limitations, had given him things to hang on to. His expertise. Staying young.

Now Ashok was telling them about the countryside in India and showing them bungalows painted intense blue and a kind of over-heated, tiring pink that any other place would be truly stomach-turning.

"Nowhere in the world is there this kind of pink!" Ashok exclaimed. "Jeffrey, we should make our beauty line this pink. Exactly this pink!"

Jeffrey looked up and could have pointed out that this was close to the very *same* pink that Ashok had so strongly objected to in the original Goddess line, but he said nothing.

"What do you think?" Ashok said. "About the pink?" He laughed. "Can you *think* pink?"

No. He could not think *pink*. Or anything.

He'd been so numb that Mom had had to pick out the tie he'd wear for the service. Black, with a skinniest, widely spaced stripe of contrasting, yes, *pink*, slightly mauvish, definitely not *that* hyper-screaming pink from India. Mom thought that all-black, once you got down to it, was simply *un*becoming. She wore a white silk blouse and one of her impeccably cut, inky-dark maroon suits. There were displays of white lilies and baby's breath, with the air-conditioning turned up deadly freezing so women could wear furs; and a polished, closed casket, pushed to the side, almost like an afterthought. Men shook his hand stiffly. No one patted his shoulder. Everything was frozen, offering as always the benign promise of sweet, Southern denial, and normalcy.

The window was open and Jeffrey tried to keep from choking in the backseat, as he had coming back from the cemetery (he'd willed himself to forget every bit of that). Now the road was blocked by a procession that must have been part of the same festival that locked the temple. John asked what it was about; Ashok said, about the festivals, he could not "remember all of them." It was like a circus, complete with an elephant and large, wildly decorated carts on big wooden wheels carrying statues, with about a hundred people walking, some chanting, and youngsters capering about energetically on the dusty edges, accompanied by a grating noise like the hijras: loud, nasal, with jingling bells inside. To Jeffrey it became the sound of India. Its colors, intense with sunlight and thick, crudely brushed pigments, stifling, combative, those annoyingly dense and aggressive colors, seemed to permeate the air and become pasted on the windshield of the stopped Rumi. He could see their hot reflections running opaquely across John's unsmiling face. They were not the colors of his paintings, which had a vivacity of deeply human, saintly freedom in them.

He felt assaulted by the colors, and sorry for John.

"Are you all right back there?" Ashok asked. "Is it too hot for you? I'm not a fan of air-conditioning, but I can turn it on if you'd like."

Jeffrey did not know what to say. All he could do was shake his head; he had no idea what else to say.

"Good!" Ashok cried. "You are fine! We'll be going soon. Then we'll make a nice turn off the road toward the river, where we want to be."

Jeffrey nodded. He was unnerved, and did not want Ashok to see it; he needed to be in control. He knew that if he closed his eyes he'd be back at the church again. Mercifully, the crowd started to thin out; he looked out his window at the flat distant countryside. Suddenly another wave of kids and old women surrounded the car in endless tides of brightly colored bodies, more people than he had first seen in this nameless procession. More colors. More smells. Where did they come from, maybe just from India itself? He wished it would rain, anything to disperse the noise and the crowd.

Finally the crowd was gone, like a rush of birds that had flown away.

They drove a short bit more, then turned off the road at the river, exactly as Ashok had promised. He parked the car, and the three of them got out.

"Just wear your underwear, as the Indians do," Ashok said, proceeding to take everything off except that. He was dark and hairy, in contrast to John, who was reddish, still pale despite India. John was muscular but wiry; Ashok was more thickset, slightly babyish though not really fat, more "juicy" as the Germans would say. He was playfully smiling.

Jeffrey watched them strip to their undershorts. Ashok took John's hand, leading him to the river, which was hidden in places by trees, then looked back at Jeffrey.

"You have to come in also. It's too hot not to."

"All right," Jeffrey said, feeling slightly nauseated. "Do we need to lock the car?"

"No," Ashok said. "I have the key. People don't steal here."

Jeffrey took his clothes off down to his white briefs. He thought for a second about Gregory Malace, hardworking but quite blank as a personality. What a wus Malace would think he was, just wading in a shallow Indian river. Malace would have to be snorkling through its murkiness, or deep diving among piranha in order to connect with his desires.

With a jolt Jeffrey realized that John van der Meer embodied everything that he had ever desired. The realization saturated his entire being. It was like India itself: physical, something in the air, the dust on the ground, the eye-stinging, compelling colors. A large tourist bus drove by, filled with Indians, coming out to see their own countryside. Some of them waved at Jeffrey in his white briefs.

He turned to them and smiled.

Chapter Fourteen

*T*he water was cleaner than he thought it would be, because it was moving quickly. A group of six or seven men stood in a shallows downriver from them, at a wider, slower place that also looked muddier, with a woman in a damp black sari watching them from the bank. Ashok and John were in a narrow finger of water, next to some trees growing out of the stream, with a higher crest of reddish clay separating them from Jeffrey.

"Come here!" Ashok called. "The water rushes here. It's very refreshing!"

"*Ja!*" John called. "It's O.K.!"

Jeffrey waded toward them, getting pushed down by the current several times, and righting himself up again. He wasn't sure he could make it, then John came over and helped him.

"It wasn't so fast when we came in," John said. "I think Ashok knows the right places."

Jeffrey grabbed him, with the river rushing around them.

"I didn't mean it," he cried out to John. "I don't want you to go. I'll do anything to be with you. Can you believe that?"

John smiled radiantly.

"Yes. I can."

"Good. I need to tell that to Ashok right now. He can't have any idea that he can take you from me. I was stupid, I know it."

"All right," John said, his whole face lit up, "I'll stay here if you want to tell him."

Jeffrey managed to wade over to Ashok fairly easily; the crest of clay slowed the current a bit, then it got faster as he approached Ashok, who was hanging on to one of the small trees.

"I used to come here and play when I was a kid!" Ashok shouted to Jeffrey in the swirling water. "Hang on to this!"

He pulled Jeffrey to him as the river rushed around them. They were on a higher spot, in the midst of a clump of struggling trees. Ashok giggled, as if he were tickled by the power of the stream.

"I won't let him go!" Jeffrey announced in a loud roar of rushing water.

"You what?"

"I said," Jeffrey repeated, raising his voice, "I've got to be honest—I won't let him go. I don't care what happens to me, but I need John!"

"That's CRAZY!" Ashok shouted. "You'll die with John! That's how the system works. It works here in India just like it works any-place. You don't even care about him. Not the way I do!"

"Why do you want—" Jeffrey's voice cracked. He could not talk above the water. It was futile to have this conversation here, and he knew it. But he was no longer using his head.

"I don't know," Ashok confessed, his voice lower, though Jeffrey could hear every word. "I just—it's the first time I ever wanted some-thing on my own. For me. Not Neji. The system. India. It's for me. You've got to see that!"

"I see it, but I can't—"

"Can't WHAT? You can do ANYTHING!"

"I—"

Jeffrey ceased talking, stopped by Ashok who was boiling with rage, as if something in him had either snapped or all the waiting violence in him had been brought together out in the open in the water. He grabbed Jeffrey and forced him down, his hands at Jeffrey's neck. Jeffrey thrashed against Ashok in the rushing stream, choking in spasms, with Ashok pulling him down as he struggled in the water. Ashok managed to bob up for air, then pushed Jeffrey down again. But some gathering and distinct relaxation, like a bubble rising from below the surface, halted Jeffrey's panic.

Harold, weightless, suddenly cradled him, his normally expres-sionless mouth murmuring words only Jeffrey could hear.

"Son, I love you. I do . . ."

The words were attached to that ease Jeffrey had always attached to Harold, which had been ripped so heartlessly apart, even before the garage. It would be death, effortlessly, in India for him. He stopped fighting, and tried to see with his eyes.

Ashok was at his throat, the water silent. But he was lifted up into Tony's mist, that space where every calm intake of air and light carried its own insights . . .

Ashok released him.

John pulled Jeffrey from the turbulence, screaming:

"I'll kill him!"

And he plunged back into the water at Ashok, and attacked him.

But Jeffrey, weak, choking on dirty water, barely able to hold himself up, came between them.

❦

Getting dressed was arduously difficult, not simply because Jeffrey's body ached but because he kept imagining a herd of Indian elephants trumpeting all over the now soggy area where the Rumi was parked. There was too much trumpeting going on in his head, too much that couldn't be acknowledged. John looked at him bitterly. They said almost nothing in the car until they got back to Mumbai, but sometimes Ashok, in a frenzy of guilt, would pop up with: "I was trying to save him. Believe me. He slipped and the river got him!"

John in the front seat said nothing, while Jeffrey in back held his silence. Sometimes Ashok played the radio, to keep the enforced quiet from driving them crazy. As they approached Mumbai, things became more normal and Jeffrey talked to Ashok about the beauty line and what more had to be done with it. Ashok went into his act of being charmingly obsequious to Jeffrey, while transparently hinting that he would try to take over once Jeffrey left India.

Jeffrey made plans for the next two days of work on "That Woman." He was more tired than even he could admit and more than ready to leave India. Though unsaid, what had passed in the river once again reinforced Jeffrey's power. Ashok understood this, evidently, and became quieter, less annoyingly charming.

Which made Jeffrey feel better. He could never haul Ashok up on charges. There would be too many questions about John and why Jeffrey had brought him there. So Ashok would get his way, with

Jeffrey's presence close behind it. And Jeffrey was only too happy to drop "That Woman" and the sad visages of Deborah Kerr and Audrey Hepburn (he could only imagine their reactions!), glitzy rhinestones, embossed gunk and all, ninety-nine percent into Ashok's hands.

Still, as they worked together the next two days, Jeffrey actually began to acquire some solid respect for Ashok. He had been right, Jeffrey realized after going over the material and prototypes several more times, about certain things. "Goddess," to be the kind of huge hit Ashok wanted, would never have worked. And Jeffrey's earlier conceptualization for "That Woman," all high fashion and style snobbism, was too high for this market. Ashok convinced him that he would be able to keep the Indian Money—which, like Money every-place, engaged a limited attention span with unlimited greed—inter-ested. He introduced Jeffrey to several Indian finance people who beamed at Ashok like proud relatives, as they said over and over again, "We're so proud of Ashok, and what he is trying to do for all of us!"

At night in the hotel, John looked at him puzzled.

"I don't know how you can stand to be around him."

Jeffrey was positive that John thought he was being weak; Jeffrey was not sure what he was anymore. He only knew that he could not hate Ashok. Ashok was young, and he and India had helped Jeffrey open the locked door to his past, just as John had opened other doors to him. It was painful, to open it, but he'd needed to do it—that was the only way he could put it: in terms of *need*.

"I'm sorry I didn't kill him," John said bitterly.

"That would only have destroyed me as well as you."

John thought for a second.

"You're right. And what would that have proved?" John looked at him. "You're stronger than I am. Sometimes that makes things diffi-cult."

Jeffrey liked hearing that, because he felt insecure now. Love, and a past he was not supposed to visit, had made him feel that way.

"I don't want to take all the credit for the this," Ashok confessed humbly to Jeffrey as they finalized the line's look and its sales concepts, getting it ready for the Money, the promotion writers and designers who would finish the details, the factories and the distributors. In the end, "That Woman" would be a lot more Bollywood than Deborah and Audrey, even with a dash of old Merle Oberon Anglo-half-caste beauty in all of the models chosen for it. The Balenciaga sleeve effect was more or less retained, but wider and thicker ribbons were added, with traditional Indian patterns. Ashok decided the rhinestones should be even flashier rubies and emeralds, adding a Mogul-jewels effect. Everything was packaged in a form that would be quickly marketable worldwide, to distributors and retailers who needed to be sold almost instantly.

"This is so exciting!" Ashok cried. "I feel like I'm on the—"

"Verge of something?" Jeffrey said dryly.

"That's it. I meant what I said about wanting to come to Germany, Jeffrey."

"Maybe you should."

"Would you permit it?"

Jeffrey looked directly at him.

"What makes you think I need to permit it? If you make a big enough kill here, the system will send you anywhere. You can write your own ticket, Ashok."

Ashok changed tactics.

"Don't act stupid, Jeffrey. We both know you'd have to O.K. a change like this."

"What do you mean 'stupid'? Do you really think I am?"

Ashok blinked. He knew when to retract.

"No. Of course not. I didn't mean that."

"You don't have to be brilliant to be in my position, Ashok. But you do have to know when someone is right behind you, and will use anything he can to—"

The elephants started trumpeting again. Jeffrey shut up, not wanting to fall into another trap with Ashok, who looked suddenly very uncomplicated, very sincere, smiling generously.

"What is it, Jeffrey?"

The hell with it, Jeffrey thought.

"You knew John had certain elements of 'rashness' in his past. Maybe I should leave it at that."

"If you still think I tried to murder you, Jeffrey, it's not true."

"All right. Let's say it's not true. Let's say you tried to do *something*—'Metaphysical' or not. Anyway, whatever you tried, you needed someone like John, someone impulsive that you could blame it on."

"That's crazy, Jeffrey. John would never hurt you, I know that. As for me blaming anything that happened on him, it's absurd. Like I said, it was an accident. I tried to help you."

Jeffrey forced himself to smile; he could be generous, too.

"All right, I get you. So you want to come to Germany? Well, you're attractive and talented; I can see that, and I can see you coming over. It's a step up in the system, no matter how you put it. I'll keep it in mind."

"Thank you," Ashok said. "I'm honored that you have so much faith in me."

Jeffrey ignored Ashok's false humility.

"Let's see how our little line does first. All right? I want it to be a success as much as you do, believe me."

John came to his room their last night in India.

"*Bis du* O.K.?" he asked, kissing him.

"I'm fine. I'm really very O.K. With you, me, and even Ashok."

John lowered his eyes.

"I still think you should have let me kill him. I don't trust him."

"But what would I do, if you did?" Jeffrey asked. "I'd have to explain his death, and how you got there. They'd catch up with you, too."

John smiled beguilingly.

"He'd be only one more body in the river. In India there are lots of bodies there, I'm sure."

Jeffrey nodded. "Then suppose I enjoy yours?"

They turned out the light and made love, feeling more relaxed than they'd been in several days now that they were ready to leave India. They ended up in the smooth, flowing embrace of mutual oral sex; John came in Jeffrey's mouth, giving him a wild, zincy shoot. Jeffrey, with his eyes closed, felt himself back in the temple with rain outside. Chanting. Drums. Peeling colors of temple gods and their consorts in sexual heat. Sacred water, darkness. And this glorious, intoxicating thing: the lingam itself, root and stalk of the male principal, shooting its thick but elegant chemistry into him.

No files: nothing could capture this.

It warmed him down to his toes.

Chapter Fifteen

At the airport, Ashok presented John and Jeffrey with garlands of chrysanthemums before they got on their plane.

"It is a symbol of my desire for you to return!" he said formally, pecking Jeffrey and John politely on each cheek.

"You taught me so much, Jeffrey. I can never forget you!"

Jeffrey smiled, thanking him coolly. John said nothing.

The young male cabin attendant offered to keep the garlands in refrigeration, but Jeffrey told him not to bother.

"I think it's better we keep Ashok that way," John said after the attendant left.

Jeffrey smiled, though he was feeling tense again. He knew he needed to see Tony and Bernd as soon as he got back. He hated the thought of having to tell Tony about John, but knew he would. Tony would figure it out, when his stress levels went through the roof. Bernd would be more on his side, he was sure, and try to work things out with him.

He could imagine Herr Dr. Ostreich saying, "Nonsense. You need a little love in your life. *Ein kleines Liebe! Ist gut für allis!*"

But would Bernd really support him in the reports his primary doctor would have to make to the system? Jeffrey would be under a huge amount of pressure, and he knew it. So much work was coming in, and he'd have to do his own report on the Indian project, detailing how it was now more in Ashok Rahman's hands than his own, without making it seem that he was giving it up. He wondered how Gregory Malace would deal with "That Woman." Malace didn't like changes, certainly not those that came with any whiplash in them. Then Jeffrey remembered that Malace would be away when he got back, having finally got his vacation time. After Jeffrey's experiences in India, he wondered what kind of adventure this buttoned-up young man would find for himself.

He thought about having John sleep with him the first night back in his apartment, then thought about the dangers of it. Everyone who came and went in his building was surveilled and recorded. John would probably find its luxuries antiseptic, and hate all the advanced toys and gadgetry Jeffrey had accumulated, all the high-end gallery art.

So he said good-bye to John at the airport, barely showing any real feeling toward him. He hated himself afterward in the private car ride into town. John would take a pubtran; now that he was back in the city, in Germany, he would not risk showing up at Jeffrey's highly secured building.

At home the first thing Jeffrey found was a message from Chris Stewart. Just seeing Chris's name displayed was upsetting. He was sure Chris was going to threaten him further about Reginald Magus's death. That episode felt as if it had happened a year ago; as far as Jeffrey knew, nothing had surfaced in his absence proving Jeffrey had seen Magus only a few minutes before terrorists hit the club. The whole thing was repulsive, with Joshua Goldmeister thrown in; the thought of it was sickening.

He listened to Chris's message.

"Jeffrey, you've got to help—please! They're putting Len in Suspension. He had a bad heart attack. He's in the hospital now. It won't be long—"

❦

He did not unpack or even shower, but took a cab straight to the hospital. It was upper-class, very elegant with art and orchids in showy display pots everywhere. It was almost unbearably tasteful and could have been an exclusive department store, except for the slight medicinal smell. Unlike the hospitals, or *krankenhausen*, built for the workers, there were no lines of desperate people waiting to be seen at clinics, no rushing, overworked orderlies and nurses with soiled or bloodstained uniforms, no crying children or demented elderly roaming about lost. Here you could have been in a great store, among groups of quiet, stylish customers. A few patients were wheeled serenely through the halls by people in spotless uniforms, with relatives or friends hovering close by.

"Did you eat today?" an old lady in a fur wrap asked her husband in German.

"What?" Then he heard her and answered yes. "Lunch was excellent. Poached salmon. Riesling. Black forest cake *mit schlag*."

She smiled, taking his wrinkled hand in her gloved one.

Chris tried to smile through his scowl, looking up from Len's bedside.

"Darling, you're here!" He approached Jeffrey, but did not touch him. "God! I thought I was going to go nuts."

"It's all right," Len interjected weakly. "I don't know why she's so upset. I had a heart attack; people get 'em all the time. They put a shunt in and they're going to do all sorts of terrifically expensive therapies on me." Len smiled gamely. "I'm a doc, so I deal with this kind of shit everyday."

"I know you do," Chris said, looking at Jeffrey. "That's the problem. You deal with it too much. The stress is killing you!"

"It's not *my* stress!" Len popped up unexpectedly, hands clenched. "Damn it, Chris. Y'know we don't need t'lead the kind of life we do. All the parties and the people. You gotta be a star, you gotta be a—"

"STOP IT!" Chris screamed. "You've put me through *enough* shit for seventeen years! What the hell are you trying to do to me now?"

"Sorry," Len said, lowering his voice. "I'm sorry. I bet I'm starting to sound like my goddamn parents, may their souls rest in pieces." He smiled softly, with some effort. "Jeffrey honey, I'm glad you're here. You need to calm my husband down. She's been having a rotten day or week. And I'm not helping."

"That's all right," Jeffrey said, quickly kissing Chris, then Len. "We all have them. I'm sure academics is not easy. And as for medicine—"

"It's killing him," Chris sobbed, breaking down. "And now they're going to—"

"They're going to make me better," Len said, trying hard to convince Chris, and perhaps himself as well.

Two young, very blond German specialists in white coats came in, talking fast, muttering to themselves, carrying paper files.

Len beamed, and shrugged. "Hans *und* Hans-Pieter. My doctors. How are you guys?"

"Ve ah ek-zellent," one said in a thick accent, ignoring Jeffrey's presence. "Ve vant to go over d'verk and vat is up ahead."

"Sure," Len said. "I guess you boys need to leave us for a moment."

"I should stay," Chris insisted. "I'm his spouse. I need to be here."

"'Fraid not," the one who talked said. "Ve'll come out and talk in a moment. If dat is O.K mit you?"

"Chris," Len said softly, motioning to the door with his hand. "It's better. Just go outside with Jeffrey."

Chris and Jeffrey walked out and shut the door. They found an attractive conversation corner nearby in the corridor. An attendant asked if they would like to have a cola or some wine with crackers and cheese.

"What room are you visiting?' he asked.

Chris told him, and asked for a dry riesling. Jeffrey asked for plain water. A moment later they were brought on a silver tray.

"It's like a resort here," Chris said. "Except that a lot of times, you don't get to check out." He started to sob again

Jeffrey sipped some water.

"What makes you think this is that time?"

"I've seen his chart. Even Len knows it. They're not going to keep him here very long, and they know that he's about washed-up. He's of no more use to the system. The problem is that we're too far up on the social scale just to descend to nothing, so the next step will be . . ."

"Suspension. But for how long?" Jeffrey asked, his heart pounding and his stomach suddenly tilting with nausea. He loathed asking the question. It was one of those questions whose answers were more terrifying than ignorance. Ignorance was not bliss anymore; ignorance was pure anxiety. But the answer to this—

"Who knows? A year. Maybe just a couple of months. I know one thing: they aren't going to try to bring him back, not even if some really cheap way is put together to keep him alive. He's not useful anymore. He's burnt out. And they sure as hell aren't going to keep him here. They'll warehouse him in some cheaper facility. This place costs by the minute."

"I can see that," Jeffrey said.

Chris was right. The system would get rid of Dr. Silverman. He was no longer worth the money put into him to keep him going, and he wasn't creating channels for big money to move in, the way Jeffrey did. They could not kill Len, but Suspension, and then . . .

"What are you going to do?" he asked Chris.

"I don't know. I should go back to the States. As long as Len is in Suspension, there will be no survivor's insurance for me, so I'll be next to broke. That's the nice thing about Suspension—they win double." He bolted down most of his wine. "I can't live the way I've lived here in Germany. I'll have to sell our apartment, and the apartment in New York too. Len's right. We've been living way over our heads." He blew his nose. "I guess I'm to blame, but I couldn't live with Len any other way."

"Why not?"

"He took too much out of me. His stress level, his craziness just added to my own. So like any good doctor's wife, I spent and spent, and had my 'salons' where I could be a star in my own world. Who wouldn't want that?"

Chris tried gamely to smile, but Jeffrey couldn't. Then Drs. Hans and Hans-Pieter came by, and the talking one, who never introduced himself to Jeffrey, informed Chris that they would "proceed wit' d'next step quick—t'morrow." Chris started to speak very fast in German to them, so Jeffrey was able to follow very little of it. Then without another word, the two men in white left.

Chris sat crying bitterly in the soft white padded leather chair. Two attendants came by, nodded caringly, and one offered him another glass of wine.

He told them no, and they left.

"What'm I gonna do?" he asked Jeffrey, slurring his words, something Chris never did. He blew his nose into a tissue. "I'm over. Jus' over. How'm I gonna say goo'-bye t'him?"

"I don't know," Jeffrey answered. "Do you want me to be there with you tomorrow?"

"They told me I can't be there when it happens. The day before yesterday, when he was admitted, they said the underwriters and the system people had been looking at his charts, his work, his billings. It's horrible, Jeffrey. I can't understand why someone like—"

He stopped talking.

Jeffrey looked at him, knowing what Chris was going to say: How could they put a surgeon in Suspension, while someone like . . . ?

Jeffrey blurted out an answer.

"I'm a useful part of all this. I know it and they do, too. I tried to tell Len this once at your house. He was scared. He saw it coming. I tried to give him advice, but he couldn't use it. I'm never sure what's going to happen. I can barely control myself sometimes. I wasn't supposed to have any kind of actual feelings or emotional life, but I do. I'm in love, Chris. And that alone may end up killing me."

He took Chris's hand, and they sat quietly for a while. Then they went back to Len's room. He was sitting up, smiling.

"Things are looking good," he announced. "The two blondies told me that they're going to do one more big procedure on me this evening, then I get to check out if I want to."

Len beamed. He sipped from a heavy crystal glass of sparkling water.

"I feel like it's the night before my bar mitzvah," he said, grinning broadly like a kid. "Soon I gotta go through all this *spiel*, then Mom, Dad, and the relatives bring on the presents!" He drank more of the water. "I can't wait!"

"Yes," Chris said, with more sadness in his voice than Jeffrey had ever heard. "That's what happens."

Jeffrey had a difficult time sleeping that night. Tossing in the darkness, he decided he would see John the next day, right after his appointment with Tony. When he finally dozed off, he had dreams like he'd not had in decades. He'd been off some of his prescriptions and heavy boosters in India, and now things from his once safely unreachable past started to leach under those stout walls that he had erected even in his dreams. He saw the stylish and respectable house of his parents at dusk, the big, well-kept front and back yards, the clear suburban sky. John was at the dinner table, attentive and sweetly behaved, with his mother speaking in that kind of dismissive Southern manner she had, talking about the neighbors, religious Jews down the street, who—"Still are not as bad as those Indians! Who'd believe, *Indians* in Alabama? I remember when *Indians* were only in cowboy movies. It's Little Calcutta all over now!"

John only smiled; she was having a cocktail, which she had introduced slightly earlier with dinner. Daddy used to drink beer when he got home from work, but she brought in cocktails in fanciful glasses, and the glasses were in the dream, with John listening to his mother, but looking at him. A moment later, they were upstairs in Jeffrey's old bedroom. John was his real age, Jeffrey about eighteen. His room looked the way it had then, down to the antique bisque dolls he had bought, after some deliberation, with his own money and his own post-Daddy freedom. Mom had declared them "so precious."

With Daddy gone, Jeffrey could collect antique dolls, and they were in his room upstairs, watching, as the drownings began: half performances, like some live "installation" in a museum, and half the intense, barely comprehendible enactments of a hidden sacrament, of some darkly sanctified physical act. First Cynthia's, her fine-boned, lovely English skin and aristocratic eyes. Jeffrey had never met her, but he knew it was she, and he could feel her writhing violently, swallowed by rushing undertows of water, held down by John's hands, exactly as he as an adult and John were making love in that overwhelming undertow of feelings that beckoned to him undeniably in his childhood bedroom, even while terrifying him. Then, in one constant surge, the flooding waters returned him to the river in India, for his own "sacrament." The churning currents became Ashok's slightly babyish face, first raging at him then turning, staring downward, outspokenly wise beyond any sense Jeffrey could have imagined in that doll-head, appearing as it would on one of Ashok's shopping bags, until the rushing waters of that infantile face calmed themselves into appeasement.

With Jeffrey being pulled dead from them, and India watching; with John crying: "Don't burn him and put him in the river!"

Jeffrey woke up sweating and shaking.

The next day at work, he went through all his messages, including videos. There was one from Gregory Malace, in a short-sleeved shirt and smiling more openly than Jeffrey was used to, which at least made him feel that Malace was enjoying his vacation.

"Hi, Jeffrey! Sorry I'm not around to welcome you back but I need a break and I'm sure as hell lookin' forward to this. Sometimes I just gotta get all my crazies out to—well, y'know like they say 'get in touch with'—anyway . . . I did a lotta work on the Mormon project. Hope you like it, and also the A-Z car for Antonio Zbatti. Chr-iiist! 'Scuse my—those people are a pain! Why don't they jus' do the damn thing themselves? I can't talk to anybody there, 'cause all they wanna do is talk to you anyway. Make sure you reach Agnetta, his 'shar-jay d'affaires.' That's what she calls herself. I hope I don't sound like too much of a dip, but th'truth is I been working my butt off. I mean it. Sometimes I don't know how you put up with it. You work even harder than I do, kiddo."

Malace paused. He looked at his handscreen.

"My battery's running out, so I better send this to you *Mack Schnelly!*"

That was it. "Mack Schnelly" was a joke they had. It was "Malacious" German, Malace's made-up version of the tongue, for *mach schnell*, as in, make it quick. Other Malaciousisms were "schliss," instead of *schloss* (castle) for a really shitty pretentious place, as in "This place is schlissy," and "scheissed," as in a verb, like, "I won't scheiss you." Meaning, I shit you not.

Jeffrey chuckled, and suddenly a huge, raucous belly laugh escaped from him as he realized that under Malace's dryness, shyness, and obsessiveness, was a more human person attempting to come out. But to what? Jeffrey had no idea. It was like that with so many people. The system sucked everything from them, except what actually worked for it.

He went through a slew of new files, then reports, recommendations, and more reports; reports on meetings that had been held to talk about more reports, and recommendations that came from those meetings. He started feeling better. Work's healing balm was that it replaced personal anxieties with its own pressing demands, allowing him some relief from John, Ashok, or even Len Silverman. Lunch was brought in, and later he had face-time with colleagues, who showed him their projects. While he was meeting with his Chinese designer, his phone rang. He didn't want to interrupt the meeting, but the caption told him whom it came from. He answered.

Chris's dead-sounding voice met him:

"They did it. You want to go see him again? You can. They allow it, the first week."

Jeffrey exhaled, nodded, and walked back into his own office.

"Are you still there?" Chris asked.

"Yep. I'm here. I don't want to go see him, Chris. Not now. I'm seeing my therapist tonight."

"Can you come by and see me later?"

"I can't."

"Why not?"

Jeffrey was not going to remind him about John, the man he was in love with.

"I can't. I'm really worn out after that trip to India, Chris. None of us are as young as we think we are. I learned that there."

"O.K. But if you don't come to see me really soon, you won't get a chance to. I'm leaving Germany."

"But you still have your classes."

"Thanks. That's a farce. Without Len, I can't even afford to teach here. Funny, my whole life was a house of cards. And he was the glue that held it up."

Jeffrey told him he was sorry. About Len, Chris's career, his life. That was all he could say. He didn't want to feel any worse. All he really wanted to do was see John.

❦

Tony smiled sweetly after Jeffrey sat down. Some extravagantly flowering cherry boughs in the big crystal vase gave a nostalgic English country feeling to Tony's living room. Jeffrey glanced over at it. Very Bloomsbury. He could imagine Virginia Woolf and her sister Vanessa, who had had a passionate affair with a gay painter named Duncan Grant, quietly conversing, sipping tea. He had some tea, a calming infusion Tony offered him.

"You look weary," Tony observed. "How was the trip? I thought you'd try to reach me, but you didn't."

Jeffrey swallowed some tea. He'd never read Virginia Woolf, but had seen films about her. He wondered what she would have thought about Tony. Full of her very qualified "life of the mind," or just "phony Tony"?

"I'm sorry. I was busy."

"That happens. How are you? Am I correct about you being weary and stressed?"

"Correct. Bad things are happening. One of my friends has just been put into Suspension."

Tony nodded, his expression compassionate.

"That is bad, but it could be worse. Suspension is not death. It's a nice alternative, actually, to much of the turmoil and misery people go through."

"People deemed not worthy of being kept alive, you mean? My friend was a doctor, a surgeon."

"And they still put him in Suspension? I guess that happens with the system sometimes. I've heard about it. Not everyone has the life you have, Jeffrey. You should be thankful for it."

"I am."

"But you're still upset, I can see that. What's bothering you? It's not that horrible situation with the man still, the one who'd attacked you? That was a while ago, you should be over it. You can't let negative influences like that destroy you. Too many people depend on you. What can I do to make you feel better?"

Tony looked at him with that beautiful Teutonic face and the eyes that seemed so opaque they could have rolled right out of his head and fitted perfectly into the bearings of some well-designed machine. He stroked his short beard and moved closer to Jeffrey.

"Should we do a massage, or perhaps call on 'help'? Remember what I said about forces that can help you?"

"Yes," Jeffrey answered slowly. "I do remember. And I think I've found one."

"Wonderful! Some kind of spiritual entity?"

"Yes. You could say that. *Spiritual.* It is something that has brought me closer to what I feel is my real self."

"What does it look like? I mean, sometimes you cannot really see them, at least that's what my wife has told me. Elsie says hers looks like a child. Very sweet, *ein kindergeist.* The child is without gender, simply this being of spiritualized energy. Is your help like that?"

"Yes. He's like that. 'Spiritualized energy.' Though not always what I expected."

"Wonderful! You've actually been able to see him? I would think India would be a wonderful place for the spirit to manifest itself. India is famous for its spiritual history. We Germans revere it for that."

"Yes. I can see him."

"Good. But you're very tense, I can tell. Did you want a massage, or just talk?"

"The massage would be good, Tony. But if I talk—"

Tony got up. "What?"

"You have to report—?"

"I only have to report your stress level, Jeffrey. Nothing else that you tell me. Now lie down. Take off your jacket and let me work on your shoulders. You may be so tense that even my touching them may hurt."

He was on his stomach, on the soft leather massage couch that was too padded to be a table. Tony kneaded his shoulders lightly, speaking softly to him.

"I want you to go into that mist, Jeffrey. That beautiful mist of yourself. Remember how we reach it, by going to that place you associate with lovely things and beautiful moments?"

"I remember. I've been there with John."

"*John?*" Tony's voice became acidic. "A man's name. Jeffrey, is this a sexual affair?"

Jeffrey's shoulders tensed.

"I can see it is. I've warned you before. You have to be very careful with these things, Jeffrey. Your place in the world separates you from many of the foolish passions that delude and direct so many people. You are an exceptional human being, and exceptional people have to be above even love sometimes."

"I can't!" Jeffrey said, bursting. "I can't be above it. I know that."

"Then, at least, can he be? Can he give you the space necessary for you to do what you need to do, and stay alive for—"

"Forever, right?"

"No one lives forever, but close to it. I'm here to help you with that; that's what the system pays me to do. Do you want to turn over?"

"No," Jeffrey answered firmly. "I don't want to face you right now."

"But you have to. You must."

Tony placed one hand firmly on the back of Jeffrey's shoulder, to turn him over. His face was so close to Jeffrey's that Jeffrey could feel Tony's warm, tobacco-scented breath on his nose and cheeks.

"Do you have any idea," Tony whispered to him, "how much I love you, Jeffrey? I don't want to see you destroyed. Please believe that. It would be so easy for someone to come in and . . . just destroy all those layers that the system has put down to keep you alive and working. I can't allow that; please be aware of it. I'm giving you this warning because I love you. As your therapist I care about you, and," he swallowed, then said, "I do love you."

"It's not enough," Jeffrey answered.

"Then it sounds to me that you won't take therapy seriously anymore. Is this true?"

"No," Jeffrey replied sincerely. "I will take therapy seriously. I will."

"Good. How soon will you see this man again?"

"Not for a long time. Maybe never."

Tony beamed.

"*Primo*, that's what I want to hear! If you were not my patient, I'd kiss you! I don't want to ever be put into some kind of situation, Jeffrey, where the system will make me say things I don't want to say.

Verstehs du allis?"

"I understand."

"Good. Did you ever go back to that place in the Blichtenwald that you said you liked? With the meadow and the lake?"

"Yes," Jeffrey lied.

"Maybe we should think about that for a while. Then we can do the test. But I must tell you, I'm thrilled that you've come to your senses."

Jeffrey nodded, closing his eyes. Tony was right. He had come to his senses. All of them.

Jeffrey lay on his back on the couch and walked in the Blichtenwald with John, while Tony, unaware, guided him. He wanted to do it in reality that night. He wanted it more than he had ever wanted anything.

❧

But even this imaginary walk did not keep his stress level lower than an eight. Tony was concerned, and they made another appointment for later in the week. Jeffrey put his coat on, then left Tony and hurried down the street. It was a long way to John's and he decided to splurge on a cab. The driver wore a turban, and spoke on his phone in about six languages, switching lines constantly while he drove.

Jeffrey asked him where the phone came from.

"Some little emirate on the Arabian coast, my friend." He laughed. "It's not part of the system. It's wonderful! And very cheap. But first you have to get one. Not easy, my friend. I can get one for you. Would you like that?"

Jeffrey looked at the driver's chubby, dark, slightly wrinkled almost sweetly cherubic face smiling in the rearview mirror. "Why would you do that?"

"For goodness." He grinned.

"In that case I don't want you to do it for me."

"All right," the driver confessed. "If you must know, I get a commission. But it's completely safe, confidential, and only you, I, and a couple of—"

"Your cousins someplace?"

"Exactly. How did you know? Only they will know about it."

"Let me think about it."

The driver, whose name was Omar, handed Jeffrey a card while looking at the congested street teeming with people going about their evening business.

"It's crazy now," he said. "So much traffic, so many people. Germany might as well be Istanbul—same mix and craziness, just German! I'm not crazy about the Germans, but it's good to do business here. It's safer than where I come from."

Jeffrey asked him where that was.

"One of those little emirates I mentioned. Just a piece of sand with oil under it. The Brits had it a long time ago. Then the Americans had it, the Iraqis, the Saudis, the Iranians. The Chinese wanted it and tried to come in. Now it's just who's got the money and who can take out the oil. But the regular people, the little Arabs with big families, they never get it. We end up driving cabs. You're American, I can tell right away. Where are you from, someplace in the South, I think?"

"How can you tell?"

"I have a cousin in Biloxi. He manages motels. It's like being where we're from, just more humid. You want the phone for your girlfriend, right? It has to be private, so your wife doesn't know about it?"

"Something like that."

"I understand. Everyone wants one for a girlfriend or a boyfriend; some men have both. I understand that, too."

"You do?"

"We're all cousins really. The only sin is betrayal. The Christians once understood that; the Arabs always do. I don't understand why everybody fights so much. To me what you believe is a private thing; it should be kept that way. What do you say about that? Mind if I smoke?"

"Smoke all you want to. Just open the window a bit." Then Jeffrey added: "I don't have anything to say about it. Do you know how to get to where I want to go?"

"Sir, I know how to get to where everybody wants to go. That's what's kept me alive!"

Jeffrey smiled, and relaxed as Omar smoked and the smoke drifted out the driver's window. His father had smoked that way, his left elbow hanging out, listening to sad honky-tonk dirges about betrayal, heartbreak, cheating lovers, and what they called in the South one's private, unnamable "miz-ries." They were tunes that left a lingering taste, the indelible taste of hunger itself, for which there was whiskey, tobacco, and country ballads. Mom did not like his father's music. A light classical fan, her taste ranged as far as Puccini arias.

"Music should fit the glassware," she asserted about parties. "You don't put on your dad's kind of music with stemware."

She was right. He found himself nodding, a boy in short pants again, sitting in the front seat with Daddy smoking, driving around town; the boy looking up to him silently. Mom could be a confidante, a conspirator: both she and he stuck giddily to the escapist rewards of clothes, the perfect house and garden, trips to museums to look at antique furniture more than pictures. Polished, beautifully tinted and moisturized, Mom glistened while Daddy had pits in his face and a dry, dull, unmoving quality, more removed than anything from Egypt. Maybe it was the smoking and drinking, but even more there was this sadness that Jeffrey had been too young for too long to approach. Harold Cooper, long dead, brought to brief approximation by Omar's cigarette smoke; he thought he would cry, and he did briefly, choking out of his own little bubble.

Soon they were in the countryside, in the lovely dusk.

"Really peaceful out here," Omar observed. "Do you want the phone? I can take a deposit in cash."

"How much?"

Omar quoted a ridiculous sum; Jeffrey offered him less than half.

"All right. For you, my friend, I'll deliver the whole thing! Where do you want it, at your workplace?"

Obviously no wife at home should know about this. Since cabs were strictly licensed by the city and took credit cards, Jeffrey felt that

Omar would not flake out on him, and the amount of money he gave the driver was too little for a serious scam. To be worthwhile, scams needed more money up front; that was common knowledge.

Soon they were at the awful back road. Omar's brow wrinkled, and he asked Jeffrey if he were sure they were in the right place. Jeffrey was sure. Then they were in front of John's small house. Jeffrey told Omar to meet him midweek at the shop in Afganistrasse where he'd first seen John.

Omar smiled and asked him if he should wait. "Just in case you have trouble. This is not the 'best' neighborhood."

"It's O.K.," Jeffrey told him.

He used a credit card to pay for the trip, which was expensive because of a large energy surcharge. He tipped Omar in cash, got out, and walked toward the door, almost trembling with excitement, he wanted to see John so much.

The door was locked; the house was dark. But John's car was there, so he could not be too far away. Jeffrey walked around to the back, near the mill stream, and found a window slightly open. He eased his way in, lit a kerosene lamp and sat on the mattress. He looked at John's paintings, transfigured by their strength and brightness, their clean and bracingly fresh colors, a quality they had that could only be called spiritual. Not meaning illustrating something religious, but spiritual in their deeply felt intimacy. They told stories directly: ones you kept locked in your own heart. Some painters painted with their eyes, others with their fingers, penises, vulvas, testicles, even their hearts. But John van der Meer painted with his soul, tortured as it was.

Then John appeared out of the darkness with a stranger. He smiled at Jeffrey, and embraced him.

"You got in! Wonderful. Sorry, I didn't know you were coming. You remember each other?"

It was Pik, the ringleader of the boys who'd attacked him. Jeffrey felt a shiver go through him.

"I didn't realize you knew each other so well," he said coldly.

John's face smarted, like he'd been slapped.

"He's going to help you, if you ever need help," he explained. "I told him about you, that you're my friend. They're not unreasonable, right, Pik?"

"*Was ist* 'unreasonable'?"

"It means, *Arshloch*, that you don't fuck with him, and I'll do favors for you if you need it. Get it?"

He mussed Pik's hair, and offered him a beer. He gave one to Jeffrey, too, and the three of them sat on the floor drinking it.

"You're a good man," Pik said to Jeffrey. "Johann told me you're good. You like boys, I mean for friends?"

"Yes," Jeffrey said softly. "I like boys."

"Good. Few people like them. They say they do, but don't. I love boys. Friends. Whatever. I have a girlfriend, but," he shrugged, "she's like a boy."

"Sometimes you can't always be a boy," Jeffrey observed, slowly drinking the beer. He felt really old now, far away from Pik, even too far from John, and any distance from him hurt. Without warning, he started crying.

"What's wrong?" John asked.

"I don't know. Maybe I'm happy just to be here."

John came over and knelt by him and consoled him. He looked over at Pik, and said: "Maybe you should go. I'll see you soon. Thanks for everything. *Danke sehr.*"

"What is it?" John asked, after Pik had left.

"I'm in love with you."

"I know," John said. "It makes me sad. I feel too guilty for love. But in those moments when I'm not feeling bad, I feel the same way. Or close."

"I'm getting you a phone for you to use. Nothing can be traced to you. I also want to get a place in the city where we can meet, just spend the night and be together, so I can continue working. I have to keep working. I'll die if I don't. Maybe you figured that out."

"Yes, I did." He tried to smile. "Does it keep you young, like, my age? Sometimes I wonder. You're not really young, are you? You're like a boy who's an old man, and an old man who's a boy."

"I'm not a boy. I've never been."

"But you can be with me. I do love you."

They made love again. It was nice, just folding into each other. Jeffrey felt that they had never done it before, he was so deeply in love. Then John drove Jeffrey back into the city, almost to his apartment building. When he got in, there was a message from Chris Stewart.

"Jeffrey, if you can, can you please come and see me tonight? It doesn't make a difference what time. I'm going to be leaving here soon, and there are things I want you to know."

Chapter Sixteen

*W*orn out, Jeffrey found another cab to take him to Chris's plush apartment building. It felt strange calling it Chris's, instead of Chris and Len's. The two of them had seemed so bonded despite their often comic conflicts. It was easy to think of Len as a comic character. His endless anxieties about money while throwing it around; the oversized yacht he pined for. Why didn't he just get himself a regular boat, stick it in a German river, and enjoy it? Len complained about Chris's extravagance and queeny ridiculousness, but obviously Chris needed a large, not always handy dose of patience and resilience with Len. The extravagance was his reward for keeping that up.

Len couldn't even stop being a dysfunctional narcissist long enough to survive. Surely, he could have put up enough of a fight to ransom himself; somewhere he must have had some leverage in this game.

Jeffrey extended his card to pay the cabby. Passing electronic surveillance, he was buzzed into the lobby, a giant bon-bon box of gilt mirrors and elaborate moldings. He got into the elevator, wondering what kind of dramatic reception Chris would give him.

But it was Azeena who came to the door. She'd been crying. There were empty crates and boxes all over the place, and what looked like a quick attempt at packing, but not much taking place.

"He's in the bedroom," she said without looking at Jeffrey. "I been waiting, sir. What am I going t'do?"

Jeffrey had no answer. He walked into the baronial bedroom, where bedclothes were strewn about, with stacks of books heaped on top. It smelled like it had not been aired out in a week. Chris lay on his side at the far end of the bed, facing a wall, away from Jeffrey, wearing only boxer shorts and a bloated T-shirt. Jeffrey walked over cautiously and switched on a light.

There were empty pill bottles on the night table, all for sleep or nervous anxiety, and an empty glass that smelled of scotch. Azeena stroked one of Chris's hands that lay inert, like something merely attached to his body.

"I found him like this," she sobbed. "I work for them for ten years. They're like m'family. Poor Doctor Len, now Mister Chris. I called the police. What can I do? They'll ask me all kinds of questions."

"Did he leave anything, Azeena? A note maybe?"

"He left a bunch o'stuff on the table, in the living room."

Jeffrey walked over and found a short note to the head of Chris's department, apologizing for "leaving without notice. But I'm sure you guys can find someone else to drag the Renaissance into a period when it's not wanted"; an equally bitter note to Angelina Harkness; and one to Len.

> My darling,
>
> I know you can't get this or know it. I had a hard time too often telling you how I felt about you. You are the only noble person I've ever known in my life. The only good one. I've been a fool a lot of the time, and pretty stupid despite publishing so much of value. But you've always believed in me and loved me, and I can't go on without you. It's as simple as that.

Finally, there was one to himself:

> Dear Jeffrey,
>
> I know you must hate me for exposing you to this. It was a dirty trick, but you are probably used to that. I never thought you had a lot of brains or talent, but you know how to get along in this world, something Len and I don't do well. He's a doctor and I'm a scholar, but you could play the bigger games with the bigger guys. I just did it with the small fry. You probably had a great time at my expense, laughing at me inside your sleeve. But I want you to know I've treasured my friendship with you, and admired you, despite all the catty things I've said from time to time. They were simply that: catty. Both Len and I have wills, and I know the system will use a lot of our

resources to keep Len in Suspension until they pull the plug. I know you are a young guy and will be around for a long time, but I want to leave you some of the art and other things in the apartment here in Germany. The places in New York and Ibiza will be sold quickly and the proceeds go to Len's family. He has cousins in Queens he was fond of. They'll get that. I always thought they were pretty jerky and a bunch of boors, but they should have the money even if they thought "Renaissance" was the name of a boat. We never had anything to talk about, but Len did. He could talk to anyone. He was a good man, that's all I can—

A hand touched Jeffrey's shoulder. It was young cop who was such a striking figure of blue-eyed, sturdy German handsomeness that he might have stepped either out of a Renaissance painting by Durer or an old SS poster. Jeffrey smiled.

"I'm Officer Hagen," he said. "Funny, we're both smiling. You're American, too, I guess?"

Jeffrey nodded. Hagen had been in the bedroom, where other cops were now gathered. Pictures were taken, then Chris's body was put into a bag and placed on a light travel gurney. It all happened smoothly, with hardly a word spoken.

"You knew him well?" Hagen asked.

"A little. It's hard to say I knew him well."

"Did he have some reason to murder himself—I mean kill himself?"

Jeffrey told Hagen about Len being put in Suspension.

"Sometimes that is worse than death," Hagen said. "It's supposed to be a prize for being important. But—I'm glad that won't happen to me. When it's over, it should be over."

"Yes."

Jeffrey signed some papers, then returned to his apartment. He tried not to think about this. It brought back too much of his father's death. The system said the past only weighed you down, yet what were you without it? A realization hit him: For decades he'd been only a cipher. A thing few people could ever see. Boyish, good looking, a walking mannequin of style.

He'd gone shopping with his mother once, and she had told him what made a dress beautiful.

"It has to move nicely with the body," she said, her manicured hands making a graceful sweep. "And it has to have a true musical feeling to it."

"Oh, not too loud. Just enough. Right, Mom?" little Jeffrey declared.

"That's genius!" she gushed, and kissed him. "I never realized you're a genius, Jeffy." He felt so warmed by her compliment and remembered the way her lips felt—not too soft, slightly stiff near their perfectly drawn outlines—and the gardenia-and-citrus perfume she wore, called "Pas d'Innocent." It was one of Mom's secrets that she could reveal so much of herself merely in the name of her perfume. The scent was expensive, with a rare, almost shockingly jarring "deep note." He had an excellent olfactory memory, and could remember that lurking scent "note," but could never quite place it. Something profound, certainly. But what was it: fresh earth? Wet clay?

Or was it deep enough to hit oblivion itself? Maybe it was just her own clay feet, coming out no matter how hard she tried to hide them. Still, she had this perfection about her, and even if he were too young to understand it, he definitely wanted it. It was that sense that you could make yourself remote and beautiful, and stay that way. He'd had to hide that desire from other boys, and especially from Daddy, who was on the other side of the moon from all that. He was real, like some barely glimpsable planet.

Maybe even like John van der Meer.

The *sotto voce* buzz among the secretaries, assistants, interns, and even some of the colleagues the next day was that no one had heard from Gregory Malace, who had not shown up as expected. Malace was usually ruthlessly punctual and hard-driven like nails. He had no family. No one knew anything about his personal life, or even if he had one aside from his brief vacations with the extreme sports he liked—the frigid ice climbing and the self-punishing cycling, stuff his ex-Marine dad would have admired. The day wore on. Jeffrey worked hard, every few hours asking his staff if they'd heard from Malace. They hadn't.

At seven, just as things were livening up as far as the increase of pressure was concerned, he got a call on his private line. The sound was scratchy and hard to understand.

"Hullo! I am Sister Saint Mohammed," a singsong, African-inflected voice announced, "calling you from the dear God's Army Hospital in the province of"—Jeffrey could not understand her—"in Kukox. I pray you understand where we are, and why we are here. What I am to tell you is of urgent importance."

"Urgent?" He thought it had to be some overseas scam. But only a few people knew his private line number.

"Do you know a young man," she continued, "very valiant and good, by the name of Gregory Malace?" She pronounced it "MAH-las."

Jeffrey's heart quickened. Had his assistant been shark-hunting there too? He told her he did.

"He's been wounded in a local war, grievously. He's here in our hospital, with lots of his face gone, poor fellow. I think his mind is not too well either. He wrote this number down for me to call you. He's been here for two days, and it's time for him to go home. He'll need money for the airplane ticket and to get out of the territory."

"Territory? What are you talking about? He has plenty of credit available; he can get a ticket anywhere he wants."

"No, sir. He owes a lot of money to the hospital, and our occupying forces, who legally have rights to this territory, have exacted a departure fee for him."

"Are you asking for a ransom, Sister?"

"No, sir. A ransom would be against the word of God. It is a legal fee that the Revolutionary People's Army of Kukox has declared Mr. Malace owes the people. For his medical services, his upkeep, and to recompense the families of men he has hurt."

"Did you say 'hurt'?" It was hard for him to believe. He could not imagine Gregory Malace hurting anyone, except himself.

"Yes, sir. Your young friend has hurt people. So he owes us money. You understand?"

Jeffrey didn't, but all he could ask was, "So what is the fee?"

She gave him a number in Kukox pounds, then translated it into the European Common Monetary Element. It was a large amount of money, equivalent to two years of Malace's salary.

"I can't get this," he told her.

"Then I am afraid Mr. Malace will probably die."

"Isn't that against God's word also?"

"Don't be blasphemous, sir. What is your name?"

He told her, and she said that she would take it down and go to the tribunal that had decided the "departure fee."

"So we can do a little dealing here?" Jeffrey asked.

"If it is for the benefit of Mr. Malace, we can attempt it," she said dryly, then hung up.

Jeffrey looked at his phone to get her number. There was no telling where she had been calling from; the call could have been retransmitted through a number anyplace, for privacy's sake. Privacy and piracy, Jeffrey thought. Funny how close they sounded. He would have to go into the system to see if they had any means of dealing with this. Perhaps they could even rescue Gregory.

Jeffrey tried to call Gladys Hawthorne, a superior in Santa Monica, California, in Human Resources for his part of the system. He'd had a face-on with her once, when she appeared at a meeting he attended on the West Coast. She was attractive enough-looking, in late middle age; but even better, she was very good about working her way through some of the more conservative and complicated aspects of the system. She oversaw a lot of Jeffrey's medical treatments and routines, and silently made decisions in his favor.

Gladys was unreachable, so he left a message with her:

"I need to know something urgent regarding my assistant Gregory Malace."

The Sister's words jumped inside his brain: "Lots of his face gone. Poor fellow. Mind, too." He panicked, like he did with Ashok in the water; but worse. He never thought he could feel this way about Gregory Malace, but his assistant had never been in such a situation before, even when he hurt his leg in Switzerland. He'd worn a large plastic splint for a month, never complaining about it, working as hard as ever. Sometimes Jeffrey could see the pain on his face, but he never uttered a word.

Gladys called him back an hour later. Her tone was no-nonsense, dead serious.

"We know all about it. He signed up for something called 'Extreme Raw Adventure.' *Extreme,* all right. The ads are in underground parts of the media, but they aren't outside the system by a long shot, so we can monitor them. You know, stuff like 'Live the way a real mercenary does! Pure adrenaline excitement!' They give kids some pseudo-military training and professional equipment, and drop them off in warring parts of Asia or Africa. I hate these things. They really muck up my job, Jeffrey. We had a girl from a really nice family—I mean, like finishing school—get herself enrolled, and she was killed in one day! You can only imagine what her parents went through. All they got back was some of her body parts. Your assistant has screwed himself, Jeffrey. I hate to put it that way, but that's the case in a nutshell."

Jeffrey was scared to ask the next question, but did:

"What are you saying, Gladys?"

"We can go into his bank account and take out any money there to bring him back. Or we can advance him some money, pure and simple. Though the system feels sincere sympathy and compassion for Gregory Malace, it does not feel that he's worthy of this kind of ransom. And we sure as hell are not going to attempt an in-person rescue. Wars go on in these African countries forever. They're basically about what faction gets to bleed the locals the most."

"Sincere sympathy." Jeffrey knew that was pro-forma, since their conversation would be electronically recorded. Basically, the system would let Malace die. Jeffrey asked Gladys how much money it would allow for Malace, and she told him that people in her group had already been contacted by Sister Saint Mohammed; in fact, the Sister knew exactly how to work her way through it. Jeffrey did not mention that the Sister had hinted to him that the Kukox Army might consider bargaining. He did ask, though, that the money be sent to his personal bank account.

"That's unusual, Jeffrey. It's kind of you to put yourself so far out for a subordinate."

"He's a good designer, and a nice young man."

"I'm sure he is. The fastest I can get that line of currency to you is thirty-six hours. How is everything else, Jeffrey? Are you enjoying Germany? I'm sure it's nothing like Santa Monica, but I've always wanted to see it."

❧

He would have to get the rest of the money from his own account. He didn't like doing it; in most circumstances, money was your only security, despite perks from the system. Having your own money gave you a degree of privacy and dignity. For this reason, he'd been secretly squirreling away money, even sending it as "gifts" to Lelia Weeks, a distant, unmarried cousin he trusted in Alabama, with the agreement that this was a "rainy day" fund for both of them. He had used his own money to get John to India, and knew he would use a lot more of it on John. But he would not simply allow Gregory to die, no matter how much it would cost him.

The Sister called back at eleven o' clock that night, German time.

"God's greetings to you! I spoke with the tribunal. They have decided to be merciful to this young man. They will reduce the liberation fee by five-and-twenty percent. I know that will be good news for you. You can wire the money into this account."

"How do I know it will get Gregory back here?"

"Do you want to come down to retrieve him? I know that in his condition, he'd be glad to see you."

Jeffrey did not answer. It would be impossible for him to fly to Kukox. He did not even know where the hell Kukox was.

"Sir. I myself will see to it that Mr. Malace gets on the plane. I am a godly person, and do not lie!"

There was no video portion of the conversation, for which Jeffrey was glad. He was afraid even to imagine what Gregory looked like. But he asked if he could speak with him, and a few minutes later

Gregory was on the line.

He was so weak, he could barely speak.

"You're going t'help me?" he whispered.

"Yes," Jeffrey said.

"Thank God. Maybe I should just die."

"Don't say that, Gregory."

Gregory choked on phlegm, trying to get his voice back while at the same time breaking down.

"I screwed up bad. I'm worthless . . . a piece of shit. No wonder nobody ever cared about me."

"I'm going to help you, Gregory. I'll get you back here. Now that I know you're alive, I'll do it personally."

Gregory only moaned, "thanks," and got off the line.

He went to see Tony, who was fairly dispassionate about the situation.

"Your friend seems to have a martyrdom complex. Some people do. What's important is for you not to get involved with it."

"I *am* involved. I'm going to have to bring him out with my own money. The system won't."

"*Ja*, it's unfortunate. Money can be an ugly issue. Will you resent this expenditure later, when he comes back to work? He'll be around all the time. The mature, responsible thing would be for him to have some plan to repay you. That should also curb this crazy desire he has to put himself at risk."

Jeffrey smiled. Tony had little idea how much risk Jeffrey had put himself in, and he'd see to it that that situation remained unchanged.

Tony placed his hand on Jeffrey's chest. They were sitting very close on his couch after a massage session. He ran his hand through Jeffrey's hair, and let it stay there.

"I've been thinking much about you," his therapist said. "Your stress levels have been high, and I don't want to see anything happen to you. This has not been a good time for you, with the problems with your friends Len and then Chris. But sadness is a part of life, *mein lieber freund.*"

Lieber freund, dear friend.

Tony had never addressed him exactly that way, with so much melting intimacy and tenderness in his voice. In his fantasies, Jeffrey had wanted to kiss Tony for years, simply to kiss him. And now it seemed possible. Tony had spoken what seemed so long ago about those forces that could help him. Unseen, almost unknowable, and yet there. Jeffrey had been aware that John was one; but in truth, was Tony one, also?

Jeffrey felt as if he were skating on ice that was at once too thin and too tempting to resist. On the kind of impulse he would allow himself only after knowing John, he decided to jump in, even though it might destroy their professional relationship.

"I'd like to kiss you, Tony."

"I know. I've known it for a while."

"Would you let me?"

"I would now."

Jeffrey smiled.

"Why now?"

"Because I care so much about you, despite my role with the system which both allows me to see you and help you, and also . . . I guess you know the rest. So I would allow it, *wirklich,* since I know what you've been through lately."

"You only know some of it," Jeffrey said. In the past he never would have said that, but now he felt very disarmed.

Tony leaned in and kissed Jeffrey softly on his lips. It was a chaste, almost brotherly kiss with a hint of passion in it.

"What's the rest?" Tony asked. "Now that we have gone this far, tell me the rest."

"I'm in love."

"With the man who attacked you?"

Jeffrey nodded.

Tony flinched.

"Damn! He's opened up everything in you, what else can I say? You might not have helped that boy Gregory, if you weren't in love."

Tony got up.

"I'm frightened for you."

Unexpected tears flowed from his eyes. Jeffrey grabbed his therapist's dark, strong hand and, rising, brought it to his lips.

"I can't protect you or help you, if you continue with this," he warned Jeffrey, then reached for a tissue for his nose. He paced about nervously.

Jeffrey sat down again.

Tony regained himself and sat with him, taking his hand.

"I won't tell anyone about this," he swore to Jeffrey. "It'll be our secret. Let me kiss you once more, just to seal it."

Chapter Seventeen

The next evening, Jeffrey went to the shop on Afganistrasse to meet Omar, and get the phone. After waiting an hour, he went back to the square where he'd first arranged to meet John. John was there under a dim streetlight, casually smoking a beedi and sketching a group of Arab boys who were lounging on a nearby bench, smiling and touching each other.

"I like the way those kids act. Not like the Dutch, who are always so serious."

"They can be serious too, just not in the same way."

He told John about the problem with Gregory Malace.

"I understand!" John said. "Sometimes the only way to feel alive is to almost invite death. This is one of the few areas of the city that's not completely canned or under system control. Yes, I can see why your friend would go to Africa to die."

"But he didn't go to die. He went to fight, and kill."

John shook his head.

"Why fight and kill unless you really need to—just for the thrill of it? It's a waste. Still, I can see why your Gregory would do it."

"They'll bring him home soon. I'll probably have to take care of him. It'll take up a lot of my time."

"Then I'll take care of him," John said. He was serious; he repeated the offer.

Jeffrey wasn't sure about this.

"He may be too injured to be so far out, where you live. He'll need doctors, a nurse maybe."

"Then you want him to stay with you, alone?"

Jeffrey thought for a moment.

"No. I have room in my apartment for the both of you. I'll tell the building management that you're his nurse. How does that sound?"

"Sounds fine. But I've never seen your building."

Jeffrey made a snap decision, like asking Tony if he could kiss him.

"You will now."

He pulled a cab over.

"You'll need I.D. to get into the building," he told John.

"I don't want them to know me," John said. "It's another part of the system. They'll track me down with it."

"Then I'll sneak you in. It's easy to get out; they never ask for I.D. when you're leaving. Just tell them you're a doctor or a nurse."

John frowned. "I don't look like a doctor."

"Tell them you're a doctor on your day off. 'Doctor' impresses these people more than 'nurse.' If you can be a Dutch filmmaker in India, you can be a doctor in Germany."

About twenty-five minutes later, they left the cab a short distance from Jeffrey's building, which like a great castle was set off by itself, surrounded by a moat of intimidating luxury in the form of waiting limousines and big sedans outside restaurants and shops.

"You live here?" John asked.

Jeffrey nodded, and the two of them entered the building. A young Spanish woman named Lucy was by herself at the front desk, doing security—a good sign. Jeffrey told her he was "going up for a short while with Dr. van der Meer."

"Do you have I.D., Doctor?" Lucy asked genially. "I'm sorry. It's security. Everyone's got to show I.D., no matter who they're with. If my boss looks at the visitor log, I'll be in trouble."

John pretended to search his pockets, then piped up with:

"I must have left it in the car!"

"Can you go get it?" she asked. "If that's not too much trouble."

John tossed his head theatrically, and smacked his brow with the heel of his palm.

"It is, I'm afraid! My wife has the car now. She's with the kids, and I'm stuck. Jeffrey wanted me to look at his new—what was the name of that artist?"

"Brinker. A new guy, from Holland, where Dr. van der Meer is from. Listen," Jeffrey promised Lucy, "I'll vouch for him. You've known me for years. We'll come back and bring his I.D. later, when his wife comes around for him."

Lucy nodded. "How many kids do you have?"

"Three," John said. "Three little ones, and are they a handful!"

Lucy commiserated with him. As John and Jeffrey walked toward the elevator bank, their images were captured continuously in a variety of retrievable formats, then catalogued according to race, height, approximate age and weight, and even some characteristics such as moles, beards, and hairstyle. On Jeffrey's high floor, they were met by polished wood and mirrors, arrangements of flowers, and high arched windows that overlooked the whole city. Jeffrey took out a card and opened his door.

"*Gott!*" John exclaimed nervously, not so much dazzled as unhinged by the effortless, coldly sterile luxury and technology in which Jeffrey lived. "How do you stand my place?"

"That's easy. You're there."

John smiled. Jeffrey invited him to take his shoes off and make himself at home. John was soon padding around barefoot on the thick carpet. Jeffrey found some brandy that they drank from big snifters.

"Where will you put your friend?" John asked.

Jeffrey had a large room for music and entertainment, like a den, that could double as a guest room. In one of the few comfortable areas of it stood a lusciously curvy love seat in a mouth-drooling, warm lipstick red, very "Dolce Vita" Italian design, circa-1963, that, if needed, popped open to a usable-enough bed. John thought the room was too posh for a very sick man to be laid up in.

"Suppose he throws up on your carpet or destroys some of your expensive furniture?" John made a big frown. "You don't know what kind of control he's going to have over his bladder or bowels."

Jeffrey had not thought about that. He decided he'd roll up the carpets and put plastic coverings on the floor and some of the better furniture, depending upon how much protection was needed.

The problem was, how to protect John? No matter what they said, getting him up into the apartment without the system having some knowledge of it would be impossible. Their betrayal by some component of the system was inevitable. In fact, making up any kind of story would only complicate things and open them up to more suspicion.

They sat close on the louche couch, which had always had a wicked sense of humor about it, as if some sexy Italian starlet in a tight dress and big hat should have been sitting there, posing for cameras. Jeffrey looked into John's green eyes.

"Are you sure you want to do this?"

John grinned. "Why not? This is perfect. You're so high up in the system, they won't be interested in doing much of a check on me."

"What makes you think that?"

"It was no problem getting me into India. And no one's followed me since then."

Why would they, Jeffrey thought, and why was John so secretive? Was he still psychiatrically committable, or had he done something else, besides murder his wife—if it were murder? Jeffrey had decided not to think about it that way. It was an accident. People drowned all the time in undertows. John had simply panicked, the way Ashok claimed he had. John might have been complicit, but certainly not completely culpable in his wife's death. Jeffrey had to live with this mystery in John's past. And he could live with it, if John could. He had been trained not to ask difficult ethical questions that could compromise the system, and he would not ask questions now.

Except for one:

"Why don't we take our clothes off and test the couch? I've never used it as a bed."

"Ah, an ulterior motive," John said. They opened the couch. When they were both naked, John suddenly jumped off it.

Half hard, he said, "I need something to drink."

He walked toward the kitchen, and Jeffrey followed him. There was some beer in the refrigerator, and John poured himself one.

"How did you know where to find the glasses?" Jeffrey asked.

"All of these places are alike, once you get used to them."

"When did you do that?"

John kissed him, his mouth pleasantly beery.

"Some time ago. I told you, my wife and I were like a magazine couple. My wife's parents lived like this. We did too, for a while."

"I see. Funny, you hardly ever use her name. It was Cynthia, right?"

John sighed wistfully.

"I don't like to use it. I've betrayed her enough. It wasn't her fault that she was the way she was. It was mine. I lied to myself, and I've had to pay for it ever since. You always pay for it when you lie to yourself. You do, too; don't you?"

All Jeffrey could say was:

"Have you betrayed me, too?"

"Fuck you!" John screamed, unexpectedly breaking into raucous laughter. "No! I haven't betrayed you. Only myself. I've betrayed me! Does that answer your fucking question?"

"Yes," Jeffrey said softly. "But do you miss all this?"

"Never. I would miss myself twice as much as I could ever miss any of this. Come on!"

He grabbed Jeffrey's hand and took the beer back to the guest room, lying back on the couch with his legs open, gazing at Jeffrey. Like a gun going off, Jeffrey exploded with sexual tension. His mouth found John's cock; he wanted to suck the very heat out of him. John leaned back, beer dribbling from his lips onto the exposed vermillion of the couch and onto Jeffrey. Jeffrey didn't care. He felt like Marcello Mastroianni: decadent, marvelous. John grabbed him by the shoulders, reversing positions, sucking Jeffrey to orgasm: like that—*presto!*—even though he had never got entirely hard, as if some pure hot voltage, coming all the way up through him, had bypassed a full erection.

"Wowww!" John said, licking cum with beer from the side of his mouth and liking the taste of it, then following it with more from the glass. "For an old guy you know how to do this."

Jeffrey smiled. "How do you know I'm that old?"

"I know. Not how old you are, but you're smart. I knew that from the start."

"Did you?"

But before John could answer, Jeffrey tickled the bottoms of his feet, making John spill more beer on the precious couch. But Jeffrey couldn't have cared less. He was too busy licking almost every inch of John.

Soon it was dark. The two of them wandered naked through the apartment, the city below them glowing and twinkling with its display of wealth and power. Jeffrey loved it, forgetting for a moment why John was there. The few guys he'd brought up to his apartment never felt at home there; it was too *luxe*, too staged, too private, and yet not nearly personal enough. Sometimes even Jeffrey felt that way. But John seemed to fit in, or the place fitted him. They were in the living room, watching stars and dark shifting clouds play hide-and-seek with the crescent moon while inside the glimmer of screens programmed with endless loops of "Art" captured their attention from time to time, but never conflicted with the view or their own closeness. Jeffrey ordered dinner; when it was brought up he realized it was getting late and it might be best if John left. Anything out of the ordinary (that John had left in the early morning hours, for instance) would be pulled into the system.

They ate, then redressed.

Jeffrey went down with John in the elevator; since Lucy was no longer on duty, he did not have to offer any explanations. He smiled to the man at the desk and several porters at the door, then walked out into the street with John. Cars passed, some with uniformed drivers. John seemed relaxed, like a film star returned to the glamour he was made for. He kissed Jeffrey, then walked to the pubtran entrance.

Jeffrey returned to his apartment. Obviously, there were aspects of John he did not know. Despite the rustic way in which he chose to live, he was comfortable in the world of wealth and power. He got into bed and thought about John; he was inside Jeffrey's skin now. But maybe there were hidden aspects that made John van der Meer more than just another impostor in a world of imposters. Aspects that made him touch Jeffrey's heart and psyche through the most direct route to them, as perhaps even a reflection of Jeffrey's own, deepest self.

As the lights of the sky and the city spun their distant witchery outside, Jeffrey's eyes fell on a large mirror not far from the bed. He drew himself up and gazed into it. John looked back at him, his eyes all green twilight, his limbs mapped with stars. Jeffrey longed to walk into this dark mirror image, to hold John and kiss him, until death itself would seem as much of an illusion as what the mirror held.

❦

Two days later in the early evening, Jeffrey went to the airport, not knowing if he'd need an ambulance for Gregory, or a hearse. All he knew was that Gregory's name was on the passenger list of a legitimate scheduled airline, not some fly-by-night African provincial operation, of which more than a dozen flew into Germany, often carrying mail-order brides for manual laborers, or girlfriends for mercenary fighters looking for romance. Jeffrey saw a group of these women in brilliant costumes and makeup get off a plane, and be herded into customs and immigration. He waited, looked at his palm screen for recent news, checked Gregory's name through the airline, and waited some more.

Finally, Gregory's plane arrived, and the time for it to gate and discharge passengers crept by. As passengers began to deplane, a young woman in an officer's uniform approached him. She was very pretty, dark skinned, and North African-looking, like Azeena. She was shaking.

"Mr. Cooper?" she said to him tensely. "Are you Mr. Jeffrey Cooper?"

Jeffrey told her he was.

"Your friend's in the back of the plane. He—he didn't make it. I don't know how they could let him fly like that. He started bleeding, running a fever. He should never have been on board. It was horrible!"

She broke down crying. "How could they do that to that man? How could they put him on the plane?"

"What can I do?" Jeffrey asked.

"Your name's on his ticket, that you'd be meeting him. That's why we allowed him on. We knew he was hurt really bad. It's a war zone. Airlines have stopped flying in; it's too dangerous. What was he doing there? Boys like him don't belong in a place like that. Maybe criminals, that's all."

"Why'd you pick him up?"

"Humanitarian reasons. This Sister called and we had dealt with her in the past. We knew he'd die otherwise, but hoped not with us. He should have been on an ambulance plane, but I guess there's no money in Kukox for that. Kukox is so poor, and always at war. This woman, Sister—"

"Saint Mohammed?"

"Yes. She put him on. The captain didn't want to take him, but she said if we didn't, he'd die soon, very septic. We gave him a row to himself and took him. I still feel terrible. He's so young."

"He was." Jeffrey could barely hold on to himself. Gregory was only twenty-seven.

"We can put him in the morgue here at the airport. They have one. Does he have family?"

"He must, someplace. Thanks for the offer. If you can do that, it would be very good. I can take care of any fees. I have enough cash, if necessary."

She led him to a small side room used for storing airline equipment. There was already a long, zippered, dark olive-green bag on a gurney.

"Do you want time alone with him? His face is mostly bandaged. From what I could see, he must have been a nice-looking young man. It's up to you, Mr. Cooper." She stopped speaking, her body still shaking, then said, "I'll give you a moment."

She left, shutting the door.

Jeffrey nervously approached the bag. He needed to say good-bye; after all, he might be the only person who would. He'd never been good at saying this. He had never had to to his dad or his mom. She had died in old age much the way she had lived: remote, stylish, her hair and face always beautifully done, with nothing said that would upset any illusions. Gregory's life had been spent in isolation, though Jeffrey wondered how much more isolated it was than most people's. He wished John were there. John—Johann van der Meer— that other mystery in his life, but one who had exploded Jeffrey's own bitter isolation.

Jeffrey struggled to disengage the first unyielding teeth of the long zipper. It finally parted, and he looked at the small exposed terrain of Gregory's face. Thick, dark, blood-encrusted bandages covered his cheeks, crossing his nose, but his expression was peaceful at last. He'd never seen Gregory, always over his head in work, fueled by coffee and resentment, look so peaceful. His resentment itself must have been awful, but what else could he feel, without the laser-eyed abilities which early on had marked Jeffrey Cooper?

Gregory had his "Release" at last; Cooper could see it on the young man's face.

"Shit!" Jeffrey sobbed, stabbing at his tears. The poor sonovabitch was fulfilled, finally. No more numbing overwork. No more "X" sports pushing him up to the gates of Hell, where the thrill was just walking away alive. Gregory had pushed beyond the gates, and Jeffrey did not know if he wanted to laugh or howl, or even hit something as John might do.

He choked back another tear. He had to hold on to himself. It was easy to imagine those bandages now on his face, covering the unchanging veneer of youth he had convinced himself he adored. He did not want to look anymore; it would be too easy to fall apart completely.

He zipped the bag up, as the young woman returned with a sheaf of papers to sign. Amazingly, they resembled a car rental contract. He handed some money to another clerk from the airport's Department of Material Holdings, for the morgue fee, then left as a rush of numbness overcame him, leaving him feeling slightly nauseated. As the numbness spread to the world around him, he wondered if Gregory had somehow existed in that same feeling for years.

Chapter Eighteen

*H*e took something to sleep that night, after injecting himself with a double dose of Bernd Ostreich's youth-retaining drugs. But that sense of intense failure, of paralysis, of numbness stayed with him. And the next day at work, he had to face telling people about Gregory's death. It was not easy, and he decided he'd assemble the whole staff and tell them, as much as he could, the truth. The system would not like it, and every word he said would be taken down, transcribed in various retrievable formats, possibly leading to a formal memo, not a real reprimand but a "Notice of Significant Language Issues" from an officer in Human Resources, like Gladys Hawthorne in Santa Monica, although possibly one not as nice and humane as Gladys.

He rarely got the whole staff together, usually just for the yearly winter holiday party, and then one in summer, that was called July Liberation Day, which was not meant to be patriotic as much as a reminder that political boundaries still had some, mostly sentimental, significance: the Americans, the French, the Germans, even the various Asian members of his staff still retained some national ties beyond basic global trading relationships.

He gazed around at the assembled faces, many of them quite young. Their expressions were witheringly serious.

"I need to tell you about Gregory Malace. We all admired Gregory. He was an extremely hard worker and dedicated to this group. I'm afraid there have been a lot of rumors about him, so I think we need to have the truth told. And the truth is, I'm afraid Gregory will not be coming back to us . . ."

When it was over, a lot of the young women had tears running down their cheeks, and some of the young men were close to it. The older people took the news fairly stoically, and Jeffrey wondered what were they thinking. Was it, "He had it coming"? Or maybe, simply, just "Poor bastard"?

He arranged for tea and cookies to be served afterward, by a German caterer with Thai and Turkish workers who smiled brightly, thinking perhaps that this might be a birthday celebration. Then, on his way back to his office, Jeffrey realized he'd have to find a replacement for Gregory. There were several possibilities lower down on his staff, but few of them had the capacity to do the drudge work that Gregory had, and none of them with real talent wanted to be sidetracked for years as Jeffrey Cooper's overworked assistant.

Then a flash came to him: Ashok.

Ashok had wanted to come to Germany in the worst way, so here was the perfect opening. Ashok could work hard, if not as hard perhaps as Gregory. He would also put a different, very useful spin on the position. He was not only young, self-starting, ambitious certainly, and talented, but capable of dealing with clients, the difficult Money, and other parts of the system, something Gregory could never approach. Jeffrey had learned in those last days in Mumbai that he could respect Ashok, even if he could not trust him totally (though in Jeffrey's world, not trusting people was simply part of the formula). He might have to hire someone else to do the drudge work, but Ashok could take a lot of the responsibility off his own tense shoulders, without threatening Jeffrey too much. And if he did threaten Jeffrey, at least the young man would be close by in Germany, not off in India.

Jeffrey liked the thought of it, especially as the success of "That Woman" approached: now they would be too entwined for Ashok even to try to pull out ahead. Ashok could be a worthy ally, one who knew him and some of his secrets, and was strong enough to withstand the regular detonations Cand blood-lettings within the system. Criticisms that used to shake Gregory to his core, Ashok would weather beautifully. In fact, professionally, he might prove to be an excellent lightning rod for them.

Jeffrey even liked the way Ashok would look in the office: an exotic, queerly dramatic presence among so many bland system people. The idea seemed almost karmically inspired. He called Ashok, jumping in exactly as John might do.

"Dear Jeffrey!" Ashok exclaimed. "I dared not imagine hearing from you at this point! How did you like what we finally did with 'That Woman'?"

"It was fine," Jeffrey said. "I think 'That Woman' will take off."

"You don't seem very enthused, Jeffrey. What's wrong?"

Jeffrey told him about Gregory.

Ashok's good-looking face fell on the monitor. Then he resumed his patient, sweet smile.

"In Africa, my God! What a spark of aggression beneath that exterior. In India, he would have been considered truly dangerous, hiding everything like that. But, Jeffrey, my friend, you're kind enough to have compassion for him. I admire that."

Ashok's face reminded Jeffrey once again of that amazing shopping bag from Neat House, the drama of which was much more intense and memorable than anything in it. After all, what was in it: just the usual tchotchkes sold all over the world?

"Do you really, Ashok?"

"I admire you, Jeffrey. You must know that. I am foolish sometimes, but I admire you awfully."

"Good. I'd like to ask you something. Would you like to work here with me? I need an assistant now. You wanted to move to Germany. Here's your chance."

After a half-second pause, Ashok exploded:

"I can't believe it! Are you for real? I would *leap* to work with you! I'd—"

"All right," Jeffrey said, not really smiling but trying to be genuinely warm. "I'll start the paperwork."

That evening he went to see Tony. Once he'd settled in, Tony said, "You look really tired. What's wrong?"

He told him about seeing Gregory, and then about his decision to hire Ashok Rahman.

"The Indian? Are you crazy? He's going to be real trouble. Why?"

"I think I need him, Tony. I can't go back to my old life. Not feeling anything, just being a part of the system that—"

Tony jolted, his face flushed with feeling.

"Shut up!" he commanded. "Don't ever say that to me. You're not just a *part* of the system. You're gifted. The system has recognized that. I'd do anything to be a part of the system the way you are."

"No, you wouldn't, Tony."

"You're not going to die, and I cannot let you. Jeffrey, please—"

He had to stop to contain himself. Jeffrey looked at him, as puzzled by his therapist as he would ever be. Tony resumed.

"If you continue like this, Jeffrey, I'll be forced to report what's going on. There's no way around it. I have to keep testing your stress levels; I have to give them some kind of evaluation of what's happening. I don't have a choice in this anymore. I'll end up in real jeopardy if I don't. I'm sorry to have to tell you that, but it's the truth."

He paused again. Jeffrey looked at Tony, feeling almost sorry for his therapist, but after seeing Gregory, devoid of any available sympathy. He said nothing. Tony went on.

"You must know that Dr. Ostreich and I, at some point, would be forced to be part of a decision we don't want to make. Sooner or later I'm afraid the decision will be taken away from us. You must know that, also. So, Jeffrey, you've got to change your attitude very, very fast. I implore you to."

"What do you think I should do?"

Tony did not hesitate.

"This man you're seeing has got to go. I mean it. He's bad for you. As for the Indian, if you think he'll be as useful to you as young Malace was, give him a reasonable probation period; and if he's not, go on your merry way."

Jeffrey smiled wryly. It felt good to be able to be able to say what he was going to say. He felt stronger.

"I'm not sure I can go on my 'merry way' anymore, Tony."

Tony lost patience. Jeffrey simply watched him as Tony's face seethed with anger, his fists clenched.

"*Gott! Es macht*—what should I do with you, Jeffrey? Let's put all the cards on the table. You're rocking the boat we're both in, and I don't like it. I swear, I don't like this!"

Silence fell between them, while Jeffrey felt oddly removed, which was probably the way Tony would have liked him to feel, advising him to step outside himself, and enter into that . . . but no. This was not because of Tony. It was because Jeffrey was becoming more sure of his real self, the one connected to a reclaimable history, with feelings flooded with a risky but truly intimate love.

The phone rang, shattering the silence. Tony's English spouse, Robert, was on the other end. Tony apologized, saying he needed to take it. He took the call in the hallway.

Jeffrey was sure that Tony only needed a moment away from him to cool down. Jeffrey looked around at the decor of the nicely appointed office, suggesting breeding and a comforting "old boy's" respect for civilization and Art. A frieze of pale, fog-gray glazed tiles stamped with reliefs of Arcadian flute players and seminude Greek youths banded the space below the windows. The old table lamps, glowing with jewel-toned stained glass in erotically suggestive flowers, always made him feel comforted. He would miss this place, and what it offered him: some release from . . .

"Usual *Scheisse*," Tony announced on his return. "It's always Robert or Elsie, or—" He smiled, delighted with himself. "Our daughter's getting married and Robert's helping with the wedding. Since Robert and I never did the *kinder* thing, now he gets to be Daddy Number Two. But you know he can be very pushy in his English way—not the same as the German way, but it's bad enough."

"What's it all about?" Jeffrey asked, not caring, but pleased by the change in Tony's face, which seemed more composed and in control.

"Like I said, 'usual *Scheisse*.' The flowers. What kind of music. What Hortense is going to wear."

"Hortense?"

Tony smiled. "Oh, you never knew my daughter's name, or did you forget it?"

"We don't talk about your daughter often."

"No, I guess not. That's the problem with therapy: I know so much more about you than you know about me."

Jeffrey looked at him. What a wonderful illusion. He knew a lot about Tony. The realization hit Jeffrey hard: He did not want to see Tony again, as dreadful and final as that sounded. But he had no idea how he'd "terminate" with him, even if the system would allow it.

Terminate. He pushed the word out of the way, then got up.

"I think I want to leave," he announced.

Tony looked startled.

"We haven't tested you."

"I know. But I don't want to stay. I hope you understand, Tony. This is our last session."

Tony's face collapsed.

"I've done everything I *can* for you."

"I know you have. You've been good."

"You can't just quit, Jeffrey. You'll need another therapist. I'll help you find one, if you want."

Jeffrey nodded.

"You've been more involved with me than anyone else, Tony. You've tried to protect me. I don't think I can do this anymore."

Tony repressed a sob. Jeffrey could almost feel it in Tony's throat. He knew what that sob was like, and how much it genuinely hurt to repress it.

"You're about to *blow* the whole thing, Jeffrey. Aren't you?"

Jeffrey closed his eyes. This was harder than even he'd imagined.

"I don't want to think that far ahead."

"All right. But I need to tell the system something. I can't lie to you. I've got to tell them *something.*"

"Tell them that I had something pressing, that you can't handle me anymore. Tell them I need more handling than you—maybe I just need to handle myself, while I've still got something to handle."

Jeffrey got up to walk out, then looked back at Tony for the last time. He looked crushed. It took all of Jeffrey's resolve not to run to Tony and hold him. But he knew that, in the end, Tony would be a part of everything that would destroy him. And he had to start thinking about preserving himself, without Tony's help.

❦

At work the next day, Jeffrey announced that he was taking time off, at least a week, before Ashok Rahman arrived in Germany to be his new assistant. He met with his colleagues in the conference room around a large polished, dark cherry-wood table that had once been venerated as a work of art in Japan, its surface a convulsive swirl of wood grain patterns, like a Rorschach test. There was something almost too formal about using this room and the table, and they rarely had meetings in it. People stared at him with questions in their eyes that they did not voice; he knew he would start getting memos almost immediately and phone calls from distant superiors, from various underwriters, and from Human Resource executives, all wanting to know what was going on. He could blame some of it on Gregory's death, although he was not supposed to respond to such events: Gregory Malace had got himself into his own "pickle," and his death was something that the system could not support. He left the meeting looking calm, but torn apart inside. He kept seeing Gregory's face in that bag.

In truth, no one had come forth to claim his body. It was still at the airport morgue.

Jeffrey called Gladys Hawthorne. Unexpectedly, she was sympathetic.

"I heard you're taking some time off." There was real warmth in her voice. Her sweet, nicely groomed face on the monitor had a brief, unguarded, "There-but-for-God-go-I" look.

He told her it was true.

"They're not happy about it, Jeffrey." She brushed back her streaked California-blonde hair back; the unguarded look vanished. "There are murmurings of 'thin ice' around here."

"You mean about Gregory?"

"Gregory. Other things. You know how people here talk. Nobody talks a lot, but they do talk."

He nodded.

He could feel that something was happening. He didn't want to face it directly. He had been taught for years not to face things directly. So he put the spin on something else.

"What can we do about Gregory? Have his parents been notified?" His eyes became more serious. "Did he have parents?"

She shrugged. "Everyone has parents, Jeffrey. The system contacted them. The truth is, they're kind of ashamed of him. His mother wants him buried in Germany, since she was from there. They're now in the Midwest, raising another family. I think they're religious people, so they feel that what he did was tantamount to suicide. People, go figure? Jeffrey, would you feel really weird about arranging for a burial or a cremation?"

Jeffrey paused before answering. The bluntness of her request bothered him. Then he realized that he should not be shocked or bothered. There had been no love for Gregory from anyone; there had always been everything but love, and only now could Jeffrey understand it. He told Gladys he would take care of everything.

Then he added, "Don't worry about me, Gladys. About me taking time off. I may not really do it. I know how much I owe the system. There's no way I can let it down. After all, it created me, didn't it?"

Gladys smiled with an almost silly, unguarded radiance, as if all of her securities were now reinforced, and God was back at home, exactly where He should be.

Chapter Nineteen

*H*e took the train and another cab out that afternoon to see John, who was wearing only a pair of briefs and working on a large picture of a nude male.

"It's about Moses and the burning bush," John said. "It's a seminal idea to me: God announces Himself in the form of energy. Potent. Violent. What always amazed me is that God asked Moses to take his shoes off and approach Him barefoot. I wonder if that meant Moses was naked when he approached God. So I'm doing him that way."

"Maybe," Jeffrey said thoughtfully, "God meant that Moses could not take things that he normally had with him; he needed to be prepared to be humbled. It's hard to say. These stories are always open to interpretation. But I like the story, I'm glad you're painting it."

"It's all about heat," John asserted. "Heat, and that moment when heat takes you out of yourself and joins you to something else."

"I see," Jeffrey said. The burning bush—and Moses—returned him to that feeling about approaching Money, power. It had to be done supremely carefully, especially when you would never know exactly what the Money looked like. He told John about Gregory, the whole story, and asked him to go with him the next day to claim the young man's body, and bring it to a crematory.

"I guess there is no need now for me to be his nurse," John said. "But I must be his"—he thought, then said, "his Anubis. That's the god of the dead, you know."

"Yes, I know who Anubis was. If you want to be that, fine. But I prefer you be the god of the living, at least for me."

"All right. Would you mind if I paint some more? The light is still good, with the lamps for help. Would you like some water? I have some very good water. I got it from the forest. Pik showed it to me;

there's a secret stream and he uses it. He's not such a bad kid. I've started to like him."

He offered Jeffrey a glass. The water was good, although it had a pronounced undertaste.

"What is it?" Jeffrey asked.

"I don't know. Some kind of mineral. Pik said the Ostfolk love it, especially the Polocks. In Poland they like what we call *Wildwasser*, water from streams and forest springs. It makes excellent beer too."

John drank a whole glass of it, then smiled.

"It makes you pee your brains out, but that's part of life!"

He went back to the painting, and Jeffrey watched as Moses's figure—large, imposing, but strangely fearful, even doubtful perhaps—came to life. Within the fire of the bush itself, faces, tongues, eyes, and other bodies appeared. And snakes, one of which coiled part of its length onto Moses's rod, then hid inside Moses's flesh, inside his thighs and groin, until its darting, almost invisible head reappeared exactly at Moses's penis.

It became darker in the room; Jeffrey had to look harder to see the painting. Finally, he said:

"It always seems to be there, doesn't it, in one form or another?"

"You mean, one of God's snakes—from the burning bush—in his cock?"

"Yes."

"Like you said, the stories are forever open to interpretation. Everyone now wants to take the life out of them, as if these men never took a shit or jerked off, even when a beautiful girl or a boy was around. To me it's sacrilegious. Your Whitman sang of the 'body electric,' but how about the body mysterious? That is what I want. I want its mysteries, and its beautiful secret perversions."

"Without symbols at all?"

John became quiet. Maybe the conversation was getting too deep, too dense, Jeffrey thought. Symbols were more his business, the business of marketing. Suddenly he hated the question.

He got up and kissed John, stripping off his briefs and kissing his cock.

"Do you have God's snake in there?" he asked, and began sucking him.

"*Ja,*" John said. "*Naturlich.* I do."

They made love. Jeffrey felt renewed by it, not so much energized as reinvented. He wanted to be recast, remade as his true self, not the artificially young one he'd been for so long, the one who'd had to jettison his feelings, his history, his self. In the middle of sex he realized that he did not know John at all, and the more he allowed his real self in, the less he knew him. In a way this was wonderful. John was even more of a stranger, fresher, intimidating even, as unpredictable as those encounters he treasured from years back in the leafy shelters of parks, bathhouses, or other places that, for the most part, had ceased to exist under the complete, protective domination of the system.

He released onto John's chest, and John took some of him into his mouth. John was slower, but Jeffrey enjoyed the petal softness of his foreskin and the pink fleshy bud within it, until John climaxed. Afterward, almost dreaming within the diaphanous tent of orgasm, John said:

"Whatever I do, you must forgive me. Tell me you will."

"Yes," Jeffrey said unconditionally. "I will."

The next day at the airport morgue, they were met by a sturdy-looking, young woman in a black dress and a middle-aged male attendant in a gray uniform. As soon as Jeffrey revealed his name, the woman acknowledged that they had been expecting him; Gregory Malace's Human Resource connections had already contacted the authorities, notifying them of Jeffrey's status as "decision maker." The woman asked if Jeffrey desired flowers to be brought in.

"We can even arrange a little service here at the airport," she said sympathetically. "It's hard losing a friend. We know."

John said something quickly to her in German, and she smiled brightly. Jeffrey asked what it was.

"I told her that he was your *colleague*; his death had been unpleasant. 'Colleague' here counts even more than 'friend.'"

"I see," Jeffrey said. It was always about work. He insisted on seeing Gregory one more time. It would be like saying good-bye to his father, he decided.

"Are you sure you want to?" John cautioned him.

Jeffrey nodded, then realized that on no account would John want to see Gregory.

"I'm sorry," John apologized. "I hate it. I don't like looking at something like this." He left the morgue.

The attendant, who was a big, beer-bellied German, opened the bag and turned away.

Jeffrey looked at Gregory closely, then without any nervousness peeled some of the bandages from his face. He realized he had never actually known Gregory, except in death. A huge sob rose out of him, like Tony's last, painful sob. Tony, who in the end had known so little about him, Jeffrey. There was only that moment when, casting so much aside, they had shared that chaste, brotherly kiss. Jeffrey looked one final time at the young man's colorless face with its stitches and scabs, then zipped the bag up.

Immediately he thought: we're all only scabs on the system.

The attendant led him into an office, where the young woman told him and John what could be done.

"There is a place not far from here. We can send him there in a special van. It will cost you less than a hearse. It can all be done in one fee. Just tell us how you want to pay for it."

"Can he use cash?" John asked.

"No," she shook her head. Her hair was dyed a brassy red, and the light bounced through it. "Nobody uses cash. The system has no way to process it."

Jeffrey took out his I.D. card, and gave her his credit numbers. She handed him a bill. It was actually fairly reasonable.

"You want no flowers, nothing like that? They can have music at the crematory, if you want."

"No," Jeffrey insisted. "That's one thing I don't want."

❧

The rest of it was almost superfluous, and he realized in the car to the cemetery that they did not need to be there for the "processing" part of the operation. But he felt that he owed it to Gregory; it was the least he could do, not to let Gregory make this last trip alone. John stayed outside the small building with the furnace. The whole thing lasted a short amount of time; they told Jeffrey they would send him the cremains, and he gave them his address in town.

He and John took a cab all the way back to John's place.

"Quite a splurge," John said. "But maybe you need it."

Jeffrey was quiet, although he held John's hand. They arrived toward the end of the afternoon, and John suggested they should take a dip in the stream behind his house.

"You need it," he said. "It will be like a rebirth for you, after all this *Totenscheisse*."

"Death shit?"

"That's what it is. I hate it. I don't like dead stuff—*death!*" He grimaced. "I want to be only alive. No matter what it costs me."

"You should be," Jeffrey agreed. They plunged naked into the stream, which was icy but felt very good. Then John helped him towel off by the stream, to get warm as soon as possible.

"What are you going to do?" he asked seriously.

Jeffrey looked at him unblinking.

"Live here with you. I've decided that. Otherwise, I can't go on living anymore."

John wore only a pair of work pants. There was still enough sun for him to enjoy it on his bare chest.

"That means giving up your apartment. Everything."

"Yes."

Suddenly out of nowhere, a cab drove up, and Omar emerged with a small package.

"I'm so glad I found you," he said. "Not easy, you guys."

Jeffrey introduced John to him.

"He has something for you," Jeffrey explained. "I decided you should have some kind of phone here."

"I don't want it," John said frowning. "I mean it! I don't."

"It's O.K., friend," Omar said. "This one is totally untraceable.

It's not a part of the system at all."

John looked furious. He disappeared into his house.

"Why is your friend so crazy? Because I'm here? I'm sorry I never got to the place in Afganistrasse. But it was one of those cousins-of-a-cousin deals. Anyway I have the phone now, and it's set up. You make the payments through this party, and no one is the smarter for it."

He opened the package and showed Jeffrey the tiny, basic, anonymous-looking device.

"See, I'll dial it. Look."

"No, don't. Let me dial it."

Without further thinking, he dialed his number at home, expecting to get his voice mail. Instead, after only two rings a flat, synthesized voice came in saying: "You have reached a non-working number. Please check the number and try again."

"See? Doesn't it work?" Omar asked, smiling.

"Yes," Jeffrey answered. "It works perfectly."

Chapter Twenty

"**W**hy were you so upset about the phone?"

"I don't know," John answered, lying on the mattress, his face away from Jeffrey. "Maybe I'm just tired. It hasn't been the best day."

"I think the system is already closing down on me. I called my home number and got a recording saying that I no longer exist."

"Maybe you don't," John said, turning and pulling Jeffrey to him. "Maybe I just made you up. Or you invented yourself, only for me."

"You're very sweet to say that," Jeffrey said, kissing him. "I'm going to age now, you know. What will you do when I'm old."

"Nothing. What I've always done." He got up quickly and announced, "I need to paint, but I think we should take a walk in the forest first."

Jeffrey looked at him.

"It's getting dark. Why do you want to take a walk now?"

"I need to get out of here. Won't you come along? It'll do you— how do the English always put it, 'a world of good'?"

"All right," Jeffrey said. He was very tired, but he felt that he should keep up with John, as long as he could.

"We'll go by that meadow you like, and the lake. We've never been to the lake together, have we?"

"No, we haven't."

Jeffrey was not sure he was dressed warmly enough, but John gave him an old sweater to wear over his shirt and the nicely tailored pants he'd worn to the airport and the cemetery.

They left the house as the light was starting to ebb; John brought a flashlight. As they walked into the forest, Jeffrey felt suddenly wonderful, with the evening air and its fresh breezes chasing away all of the recent images and events that had bedeviled his mind. The setting sun's rays cut dramatic shafts of light through the trees and chalked the outlines of low clouds with silver. He was excited about going back to the meadow and the lake, places he had first talked to Tony about, during that difficult session after John had attacked him on the pubtran platform. These places seemed to invite or even incarnate so many helping spirits, those powerful "forces" Tony, at one of his most endearing moments, had revealed to him, which in turn had begun Jeffrey's opening up to himself.

They took a twisting, unpaved road not much wider than a bike lane, lined with evergreens, and were soon within the heart of the woods.

"Where are we?" Jeffrey said. "I'm lost."

"It's all right," John assured him, clutching his hand. "The meadow is a short way over there—" He pointed to a direction obscured by trees, with a glimpse of an even narrower way through it. "When we're in it, you'll feel much better. Then there will be the lake."

"O.K. But I want to go back after that. I'm really tired."

They walked along the narrower path, which was darker with dense trees but nicely cleared, as if it had been prepared especially for night hikers. John released his hand.

"You miss your old life, don't you?" he asked.

"I've hardly left it."

"I mean in Alabama," John asserted. "That life that you had to squeeze out in order to stay young."

"Sometimes. But I don't feel that way now. How did you know about that life?"

"I knew about it. Not a lot, but I knew."

Jeffrey saw diffused light up ahead, and was sure it was because the meadow's moonlight was gaining on them. His heartbeat quickened as he recalled that the meadow was part of a park inside the forest. How German to place a park there, with a tended lake edged with lily pads, adding some human styling to the uncertainty of nature. He looked ahead, sure there were beams of light bouncing off water. The light gave him a sense of security, and he thought: My whole life has been about injecting security, embodied by style, into the unknown market, which always offers the beguilements of success or the terrors of failure.

We know nothing at all, he decided, walking close to John; all we can do is make up stories about what we don't know. Everything was a fabrication. What is a chair and why does it have to look this way? There's a chair for the rich and one for the poor. A chair for the unnecessary house and a chair for the home you've dreamed of all your life, the reality of which contains only one certainty: that chair. That it will look a certain way and be what you wanted it to be. That was the only thing you could count on. And Jeffrey, as his own gift, had made it. He thought that, smiling.

They were almost out of the trees. Intense lights approached them, held by kids guarding the meadow.

"They're the same boys, aren't they?" Jeffrey asked nervously. "The ones who tried to kill me. Their leader—you know him, right?"

"Pik. Sure. He's around. He'll come out soon. Don't worry, they're going to let us get to the lake. They may even follow us."

Jeffrey swallowed hard. He had no nerve left.

"Why are they here?"

"It's their territory, I'm afraid. I live in it, but I'm only here because they allow it. Don't worry. You're protected by me. We'll go to your lake, then they'll be gone."

Suddenly Pik appeared out of some dark fold of the meadow and smiled at John. John waved at him.

"Take your clothes off," John told Jeffrey.

"What?"

"I mean it. They want us to take our clothes off. To show them we're not armed, that they don't have to be afraid of us. That's why I was running naked that time in the forest. Can you understand now?"

Jeffrey stopped walking.

"I don't want to do this. I want to go back."

John shook his head sadly.

"You can't, my friend. I'm afraid you can't go back."

"What's going to stop me?"

"They will. Believe me."

Jeffrey took his clothes off—everything, even his shoes. So did

John. John took his hand, and they walked through the meadow to the lake, pure silver in the moonlight.

"I knew you couldn't live without the system," John whispered. "Even I couldn't, to tell the truth. See, I'm a sham, Jeffrey."

"What are you talking about?" Jeffrey asked bitterly, but still holding on to John's hand.

"I didn't lie to you. I feel good about that. I killed my poor Cynthia. Drowned her. And they know that. Oh, *Gott*, I could fool no one. I'm really *branded*, that's it. Funny way to put it, isn't it? They allow me to live here with these boys, like in the Garden of Eden or Neverland, in the most twisted way." He paused, biting his lip. "Still, innocence here is no good. It's its own worst evil."

John was making no sense to Jeffrey. He did not even want it to make sense, because then he would have to believe it.

"What are you talking about?" he screamed. "What in hell are you talking about?"

John did not answer.

They were at the lake, now watching the crowd of boys come closer, their hungry eyes, clenched fists, and charcoal-smeared bodies emerging from the darkness.

John sank down onto the wet bank, hunching over.

"I hate myself. I must tell you that. The system wanted me to attack you. They've known about you for years, that you were slowing down. You couldn't fight the stress anymore. But you always thought you could fool them. So they came to me, a nutcase who lives out here with these cast-off kids, and told me that if I—I can't remember their exact words—but if I led you here, did good with you, and got rid of you, they'd let me remain here. On my own, in my own way. I could stay independent. The true artist, true to my own fucking self."

A sordid, bitter laugh scraped out of him.

"But I would do anything for you," Jeffrey said, standing. "Money. Anything. I can do all of that."

"It doesn't last. Believe me, they get you. That's why I had no phone, no means of letting them have me. But they do it anyway. You know that."

"Are you an assassin for them?"

"No." John cried. His whole body shook. "A pawn, just a stupid pawn."

"Why didn't you let Ashok kill me in India?"

"Because I wanted to protect you until there was no way out. I didn't think they'd do this so fast. I thought we'd get to spend more time together. I wanted that. You'd get old. I was planning on poisoning you. That water, you remember? I'd do it slowly with the water. But now it's time. Pik came to tell me; he got in on it, too. He and his gang are going to do it. They'll make some money from it, and the system will leave me alone again for a while. At least until something else happens, and then I'll have to attack another poor fool on the pubtran."

Jeffrey couldn't help smiling. Tony had been right. These would be his *good* forces at last, here by the lake. And the final carnal sacrament in Jeffrey Cooper's life would be his own existence.

"Do me a small favor," Jeffrey asked, looking down at John. "Kill me yourself."

John got up. "I was afraid you'd ask that."

"I'm tired," Jeffrey admitted, holding on to John's arm. "Where are they going to do it?"

"They'll pull you into the lake and drown you."

"Then I'd rather you did it. Like you did your wife."

"I can't," John said, sobbing. "You don't know the hopelessness of this. There's no way I can survive it, without you going down."

The boys were now surrounding them, and Pik's gaunt face appeared.

"Remember me?" Pik asked.

Jeffrey did not answer.

"You don't like us, do you? You Americans think you're better than everybody. Right ways, right words. Right everything. Shit! Nothing's worse than American *Schwulen*! You got everything right. Right?"

"No!" Jeffrey said. "I don't have it *right*—what is it you want, money?"

"*Ja*!" Pik shouted. "Money's everything. Bread, blood, even—"

he asked a boy next to him something. Then Pik shouted, "Soul! Money's soul! The soul of everything, you stupid shit! *Scheissekopf*! That's what you think—but we hate you more than we like the money!"

Bursts of large sharp stones hit Jeffrey. Blood streamed from his head, blinding his eyes. They dragged him waist-deep into the lake, then kicked and forced him face-down into the silty water. He struggled, as he had in the river with Ashok, but this time it was futile. There were too many of them; all he could do was open his eyes to watery quivering moonlight, its silvery dancing reflections, and the truth, in its loneliest apparition, as death approached him, manifesting its large, almost consoling self.

Jeffrey felt the difficult, struggling weight of himself, even with the boys attacking him, relax. Everyone he had lost floated to him. Mom in her suit. Harold, who loved him and could never protect himself. Sad Gregory. Len. Chris.

And finally John. Real.

Pushing himself in, blocking the boys drowning him, his body shielding Jeffrey, even as the kids tried to drown John, too.

John pushed him away, to safety, and immediately the youths grabbed for John's throat, with even more boys rushing in to hold him down. Jeffrey had to come up or water would fill his lungs. He was choking but he could see in the watery muck that John was sinking as the boys attacked him. Jeffrey pushed himself up, breathing, then slowly went back down into the gray depths again.

The boys had disappeared, sure they had killed John. Jeffrey groped almost without sight until he found John suspended in the reaches of a large sunken tree, not far from the muddy bottom. He managed to pull him over to the bank, by lily pads sunk into the ooze. John coated in slime looked like some dead primeval creature. Jeffrey pressed firmly on his chest and blew hard into his mouth, holding John's nose, over and over again, refusing to give up, even though he was almost out of breath himself.

Finally John breathed.

They lay on the cold edge of the water for what seemed like hours but was only a few minutes. The moon disappeared. Jeffrey could hear the loud distant voices of the kids out in the dark. Their shouts terrified him, but he couldn't leave.

John opened his eyes.

"I couldn't do it. I'm a coward. I know it. They think I'm dead. Soon they'll come back and kill me for real. They'll come to the house and burn it down and won't stop until they get me."

"Your paintings?"

Slowly, John managed to get up. He shrugged.

"They were a way of giving myself a past. At least the system won't get them."

Jeffrey got up and John grabbed his hand tightly.

"Would you marry me?" he asked. "Right here? Now?"

Jeffrey hesitated.

"Shouldn't we go back to your house, before the kids get there? We can save what we can, we—"

"No. I want you to marry me here. I want you to pledge that you will always be mine, be my—I don't know—but I need that. I need that more than any of the paintings and anything. Even more than my life."

"O.K.," Jeffrey said quietly, and fell into that oblivion of love that seemed as deep and vast as death itself, kissing John's slime-coated face, his hands, his pliant Dutch lips; until he emerged from this oblivion reborn, rescuing, finally, his own innocence of heart. They knelt in the cold damp earth, holding hands, and Jeffrey pledged to John solemnly, recalling any part of the marriage service he could from Alabama—

"I will take you John van der Meer as my equal and my love. I will hold you and protect you and love you until I die."

"*Gut,* I will do the same for you, Jeffrey Cooper."

He kissed Jeffrey's mud-covered hand, and they walked back still naked in complete darkness to John's house. It was ransacked and trashed, the paintings attacked with knifes, left in tatters. John's car was stolen.

John nodded his head sadly.

"They were really angry. Those kids are like a storm. It's not something you can control. They wanted to kill something, even more than they wanted the money."

Suddenly he smiled.

They washed in the stream, as dawn broke.

"What should we do now?" John asked. "I know this: The system is worse than the kids. It will destroy us more completely. We can try to stay here for a few days. They'll retake your apartment, and everything else in your life."

They went back into the house. John found some candles and lit them, and Jeffrey dug through the wreckage long enough to find the cell phone Omar had brought. Omar had left his number with it, and he dialed it.

Omar was half asleep.

"Can you pick us up?" he asked. "You know, at the house?"

"I figured you'd call me. What else can I do? You have things you want to sell? You want to leave the country, right?"

"Yes," Jeffrey said. "To both. I want it a lot."

He clicked off, and smiled.

"I don't know how much longer I've got to live," he said softly to John. "I guess you must know that I'm a lot older than I seem. I can keep myself going, if I have to. Some people do—on the black market. But," he paused.

"What?"

"Would you be bothered if I got old fast? Would that bother you?"

"No. You'd be more human. More real to me. Besides, I'm yours. You know that."

"Good. Then Omar will take me back to my apartment and I'll sell everything I've got while it's still mine. I've kept some money there; it's mine, away from the system. And I have money in Alabama, in a small town. No one can touch it except a cousin and I. It's safe, I know it. You and I need to go someplace. If we made it to India, we can go anywhere. This is going to be very interesting—I'm not sure where we'll end up, but it's got to be some place strange and yet safe. And some place where there are people still violent and backward and smart enough not to get trapped in the system."

John nodded.

"Any suggestions?"

"Yes," Jeffrey said. "Where I'm from. America."

the end

Foreign Words and Phrases

All words and phrases in German, unless otherwise noted.

Ach, Ah!

Allis ist, everything is

Arz, doctor

beedi, Hindi, Indian cigarette, often strong and spice scented

bimah, (Hebrew) altar

bitte, please

boychik, (Yiddish) young boy

Büro, office

C'est la guerre, (French) "So goes the war."

Danke sehr, very much thanks

Der Rosenkavalier ("Cavalier of the Rose"), opera by Richard Strauss (1864-
1949) about an older woman who is taken with a young boy.

Deutschland für Deutscher, Germany for Germans

dreck, (Yiddish) shit.

Dumkopf, dummy, stupid

Ein geschmeck, a taste

einfach, easy

Entre nous, (French) between us

Es geht, es geht nicht, It goes, it doesn't go.

Fasching, Carnival season

fortepiano, early version of piano

fress, eat (very pejorative, as in how animals eat)

Ganesh, the elephant-headed god of wisdom

ganz fremd, really strange

ganz, whole, completely

gern, gladly

geschichte, past, story, or history

Gott, God

grand mal, (French) serious illness

Gut, good

Guten abend, Good evening

Guten tag, Good day

Has du Gelt, Do you have money?

haut bourgeois, upper middle class

hier, here

Ich verstehe, I understand

Ja, yes

Judenkeit, Jewishness

Komputerkunst, computer art

köstlich, gemlike, very rare

Kultur, culture

kvetch, (Yiddish) complain

landsman, (Yiddish) countryman

lederhosen, leather pants, traditional German.

Liebchen, little love, term of endearment

liebe, love

lieber knabchen, young boy who is my love

Lieber, dear, term of endearment

macher, literally a "maker"; a "mover and shaker."

Mein freund. Beschftig, My friend. Busy?

mit schlag, with whipped cream

mumsers (Yiddish), bastards

nafkee. (Yiddish) low thief, or horse thief

Naturlich, naturally

Neges, blacks

Nein, no.

omelette au fromage, (French) cheese omlette

Primo, excellent

puja, prayer or blessing

pukka, Indian term for "fine" or acceptable

putti, tiny angels

Richtig, correct

riistafel, Dutch, "rice table," an Indonesian meal with many dishes

satsang, Sanskrit, blessings

schade, pity or shame

scharf, bitter. Scharfscheisse, bitter shit (worse)

scheisse, shit

Scheisse, shit. Commonly used expletive.

scheisseliste, shit list

Schlect, bad

schlock, (Yiddish) cheap merchandise

schmaltz, (Yiddish) literally, chicken fat; meaning, greasy.

schmertz, pain

Schön, beautiful

Schwul, queer or faggot

Schwulescheissekopf, faggot shithead

sehr unhöfflich, very discourteous

sehr, very

Sind Sie fürloren?" Are you lost?

spas, fun

spitz klasse, highest class

strassenklassen, the street classes, or regular working classes

stücke, piece (of action)

sussekeit, sweetness

Tiergartenstrasse, literally: Zoo Street

tiffin, (Victorian English expression) lunch

total verukt, completely crazy, totally nuts

Ubermensch, Superman

universalarbeit, universal work

vekachte, (Yiddish) shitty

Verstehen allis, Understand everything

Verstehen Sie, Do you understand?

Was kan Mann tun, What can one do?

Weiss nicht, Don't know

Wer sind Sie? Who are you?

Wie Deutsches ist es? "How German is that?"

Wie geht's, how is it going?

Wie kennst du, How do you know?

Wirklich, truly

wo ist deine höfflichkeit, Where are your manners

woll, "complete," but also O.K.

Wunderschön, wonderfully beautiful

zu viel Deutsch für, too much German for—

zum beispiel, for example

Perry Brass

Originally from Savannah, Georgia, Perry Brass grew up, in the fifties and sixties, in equal parts Southern, Jewish, economically impoverished, and very much *gay*. To escape the South's violent homophobia, he hitchhiked at seventeen from Savannah to San Francisco—an adventure, he recalls, that was "like Mark Twain with drag queens." He has published fourteen books and been a finalist six times in three categories (poetry; gay science fiction and fantasy; spirituality and religion) for Lambda Literary Awards. His novel *Warlock* received a 2002 "Ippy" Award from Independent Press Magazine as Best Gay and Lesbian Book.

He has been involved in the gay movement since 1969, when he co-edited *Come Out!*, the world's first gay liberation newspaper. Later, in 1972, with two friends he started the Gay Men's Health Project Clinic, the first clinic for gay men on the East Coast, still surviving as New York's Callen-Lorde Community Health Center. In 1984, his play *Night Chills*, one of the first plays to deal with the AIDS crisis, won a Jane Chambers International Gay Playwriting Award. Brass's numerous collaborations with composers include the poetry for "All the Way Through Evening," a five-song cycle set by the late Chris DeBlasio; "The Angel Voices of Men" set by Ricky Ian Gordon, commissioned by the Dick Cable Fund for the New York City Gay Men's Chorus, which featured it on its *Gay Century Songbook* CD; "Three Brass Songs" set by Fred Hersch; "Five 'Russian' Lyrics, set by Christopher Berg, commissioned by Positive Music; and "Waltzes for Men," also commissioned by the DCF for the NYC Gay Men's Chorus, set by Craig Carnahan. His latest musical collaboration, "The Restless Yearning Towards My Self," set by opera composer Paula Kimper, was commissioned by Downtown Music.

Perry Brass is an accomplished reader and voice on gender subjects, gay relationships, and the history and literature of the movement towards GLBT equality. He has taught numerous workshops and classes in writing and publishing fiction, and the hidden roots of gay culture. He lives in the Riverdale section of "da Bronx," but can cross bridges to other parts of America without a passport.

OTHER BOOKS BY PERRY BRASS

Sex-charge

". . . poetry at its highest voltage . . ." Marv. Shaw in **Bay Area Reporter**.

Sex-charge. 76 pages. $6.95. With male photos by Joe Ziolkowski. ISBN 0-9627123-0-2

Mirage

ELECTRIFYING SCIENCE FICTION

A gay science fiction classic! An original "coming out" and coming-of-age saga, set in a distant place where gay sexuality and romance is a norm, but with a life-or-death price on it. On the tribal planet Ki, two men have been promised to each other for a lifetime. But a savage attack and a blood-chilling murder break this promise and force them to seek another world, where imbalance and lies form Reality. This is the planet known as Earth, a world they will use and escape. Finalist, 1991 Lambda Literary Award for Gay Men's Science Fiction/Fantasy. This classic work of gay science fiction fantasy is now available in its new Tenth Anniversary Edition.

"Intelligent and intriguing." Bob Satuloff in **New York Native.**

Mirage, Tenth Anniversary Edition. 230 pages. $12.95. ISBN 1-892149-02-8

Circles

THE AMAZING SEQUEL TO *MIRAGE*

"The world Brass has created with *Mirage* and its sequel rivals, in complexity and wonder, such greats as C. S. Lewis and Ursula LeGuin." **Mandate Magazine**, New York.

Circles. 224 pages. $11.95. ISBN 0-9627123-3-7

Out There

STORIES OF PRIVATE DESIRES, HORROR, AND THE AFTERLIFE.

". . . we have come to associate [horror] with slick and trashy chiller-thrillers. Perry Brass is neither. He writes very well in an elegant and easy prose that carries the reader forward pleasurably. I found this selection to be excellent." The **Gay Review**, Canada.

Out There. 196 pages. $10.95. ISBN 0-9627123-4-5

Albert

OR THE BOOK OF MAN

Third in the *Mirage* trilogy. In 2025 the White Christian Party has taken over America. Albert, son of Enkidu and Greeland, must find the male Earth mate who will claim his heart and allow him to return to leadership on Ki. "Brass gives us a book where lesser writers would have only a premise." **Men's Style,** New York.

"If you take away the plot, it has political underpinnings that are chillingly true. Brass has a genius for the future." *Science Fiction Galaxies*, Columbus, OH. "Erotic suspense and action . . . a pleasurable read." *Screaming Hyena Review*, Melbourne, Australia.

Albert. 210 pages. $11.95. ISBN 0-9627123-5-3

Works

AND OTHER 'SMOKY GEORGE' STORIES, <u>EXPANDED EDITION</u>

"Classic Brass," these stories—many set in the long-gone seventies, when, as the author says, "Gay men cruised more and networked less"—have recharged gay erotica. This Expanded Edition contains a selection of Brass's steamy poems, as well as his essay "Maybe We Should Keep the 'Porn' in Pornography."

Works. 184 pages. $9.95. ISBN 0-9627123-6-1

The Harvest

A "SCIENCE/POLITICO" NOVEL

From today's headlines predicting human cloning comes the emergence of "vaccos"—living "corporate cadavers"—raised to be sources of human organ and tissue transplants. One exceptional vacco will escape. His survival will depend upon Chris Turner, a sexual renegade who will love him and kill to keep him alive.

"One of the <u>Ten Best Books of 1997</u>," **Lavender Magazine**, Minneapolis. "In George Nader's *Chrome*, the hero dared to fall in love with a robot. In **The Harvest**—*a vastly superior novel*, Chris Turner falls in love with a vacco, Hart256043." Jesse Monteagudo, **The Weekly News**, Miami, Florida.

Finalist, 1997 Lambda Literary Award, Gay and Lesbian Science Fiction.

The Harvest. 216 pages. $11.95. ISBN 0-9627123-7-X

The Lover of My Soul

A SEARCH FOR ECSTASY AND WISDOM

Brass's first book of poetry since *Sex-charge* is worth the wait. Flagrantly erotic and just plain flagrant—with poems like "I Shoot the Sonovabitch Who Fires Me," "Sucking Dick Instead of Kissing," and the notorious "MTV Ab(*solutely*) Vac(*uous*) Awards, *The Lover of My Soul* again proves Brass's feeling that poetry must tell, astonish, and delight.

"An amazingly powerful book of poetry and prose," **The Loving Brotherhood**, Plainfield, NJ.

The Lover of My Soul. 100 pages. $8.95. ISBN 0-9627123-8-8

How to Survive Your <u>Own</u> Gay Life

AN ADULT GUIDE TO LOVE, SEX, AND RELATIONSHIPS

The book for <u>adult</u> gay men. About sex and love, and coming out of repression; about surviving homophobic violence; about your place in a community, a relationship, and a culture. About the important psychic "gay work" and the gay tribe. About dealing with conflicts and crises, personal, professional, and financial. And, finally, about being more alive, happier, and stronger.

"This book packs a wallop of wisdom!" Morris Kight, founder, Los Angeles Gay & Lesbian Services Center. Finalist, 1999 Lambda Literary Award in Gay and Lesbian Religion and Spirituality.

How to Survive Your <u>Own</u> Gay Life. 224 pages. $11.95. ISBN 0-9627123-9-6

Angel Lust

AN EROTIC NOVEL OF TIME TRAVEL

Tommy Angelo and Bert Knight are in a long-term relationship. *Very* long—close to a millennium. Tommy and Bert are angels, but different. No wings. Sexually free. Tommy was once Thomas Jebson, a teen serf in the violent England of William the Conqueror. One evening he met a handsome knight who promised to love him for all time. Their story introduces us to gay forest men, robber barons, castles, and deep woodlands. Also, to a modern sexual underground where "gay" and "straight" mean little. To Brooklyn factory men. Street machos. New York real estate sharks. And the kind of lush erotic encounters for which Perry Brass is famous. Finalist, 2000 Lambda Literary Award, Gay and Lesbian Science Fiction.

"Brass's ability to go from seedy gay bars in New York to 11th century castles is a testament to his skill as a writer." **Gay & Lesbian Review.**

Angel Lust. 224 pages. $12.95. ISBN 1-892149-00-1

Warlock

Allen Barrow, a shy bank clerk, dresses out of discount stores and has a small penis that embarrasses him. One night at a bathhouse he meets Destry Powars—commanding, vulgar, seductive, successful—who pulls Allen into his orbit and won't let go. Destry lives in a closed, moneyed world that Allen can only glimpse through the pages of tabloids. From generations of drifters, Powars has been chosen to learn a secret language based on force, deception, and nerve. But *who* chose him—and what does he really want from Allen? What *are* Mr. Powars's dark powers? These are the mysteries that Allen will uncover in *Warlock*, a novel that is as paralyzing in its suspense as it is voluptuously erotic.

Warlock. 226 pages. $12.95. ISBN 1-892149-03-6

The Substance of God

A SPIRITUAL THRILLER

What would you do with the Substance of God, a self-regenerating material originating from Creation? The Substance can bring the dead back to life, but has a "mind" of its own. Dr. Leonard Miller, a gay bio-researcher secretly addicted to "kinky" sex, learned this after he was found mysteriously murdered in his laboratory while working alone on the Substance. Once brought back to life, Miller must find out who infiltrated his lab to kill him, how long will he have to live—and, *exactly*, where does life end and any Hereafter begin?

Miller's story takes him from the underground sex scenes of New York to the all-male baths of Istanbul. It will deal with the longing for God in a techno-driven world; with the persistent attractions of religious fundamentalism; and with the fundamentals of "outsider" sexuality as both spiritual ritual and cosmic release. And Miller, the unbelieving scientist, will be driven himself to ask one more question: Is our often-censored urge toward sex and our great, undeniable urge toward a union with God . . . the *same* urge?

"Perry Brass has added to the annals of gay lit." **Book Marks**.

The Substance of God. 232 pages. $13.95. ISBN: 1-892149-04-4

At your bookstore, or from:

Belhue Press

2501 Palisade Avenue, Suite A1

Bronx, NY 10463

E-mail: belhuepress@earthlink.net

Please add $2.50 shipping for the first book and $1.00 for each book thereafter. New York State residents please add 8.25% sales tax. Foreign orders in U.S. currency only.

You can now order Perry Brass's exciting books online at www.perrybrass.com. Please visit this website for more details, regular updates, and news of future events and books.